SAVAGE BEAST

SAMANTHA BARRETT

For Kylie Kent and Mel Bennett,
Kylie you are a boss, and I am in awe of you, thank you for all that you have done for me!
Mel, babe you are so amazing, and I love you dearly.
Thank you for everything, I couldn't have done half of this without you.
From the bottom of my heart thank you both!

CHAPTER ONE

Belle

I avoid physical contact at all costs, I've hated this *gift* since I first saw our mother's death. My dad and brothers tell me it isn't a curse it's a blessing to see others' lives. I don't just see their lives; I see from the moment they take their first breath to their last. I would give anything in the world to just be a normal wolf shifter, I mean *anything*. I am the daughter of an alpha and yet I cannot shift, my three older brothers are strong and formidable wolves who are a force on two legs but on four, they are savage.

Growing up in a pack hasn't been easy, just because I am the alphas daughter doesn't make me exempt from snide remarks or sly looks from the others. I know the pack doesn't accept me because of my abilities, they fear what they don't understand. I scare myself sometimes, now days I don't even need to make contact with someone for a vision to happen. For the past eight or so months now, I've been dreaming about a man, I never see his face just his life, he's in so much pain but it's not physical. He's strong and fierce but inside he's so broken––lost.

My dad and brothers try to help me figure out my visions, they aren't always clear to me. Sometimes it's like a puzzle and I need to fit the pieces together before I can see the whole picture. I'm not a medium if that's what you're thinking, I can't speak to the dead or see them. Given the choice I would rather deal with the dead than the living.

"How you doing, sis?" I turn away from the stove and smile at Cass, he's the oldest. He may be big and bulky and look scary to others, but to me, he's just a huge teddy bear. Cass is a real ladies' man; he leaves trails of broken hearts where ever he goes. My brothers inherit their black hair from our dad, Cass, dad and Blake all have green eyes. Hunter and I take after our mom with blue eyes, I'm the only one with long brown thick hair. I used to keep my hair short, but dad begged me not to cut it since my hair reminds him of my mom. I know it sounds silly, but my long hair makes me feel like a part of her is always with me. I never got the chance to know her, the guys always tell me stories of her, and those are the only memories I have.

"I'm good, just preparing some supper. How long before dad and the others get back from the meeting?" No sooner have the words left my mouth do the other two giants I call brothers walk in; dad stands at shoulder height compared to his sons as he wrestles his way between them, smiling brightly as he heads my way to engulf me with a big hug, Blake and Hunter both snicker and roll their eyes, what can I say I'm a daddy's girl.

"How is my favorite girl today?" Dad asks as he pulls back, I smile and roll my eyes.

"I'm the only girl dad."

"He never calls us his *favorite boys*." Dad winks at me before turning around to face the boys, Blake is the second oldest and Hunter is the youngest. Hunter loves to wind us up and never takes anything seriously.

"I thought we established this, Cass is the favorite boy Monday and Tuesday. Blake is Wednesday and Thursday and your Friday and Saturday." Hunter playfully narrows his eyes and gestures between him, Blake and Cass.

"But who is Sunday?" Cass laughs and takes a seat at the dining table, Blake joins him. This is a weekly debate in our house, and we've all learnt to tune Hunter out.

"My boy, I told you Sunday belongs to God, so he's my favorite on Sunday."

I finish dishing supper and join the others at the table, all four men are boasting about how amazing it smells before they dig in. Being wolves, we consume a lot of calories, well they do. Due to being a non-shifter I graciously eat like a human, to feed four male wolves is the equivalent of feeding a family of twelve humans. I love this time of day where we can all come together as a family, dad has been so busy lately dealing with pack stuff.

"What are we going to do about the rogues?" Hunter asks, the carefree atmosphere is shattered by that one question. "They're getting closer." Dad tenses at the mention of how close these rogue wolves are getting to us. No one knows what they want or why they are raiding packs. They never take anything and as far as we know they try to keep all injuries to a minimum. Rogue wolves tend to be rabid and uncontrollable, but this specific pack seems to be organized and calculated almost like they're looking for something or someone.

"We are trying to work out the best options and we have doubled the patrols around the perimeter." I can clearly see the stress in my dad's eyes.

"We have to act now before they come for us. We can't be seen as weak; they have already taken control of at least twenty packs that we know of." The growl in Cass's voice tells us all that his wolf is close to the surface. Cass is the heir to the pack and will take over when dad steps down. The thing is though, Cass is wrong. Hunter told me that they don't claim the packs, they subdue them then––leave.

"Cassius, being perceived as weak is not the problem here. The safety of the pack is my main concern––." Cass slams his fist down on the old wooden table, I jump in freight. He levels dad with a stern look, which dad meets with one of his own.

"We need to take the fight to *him*!" I look to Hunter and Blake and see they both are staring at Cass and dad in confusion.

"Him?" Blake asks, dad and Cass won't break their stare off. Hunter turns to me with pleading eyes, being I'm the only one who's the calm before the storm. I nod to Hunter and rise to my feet, Cass and dad finally break their stare off and turn to me.

"Cass, unless you want to fight dad for alpha you need to back down." Cass reluctantly nods, it is known that if you hold a wolf's gaze for too long it is seen as a challenge. "Dad, please enlighten us as to why you both think this is just one man?" Dad sighs, he looks to Cass and gives him a stiff nod as I take my seat. Cass turns worried eyes to me, he reaches his hand out and I stare at it for a moment. Over the years I have become somewhat immune to my family's touch, sometimes a vision will strike but normally that only happens if they veer off the course of their destiny. I tentatively place my hand in Cass's and then a vision hits me–––hard.

CHAPTER TWO

Belle

I *see Cass running in wolf form, he's being chased by at least eight wolves. These wolves are strong and huge. One of them nips at Cass's flank but he dodges and leaps over the small creek. Cass runs to the top of the hill on the other side where Hunter, Blake and the rest of our pack wait for him. Once Cass is at the top he stops and turns back to the other wolves below. The huge black and white wolf with onyx eyes stares up at Cass, his lip pulled back in a snarl. This wolf reeks of power and dominance, more wolves come out of the woods behind him.*

Cass shifts and is now standing there naked with a fierce angry look on his face.

"You will not take her from us." Huh? The sound of bones cracking has me turning to the black wolf who is shifting back to human form. I gasp, my body urges me to go to him. Standing in front of me is the most breathtaking creature, messy black hair that's long enough to run your fingers through. Piercing blue eyes as bright as the sky. He's tall, maybe a few inches taller than Cass, his body is a work of art. Tattoos cover his arms and chest, he must work out because the muscles on his body are rippling with rage.-

"She is mine, I will kill you if you stand in my way alpha. Gabrielle Wilder belongs to me!"

I wrench my hand from Cass's and nearly fall out of my seat, dad reaches over to help me but I flinch away from his touch. I scrub my hands down my face as I try to rub away the vision. The rogues are coming for me, why?

"What did you see Belle?" I shake my head avoiding Blake's question. This vision felt too real, I didn't see death, I don't even know what I saw. Over the past eight months my visions have been changing, I don't just see death or some one's life, now I see other things and it's making it hard to decipher what these visions mean. If that man called Cass alpha, then that means...where was dad? I look around the table to see everyone staring at me with concern and worry, I try to smile reassuringly but fail.

"I'm sorry." Hunter shakes his head.

"Don't ever be sorry Belle, this isn't your fault. Cass shouldn't have done that!" Cass and Hunter glare at each other.

"I didn't mean to!" Cass defends, Hunter scoffs and rolls his eyes.

"Bullshit, you did that on purpose hoping she could foresee your future. If you're gonna bullshit, at least try harder to make us believe you."

"Enough!" Dad cuts in before things escalate, wolves are naturally moody, so fights break out often when you have four alpha males in your house. "What happened, what did you see?" I cut my gaze to Cass briefly before settling back on my dad, I don't know how to tell him what I saw. I can't lie either, so I take a deep breath and explain.

"Wow, shit." Blake can say that again.

"Belle saw the alpha of the rogues, didn't she?" Dad turns tired weary eyes to me as he answers.

"Yes." I inhale a sharp intake of breath; the creek I saw in my vision is near our territory so the rogues will come here but...when? I tune out as dad and the guys launch into discussion about how they will proceed from here. I can't get that man out of my head, he seems so familiar, like I know him. It was a vision, but I felt so connected to him, I have never felt connected to anyone in a vision before not even my own family. In a daze I rise and start cleaning, my appetite is long gone now, as I'm washing the dishes and still lost in my thoughts a hand lands on my shoulder and shocks me.

"Gee, calm down sis it's only me." I wave away Cass's concerns and plaster on a fake smile.

"Sorry, just lost in my head." Cass narrows his eyes; I'm a shitty liar and my brothers always know when I lie, they say I have a *tell*.

"Don't lie to me, what are you really thinking about?" If anyone can help me figure this out it's my brothers.

"The guy in the vision, I felt so−−."

"Scared, I know belle, and don't worry I will make sure he never harms you." Before I can correct Cass and say what I really wanted to, Hunter comes in and tells Cass it's time to go. Dad set up an emergency meeting with the pack elders, I have saved this pack and its members time and time again because of these visions. No one outside of our pack knows what I can do, dad issued an alpha order to keep everyone silent. Dad always said that if anyone found out about me, they would use it to their advantage, I didn't protest as far as I was concerned the less people that knew the better. I didn't need any more people looking at me weird and whispering behind my back, my family kept me sheltered and hidden most of my life. I've never left the pack grounds, my only escape is reading a book and getting lost in the main characters world. I have never felt the intimate touch of a man or even been kissed for that matter. No one wants to be seen with the freak, plus no guy wants to piss my brothers off by pursuing me.

After I cleaned up I decided to shower and change into my PJ's, I had nothing else to do, so I decided to chill and watch *Sexlife on Netflix*, one of my favorite authors BB Easton's book is now a series and I'm excited as hell to watch it. I'm three episodes deep and when *that* specific scene appears I scream and cower behind the couch cushion. Holy cow!

I mean...I can't even...that was. My mindless inner monologue is cut off when the front door opens, I scramble to find the remote and quickly click the TV off. My dad and brothers do not need to see me watching that show!

"We have to do it now."

"We can't Cass, we need to be smart."

"Dad, Cass might be right."

I peer over the back of the couch and watch as they argue between themselves about when and what to do. Sick of hearing the back and forth I stand and make my way over to them. They all stop bickering the moment they see me standing there with my hands on my hips and a firm look on my face.

"All your pack politics stays the hell outside. You know the rules––."

"Don't bring pack shit home!" They all cut in and say in unison, I fight the smile that wants to break free. They may be big burly guys, but when it comes to me, they always back down, I like to think it's because they're scared, but truth be told, they don't want to upset me. If anyone of them see so much as a tear roll down my cheek, they're beside themselves with panic, they have no idea how to deal with a woman and her emotions. Dad ushers us back into the lounge room, the four of us drop down into our seats while dad stands and paces back and forth across the rug. After a few minutes I turn to Hunter and raise my brow in question, he shrugs his shoulders. I turn to my other side and do the same to Blake, he raises is pointer finger to his temple and circles it, I narrow my eyes while he smiles. He is such an ass, dad isn't crazy, he's just stressed and worried.

"Dad?" Cass's voice halts dad in his tracks, he turns to face us, and I see worry lines marring his forehead. Whatever happened at that meeting has put dad on edge.

"Okay Cass, you get what you want. We prep for attack––." Cass tries to cut in, but dad stops him and shifts his gaze to me. "Belle, for your safety you will stay in this house, you are not to leave under any circumstances. We will fight to hide you."

"No! I will not let you four get hurt for me, just tell them that I can't help them dad. I can't control these visions so I'm of no use to them!" Dad's eyes soften and his shoulders sag, I know he wants to protect me, but I will not let them go to war for me. I'm not worth dying over.-

"Belle, when have you ever seen us beaten?" I lean around Hunter and look at Cass, his eyes shine with arrogance, but he doesn't get it!

"You don't understand, in my vision I felt his strength and determination. His power is potent and his dominance is unlike any I have ever encountered before Cass. This guy isn't some weak alpha or a crazed rogue...he's...different." Cass stiffens.

"He will fall like others before him, Wilders don't lose––ever."

CHAPTER THREE

Belle

I didn't get much sleep last night thanks to my mind wondering everywhere. I tried to let sleep claim me, but all I could see was so much pain lingering in the depths of his beautiful blue eyes. The way he said I was his, held so much meaning, almost like he really believed that I do belong to him. I shudder at the thought, for once I hope my vision doesn't come true. Ever since I turned fourteen, I have been able to better understand my visions and learn how to read them. They come to me in flashes sometimes, and other times it's like a movie, my family support and help me as best they can, especially with the amount of death I have seen but nothing seems to work.

Dad and Cass have stopped searching for ways to stop my visions, I am grateful that I have been able to help my pack with these visions and save lives, but it takes a toll on me. I will never be able to feel the intimate touch of a man or simply hold hands as we stroll along a beach. I am destined to be alone and live-in isolation, whenever I'm in the company of other people aside from my family I'm assaulted with visions. Hence why a majority of my time is spent indoors. When my dad and brothers emotions are too high it can trigger me off, over the past few years, I have learnt to build a shield of sorts to block them out. Sometimes, like last night that shield can be broken. I have had many visions over the years but one thing I have come to learn is that the only death in my family I saw was my mothers. Fortunately, I have never seen my dad or my brother's deaths which I am grateful for. I don't know how I would deal with that if I knew when and where one of them would die. I wish I could have stopped my mother's death from happening but in the end, I learnt that when your time is up, death will always find a way to claim your soul.

"Belle, breakfast is ready." I smile, Blake cooked this morning, who I might add is the better cook, Hunter's talent is baking. I scramble out of bed and race downstairs to the kitchen. Dad, Hunter and Cass are already dressed and seated at the table awaiting their breakfast. I drop into the seat next to Cass and eagerly wait for whatever delicious meal Blake has made us this morning.

"We have to head out for the day, your brothers and I won't be back until nightfall." Blake continues to serve our food as I glare at my father startled by what he just said. I have never been left on pack lands alone before. Theres always one of them that stays behind, so the fact that they are all leaving worries me.

"Why do the four of you have to go?" I ask, dad swings his gaze to Cass then back to me. I grit my teeth; hiding things from me enhances my annoyance, instead of telling me the harsh truth.

"We need to scou out the area where we plan to cut off the rogues, you have to remain inside and under no circumstances are you to leave the house." Dad's using his authoritive alpha tone right now, has tried for years to use his alpha command with me but it never works. When an alpha delivers an order to his pack it must be followed whether you like it or not but because I can't shift it doesn't work on me. I nod my head, there is no point in arguing with him. If I voice my opinion my brothers will jump in and defend him, so I bite my tongue and start to shovel the yummy food into my mouth.

Dad and the guys leave not long after we clean up the breakfast mess. I know they are only traveling half an hour away to set up, I'm disliking the thought of being alone already. To distract myself from my silly thoughts I decide to have a shower and clean the house. Cleaning is my way of de-stressing, I find it very therapeutic and calming.

After my domesticated duties are finished, I decide to engage my brain in some studying. I know in reality I'll never have the opportunity to attend college, so I'm taking classes online. I'm not your typical nineteen-year-old girl, Cass, Hunt and Blake had the option to go to regular school, unlike me I didn't. Cass declined college after he graduated, Hunter and Blake study online as well. They were both given a choice, college, or being at home where it wouldn't upset me, they chose the latter. They cover their lie's by saying it's because dad and Cass need them, but we all know its bullshit.

Cass has always dreamed of being alpha and leading the pack, he's twenty-eight now and still his dream remains the same. Blake is twenty-six and has always wanted to be an electrician, he only has another few months left before he graduates his online classes. Hunter is twenty-three and isn't sure what he wants to do, so he opted to take a business course. He said it was better to have something rather than have nothing, dads proud that Hunter was smart enough to realize that. I support my three brothers in their choices for life, as they do me. Originally, I wanted to be a vet, in order to help the pack, but quickly changed my mind when I realized even in animal form if I touched someone I would be thrown into a vision. Now I'm studying psychology, the brain is an interesting organ and I'm curious as to how it works. Maybe through this course I can learn to control my visions.

A loud bang sounds outside, I jump to my feet in fright. I stand there staring around the room, I'll admit I'm a chicken and I am home alone, so that just amps up my nerves. I start to relax when I don't hear any further noises, but all of a sudden, I'm hearing multiple bangs. I rush over to the window near the bottom of the stairs so I can peer out, the sound of the last bang came from this direction. All I can see is smoke, we don't live like you would imagine wolf packs do. Each house is different and made of different materials. No two houses are the same, some are brick, some are wood, and the rest are cabins. I notice one of the cabins on fire, I hear shouts and screams, people running in all directions. I race away from the window to recheck that the front door is locked, after checking that one I race toward the back of the house and make sure that one is locked as well. I make my way back to the lounge and quickly snatch my phone from the couch and dial dad––voicemail, shit. I try Cass, then Hunter and Blake, they all go to voicemail! Fear starts to spread throughout my body, I hear the screams of the woman and the hurt cries of the men coming from outside. Tears gather in my eyes; If I go out there, I will be brought to my knees by the number of visions that I will have. The shrill ring of my phone snaps me from my thoughts, I nearly scream when I see its Cass, I quickly push the green button.

"Cass where are you guys?"

"We're coming Belle!" He's panting and out of breath.

"Cass something is going on out there––"

"Ignore it, go to your room and lock the door. Do not come out Belle." I can hear a hint of fear in his voice and that scares me more than the screams outside. Cass is never scared.

"Cassius, what is going on and please don't lie to me." A loud growl sounds from Cass and I flinch.

"He tricked us somehow Belle, he's here and he's come for you."

CHAPTER FOUR

Belle

I nearly drop my phone; my ears begin to buzz and I'm immobile with fear. How was I wrong? The vision was cold, and I could see bits of snow, winter isn't until a couple of weeks away. How did I get this so wrong, dad has taken my brothers and most of the pack guards with him, the rest of us are here defenseless.

"Belle!" I shake my head and try to focus on what he is saying. "We're not far, just stay inside okay." My bottom lip begins to tremble.

"Cass, if anything happens to me––." Loud growls from his end cut me off, I know Hunter, Blake and dad can hear me, but I have to say this. "I love you guys––."

"Don't say that shit like it's a goodbye! You will not be taken Gabrielle; we will die before we let anyone take you!" There is so much conviction in Cass's voice, but he has to know I will never let them die for me.

"Give that to me." Hunter snaps, a moment later his voice comes over the speaker. "Belle, our job as your older brothers is to protect you. Stay inside and hide okay, I promise everything is going to be okay." Just as Hunter finishes speaking a loud booming voice begins to shout outside.

"We are here for Gabrielle Wilder, surrender her to us and no one will be harmed, you have my word." That voice sends shivers down my spine.

"Belle, don't you dare listen. You stay the fuck inside do you hear me. We're nearly there!" I end the call and quietly move toward the front of the house and ignore the incessant ringing of my phone. I move the net curtain back a tiny amount so I can peek out, I stifle my gasp. The whole pack, women, children, elderly and even the men are on their knees in front of the man from my vision. He is surrounded by at least a dozen hulking shifters, women are among them as well. Fear crawls through my veins, I can't see him clearly from this distance, but I can see the anger emanating from the stiffness of his body.

"Give her up and you will all be set free, no one has to die here today." Tears gather in my eyes; they may fear me, but they are loyal to their alpha and will protect me! They are all aware that I am hiding inside my house like a coward, while they are all out there on their knees with their lives on the line. I refuse to let them do this, they don't have a choice, none of them can go against an alphas order. I blink away my tears and stand up straighter, I take a few steadying breaths and head toward the front door to give myself up in exchange for the safety of my pack. Just as my hand touches the door handle a familiar voice shouts out and I quickly make my way back to the window.

"Leave now and *you* will live!" I see Cass, dad, Hunter, Blake and the rest of the men coming from the woods on the east side, I sigh in relief. We're going to be okay; dad and the guys will make sure of it. The man from the vision turns toward the men emerging from the woods but shows no fear.

"We are not leaving without Gabrielle Wilder." The man booms, the way he says my name is like a prayer or something.

"There is no one here by that name." Hunter shouts, a dark smirk appears on the man's face. The women that stand either side of him shake their heads if they were expecting that answer.

"Is this not the Wilder pack?" He retorts, Cass and the others now stand behind the kneeling pack members with their backs to me. All the men are coiled and ready to shift at any given second. Their frames are blocking my view of my dad and my brothers.

"It is, I have no daughter though only three sons." Dad sounds like a real boss and is using his scary alpha voice.

"I think you're lying old man." I flinch at his cold tone, the men with dad let loose growls of anger for the blatant disrespect against their alpha.

"And I think you have a death wish, leave these lands now or you leave us no choice!" I reel back in shock, I have never heard Hunter sound authoritative and scary, he's the carefree jokester brother.

"Not without the girl!" A woman snaps, I can't see her face properly, but I can see she is the blonde-haired woman beside the man, whose name I don't even know.

"Then prepare to die!" Cass shouts, and before I can blink the men shift and start to attack, I can't keep track of them. I try to spot my dad and brothers wolves, but I lose sight of them in the chaos. The men that were kneeling have now shifted and join the fight, growls and snarls fill the air followed by yelps and screams. More wolves that I have never seen before come running from the woods behind where the man once stood. There is so many of them! Panic seeps into my bones, I have a bad feeling a...really bad feeling, that we will not win this fight. As more wolves keep coming, I can tell this fight is already over before it began, this man didn't come unprepared. He knew we would retaliate, making sure he has enough power behind him to overthrow us. Tears trail down my cheeks as I see members of my pack in wolf form and human injured on the ground. I have to stop this before more people get hurt, or worse die.

I stand here and contemplate what to do, the man's voice booms through the chaos.

"Stop now or your alpha dies!" I gasp and screen through the bodies trying to find my father. I can't see anything due to so many bodies blocking my view, a tense moment passes before members of my pack shift back to two legs and drop to their knees. I cover my mouth with my hand in shock, not only are they on their knees, but each of them are also bowing their heads in the ultimate display of submission. I dart my eyes around searching for my brothers. My eyes finally find my dad and tears of horror stream down my face, he has my father on his knees with his hand wrapped around his neck. I glance at Cass, Blake and Hunter hoping that one of them has an idea about what to do.

"Let him go and take me." Hunter shouts, the man's cold eyes swing to Hunter as he shakes his head.

"You have three seconds to give me Gabrielle or your alpha dies." Oh my god, what am I going to do? My brothers share a look, but I can't see their faces to gauge what they are thinking. "3...." I race to the front door and grip the handle. "2...." Just as he's about to say one I wrench the door open and run to the edge of the porch.

"STOP!" I shout, my eyes meet the man holding my dad for a second then it hits. I scream and drop to my knees clutching my head between my hands. Buzzing begins in my ears as the stabbing pain in my head intensifies. You ever had a migraine where light hurts your eyes, and your head feels like it's going to explode? That is what this feels like, but ten times worse, it feels like my head is cracking open. There are so many people out here and it's overwhelming my senses. Visions of pack mates and strangers I have never met begin to flash behind my eyes, I scream out. It's too much I'm gonna break soon, I can't handle it. I feel myself being lifted but I can't hear or see anything, we're moving but I don't care where, I just hope whoever it is, *is* taking me inside so the visions will stop.

Minutes tick by and finally my head stops pounding. it's now just a dull ache. I still can't open my eyes, more out of fear than anything. The buzzing sound in my ears has faded, I hear footsteps around me, still clasping the sides of my head afraid to let go just in case it falls apart. I saw so much pain, death and suffering, these visions are a curse!

"She needs us, move now!" I know that voice and it brings me comfort to know he is okay, my eyes still won't open. I haven't experienced that much pain from visions in years.

"Why should I let you?" That voice belongs to the alpha male who gave me no choice but to exit my safe haven in order to save my father.

"Because she is my daughter, we are the only ones who can help her. Allow me to do this and then I will...let you finish what you started." Growls sound out.

"I don't want to kill you, Gabriel; I just need your daughter." I shudder, moments later I feel a presence in front of me but still don't open my eyes.

"Belle, we're right here your brothers and I are fine. Can you open your eyes please?" I shake my head; I'm still fighting against the pressure that is making me feel like my head is going to crack open. which means there are more people around me.

"You need to get back! You're all too close to her." I'm beyond grateful that Cass is able to pick up on my distress and knows exactly what I need.

"And risk you escaping with her? We'll pass." Comes from a woman.

"No, you dumbass, she has to have space so the visions will stop. If it's her help that you seek, refusing to back away will not help the situation."

"The rest of you wait outside now, I'll stay." I hear footsteps and then a door slam, my stabbing pain at the base of my skull begins to lessen. I slowly start to blink my eyes open. Once I'm sure that no more visions are about to assault me, I drop my hands. I sigh in relief when I see my dad and brothers standing in front of me, dad moves forward to hug me, but I shake my head, sighing he drops down next to me on the couch.

"Belle––." I can see from the look in his eyes that he feels immense guilt for what I did.

"Dad, stop. I did what I had to do; I would never let you." I look to my three brothers. "Any of you die for me." Hunter darts his gaze behind me, and that's when I remember the man is still here. I jump to my feet and spin around to face him.

Oh my god, it's him!

CHAPTER FIVE

Belle

I stand there mouth agape just staring at him, I don't know how I didn't put it together earlier when the vision of him saying he was here to claim me. I have never seen his face before, but a feeling deep inside me tells me that he is the man I have been having visions about for months. The man standing before me doesn't look broken or hurt like in the visions, this man looks cruel and mean. He wears a mask around his emotions, he has hardened himself to the world and refuses to let others in. His eyes narrow but he won't look away, I'm no threat to him because I'm not a wolf. His eyes stare through me, he isn't looking at me, it's like he is looking inside me and that is unsettling. As he comes closer and is illuminated by the light I can see him better, his chest is bare, and he only wears a pair of shorts. Tattoo's cover his arms and chest, he has a body to die for! He has long black hair that is slicked back and striking ice blue eyes that sear you with an intensity. He has high cheek bones and a straight nose, black perfectly shaped brows, full lips the size women pay money for. This man carries an aura of power with him.

"I will die before I let you take my daughter from me!" My dad's voice has me snapping out of my thoughts, I turn toward him and melt at the look in his eyes, he looks so defeated and that isn't a look I am used to seeing on him. I move so I can comfort him but stop when a growl pierces the still air, every fiber of my being feels taut and strung out. As if I am compelled by this beast of a man, I slowly turn back toward him, even though my mind screams at me to run to my family for safety. I feel Cass and Hunter press in close to me and watch as the man narrows his ice-cold gaze at us. Not wanting to poke the bear, I step forward, he watches me with an intensity that makes me feel as if he is trying to gauge my thoughts.

Goodluck, my mind is the last place you would want to be.

I don't stop moving until there is two feet of space between us, I run my gaze over him, and he does the same. I can feel his eyes lingering over my body as I can feel every part of me heating under his inspection. What seems like an eternity is over in a second, that's when I see it, the pain in his eyes sears me.

He seems way too young to have such a broken look in his eyes. His body is ridged and tense, the tattoos that cover him are like a road map to his life. I want to inspect them further and gauge each of their meanings from him, but I doubt now is not the time for that, the fact I am standing so close to him and not being plagued by visions is...weird.

"Why have you come?" I whisper, his body seems to tense further at the sound of my voice.

"Because you seem to be the answer to a lot of my problems." My brow furrows in confusion. Something about this man is throwing me off, my visions may give me a glimpse into the lives of others, but it didn't prepare me for meeting him in *real* life.

"I don't know who you are or why you have been raiding other packs, whatever it is you think my sister can offer you, she can't. If it is soldiers you need then my brothers and I will take her place." Tears cloud my vision as I turn to face Blake.

"No, I won't let you guys do this––."

"Shut up!" I stumble back toward my father and brothers and begin to tremble, the anger that coats his tone and the way he is vibrating with rage terrifies me. "No one is going anywhere until I say!"

"I won't let you harm my children!"

"Who said anything about harming your children *alpha?* I am not here to hurt anyone, all I need is the help of your daughter, and then my pack and I will leave and never return. You have my word." To my horror a snort escapes me and the broody giant snarls at my insolence. "Got something to say?"

"I have seen you for months and there is no way you will walk away empty handed, you're not here for yourself and you don't raid for power. What is it that you seek alpha because I can assure you nothing here will help you in your journey to save the one you *think* you love most?" He tries to hide it, but I can see in his eyes that I have shocked and rendered him speechless, I have had many visions over the past few months. I couldn't make sense of it. I saw things that I assumed must have been a lie, but I won't tell him that, my brothers know all about what I've have I seen. They thought I was crazy when I told them, but standing here now, I know what I saw is true. I just need to keep up the timid act a while longer, and when he least expects it, I'm going to turn his world upside down like he did mine.

"You are more astute than I originally thought, all you have to do is comply with my demands and we will walk away and leave you be." I hear truth in his words, but I can tell he still isn't being completely honest with us.

"So, you have come all this way for my help?"

"Yes!" He grits out through clenched teeth.

"What the hell do you want then?" Cass shouts, my dad gently grips my elbow and pulls me backward until I'm in the protective barrier of my family. My three brothers move to block my father and I from his view, I think the newcomer feels intimidated by this maneuver, his growls and the flickering of his eyes semi changing to his wolf sends us a warning.

"You would be wise to remember who just made your pack submit." Cass and Blake both tense at the reminder of what transpired mere minutes ago, our numbers are minimal, but we stand with strength!

"In case you haven't noticed, but you're standing in our home alone and un-protected, what is to stop us from tearing your throat out right here and now?" Hunter sounds cocky, the sly smirk that graces our captors face tells me that he is prepared for such a move. The front door bangs open, and the woman warrior accompanied with a hulking male enter our home. This woman is stunning and looks fierce, she has pixie cut blonde hair and muddy-brown eyes. She is petite, her vibes tell me she isn't someone who you should underestimate. In my visions she is always with him, whenever in battle, she fights alongside the alpha. He views her as his equal, and I hate that I am going to be the one that shatters him when he learns the truth about her.

"Touch him and I'll slit your throat while your father watches." She says this with a gleeful smile on her face that sends shivers down my spine. She seemed less...scary in my visions.

"Try not to threaten Cairo, Sky gets very...blood thirsty." Cairo...that's his name, it's such a strong name and suits him perfectly. The man beside him chuckles and shakes his head, his black hair flops onto his forehead and his blue eyes sparkle with mischief. I'm pulled from staring at the three strangers when dad releases my arm and pushes between my brothers so he can face our...guests?

"What do you want from us? If it is power that you seek then I'll give it to you——."

"Dad!"

"No!" Dad ignores Hunter and Blakes pleas.

"Under one condition, you let my children go." Cairo is already shaking his head before dad finishes.

"Power means nothing to me alpha, I don't need or want it."

"A man who seeks nothing is a man who cannot be trusted." Cairo smiles at my father before cutting his gaze to me. My breath hitches and I tense in anticipation, he rakes his gaze up and down my body, I see the heat in his eyes.

He frowns and shakes his head slightly, he finds me attractive but hates it, you won't hate it when you find out though, alpha.

"She is what I came for." Before I can utter a word, my brothers attack in unison, they battle with the three strangers as dad spins toward me. I see the fear and panic in his eyes as he meets my gaze.

"Run Belle——."

"No, daddy——."

"That's an order, run now!" I cut my gaze to my brothers as tears spring to my eyes, I face my father again and nod then I take off toward the back door. I unlock it and then throw it open and freeze, I look both ways but see no wolves patrolling the back, they must still be out the front. I snap out of it and jump down the stairs; taking off toward the woods. I hear shouts behind me, not daring to look over my shoulder to check how far they are. I pump my arms harder and push my legs to their limits, I jump over a fallen log and stumble slightly but manage to right myself quickly.

"Stop!" I hear someone shout from behind me, but I ignore them and keep pumping my limbs hoping upon hope that I will be able to outrun a shifter. I see the creek up ahead; all I have to do is get through it and climb the incline on the other side and reach the road. I begin to pray that a car will be passing, or I'm screwed. Just as I near the edge of the creek I crouch slightly readying to jump, but before I get the chance, a pair of arms wrap around my waist, and I scream out when a vision hits.

Chapter Six

Belle

*I*t's so dark and I'm cold, I push up from the damp ground and look around. I gasp when I see the bodies that litter the ground, numerous lifeless eyes stare back at me. I jump to my feet and watch in horror as I see Sky standing amongst the dead covered in blood, her eyes are as black as night and black lines that resemble veins cover her exposed arms and face. Her gaze cuts to me and I still, no one has ever been able to see or hear me in a vision, but I feel as though she is looking directly at me. A haunting smile graces her face then she throws her head back and laughs like a maniac.

I look around and see that we are in the woods somewhere, wolves lay dead, and bodies are scattered around with their lifeless eyes staring up at the night Sky. What the hell happened here?

I bolt upright and scream, I see an arm coming toward me and shrink away. I look around and notice I'm back at my house on the couch, I see my brothers tied to three chairs, my father kneels in front of me with a worrying look on his face.

"You're okay, deep breaths." I do as dad instructs and take some steadying breaths. I can feel the light sheen of sweat that coats my body, that vision is unlike anything I have ever seen before. I felt the darkness coming off Sky in waves, whatever that was inside it's horrible and frightening.

"How the hell do we move her if we can't even touch her?" I turn to peer over the back of the couch and spot Cairo, two men and Sky, when her gaze meets mine, I quickly turn away. I hear a scoff and know it came from her, the carnage that I just witnessed is still so fresh in my mind, I bite my tongue to hold in my snarky retort.

"How do we move her?" One of the other guys says, I grit my teeth and push myself up so I can stand. Dad tries to help but I raise my hand, still too fearful of his touch causing another vision. Once on my feet I frown at the sight of my brothers, Cass shakes his head in warning, but I ignore him turning to face the four asshats. I take a deep breath and square my shoulders as I meet Cairo's gaze, he quirks a brow at me which has me grinding my teeth in annoyance.

"I am right here! And the *her* is not going anywhere with you lot! If you want help, then just bloody ask, but my family and I will not let you bully us––." My tirade is cut short when Cairo stalks toward me, when he is mere feet away, I step back until I hit the wall of the fireplace. I raise my hand to stop his advances, to my utter surprise he does. His breaths are coming out in fast pants, and I spy my dad over his shoulder and see the two men have a grip on each of his arms holding him in place.

"Don't touch her!" I turn to the other side and see my brothers fighting against the chains that hold them in place. I shake my head at Blake urging him to remain quiet.

"You will do as I say, when I say and how I say!" I lift my gaze slowly to meet his, twitching my upper lip in a snarl.

"If you let my family go, I will do whatever you ask."

"Release them." My eyes widen in shock, I didn't think he would actually listen to me!

"Gabrielle no!" I meet my dad's gaze over Cairo's shoulder and smile sadly.

"You would all do the same for me."

"Take me, I'm heir to the pack and stronger than she will ever be. I'll fight any battle you want, and kill whoever you want, just leave my sister here!" Tears spring to my eyes at Cass's words, he doesn't mean to belittle me, he is talking himself up to be the better choice. Cairo's gaze remains locked onto mine as he answers.

"You will never be as strong as her. Skylar release them and stay here while I take the alpha for a...chat." Panic fills me, he is going to hurt my father! I do something I haven't done in so many years, he turns to walk away, but I reach out and grip his arm causing another vision to hit, I scream out before everything goes dark, again.

I see his wolf; he runs over the bare land as if he is chasing something that he won't let escape him. I hear the screams from beyond not bothering to catch up, as soon as he is out of sight my visions move with the person. We clear the tree line and then I see it, we're back with the bodies and Sky standing on the top of the hill laughing. Cairo releases a horrible broken howl and Sky's laughter cuts off as she faces him. He shifts back to human form, and I get a clear view of his bare backside.

"Let me help you." Sky's black eyes crinkle at the corners.

"You promised me you would never let this happen——."

"Please let me help you." I can hear the devastation in his voice.

"Your council is dead; your chosen mate is next——." A growl tears from his chest and he begins to vibrate with unbridled rage.

"You take me! You leave her out of this and take me instead, I'm the one you want, not her."

I groan, the pounding in my head from all these visions is crippling me. One vision a day takes it out of me, let alone this many in a short amount of time is unthinkable. My head feels like it is going to crack open, I bite my lip to stop the whimper. I blink my eyes open slowly and regret it instantly when the stabbing pain in the sides of my temples intensifies. I don't know what the hell I was thinking by touching him, I continue silently berating myself while conversations carry on around me, my mind falls back into the two visions. The destruction caused by the two of them is horrifying, I could feel the pain radiating off them, something is wrong. I could feel Sky's reluctance to embrace this unknown power, her fear was so potent I could almost taste it. Cairo's pain and anguish was debilitating to say the least, I could feel the hatred he had toward himself for the mayhem that Sky caused.

"Belle?" I take a readying breath and brace myself for the pain that is about to hit me when I open my eyes and face my father. I grit my teeth to stop any sounds escaping me, but it's no use, a hiss breaks free, and worry clouds my dads' eyes. I push myself into a sitting position and find I am once again on the freaking couch. "Here." He hands me a glass of water and Advil to go with it. I thank him, then swallow the pills. The pain killers help to numb the pain but it never gets rid of it.

"How long was I out?" Dad tries to mask it, but I see him cringe.

"Just under two hours." My turn to cringe now, I turn to the side and notice that my brothers are still in chains, my anger starts to peak.

"Settle down Charmed one." I swing my legs off the couch to see who spoke, I haven't seen this man before. He seems more relaxed and easy going compared to the others, he has a genuine smile, and eyes that shine with laughter. Stunningly handsome, with shaggy brown hair and sparkling green eyes, I get a feeling he's quite the prankster. He isn't as tall as Blake and Hunter, but this guy is broad and built like a wall of muscle. "Keep checking me out sweetheart, it's great for my ego." The growl that comes from someone in the kitchen causes him to laugh and shake his head. "I'm Cole."

"I'm Belle." He smirks and winks as he says.

"I know, you're a bloody hard person to find Belle. Took us months to hunt you down." He says like it isn't creepy being hunted by a pack of wolves.

"Why?" My dad claims the seat beside me but makes sure to leave enough space between us so we don't touch, I don't think I can handle another vision right now.

"Because sweetheart, we need your help." His honesty is a breath of fresh air.

"You want me to help you, in yet you chain my brothers like dogs." I scoff and slouch back crossing my arms over my chest. He clicks his tongue then makes his way over to Cass, I fight my reaction to tense and demand he stay the hell away from him. I know if I do that, I would show him that he bothers me and that is never something you should do when being held prisoner.

"Colton!" I can hear the warning in Cairo's voice and feel his presence directly behind me, I keep my gaze locked on Cole as he begins to unbind Cass.

"You want her to help?" Cole asks.

"Yes!" Cairo growls. Cole smirks at him as he releases Cass from the chains and begins to work on freeing Hunter.

"Good, then maybe you should start by not being a dick and treating her family like shit. Isn't that right sweetheart?" I nod my head like an idiot at a loss for words. "How about I let Belle and her brothers take me on a tour of their lands while you hash out the details with dear old pops over there?"

"I can't go outside!" I rush to say in a panic.

Cairo shut down Cole's idea of a tour, which I am thankful for, but of course I didn't let him know that. I have made sure to keep my distance from Cairo and his pack mates in the hopes of not setting off another vision. Seeing him for the past eight months doesn't mean I know him, *know* him. I'm getting over waiting for them to say something, dad and my brothers are sitting on the couch tense and silent. Tension and fear is coursing through my body which is enhancing another vision that I cannot handle right now, so I choose to break the silence.

"Can one of you please just tell us what you want or need from me so then you can all leave? My family and I have done nothing wrong and I'm tired and hungry!" Cole, Sky, Cairo and the two others turn toward me, I refuse to cower under their intense stares. I admit my resolve starts to waiver when it's Sky who makes her way over, I fight the shiver that wants to break free when her gaze meets mine. Her eyes seem almost darker, her face is devoid of all emotion, she has the look of a cold-blooded killer.

"What we need from you, you will not be willing to give."

"You don't know me!" I grit out and glare at her.

"Let me list off what I know then, you're the baby of the family, daddy's little princess, spoiled by her brothers. Lived a sheltered life, never had to want for anything, always had a warm place to sleep and never had to worry about where your next meal is coming from? You're like every other entitled princess, you think your special, but you're not, you are a means to an end and that is it." Her cold heartless words have tears springing to my eyes, the pain and anguish I felt for her in my vision has just been obliterated by her cruelness. I blink my tears back refusing to show this bully that her words hit their mark, I steel my spine and make sure to keep my face expressionless.

"You're right, I am all of the above." A knowing smile graces her beautiful face. "But what pisses you off more, the fact that I had all of those, or the fact that you didn't?" The smile vanishes in an instant, never breaking eye contact, I hear the others begin to snicker. Something about Sky tells me it would be a fatal mistake to ever turn your back on her, she steps closer to me, and I brace myself for a vision to hit, given her close proximity, but it...doesn't. Her face holds no anger or any emotion, this woman has an amazing poker face.

"I wouldn't expect a Barbie like you to know what struggling is, you want the truth? We need you to help us find the council and end a curse that has long plagued my pack. Do those two things and you and your family will be free." I dart my gaze to my brothers to see they are just as confused about these demands as I am.

"I can't just bring on visions about people I have never met or been near, it doesn't work like that. Also, I can't help you break a curse, I'm a shifter not a...witch." The mask drops from her face, I see it plain as day––fear. Something I just said evoked a deep-rooted fear in this fearless warrior and I plan to find out what it is.

"Enough!" Sky turns and heads toward Cairo and the others, my family must sense the shift in the air as well. My dad and brothers move to stand near me. "You will have to come with us then––."

"No! she cannot leave here." Cairo narrows his eyes at my father.

"She is coming with us whether you like it or not. Once her job is finished, we will deliver her back to you safe and sound." Fear thrums through me, at the thought of leaving my home, visions will assault me constantly and it will kill me.

"She will die!" Cass's voice booms around the room, I flinch at the reminder. All I have ever wanted my entire life is to go on an adventure, make friends and travel abroad, but unfortunately, they're only dreams. that isn't possible for me.

"No, she won't." I snap my gaze to Sky; she sounds so sure of herself, and I hate to admit it but a part of me is hoping that these people may have a solution to grant me my freedom from this gilded cage I call *home*. I can see dad opening his mouth out of the corner of my eye, I know he is about to deny them, so I cut him off.

"If you have a solution to stopping the visions from assaulting me when I leave the house, please say so." I can feel my families eyes on me, but I refuse to take my gaze from Sky.

"We do have one."

"Then, you have my *word*. If this works and no visions crash into me as soon as I step outside, I will help you."

Chapter Seven

Belle

"I cannot let this happen, you are my daughter, and I will not let you put yourself at risk for me Gabrielle. You can't trust these fools––."

"I know daddy, but I gave them my word that I will help, if they could come up with a solution, and they did!" My father stares at me with a blank look.

"What has gotten into you? Two days ago, you wouldn't have entertained the idea of leaving the house with your brothers let alone a group of strangers. No, not strangers' kidnappers, that is what they are Belle. In all the years you and your brothers have been alive have you ever heard of another subduing anyone only to take one person who isn't even the alpha?" I hear the anger in his voice, but I know it is just a mask for his pain, he feels powerless to stop this from happening. My dad has always been a fixer, whether it be an object or a person, he will endeavor to find a way to amend what is broken. My heart wants me to reach out and hold his hand, but not with my visions being the way they are today.

"I know this is hard for you––."

"Hard?" He whisper shouts, I peer over my shoulder to see Cairo and his friends in the kitchen talking amongst themselves. My brothers bolted out of the room to head upstairs when I announced that I would be leaving with Cairo. "You are but a child Gabrielle, you have no idea what horrors this world holds. You are my daughter, and I cannot let you go off with a blood-thirsty alpha and his pack of savages!" I flinch at the venom in his tone.

"She won't be alone Pops." I spin around to see my three brothers standing there, each of them has a bag slung over their shoulder and a sad smile on their faces.

"Cassius, what are you doing?" Cass moves toward dad and places his large hand on his shoulder.

"You're right Pops, she can't go with them alone. Blake, Hunter and I will go with her to make sure she is safe." My dad's face drops, he looks so...hurt and it guts me to see him like this.

"I–I, No. You three stay I'll go––." Cass shakes his head and cuts dad off.

"You said I needed more experience outside of the pack before I can lead, so this will give me that opportunity. You're the alpha dad, your responsibility is here. I swear we will keep her safe, and as soon as this is all over, the four of us will be back before you know it." I just about burst into tears when my father's tear-filled gaze lands on me.

"We have to do this now and head out before nightfall." The moment is shattered by Cairo's interruption.

"How do we do this?" I ask.

"Take Sky to your room and she will explain everything." I don't bother to question him; we head to my bedroom and take a seat on the edge of my bed. She doesn't look around just places her hands on her hips and stares at me.

"Close your eyes and don't open them." I furrow my brow in confusion but do as she says. I know this is necessary, I just hope that the vision I had a few weeks ago is right. I never told my family about that vision, it just seemed so...intimate to share with anyone. I have no idea what the meaning is, I just know with every fiber of my being that it was Sky, and I have to do whatever I can to try and stop what is coming.

"Done." I blink my eyes open and stare up at her in shock.

"What?"

"Are you deaf?" I shake my head like an idiot. "It's done. Now let's go, quicker we get out of here the better." I stand ready to follow her, but she raises her hand to stop me. "Pack a bag, you'll need it, or Callie will wind up dressing you." I quirk a brow at her, she rolls her eyes and adds. "You'll thank me for this later, now hurry up."

My brothers and I stand on the front porch facing our father with our bags in hand, dad runs his gaze over each of us like he is committing everything he sees to memory. I've been tense ever since I stepped out the front door, afraid visions would hit me, and I would be whisked back inside. I've never been able to stand outside like this, and with no pain, it's strange but also exhilarating.

"You remember what I said Cassius?"

"Yeah Pops. I'll make sure it doesn't happen." I dart my gaze between the two them, clearly, they are talking in code. Sometimes I wish my visions could be useful and show me things that I actually want to know.

"Good. I hope it doesn't happen, just be ready in case it does." Hunter cuts dad off.

"What the hell are the two of you going on about?" Dad relaxes his face and smiles at Hunter.

"Nothing for you to worry about. Make sure you all look out for each other and stay together." We all agree, my brothers each bid dad goodbye and then head down the porch steps to wait for me. As I stand in front of my father, a lump begins to form in my throat, I've never left home before. "I wish I could hold you, even for a moment." The longing in his voice is what causes the first tear to fall.

"So do I." I choke out.

Dad smiles sadly at me. "Go have your adventure Belle, just know I'll be here for you and whatever you discover out there, never forget that I love you my sweet girl."

"I love you too daddy." I sob out, dad clears his throat as he fights so hard to hold back his tears.

After trekking through the woods for a couple of miles, we emerge into a clearing of sorts where there are numerous Hummers parked. My brothers and I haven't spoken a word since we left our father. Cairo moves toward the one at the front and motions for me to follow him, I feel my brothers close in around me.

"You three aren't coming." I skid to a stop, Hunter and Blake creep in closer to my sides, I can feel Cass at my back, he releases an angry growl.

"She stays with us!"

"What the fuck makes you three think you'll be coming with us?" Hunter steps in front of me, I see Cairo's pack begin to move in closer to their alpha.

"Where she goes, we go. If you want to fight us on it, then so be it." Hunter and Blake drop their bags, Hunt grips the bottom of his shirt but stops at Cairo's words.

"You really think the three of you could win against my pack? Did we not just subdue your whole pack in a matter of minutes?"

"Fuck you!" Cass growls, Cairo's pack begins to growl, and I can see from the look in some of their eyes that they are ready to shift at the drop of a hat if my brothers try anything. I take a steadying breath and step out from behind Hunter and meet Cairo's gaze.

"Even if you won't let them come with us, they will follow me to the ends of the earth. There is no place in this world you can hide me where they wouldn't find me. It will be easier for you to just allow them to travel with us, I gave you my word I would help you, but it's now up to you whether or not I do it happily, or challenge you at every turn?" Cairo's brows raise nearly hitting his hairline.

"Are you blackmailing me?" Cole chuckles beside him.

"Of course not, I'm simply stating the facts and telling you what I think is in your best interest." I smile sweetly, the angry look he gives me tells me he isn't pleased with how I just strong armed him. The thing is, I wasn't lying, my brothers would hunt me down until they found me. My family is loyal, and we always back each other no matter what, it's how our father raised us, that if one of us battles, then we all go to war.

Never leave a Wilder behind. Is what father has always instilled in us since we were young pups.

Chapter Eight

Cairo

She is insufferable and so are her brothers, whatever she saw in that vision has Sky on edge and avoiding me. I grit my teeth and white knuckle the steering wheel, the four of them have remained silent since we got in the car, she sits in the middle of her brothers while her oldest brother rides shotgun next to me. I don't know why I allowed them to tag along, something in her gaze told me that she wasn't joking when she said that they will track her. I don't like the idea of taking three grown male shifters back with us but truthfully, I don't know how to deal with her and her visions without them. It seems that everything or anyone she touches aside from her *family* sets off a vision, I wish I could be inside her head when she has them. I want to know what she saw about Sky, no, I need to know what she saw about Sky, I promised my sister that I would take down the council for what they did to her and our family, but right now, my main concern is Sky. The only person who knows the truth about who and what she really *is*, is me, Callie is her *mate*, but even she doesn't know. We have about another five hours before we reach my sisters pack, and with the amount of tension in the car it is sending my wolf nuts, he wants to make them all submit to him.

"Where are we going?" The sound of her voice snaps me from the inner monologue with my wolf, I meet her gaze in the rearview mirror, I quickly tear my eyes from hers.

"Rosewood."

"Wait, isn't that the place where the first female alpha lives?" I grind my teeth in irritation at Hunter's question, I don't like that he knows about my sister. I open my mouth to answer, but snap it closed when Belle gasps, I feel her eyes burning into the back of my head.

"What is it?" I can hear the worry in Cass's voice, it's the same tone I use with Jess when I'm worried about her.

"She's, his sister!" I grit my teeth; I can feel all their eyes on me but refuse to acknowledge them. "I know her, well... I don't know her, but I have seen her and her family." That gets my attention.

"How the fuck do you know about her family?" I meet her gaze in the mirror and see her flinch at my cold tone.

"You may be the one holding us hostage, but you don't ever fucking speak to her like that!" The venom that coats Cass's voice has a smile playing on my lips, this fucker is going to learn fast that I am the only one who calls the shots around here.

"You will shut the fuck up and sit back before I kill her and make you watch!" He tries to lunge at me, but I'm faster, I snap my arm out and clamp it around his throat and squeeze the car starts to swerve, Belle screams but I don't let up. "Don't ever fucking question me again asshole." I release him with a shove and quickly right the car before we go off the road. I ignore his coughing and spluttering beside me, fucker needs to be taken down a peg or two.

"You want to kill me, fine! But don't you ever touch my brother like that again or I will kill you with my bare freaking hands." I scoff.

"I'd like to see you try beauty, I'm the baddest fucking beast there is, and you will learn that soon enough. Do as you are told, and you'll be back with daddy dearest before you know it."

"Then just tell me what it is that you want, and then we can be done! I'm not some side-show act that you can use whenever you feel the need––."

"I will use you until you give me what I want." I glance at her in the mirror and when a look of hatred enters her eyes I tear my gaze from her, good she needs to hate me.

She isn't the enemy Cairo.

Fuck off Bex.

My wolf–Bexley and I haven't been seeing eye to eye since meeting the little devil in the backseat, Bex is an alpha through and through and demands respect and submission. Yet, he doesn't seem to mind Belle's smart mouth and ill temper.

"She doesn't have long." Being a shifter means I have impeccable hearing; she may have mumbled the words under her breath, but I heard them loud and clear as did her brothers.

"Who, sis?" Her eyes meet mine in the rear view as she answers.

"When the snow begins to stick to the ground is when it happens, the path you are on is what will lead to her demise." I growl low in my throat; she has no fucking idea what she is saying. "*She* is the reason I'm here, isn't she?" I tear my gaze from her and ignore their chatter.

What if she is right?

She can't be, Sky knew about the control thing long before this.

If she turns––

Fuck up Bex, I won't do it.

I close off the link between me and Bex, I won't even entertain the idea of what he is suggesting–– I can't. Not to her, I could never do that to her.

We arrive at my sister's pack later than I expected, I spy their guards in wolf form patrolling their lands. I follow the long drive up to the back of the property where Creed built their new house, I never thought I would see the day Credence Reeves settled down. I'm proud of him and my sister, after everything they have been through, and the shit Creed put her through, they deserve this. I was unsure if he would step up and be the mate she deserved, but over time he has proven me wrong, I couldn't have asked for a better brother-in-law. I stop the car in front of their house, Jess never wanted to leave their small cabin, so Creed decided to just build her a bigger one. It's a three-story cabin, it almost reminds me of the Dutton's house from Yellowstone. Got to give it to the bastard, he is a bloody talented architect as well as a builder, since opening his construction company he's profited an insane amount of cash, which has helped cover the costs of the builds he has been doing for the pack. I hop out of the car and leave the four of them there, they can either choose to follow, or sleep in the car for all I fucking care.

"And the ghost of my past returns." I spin around to see Creed walking toward me, carrying a load of wood in his arms, the fucker has the lumberjack look going on. His Brown hair swishes around as he shakes his head, I see nothing but happiness in his hazel eyes. He always looked so haunted and worn out as a teenager but ever since getting with my sister, he seems more...free. "You gonna help or just stand there?" I reach out and pluck a couple of logs from his arms, his mouth drops open when he spots someone over my shoulder.

"Hello, brother."

"Colton." I grab the rest of the logs from him so he can go greet his brother, no sooner have I taken the last log from him does he brush past me and rush toward his brother. I smile as I watch them embrace each other, before Cole decided to leave with me and my pack, he and Creed weren't exactly getting along, given the fact that Cole sort of has a thing for my sister. I don't blame Creed for wanting to pummel his brother. I spy Callie and Sky making their way around the car with Z in tow, the others traveling with us were given instructions to stay back by Creed and Jess's pack. Creed spots his sister and a wide grin spreads across his face as she runs toward him and jumps into his arms, he catches her with ease.

"Big brother, I missed you!" Sick to death of holding these logs I motion for Z to get his ass over here so he can carry this shit inside for Creed. Once he has the logs I move toward Creed and the others.

"I missed you to California, you better get both your asses down to mom's house before she finds out from someone else that you're here." The twins both cringe and nod their heads, Callie places a chaste kiss on Sky's cheek before following after Cole. As soon as they are out of hearing distance, Creed spins and shoves me hard in the chest, I automatically brace for a fight, Bex lunges forward and growls, my eyes shifting to those of my wolf's.

"Stand down now, or I will make you!"

"Stay out of this Skylar!" Creed snaps.

"The fuck is your problem, Reeves?"

"You are, why the fuck did you bring them here?" He points to the car I arrived in. "My wife and son are inside, and you bring fucking trouble to their doorstep, if anything happens to them because of your shit Cairo, I'll rip your fucking heart out myself!"

"Fuck you, Reeves." His eyes flash to the blue of his wolf and I prepare for him to charge me, each of us take a step toward the other.

"Ro-Ro!" I immediately halt in my tracks, his eyes return to his normal color, Bex recedes inside me, and I spin toward the house to see my nephew running across the lawn, I crouch down and open my arms waiting for the greatest joy of my life to slam into me. I wrap my arms around my nephew and hold him close, I inhale his scent and instantly relax, the anger from a moment ago is gone within seconds.

"I missed you monster."

"Me to, you were gone a *loooong* time Ro-Ro." I smile at my nephew; he's grown since I last saw him.

"I know Monster, but I'm here now and——"

"He's right you know; you were gone a long time." I stand and lift the monster on my shoulders as I look at my sister, she stands there with a frown on her face and her hands on her hips.

"Hey smalls." She scowls at me.

"Don't you dare *hey smalls* me! You were supposed to text or call every second day, I thought you were dead you...you——"

"Eggplant?" She snaps her angry gaze to her mate, I smother my laughter behind a cough, clearly Reeves hasn't learnt to keep his mouth shut.

"Unless you want to be sleeping on the couch, you will stay out of this!" Creed visibly flinches and then turns to me.

"I tried." I glower at the dick.

"Pussy."

"Mommy Ro-Ro said daddy's a *pussy*." I cringe when my sisters angry gaze swings to me.

"If you weren't holding––" Jess's reply is cut off when the doors to my Hummer open, I take a steady breath and watch as Creed moves toward me and plucks his son from my shoulders.

"You better hope you know what you're doing bringing *her* here." He whispers low enough for only me to hear. Sky and Z make their way over to stand on either side of me, as we watch the four Wilder siblings round the car. I hear my sisters gasp, but I don't turn to her, she will see the truth in my eyes, and I can't let her kind heart sway me from what needs to be done.

"You found her?" I hear the awe in Jess's voice, Cass and the others move slightly to shield Belle from our gazes, a growl sounds out from behind me, it's Creed sending the three brothers a warning.

"You so much as lift a hand, or even think about doing something stupid while my son and mate are here, I will end the four of you without any remorse." Pride swells inside me at how much Creed has changed, Jess and Harlem are his life, and he would have no problem setting the world on fire for the both of them.

"Who the fu––." Jess cuts Blake off.

"No cussing in front of Harlem!" She snaps, she steps away from Creed, he tries to reach for her, but she slaps his hand away and growls. She moves toward the four of them, but I block her path, her blue eyes shift to the yellow of her wolf. Bex rears his head, but I push him down, I won't let him hurt my sister.

"Smalls." I growl out in warning.

"Don't you dare, you are not in my good books for going MIA for months. You brought them to *my* pack lands so as the alpha of this pack I am telling you to step aside so I can greet my...guests." I grind my teeth in frustration ready to snap at her but Sky grips my arm and hauls me backward.

"Let her do her thing." I don't bother answering Sky, instead I stand back and watch as my sister approaches her *guests*.

Chapter Nine

Belle

A female alpha, I mean I knew she existed but to see her in the flesh is something else. Every shifter around the world has heard the rumors about Jessica Cruz, well she's Jessica Reeves now. She is stunning, shoulder length blonde hair, piercing blue eyes that shine with nothing but kindness. Seeing her in visions didn't do her beauty any justice, something inside me says that I can trust her. I turn to look at Cairo, he and Jess are polar opposites, he is dark and dangerous, where she is light and kind. Her mate releases a low growl, the closer she gets to us, her mate is handsome, if possible, he looks even better with a kid on his hip. Her chuckle has me snapping my gaze from him back to her, she eyes me knowingly and I can't fight the blush that stains my cheeks.

"He's hot right?" She says with a wink, hiding my embarrassment behind a grin, as she moves closer my brother's tense. "I'm not going to harm her, I swear." The truth in her words rings out around us, I lift my gaze to find that she is standing directly in front of Cass and Hunter.

"It's okay, you guys can move." Cass turns to peer at me over his shoulder and I can see the concern in his gaze.

"You can't take any more today, Belle." It irks me that my dad and brothers think I can't handle anything let alone my own visions!

"I know what I'm doing Cassius––." Jess groans and snags my attention as she throws her arms in the air, I furrow my brow in confusion.

"Why does everyone I know have a cool name, and my mother decides to name me plain old *Jessica*." I can't help but chuckle, the others except for my brothers do the same. "Please tell me the rest of you have boring names like *Tim* or *Joe?*" Hunter laughs and shakes his head.

"I'm Hunter, and this is Blake and Cassius." He motions to each of our brothers, he steps aside allowing me room to slip past Cass without touching him. "And this is our baby sis Gabrielle." Jess groans and throws her head back.

"Why couldn't you have stink names!"

"Your name is hot babe." She snaps her gaze to the side of us and a huge smile splits her face as she takes off running toward Cole, her mate snickers and growls as she throws herself at his kid brother. We heard everything that was said while we were in the car, joys of my brothers being shifters.

"I missed you!"

"I missed you to babe, divorce that asshole brother of mine and mate with me instead." Jess chuckles at Cole's joke but her mate isn't having any of it.

"Say that one more time and mom will be burying her youngest son tomorrow morning. Princess, step away from the mongrel before Corbin kills him." Jess shakes her head and steps out of Cole's embrace only to be engulfed in another hug from Callie, the three of them make their way back over to us, Jess finally greets Sky, and even hugs her brother, but when she stands in front of the other guy Zeke, the tension in the air skyrockets.

"Hey Z." The guy's shoulders droop and a sad smile crosses his face.

"Hello Jess." She sighs then turns to face us with a small smile on her face.

"Okay well this is awkward; do you want to come inside and get warm because I'm freezing, plus I have to put my son to bed." I look to each of my brothers waiting for their decision, but a throat clearing has my gaze snapping back to Cairo. Yeah, of course, we don't exactly have a choice in the matter do we?

My brothers and I stand in the corner of the huge lounge room, the house is freaking incredible! It has a rustic old vibe to it, you can tell everything is new, I can't stop staring, whoever made this cabin is so talented. I watch as Cairo, Sky, Zeke and Cole huddle to the other side of the room talking in low tones, so we are unable to hear them. Creed and Callie sit on one of the couches sharing stories of their time apart, the tension returned as soon as Jess left to put her son to bed. I envy her strength; I wish to one day be as bold and courageous as her. How she stood up to her mate and to Cairo is awe inspiring, I have never seen a female shifter hold her own like that against a male alpha.

"We need to find a way out of this." I shake my head and focus on my brothers; we speak low enough that the others can't hear, even with their shifter hearing.

"We can't let our guard down Belle, do you know what they want?"

"It has something to do with Sky, that's all I know Blake."

"There has to be more, it can't just be about some chick he wants to fuck." I flinch at his crass words, Blake is wrong. I've been having visions about Cairo for months, and never once have I felt or seen him be untoward Sky. Plus, she is mated to a female, that has to mean something right?

"We wait till they are asleep, and then we make our move."

"And go where Hunter? We are in the most secluded pack in the whole country and the fucker still found us, we can't go home!" I hate to say it, but Cass is right, Cairo will hunt me down again and next time I don't think he will be as...accommodating.

"We can't just wait around and see what happens Cassius."

"I know Hunt, but we have to play this smart and think about each move, because Cairo doesn't seem like a guy who leaves anything to chance. He has a plan for Belle, and we have to figure out what said plan is." Cass snaps his mouth closed when we hear the sound of footsteps coming down the stairs, we all turn to face Jess as she enters the room. Her eyes dart around, and a frown begins to form on her face.

"Are we in freaking high school?" She grits out.

"What do you mean?" Callie asks.

"Why the hell are you all divided, did any of you offer them a drink? Food? Show them where the bathroom is?" They all avoid Jess's angry stare; she growls loudly, and her mate is on his feet within a second standing in front of her.

"Princess——."

"Don't you dare *princess* me; I know who she is Credence, I was just waiting for one of you assholes to fess up and admit the truth!" I hear the venom that laces each of her words, the six, no make that five because Cairo just looks uninterested, at least the others have the decency to look sheepish. She brushes past Creed and moves toward us; my brothers tense automatically, and she scoffs. "If we were going to hurt you, I'd never have invited you into my home while my son is asleep upstairs." She sticks her hand out toward Cass and speaks. "I'm Jess." Cass eyes her hand for a beat before putting his much larger hand in hers.

"Cassius."

"Nice to meet you, I know you told me your names outside, so I thought the polite thing to do is re-introduce myself officially." She smiles sweetly at my brother, and he laughs, like actually throws his head back and laughs. Seeing my brother laugh warms me, he never smiles or laughs anymore, and I don't know why. He used to be happy and carefree growing up but now he is this walled off detached guy that won't let anyone get close to him. Jess moves along the line and does the same to my other brothers, but she stops in front of me, my breath hitches when she extends her hand. I can feel my brothers' gazes on me but the one that burns the most is Cairo's, I can feel his eyes burning into the side of my head waiting, watching to see what I will do. I take a deep breath and slowly lift my hand to place it in hers, I hate that normal contact scares the shit out of me. I don't over think it, I place my hand in hers and then scream.

I stare in horror as I watch Jess being beaten in a cage, both men and women are punching and kicking her. I scream out for them to stop but I know it's useless, they can't hear or see me. I round the cage but come to a stop when I see a man standing there, watching but he does nothing to stop them from hurting Jess, even as she screams for someone to help her.

I move so I am standing in front of him, his rancid breath hits me, and I fight the reflex to gag, his teeth are crooked and yellow, and he wears an ill fitted suit, but as I lift my gaze to inspect the rest of his face, thanks to the darkness, I can't see anything else. Something about this man doesn't sit right with me, Jess lets out a blood curdling scream, and I watch as a satisfied smile stretches across his face. As he slinks back into the darkness, I follow, I stumble up the stairs after him, when he opens the door. Light assaults me, I blink rapidly so I don't lose sight of the man, he pauses to speak to someone, but their backs are to me, when I see his eyes, a shiver runs down my spine. They are a soulless pit; this man is pure evil.

"Phillip." I turn to see another man enter the room, something about him seems so familiar.

"Ah, Jacob. I was wondering where you got to."

"Had to sort that bitch that I call daughter out."

"Alexander will be pleased to have the alpha bitch and your daughter as a gift."

"You just make sure the council keeps their end of the deal." Philips eyes narrow and his lip pulls back in a snarl.

"Don't doubt me again, I was the one who figured out how to track Alexander and brought him to Rosewood. He has agreed to give us his blood if we give him the two girls and help him find––."

I bolt upright panting; a light sheen of sweat covers my body. I slam my eyes closed to get a grip on myself and calm down, but when I register who those voices belong to, I snap my eyes open and turn to the side, a shriek escapes me when I see Cairo leaning against the door with his arms crossed over his chest. My brothers continue to shout, but all thought flees my mind when my eyes meet Cairo's. He isn't looking at me though, he's looking...through me. Whatever he sees he clearly doesn't like, because his brow furrows, I pull my gaze from his to look around and that's when I notice I'm sitting on a bed, we're in a bedroom. There is a window off to the side, a couple of dressers, a chair and that's it. I ease off the side of the bed and stand on wobbly legs, I give myself a minute to regain my equilibrium before releasing my hold.

"Can you stop staring please."

"What are you?" My brow furrows.

"I'm a shifter, just like you and my brothers."

"Gabrielle!" I flinch at the anger in Cass's tone, I take a step toward Cairo hoping he will move and let me out so I can calm my brothers, but he just shakes his head and I freeze.

"What did you see?" I shudder, what I saw in that vision was horrible and I know it's not the future, it was the past. Don't ask me how I know, but the older I get, I am able to tell a past vision from a future one. Something about that vision doesn't sit right with me, and I need my brothers to help me figure it out. "Answer me!" the anger that laces his tone has me shrinking back a step.

"I-I can't." I drop my gaze to the floor unable to maintain eye contact with him, he growls which causes me to snap my gaze back to him. His eyes have changed from blue to onyx, the color of his wolf's eyes. I gulp loudly, he stalks toward me and every step I take backward, he takes one forward, until the backs of my legs hit the side of the bed and I have nowhere else to go. He keeps a foot of space between us, I drop my gaze not wanting him to think I am challenging him. His arms are littered with tattoos, and I have the sudden urge to reach out and trace my finger over the intricate lines but stop myself at the last minute. He reaches out and I tense when his fingers grip my chin, I wait with bated breath for the vision to slam into but...it never happens. My eyes widen in shock, his eyes return to their normal blue, we stand here in stunned silence with his hand on me, but no vision comes. "What's happening?" I whisper.

"Fucked if I know, now tell me what you saw?" I shake my head but stop when his grip on my chin tightens to the point of being painful.

"I can't!" I grit out.

"Why?" Tears cloud my vision.

"Please." I'm not sure if I'm begging for him not to push me or for him to release me.

"Begging isn't becoming of you *Beauty*." Hearing that name come from him has my tears drying instantly and anger welling inside me.

"Is this some sick game to you?" I don't give him a chance to answer. "You trying to live out a sick fantasy of Beauty and the Beast?" I laugh but there is no humor to it. "I will never be as dumb and naïve as that *Belle*; this beauty will *never* fall for the *beast*." I spit the words at him, he drops his hold from my face and I use his momentary shock to my advantage and dart around him, I have the doorhandle in my grasp ready to tear it open and run to my brothers but his strong-arm wraps around my waist and hauls me back against his chest, I scream out in frustration and start to kick and throw my arms around hoping to get him to loosen his grip enough that I can flee. "Let me go asshole."

As soon as the words escape me, I freeze, all the flight flees my body and sag in his hold, *in his freaking hold*! He's touching me, my back is plastered to his chest and still I haven't been assaulted by a vision. Before I can get too lost in my thoughts, he pushes me forward and I stumble using the wall to balance me but before I can sigh in relief he's there, spinning me around until my back is flat against the wall, my arm snaps out and a satisfying *thwack* sounds out around the room, I smile when I see my handprint begin to take shape on his cheek. His eyes flash to the onyx again, I steel my spine and meet his gaze head on, I will not cower.

"You just made a huge mistake!" The threat in his voice is clear but I refuse to back down.

"No, you did, when you thought you took a docile captive! I will never willingly become your sideshow act and perform for you whenever you so choose, I will fight you every step of the way until you let us go!" An evil smirk crosses his face, a shudder runs through me when he leans down and runs his nose along the crook of my neck, I gasp at the contact. I have never, I mean never been touched like this in my life! Of course, the first man that is able to touch me in this way happens to be a psycho, that is just my freaking luck!

"You smell so good." He nips at the tender flesh between my shoulder and neck causing me to gasp, he licks a trail from my neck to my ear causing a shudder to run through me, I'm embarrassed to say that I don't shudder out of fear. He pulls back and ghosts his lips over mine, his eyes drill into me, daring me. It's in that moment that clarity slams into me like a bucket of ice water, I place my hands flat against his chest and smile sweetly as I lift my knee and ram it into his balls. He crumples like a sack of potatoes, I don't waste any time as

I take off toward the door and wrench it open, my brothers fight against Cole, Creed, Sky, Zeke and Callie, they stiffen at the sight of me.

"Belle." My name is like a prayer on Hunter's lips, I release a ragged breath and smile triumphantly.

"Fuck!" I still at the sound of his angry voice before quickly rushing forward, the other's part for me so I can get to my brothers, without overthinking, I jump at Cass, he catches me. I'm passed to Blake and then Hunter, my family has always been the only people I have been able to touch, sometimes visions hit but right now that is a risk I'm willing to take. I freeze in Hunter's arms when I hear the sound of thundering footsteps behind us, I pull back and meet my brothers gaze, I can see the worry lines etched into his features. "You dirty little devil." I cringe at the aggression in his voice, Hunter's arms band around me tighter as he pulls me closer to his chest. I feel Blake and Cass close in beside us, I don't know what came over me back there but something just...snapped. I couldn't let him pressure me or push us around like we are his toys to play with. My daddy didn't raise no doormat, he always told me to fight back and never submit to no man, no matter the cost!

"That's enough!" I turn out of Hunter's hold to see Jess standing on the other side of Cass.

"Stay out of this, smalls!" Cairo growls, Creed shoves Cairo in the chest, he stumbles back growling.

"You forget who's fucking house you're in, she may be your sister, but she is my mate, and you will not fucking speak to her like that!" Growls sound out in the narrow hallway, Hunter pulls back and pushes me behind him, my three brothers form a wall in front of me cutting off my view of the others. I hear shuffling and then Cass and the others move so Jess is now standing in front of me with a sad smile on her face.

"I don't know why you agreed to help my grump of a brother." My brow furrows.

"It's not like we had a choice." I sass, Jess looks confused.

"Don't poke your nose where——." Jess cuts her brother off.

"What do you mean?"

"We're not here on our own freewill, put it that way." Her mouth drops open and her brows just about hit her hairline in shock. She spins and faces her brother with a growl tumbling out of her.

"Tell me she is joking? You did not just kidnap four freaking people and then bring them to my home, where my son is!" The dominance and anger in her voice has me wanting to submit to her but not Cairo, he squares his shoulders and meets her gaze with a determined look.

"I did what I had to do to fulfill my promise to you, she is the key to helping us find Philip and the others." A gasp slips from my lips, my brothers are on me within seconds thinking that a vision is about to hit, I wave them away and look directly at Cairo. "You know something don't you little beauty." My cheeks heat, I don't like him calling me that especially with everyone watching.

"I-I uh...yeah." My shoulders sag, I see Jess lift her hand to touch me and I automatically shy away. Guilt eats me when I see a look of hurt cross her features. "I'm sorry, I, um—."

"Physical contact sparks visions for her, that's why she doesn't touch anyone." Recognition shines in her eyes as she nods her head.

"Thank you for telling me Hunter, well how about we all call it a night and then tomorrow you can tell us about what you know Belle." Relief courses through me, I honestly don't think I could have gotten through explaining everything from the vision tonight. I'm exhausted and just want to sleep; no not *want,* I need sleep.

"There is no time—."

"Ro, they are exhausted, and Belle is dead on her feet. I'm sure after the ordeal you have put them through, they need a night to rest and...think." I appreciate Jess so much in this moment, now that the adrenaline has worn off, I really am dead on my feet. My gaze swings to Cairo, his jaw is stiff, and his eyes are narrowed, I can see he wants to fight what his sister says but to my surprise he doesn't.

"Fine, she stays with me." My eyes bug out of my head.

"Fuck no, my sister isn't going anywhere near you!" Hunter snaps, then takes a step toward Cairo but is stopped when Sky blocks his path. This woman scares me, there is so much more to Sky than you see on the surface, I just know she is the main reason why I am here, but Cairo is hiding it—Why?

"You might want to rethink what you are about to do, little pup." Hunter bristles at Sky's condescending tone.

"What are you, his Chihuahua watch dog?" I groan internally, Hunter is only going to make this situation worse with his remarks. Sky chuckles but there is no humor to it, her eyes swirl with anger.

"You want him, you go through me first and believe me when I tell you, I have no guilt in putting you six feet under." I can't do this anymore.

"Please." All their eyes turn to me but ignore them as I stare at Cairo, something tells me this only stops when he says it does. "I don't want to fight; I'll stay with you—."

"Belle, no."

"Fuck off." I ignore my brothers worries and push on.

"If you can assure me that my brothers are close, I need them...without them I can't decipher some of the visions I have." I can see the cogs turning, he's trying to weigh up his options, but he really doesn't have any if he wants my help.

Chapter Ten

Cairo

I slouch down in the wingback chair and just stare at her while she sleeps; how can this tiny wee thing hold so much power. Bex got carried away before and it shocked the shit out of me when I felt how aroused he was by her, something about her is calling to him. She isn't even a fucking shifter, and she has no idea that those fuckers aren't even her brothers! She claims to need them, but what happens when she finds out the truth? A quiet knock at the door draws my attention, I move to open it only to find Creed and Jess standing there. They step aside to let me exit the room and I close the door quietly behind myself as I follow them down the hall to the lounge room. I grind to a stop when I see Cass leaning against the wall with his arm outstretched gazing into the fire, I thought he went to bed hours ago with his brothers. I know he can hear us enter the room, but he still refuses to look at us, I cock a brow at my sister in question, but she just shrugs and follows Creed over to the sofa and drops down beside him. I open the mind link I share solely with Sky.

Are you awake?

What do you need? Some of the tension flees my body at her reply.

Come to the lounge room, Cassius is here.

On my way.

Sky is the one person in this world I can say I trust with my life; I know people say that all the time, but they never really mean it. Sky has been there for me since the moment I ran from Jacob and became a rogue, Sky never gave up on me, never doubted me––not once. I wouldn't be the man or the alpha I am today without her. There is so many things that she and I have kept hidden from the others, Sky isn't like any of us, she's...special. As soon as she enters the room Jess shakes her head.

"I should have known." I smirk. "Next time I'll wake you both at the same time." Sky just nods, she isn't a woman of many words, when she speaks, she has a reason or need for it.

"Why are we here?" I ask, Cass lets out a loud sigh and straightens as he turns to face me. We stand here staring at each other, Cassius is a big guy, and I can

43

tell loyalty runs deep in him for his family. As the oldest he is the next in line to become alpha of his father's pack.

"My sister can't help you Cairo." I glare at the bastard.

"You got my sister to pull me out here just so you can say that?" I growl.

"No, I asked her to help me convince you to change your course." I turn to Sky and find that she looks just as confused as I do.

"Our fates are sealed––." Cass cuts Sky off.

"No, they are not, Belle is...a loophole to nature. What she can do means she can alter...destiny I guess you would call it, but it costs her each time. She thinks I don't know but every time she has a vision––."

"That's enough Cassius!" I spin around to find a seething Belle standing there with her fists clenched at her sides glaring at her brother, her angry mask doesn't fool me, I can see the betrayal in her eyes.

"Gabrielle––."

"No Cass, that is not your story to tell! You promised me you would never say a word to anyone." The watery tone of her voice tells me that she is close to tears, a pained look crosses Cass's face.

"You can't do this; I won't let you, and nor will dad." She throws her hands in the air.

"Where is dad now Cassius, hmm? He isn't here to stop them," She points in our direction. "Or to stop me, I'll do this so they can let us go, I will not risk you, Blake or Hunter, do you understand me?" Cass's shoulders droop as he approaches her, he lays his big hands on her shoulders and stares down at her with a pitying look.

"This is too much Belle; I don't know how to bring you back if––."

"Enough Cass, we will figure it out, we always do big brother." She steps out of his hold and runs her gaze over each of us before finally settling it on me. "I'll tell you what I saw, do whatever you want me to, but you *do not* ever use my brothers again. You have my word that I will not fight you or try to escape if you allow my brothers their freedom."

"Gabrielle––." I cut Cass off.

"Agreed."

"We won't leave her; she is our kin and my brothers and I will fight to the death for our sister." I smirk at the big fucker.

"I would expect nothing less but, she still stays with me until...I say." I can see that he wants to fight me on this but relents when Belle grips his hand and begins to lead him from the room.

They are hiding something.

I know Sky, I guess we have our secrets and they have theirs.

We need to figure out what she is hiding, it must be big if her brother came to us.

"Whatever shit you are into Cairo it better not blow back on my pack."

"I'm just upholding the promise I made to your mate." He scoffs at my reply.

"What the hell does she have to do with anything? Does Davina know she is here?" I glower at him; his eyes widen just a fraction, but I catch it before he schools his features. "You idiot, she is going to find out that she is here."

"Not if you don't tell her!" I grit out.

"Alexander is after her." Creed hisses, Jess places a hand on his chest trying to calm him, but it doesn't work.

"I know, we need to find out why and what part Davina plays in all of this!"

"Don't lie to me Cairo, there is more to this than just Davina wanting the girl. I knew it from the moment you agreed to help her track Belle down, the only thing that has me stumped is why?"

You can tell them––.

No Sky, it is not their business, this is something I need to do on my own. I told you I would fix this and I meant it!

"She is only here to help us locate the council, nothing more, you are reading way too much into this. I'm going to bed; I suggest you both do the same." I turn and follow Sky out of the room but pause at my sister's words.

"You either tell her the truth or I will." I grunt in reply.

My back and neck are stiff from sleeping in the chair, I refused to share a bed with the she devil. She isn't here for my enjoyment much to Bex's dismay, she has a purpose and once that is fulfilled then she will be sent packing back to her father. I watched her sleep for longer than I want to admit, when I came back to the room, she was fast asleep with her brother standing guard, I kicked his ass out and locked the door. I know they will try and flee the first chance they get which is why I left a couple of my guys behind to...watch her father. He was way to calm to let his whole bloodline leave with me, how does she not know the truth? How has she lived as one of them for so many years and never killed? The vibration of my phone pulls me from my thoughts, I fish it out of my pocket and stifle a groan.

Vince – We picked up Alexander's scent, he's on the east coast.

Why the hell would he be over there? I quickly type out a reply.

Me – When you and your master start telling me the truth about the girl and who he is to her, is when I will tell you what I found.

His reply is almost instantons.

Vince – You have her?

Me – No!

Vince – Don't lie to me Ro.

Me – Fuck you! Get me my answers and I'll get you the girl, until then, fuck off Vince.

I hit ignore when he tries to call, I know Creed and the twins have come around to the idea of Davina, well, Creed more so than the twins, but something doesn't sit right with me. She is hiding something, and I want to know what the fuck it is, Belle plays a part in whatever Davina has planned. Until I find out what that is, the girl will remain with me, we also have to hunt the council, find dear old Alex and figure out what he is up to. I scrub my hands down my face in frustration, this shit is just too much! I miss my old life, my home and how simple things used to be. I never had to worry about any of this shit, my pack was happy, and I was...I think I was happy.

"You look stressed." I drop my hands and look up to see Belle sitting up in the bed with the sheet clutched to her chest. I fight the smirk that wants to break free, I can overpower her in a heartbeat.

"Get dressed, we need to talk." She scrunches her face up but doesn't say a word, I scowl at her when she stands from the bed, I see she changed into an oversized shirt that stops mid-way on her thighs. "Who the fucks shirt is that?" She stumbles back a step looking at me in shock.

"W-what?" I storm over to her and grip the collar of the shirt in my hand yanking her closer to me, so we are nearly nose to nose.

Bex! I growl in warning.

She is wearing another male's shirt!

Let her go now, she is nothing to us Bexley!

I'm too lost in my inner argument with Bex that it shocks me when her hand cups my cheek. My eyes return to my own and Bex relinquishes control back to me, I stand here and stare at her waiting to see what she will do next.

"I-I've never...touched anyone before." My brows crease.

"What?" She takes a shuttering breath and blinks a few times.

"Every time I touch someone I...get a vision, but when you...touched me last night––."

"Nothing happened." She nods. "Why?" She shakes her head as she answers.

"I truly don't know; I have to speak with my brothers about this and see if they can help me understand－－."

"You make me sound like a lab test." She chuckles and something inside me crumbles at the sound.

"You are no lab test, if anything I can see you being the mad scientist." I bite my bottom lip to stop the smile that wants to spread across my face.

What the fuck? I drop my hold on her and stumble back a step, what the fuck was I thinking? A frown mars her face and I shake my head pissed at myself. I snap at her to change and storm out of the room to go in search of Z and Cole, I find them sipping coffee in the kitchen with Callie and Jess.

"Where's Sky?" I mumble as I pour myself a cup.

"Well, good morning to you to, angry pants." I glower at Callie, she hides her smirk behind her cup, ignoring her I turn to my two guys and quirk a brow.

"She went with Creed."

"To do what?" I growl.

"Hey, we didn't know you needed her this morning." Zeke's right, I shouldn't be taking my anger out on them.

"It's fine, where are the three clingers?" Jess snickers but doesn't say anything.

"They went for a run this morning not long after Creed and Sky left." I balk at Cole.

"You just let them go and wonder around my sister's pack lands?" Cole's eyes shift to the color of his wolf.

"It's my fucking homeland, and my brother is alpha here to asswipe. You gave them their freedom according to Jess so who am I to stop them?" I grind my teeth in irritation.

"I'll call Sky and tell her to come－－."

"Uh, hi?" I snap my gaze to the other side of the bench to see Belle standing there, my gaze travels down the length of her body and an irrational urge to demand she change washes over me. She's wearing a yellow crop top that hangs off one shoulder and displays her toned stomach, jeans that fit her like a glove and show off her curves. Judging by the looks on Cole and Z's faces they don't mind the view at all, and it pisses me off!

"Hey Belle, can I get you some coffee and breakfast?" Belle looks shocked by my sisters offer and nods her head shyly.

"That would be great, thank you."

"Come have a seat." Cole taps the empty stool between him and Z, Belle tenses before cutting her gaze to me as if asking permission. I open my mouth to speak but Jess cuts me off when she hauls another stool around the corner of the kitchen and plants it at the end away from everyone.

"I thought you might prefer to sit down here so you don't risk anyone bumping you, and you know..." Belle releases a whoosh of air before smiling and making her way over to Jess and plopping down. Her hair is loose and acts as a shield when she looks down at the counter, Callie nudges me in the ribs and flicks her head toward Belle indicating that I should say something.

"Where's the monster sweetheart?" Saved by Cole.

"He's at school, he'll back later with Meg." Jess places pancakes, bacon, eggs, syrup and biscuits on the counter for everyone. Just as the guys and I are about to dig in, she slaps Z's hand and speaks. "Ladies first, Callie, Belle?" Belle snaps her gaze to my sister darting her eyes around at the rest of us unsure whether or not she should eat. What the fuck is that about? She stands gingerly from her stool and makes her way over to us, I'm standing by the edge of the bench and as she grabs a plate, she tries to move past me but her arm brushes mine and jumps back in shock only to smack into my sister, she cries out as her eyes roll into the back of her head. Without thinking I drop my cup and reach out to catch her before she falls, I lift her in my arms and carry her bride style over to the couch, I block the others conversation out and wave them away when I lay her down on the couch.

"I didn't mean to touch her!" I tear my gaze from a withering Belle and look at my sister, she has tears in her eyes, and I can see she feels guilty, but this isn't her fault...it's mine.

"It was an accident, smalls, it's not your fault." I turn to Z and Cole and say. "Go find her brothers and bring them back." I turn to a pale looking Callie next. "Find Sky and tell her to get her ass back here now." The three of them rush out of the house to do as I ask.

"Cairo, she can't be here——."

"She is the only way we find those council scum smalls."

"There is more to it isn't there? I can see the look in your eyes Ro, what aren't you telling me?"

"Alexander is on the east coast, Davina and Vince have trailed him there. Belle means something to Davina and Alex, and I want to know what it is Jess."

"Why?" She yells in frustration.

"Because! After everything we fucking went through Jess, I have to know if our mother and fathers' deaths were worth this girl's life! They died because Alexander was protecting this girl, and I want to fucking know why!" She stumbles away from me; my breaths are coming in short rapid pants. Jess is struggling to stay in control and keep Sheba at bay, but I can tell she is struggling––shit! I run a hand through my hair and tug on the strands. "I'm sorry smalls." I whisper.

"I didn't realize their deaths meant...that much to you." I exhale a long breath and speak the truth.

"I didn't have anyone to step in and raise me like you did, I was on my own until...Sky. I want to know why they died, why the council tore my family apart and what part this girl plays in it all." I hear her sniffle and I snap my gaze to her to see tears streaking down her cheeks.

"I'm so sorry––." I march over to her and wrap her in my embrace as she sobs into my chest, a second later the front door slams open and Creed, Callie and Sky race in. Creed takes one look at his wife crying in my arms and worry turns to anger as he pins me with a death glare.

"The fuck did you do?" He growls as he shoves me back and cups Jess's face between his hands, he bends down so they are eye level. "What did he do princess?" She shakes her head.

"N-nothing."

"Don't lie to me." I scoff, he turns to glare at me.

"That is fucking rich coming from you." Creed drops his hold on Jess and goes to move toward me but is stopped when Sky blocks his path.

"I can't let you do that." He glares at Sky and opens his mouth, but Callie cuts him off.

"You so much as think about saying something hurtful to her, and I swear to god Credence, hurricane California will fucking end you." Creed cringes slightly, he snarls at Sky before turning around to hold my sisters sobbing form. Sky moves over to me and gives me her infamous *the fuck did you do* look.

"I told her why I wanted to find the council and figure shit out."

"Oh." I stare at the dumbfounded look on her face.

"What?"

"I didn't think you would tell her so easily." I groan as I throw my head back and stare up at the ceiling. The sound of thundering footsteps draws my attention to the door, Z, Cole and the three Wilder brothers rush through the front door. They survey the room until they see their sister passed out on the couch, they rush over and drop down beside her except for Cass, as soon as he sees me, he marches over and shoves me in the chest. I hold strong and glare at the fucker, we stand eye to eye growling, his eyes change to his wolf's and mine do the same. Bex is thrashing against my ribs demanding I let him out to teach this fucker a lesson for ever thinking he can challenge me!

"The fuck happened to her!"

"Take the bass out of your fucking voice when you speak to me!"

"Fuck you Cairo!"

"I prefer cunt to cock Cassius." I retort, a growl of warning tears from him, he cocks his arm back ready to take a swing at me but stops at the sound of Jess's voice.

"Stop it! Please don't do this, it was my fault." Cass spins around to face my sister, Creed moves so he is partly shielding her and growls at Cass.

"You come for her, and I will fucking tear your throat out." He would to, I give him a lot of shit, but Creed really would kill without batting an eye for my sister.

"Creed stop." Jess moves out from behind her mate, much to his dismay and looks up at Cass who is vibrating with rage. "I accidently bumped into Belle, I swear I never meant to hurt her, Cairo caught her before she fell and hit her head. He didn't do this."

"Bro, stop. You know Belle wouldn't want this; this isn't their faults."

"You're right Blake, it isn't their fault, it's his fucking fault!" Cass pins me with a look of hatred, Bex shoves forward and my eyes shift to his.

"Anytime you want to step up to the plate I'm ready!" My voice isn't my own, it's rough and course due to the partial shift.

CHAPTER ELEVEN

Belle

I startle awake, I blink my eyes a few times to adjust to the light. I hear movement to my left and slowly turn but groan when the pounding in my head intensifies and slam my eyes closed again. It's getting worse, each vision is taking a toll on me, and I don't know how much longer I will be able to handle it, dad and Cass are right. I hate to admit it to myself, but I may have no other choice than to do as they say, I don't want that life, but I don't see another option.

"Here sis, take these." I can tell it's Hunter from the sound of his voice, he lifts my hand and places the pain killers' in my palm and gently guides them to my mouth. He helps me to sit up so I can swallow the water he gives me, after which he helps me to lay back down as I fight another groan. "What happened Bells, you were out for nearly four hours." I cringe, not only is the pain getting worse, but the time is also getting longer––great. I take a minute to gather myself and my thoughts before I try to open my eyes again, the pain is still there but the pills are kicking in quickly, which I am grateful for. I see the look of concern on Hunter's face, and I reach out to smooth the frown lines.

"I'm okay, I promise."

"You're not okay Belle, you can't do this." He whispers low enough for only me to hear, but it still annoys me, it is my life, and I will choose how I want to live it––for as long as I can.

"You can't fight this battle for me Hunt–."

"Like hell I can't." He jumps to his feet and storms away from me, I close my eyes and take a shuddering breath.

Why can't I just be normal?

"Where's the fun in being normal?" I squeal in fright; I didn't mean to say that out loud! I look to the corner and see Cairo standing there with his arms crossed over his chest and one leg kicked back against the wall, he just stands there staring at me. The pressure of his gaze has me squirming, I sit up and drop my legs off the side of the sofa just for something to do other than look at him. That vision wasn't like anything I have ever experienced before, I was jumping from one scene to the next, but I was seeing different people's past. I'll admit it frightened me, I couldn't pull myself out of it or even stop myself from vision jumping.

"I would give anything in the world to just go outside and not scream in agony. Do you know what it's like to see people kiss and not be able to ever experience that yourself?" I don't give him a chance to answer. "See, I bet you have had sex, I will never get to do that, because it will fucking kill me!" I scream the last at him, I'm panting and mildly mortified that I just confessed that all to him, but it has been a hell of a day already and all this is his fault. He still shows no emotion or even an ounce of care, he stands there with his arms crossed looking at me like I'm an annoying fly. I sag in defeat, no one will ever understand what it feels like to crave human touch and never be able to have it.

"You can touch me." I whip my head up so fast and balk at him, he shrugs his shoulders like the implication he just made is okay.

"I would rather eat dirt, than let you kiss me." He scoffs and pushes off the wall, he stalks toward me like a true alpha wolf, his power radiates off him in waves. "Don't come any closer." My resolve begins to weaken the closer he gets; he stops when there is just a sliver of space between us.

"What are you going to do when I trample through all the walls you have up? I didn't get to be where I am or who I am today by letting others dictate the outcome of my future." I choke on air at the audacity of him, after what I just saw, I know he is full of it! I square my shoulders and meet his heated gaze with one of my own.

"For someone who doesn't like the word *no* you sure seemed to take it like a champ when it came from Skylar Cage." His eyes widen and he moves back a couple steps allowing me to breathe slightly easier. When he is close to me it's like he has sucked all of the oxygen out of the room, Cairo is a dominate alpha and if the stories are true about him, I really need to stop provoking the beast within.

"You have no fucking idea what you are talking about!" I roll my eyes, he growls and in a split second the space between us is gone, his hand is around my throat tight enough for me to begin to panic and claw at his arm. "You know nothing about me or Sky––."

"Get the fuck off her now!" I dart my eyes to the side to see Blake storming toward us, Cairo turns his head toward my brother and releases a growl of warning. Blake ignores it and continues toward us; my eyes widen in horror when Blake is sent sailing through the air by Zeke.

"P-please d-don't." I wheeze out, he snaps his gaze back to me with his lip pulled back in a snarl. His eyes are his wolf's and shine with malice.

"All you have to do is show me what I want to see and then you are free to go, whatever else you see, you keep your mouth shut!" The threat in his voice is clear, I try to nod but can't thanks to the grip he has on me. He releases me with a hard shove, and I stumble back a step coughing and spluttering, I spy Cass out of the corner of my eye, but I can't get the words out to tell him to stop. His fist connects with the side of Cairo's face, he tries again, but Cairo is quick on his feet and manages to dodge the hit and swivels around to land a hit against Cass's ribs. The others rush in, Cole and Creed haul Ro back while Blake and Hunter wrangle Cass back. Both of their eyes have changed to the color of their wolves, I fear they will shift any minute and wreak havoc in here. Before I can even think too much about it, I shout loud enough that they will all hear me over the growls and screams.

"I know where the council is!" All the shouting and growls stop upon my admission, every pair of eyes in the room is on me. I begin to fidget under the scrutiny of their watchful gazes, I hate being the center of attention, and I know that sounds stupid considering I have visions and faint at the drop of a hat. I wish I had of waited to let that information come out, but I didn't have a choice. My plan was to let Cairo figure things out on his own but given the tension between him and us, I fear I may have to just tell him––soon.

"How?" I turn and see Jess standing beside Callie and Sky on the outskirts of the living room. It's then that I notice each of them are holding Sky back, Sky looks like she is ready to commit murder, this woman scares the living daylights out of me.

"When I touched you, I...saw things." I cringe at how meek and unsure I sound but I don't want to blurt the details of her past out in front of everyone. What I saw in those visions about Jess will haunt me, what she endured and suffered isn't something anyone should have to go through.

"What things?" I don't take my eyes off Jess as I answer her mate.

"Things from your time as a...captive." Jess pales at my admission, a hiss escapes Creed and guilt begins to build inside me. I hate that I feel guilt when I'm in these situations, but I can't help that I can see into people's pasts and futures. Jess's features harden as she drops her hold on Sky and moves toward me, I can feel the alpha power rolling off her in waves.

"If you hurt her––." Cass is cut off when Jess swings her gaze to him and growls.

"I would never hurt an innocent!" She turns back to me, and I can see the fear in her eyes, that look sends a cold shiver down my spine. "How much did you see?"

I swallow loudly.

"All of it." She bites her bottom lip and nods.

"Okay, well given that this is my story, I think it's only fair that we discuss this in private." Jess doesn't bother to wait for a response, she heads down the hallway with me following after her and up the stairs. We come to a stop in front of a closed door, she pulls a key from her pocket and unlocks it ushering me in before her. I marvel at the room, it's her very own library, I run my hand along the spines of the books closest to me and inhale. The smell of worn leather and old books is like a balm to my battered soul, I don't care what anyone says there is no better scent in this world than old books! "Have a seat." I follow her over to the couches set up near the window, the tension amplifies as we sit here and stare at each other, to say this is an awkward moment would be an understatement.

"I'm sorry." I blurt.

"Sorry for what?" My temper begins to spike.

"You misunderstand me, I am not apologizing for seeing what I did."

"Then why are you sorry?"

"Because I saw what you endured at the hands of that man Jacob, no one should ever go through what you did." She inhales a sharp intake of air, clearly, she wasn't expecting that response.

"You aren't as meek and timid as you portray yourself to be, are you?" I smirk.

"I was raised by an alpha and have three alpha heirs for brothers, I have learnt pretty fast how to cope with making myself seem timid and less of a threat to their beasts." She sits back and crosses her leg over the other, she runs her gaze over me as if trying to gauge my deepest secrets, she won't find what she is looking for, I'm used to keeping all my feelings locked away.

"Why do I get the feeling that you wouldn't be here with my brother if you didn't want to be?" I make sure to keep my face blank.

"I don't know what you mean." Her features harden and her eyes flicker between hers and her wolf's.

"Cut the shit, you know exactly what I mean." Her voice is course from her wolf being so close to the surface, I can see she is used to everyone submitting to the alpha in her, but she won't get my submission—–She can't."

"I owe you nothing."

"Finally, now your true colors are starting to shine. You can try to keep up this sweet and innocent act, but it won't work on me, why the hell are you really here Belle?" I lean forward and rest my elbows on my legs making sure to meet her gaze.

"My reasons are my own––." She growls in annoyance.

"If you plan to hurt my brother––." I cut off her bullshit spiel.

"I'm not here to fucking hurt him, I'm here to stop him and *her* from ruining the shifter race. I promise you that once I do what I came here to do, I will leave, I will never return to your pack lands, and in return, no one will ever come for me or my family again!"

CHAPTER TWELVE

Cairo

I refused to eat dinner with the others, Jess and Belle both refused to tell any of us what was said earlier between them. I didn't push my sister for answers and the three bitches that came with Belle made sure she was tucked away from me until I disappeared into my room. Jess, Creed, Sky and the twins are having dinner at Meg's house tonight and I overheard Zeke telling Cass and the other two that he would take them out tonight so they could shift, which means it will just be me and Belle here, which gives me the chance to make her tell me what she saw and what she and my sister spoke about earlier. Before I can get too lost in my own head my phone vibrates, I pull it out of my pocket and see that it's Bodie.

Bodie – We have set up on the east side of the property in the woods so we can shift.

Me – Make sure that you all stick to the outskirts of the property and don't come inland.

Bodie – Yes alpha, I'll debrief you on the pack run in the A.M.

I drop my phone on top of the comforter and decide to take a shower before going in search of Belle. That girl has me second guessing everything, she sees more than she lets on and I know she hates it. I have seen the look in her eyes after each vision she is plagued with––My phone starts ringing this time and I curse. Thinking it's Bodie again I don't even check the caller I.D as I answer.

"What?"

"Where is she?" I stiffen at the sound of her voice.

"Davina, how lovely to hear from you." She hisses in annoyance which just causes me to smile.

"Don't you dare patronize me Cairo! We had a deal––." My temper spikes.

"No, you fucking heard what you wanted to hear. I told you I would find the girl and then take the council out, I never said I would hand her over."

"You little shit! You don't need her to find the council."

"Oh, I know that, but I also know she is important to you, and that Alexander is after her."

"Cairo, Alexander is not someone to be messed with– –." I growl out my annoyance.

"He is the one that tried to save us and my father, I want to fucking know why. I'm banking on him coming for her and when he does, I'll be right here waiting."

"Oh my god, you're at Creed's, aren't you?"

"And if I was, what's it to you?"

"Jess will tell her everything! She can never know Cairo, if she does it will send her spiraling and none of us can bring her back from that." I can hear the fear in her voice.

"Why do you care so much about this girl?"

"Because she is one of the originals–."

"Don't fucking lie to me Davina!" I shout.

"I'll be there in 5 days, keep Jess away from her." Before I can respond she disconnects the call, I'm so pissed off I want to throw my phone across the room.

She means more to Davina than her own children.

I know Bex, we need to find out why!

I close the link between Bex and I, I hop in the shower and hope that the water will wash away the stress of the day. I know time is counting down, Sky and I have banked everything on this girl because of what Vince said back on the island. If she is as powerful as they say, then she should be able to tell me when and where the event happens. I have lied to everyone about what I am really up to, the only one who knows the real truth is Sky. She knows me better than anyone, so when I announced we were going after the council she knew it was a cover. Time isn't on my side; I have to stop handling Belle with kid gloves and pull the truth from her.

You can't though, can you?

I slam my palm against the shower wall and growl in frustration, Bexley is right. I don't know why I can't bring myself to harm her, I would blow this world apart for Sky, kill anyone in my way except for...her. I shake the thoughts away and quickly get out; the shower done nothing to relieve my stress. I wrap my towel around my waist and leave the bathroom, I stop short when I see none other than Gabrielle Wilder sitting on the end of my bed. She lifts her head slowly and runs her gaze over my naked chest, her pupils are blown wide, and I can hear the change in her heart rate– –I affect her. I pull my gaze from her and head toward my duffle bag in the corner and grab out a pair of sweats, with my back to her I drop the towel and relish in her gasp. Once I have my sweats on, I turn and lean back against the wall, a blush coats her cheeks, her hair falls forward as she drops her gaze blocking her face from my view.

"What are you doing here?"

"You wanted to see me." She slowly lifts her gaze to mine; I cock a brow in question, and she rolls her eyes. "I'm not stupid, I know with the others gone it gives you the perfect opportunity to interrogate me so, please don't act dumb it doesn't suit you." I grind my teeth in annoyance while Bex chuffs inside me, he likes her smartass banter.

"You have no idea what suits me and what doesn't, let's not forget who the captive is here." My tone is course and full of warning, she is playing a dangerous game and I will not have her thinking that she has the upper hand.

"I am only a captive if I choose to be." She stands and moves across the room toward me leaving a couple feet of space between us, her eyes flicker side to side as she takes in the ink that marks my body. As her eyes travel across my exposed skin, it begins to heat, I grit my teeth angry as fuck at myself for letting her affect me. "You have so much pain and anger inside you––."

"You know nothing about me beauty, I am not a puzzle you can solve. Don't get shit twisted, you are here to do a job and that's it."

"They are here in the States." My eyes widen in shock, the cocky smirk that graces her face tells me my reaction is exactly what she wanted.

"Where?" The smirk vanishes, her eyes lose some of the light in them and her shoulders droop slightly.

"They will come to you."

"What?" Her eyes meet mine and I can see so much regret in them, it astounds me. How can she give me *that* look when she knows nothing about me?

"You can't save her, Cairo." I snap, I have my hand around her throat and her slammed against the wall within a second. I crowd her space, we are nearly nose to nose, I release a growl right in her face. She doesn't flinch or cower in fear, she just looks at me with pity, that look fucks me off more than if she spoke the words again.

"You know fucking nothing––."

"No matter how many times you say that, it won't make it true, you brought me here because of what I can see. Trust in that and know that I am not saying this to hurt you, but to prepare you for what is to come." I search her gaze for any mistruth but find none, I release my hold on her neck and move back. She doesn't reach up to grab her throat or even acknowledge the position I just had her in, she squares her shoulders and stands tall, the silence stretches between us, but I refuse to be the one to break it. I release a long sigh and run my hand through my hair, this woman frustrates me, but she is also so alluring and the fact that she doesn't drop to her knees and worship me because of the rumors that have circulated about me over the years has me wanting to know...why she is different to the others. I head over to the bed and take a seat on the edge resting my elbows on the tops of my thighs, I hunch forward and get lost in my own head for a long time before I cave and break the silence between us.

"What did you see earlier?" My voice is barely above a whisper.

"Do you really want to know?" I lift my gaze slowly to hers, the fierce look in her eyes has me tensing.

"Yes."

"I saw what happened to your sister and I know where your council is, also what they have planned. The man leading them is named Phillip and he is trying to find a way to take your family and the Reeves down. His hate for your father has bled over into you and your sister, I don't know why he hated your father though." I can see it in her eyes that there is more she has seen.

"What else?" I see the way she tenses and hear her heart rate spike; I can tell when she opens her mouth, she is going to try and deny it, so I push on. "Don't lie to me beauty, whatever it is that you saw I...need to know." A whoosh of air escapes her and her shoulders hunch forward slightly.

"I don't get to pick and choose what I see, my visions are...changing." My brows furrow in confusion.

"What do you mean?" If I wasn't paying such close attention to her, I would have missed the look of fear in her eyes before she quickly masked it.

"You don't need to worry about that−−."

"Tell me now or so help me−−."

"I know you're in love with Skylar Cage." My mouth drops open in shock as I stare at her. "I saw everything Cairo, I know you love her and I'm so sorry that she..." I block out the sound of her voice as I get lost in my own thoughts, I have never admitted shit to anyone about Sky. My pulse begins to spike, and my heart rate accelerates, I can feel Bex pushing against my ribs urging me to shift and allow him to take over so he can clear my mind and block out my emotions. I can't take this shit; I jump to my feet and make sure she can see nothing but anger and hatred in my gaze. She knows nothing about me or what the fuck I feel, I will never allow myself to care for another person, Jess and Harlem are different they are the last family I have left. I can't let her unravel all the work I have put in to keep myself closed off from ever feeling anything again or having someone psychoanalyze me.

"Stay the fuck away from me, you are a means to an end and that is it. You ever breathe a word of this to anyone and I'll make all your nightmares seem like a daydream." Her eyes widen as a gasp escapes her. "I'm not some broken toy you can fix, your job is to focus on the council and that is it, do I make myself clear?" My fists are clenched at my sides, anger is wafting off me in waves and Bexley is just below the surface I have to shift––soon.

"Message received loud and clear."

"Good. Now, get out!"

I couldn't stay inside the house with her, I needed to get out and shift, Bexley was restless. We have to stick to the outskirts of the property, or I risk a fight breaking out, Bexley and Sheba can't be near each other. My sister and I both have dominant alpha wolves and having them together will end in blood shed. I've been out for a few hours running, hunting and just being free of all thought. Bex is simple and carefree, wolves don't process emotions like humans, they only care about dominance, hunting and fucking. I needed to escape out of my own head and there is no better way to do that than shift, I used to spend more time as a boy in wolf form than I did on two legs. I was never cold, lonely or hungry, I may not have been old enough to survive after being cast out, but Bex was ready for it. Without him I would have died after Jacob took over my father's pack, seeing his corpse and knowing that he was wiped from this earth was freeing, some think me sending his head to Russia was overkill but to me it was...fitting.

The death of my father haunted me for years, I wished that I was older, stronger even to fight against Jacob. I hated being weak and having to watch the horror unfold in front of me, I watched as that cunt killed my father. I vowed to myself the day I ran that I would never be weak again, I would train day and night to make sure I was the strongest. I kept that vow, to this day I have never lost a challenge, I'm not seen as weak because I had no weakness––well, until Creed brought my sister back to Rosewood. Having her around doesn't weaken me though, her and Harlem give me a reason to fight harder to ensure their safety.

I trek back along the creeks edge, I pause and scent the air, I've spent most of my life away from Rosewood but coming back here and smelling the same smells I did as a child brings a calmness to me. Unlike Jess, I actually have vague memories of our father, for some reason I never picked up on Shelley being our mother. I thought she looked familiar but that's as far as it went, I never talk about my parents but a part of me hates them for leaving us. I hate that I never got a childhood, I envy my sister for being taken away from here and getting to live her life carefree. Don't get me wrong I'm glad one of us got to have some sort of a life away from all of this shit, but while she was out there with Aunt Kat, I was struggling to find my place. I never wanted to be an alpha but when Sky came along——everything changed. I wanted for things for the first time in my life, I didn't want to live in the woods anymore I wanted a roof and bed, something to call my own. Sky stuck by me through everything, her and Zeke became my family, we built a home for ourselves and eventually the rogues found us and somehow, I stepped into the role of alpha without even realizing it. I didn't want the title, but Sky reminded me that being an alpha meant I was strong, the little boy inside me jumped at the idea of a pack turning to me for their safety. The other half of me though still hates the title, I don't think we need a leader, I believe the packs should live equally. I find my way back to the log where I left my clothes but sitting next my pile is none other than the woman who takes up too much time in my head. She runs her gaze over my wolf and smirks.

She isn't the one, Cairo. I sigh internally, he's right but it doesn't make it any easier.

I know Bex, shift back so I can sort shit with her and make a plan.

Bex relinquishes control back to me and within seconds I'm back in my skin, she turns her head to give me a modicum of privacy while I pull my sweats and shirt on. I drop down on the log next to her, we both remain silent for a long time, neither of us willing to address the thing we both know will cause us to argue. I fucked up and I'm the reason there is this divide between us, I know she doesn't feel the same way about me and that stings more than anything.

"I can feel it you know." I turn and stare at her, she keeps her eyes facing forward as I take her in.

"Feel what, Sky?" She faces me and I can see resignation in her eyes, and it guts me to see that look.

"The power inside me is surging, ever since I healed Jess and excreted myself it's been harder to keep under control." A whoosh of air escapes me, she reaches over and clasps one of my hands in hers. Her touch calls to a part of me that no one else has ever been able to reach before. "You can't change my fate, Ro, I need you to be the one to do it." I tear my hand back and jump to my feet growling at her, she deflates but holds my gaze like the stubborn ass she is.

"I'll never fucking do it Skylar, do you hear me?" I shout, she stands and moves toward me, I hold my ground even as she places both her hands against my chest.

"It has to be you––." I rear backward and glare at her, her hands fall to her sides as she shakes her head in exasperation.

"I won't do it...I-I can't."

"From the day I freed you of being led a part of me has lived inside you, you are the only one who will be able to get near me when the time comes." I snap, I stalk toward her and clasp her face between my hands. She holds my gaze and the pleading look she gives me breaks my heart.

"You are the only woman I have ever loved Sky––."

"Ro, please don't."

"I need to get this out, please let me?" She sighs and nods her head stiffly. "I know you don't love me the way I love you." I see sadness and guilt cloud her vision and I hate myself for putting that look in her eyes.

"I do love you Ro." I smile sadly and brush my thumbs across her cheeks.

"I know you do darling, just not the way I want. I will find a way to stop the surge Sky, I swear I won't rest until I do." She shakes her head and pulls my hands from her face; she holds them tight as she says.

"Don't put your life on hold for me, I want to enjoy the time I have left with you and Callie. You may not be able to see it or even feel it yet, but that girl back there, she isn't your enemy Ro, she knows a lot more than you give her credit for."

"Are you seriously trying to push me away and force me to go after Belle?" She sighs and rolls her eyes, a smile tugs at her lips.

"I'm not forcing you to do anything, I know you Cairo Cruz and I can see the way you track her every movement; do you know you subconsciously gravitate toward her?" It's my turn to scoff, she chuckles. "Well let's just blame it on Bex then, huh?"

"She isn't my mate Sky, she can't be, she isn't a shifter." She huffs out a frustrated breath.

"And neither am I Ro, what you feel for me is gratitude, not love, you love the idea of me and you because you view me as your equal. I'm not the girl you want to wake up next to every morning and make love to every night."

"You didn't complain about me fucking you years ago!" Sky flinches and I cringe, that was a low blow and I know it. Sky and I slept together a few times years ago, she put a stop it when she figured out that she wasn't being true to herself and her wants. It gutted me, but I respect her too much to be salty, she always made jokes about me turning her off men.

"That was then, and this is now."

"You're right, I'm sorry I shouldn't have said that. I know you love Callie, and I will never do anything to hurt either of you, just please don't give up the fight. Give me some time to get the answers we need from Belle."

"She can't stop it Ro, the others will figure out that she isn't here to help find the council." My eyes widen in shock. "Yes, I know you Cairo and I know the council doesn't mean shit to you. They were just a cover so no one suspected why you wanted the seer, what you didn't think about though is bringing her here to your sisters pack, means Alexander will follow her here, in turn Davina and her vamps will come to."

"Shit!"

"Yeah, didn't think this plan of yours through properly did ya?" I glare at the smartass.

"What do you suggest then old wise one?"

"That you be honest with the others, tell them why Belle is really here, I have to prepare Callie, she has a right to know that I am going to break her heart." I can feel the tears building behind my eyes, just the thought of never having Sky by my side or even losing her is unthinkable "I love her Ro; she constantly asks questions; and I am tired of deflecting them because of a promise I made to you when we were kids." I can hear the watery tone of her voice and it makes me feel like shit under her boot. She has been lying to the woman she loves because of me, and no one should have to do that to their significant other. Part of me wants to tell her that she is wrong and that nothing is going to happen to her, but the other part of me is scared shitless that she might be right, she may actually die, and I don't know if I would survive losing her, my best friend...my soul mate.

CHAPTER THIRTEEN

Belle

I barley slept a wink last night, after Cairo left, I decided to lay down. I'm so confused and angry at myself, I knew Cairo was going to be hard to get through to, but I didn't think it would be this hard. He has built so many walls inside himself, and refuses to let anyone in, I don't know how I am supposed to help someone who doesn't want to help themselves, all the visions I have had of him tell me that he is in pain. I know that I am here because he needs my help with something to do with Sky, but I don't know how my visions can help stop the carnage I have seen her cause. My visions are coming more frequent, and I know the more I have the worse off I will be. I made my brothers swear that they wouldn't say anything. I'm worried that if Cairo finds out the truth and I can't...perform we will be of no use to him, and he will harm my brothers. I am slowly starting to learn that whenever I tell another about a future vision, it changes. Cairo won't understand that if I tell him, it is better for me to keep it to myself sometimes or ask my brothers for help and not...alter the future more than I already have.

My phone begins to ring, I roll over and quickly answer.

"Daddy!"

"Belle, it's so good to hear your voice." Tears spring to my eyes, I miss my dad so much.

"I miss you daddy."

"And I, you my darling girl. How are you all holding up?" A whoosh of air escapes me.

"We're...hanging in there, how are you and the pack going?" Dad chuckles.

"You four are being held captive and you're more worried about me and the pack?" I chuckle and shake my head.

"Yeah, I guess that does sound silly, huh?" A beat of silence passes before dad sighs and asks.

"How are you all *really* doing?" I nibble on my lip debating on if I should sugar coat things or be honest, I decide honesty is the best policy.

"I'm taking longer to recover from the visions, Cass, Blake and Hunter are trying to find a way out but even if they do, he will come after us."

"You know what he wants don't you?" Dad knows me better than anyone.

"Yeah, it's more...complicated than I thought. He has so many walls up and I can't get through them to help him." Dad splutters.

"Gabrielle what are you saying? You actually want to help this mad man? he kidnapped you and your brothers and nearly killed our pack!" I flinch at the disappointment in his voice, but I won't lie to him.

"Dad please, something inside me is telling me that he needs my help and I...can't walk away––."

"You can and you will! Cass and I have been working on a plan––."

"What?" I shriek. "I just told you he will hunt us down; I won't risk my brothers or the packs safety just because you want me out of here."

"As your alpha I am ordering you––." I growl as best as I can.

"I can't even shift so your orders don't apply to me! I am old enough to make my own decisions and I am telling you that I will help Cairo––."

"Oh god, you're on first name basis with him now. He has brainwashed you Belle; can't you see that?" A noise outside my door draws my attention and I quickly end the call and quietly hop out of bed and pad silently over to the door and wrench it open. Cairo stands there with his arms crossed over his bare chest glaring down at me, the angry look in his eyes has me stumbling back and gulping. He takes a step forward and I step back, every step he takes toward me I keep backing away until I hit the edge of the bed, again.

"W-what are you doing here?" He cocks a brow at me, but he still has that angry look in his eyes, the room feels so small now that he is in it. I wish he didn't close the door; I could have side stepped him and escaped to the safety of the others.

"*Daddy* doesn't seem too pleased with you being here with the big bad beast." I glare at him; he does not get to look down his nose at my father.

"He is a good man and a great father; he's just worried as any good parent would be!" An angry growl tumbles out of him, and his eyes begin to flicker between his and his wolf's.

"Wouldn't know beauty, my father was murdered when I was nine and my mother fucked off with the council." I gasp, I cover my mouth with my hand. No wonder he is so angry and bitter, he has all these walls built around himself because of the pain he has endured since he was a child. I drop my hand and stare up at him, I can see it now, he uses his anger and need for vengeance to mask the pain he has suffered since a young age.

"I'm sorry, I didn't know."

"You never asked."

"You never gave me a chance." I volley back.

"Touché, I don't want your pity beauty, I need your skillset and I need it now. We don't have a lot of time left before the calvary arrives."

"The what?" He runs a hand through his hair and sighs, I can see some of the tension ease from his shoulders.

"You'll meet them soon enough; all you have to know is that...Fuck." He spins around and heads toward the door, I sit here confused as hell. He pulls the door open and then peers back at me over his shoulder and says. "Get dressed, you and I are going for a stroll."

The tension between me and Cairo is palpable, we walk side by side through the woods that surrounds Jess's pack lands. My brothers weren't happy to be staying behind, they made threats and told Cairo if I wasn't back by lunch, they will hunt me down, it goes without saying that Cairo didn't even bat an eye at them. We have been trekking through the dense brush of the forest for what feels like forever, I chose the wrong shoes to wear that is for sure, Jordan's are not made for hikes. I'm wearing cut offs and a teal crop top, the humidity is stifling, I sniff the air and I can smell that it's going to rain, I love rainy days, nothing beats curling up reading a book with the sound of rainfall in the background.

"You're right you know." I peek over at him and find that his face is scrunched up like he is bothered about something, but he doesn't slow his pace, I turn away from him as I answer.

"About what?"

"If you fled with your brothers, I would hunt you down, and *when* I caught you, I wouldn't be as hospitable next time." I splutter.

"You're not exactly warm and welcoming *this* time!" I stumble and come to a halt at the sound of his laughter, Cairo doesn't strike me as the type of man to just giveaway smiles or laugh freely, so to see him laugh is like the sun coming out on a rainy day. His laughter stops a few seconds later, his gaze lands on me and a strange look contorts his face.

"Why are you smiling at me like that?" I shake my head to clear my thoughts before I answer.

"You don't seem like you laugh often enough."

"Coming from the girl who lives inside 24/7?"

"I don't have a choice, but you do. Life is plenty hard Cairo; you don't need to make it any harder." His eyes widen slightly as if my words have actually registered for the first time.

"I...uh...I never really thought about it like that." He leads me over to the edge of the creek and drops down extending his legs in front of him, he looks up and motions with his hand for me to do the same. I'm woman enough to admit that I am apprehensive of this side of him, he isn't yelling or demanding, he is...asking. I decide to take the plunge and see where this will go, I cross my legs under me and hunch over to pluck blades of grass for something to do. I don't know why I feel this burning need to help Cairo, he is a complete jerk and has threatened me more times than I can count. The visions I had of him showed me that he is desperate and scared, but the man sitting beside me doesn't show those fears, I can tell he is stressed but I see no fear or desperation in his gaze. We sit here for a long time lost in our own thoughts, the silence isn't uncomfortable, it feels surreal to sit next to someone who isn't my father or brothers and not be assaulted by visions.

"Can I ask you something?" A resigned sigh escapes him.

"You want to know why you are really here?"

"Yes." I feel his gaze boring into the side of my face, but I choose to ignore it.

"A part of me wants to be the one to shatter your realty so you would rebel against your family in order to do as I ask. But, the other side of me doesn't want to see any more harm come to you." Now I do meet his gaze, I hear the truth in his words, and I am beyond confused as to how he can want to harm one minute and then, admit he doesn't want to see me in pain.

"What does that mean?" I can tell from the way his eyes dart away from me that he isn't going to answer that.

"You're here because I need your help to save Sky." My mouth opens to speak, but he shushes me by continuing. "I lied; the council was never the end game; they were just the cover so no one would find out about Sky."

"I don't understand."

"Everyone thinks I brought you here to help me track the council so I can end them, I let my sister think I wanted to do this because they killed our parents. Truth is, I don't give a flying fuck about them, I just needed everyone to believe that, so they wouldn't ask questions."

"So, the council is your cover story?"

"Yes, you are really here to help me save Sky, I cannot let the surge happen if it does...I-I just need to stop it." The vision I had about Sky comes to mind, I hold his gaze as I tell him about what I saw. "Fuck!" He roars, I flinch back as he shoves his hand through his hair and yanks on the strands, I wish I was brave enough to reach out and place my hand on his to offer comfort, but I'm petrified of human touch even though I long for it. Stupid, huh?

"I'm sorry––."

"How accurate are your visions?" I cock my head to the side in confusion. "Are they ever wrong?" I think on that for a moment, they aren't always on point and may vary, but the end result is always the same. I can see the pleading look in his eyes, he wants me to say that they hold no mirth or truth, but I can't lie to him.

"I have only ever been wrong once." A look of defeat crosses his features. "I'm sorry Ro." His eyes widen slightly, and I'm taken back by that look.

"That's the first time I think you have ever called me *Ro*." I stiffen, I can feel the blush fighting its way to my cheeks, so I turn away from him. We aren't friends, not even remotely close to it we're more...acquaintances.

"It won't happen again." I blurt out.

"I like how my name sounds when you say it." I snap my gaze back to his so fast I feel a muscle in my neck pinch.

"W-what?" He doesn't answer just shrugs his shoulders. I'm sitting here reeling from his little declaration while he doesn't seem bothered in the least.

"Close your mouth beauty, some might take it as an invitation." I gape at him in horror and quickly snap my mouth closed, did he just make a crude remark––toward *me*? "Don't get lost in your head, you spend way too much time inside your own mind." What the hell?

"How the heck would you know anything about me?" He slowly drags his gaze back to mine.

"I didn't just show up one day and take you. I researched you for months while we were tracking you, I may be rash and crazy sometimes, but I never go anywhere unprepared." His revelation shocks the hell out of me.

"Here I was thinking you just heard about the circus freak and showed up." I try to sound noncoherent, but he hears the bitterness in my tone. He meets my gaze and I see anger swirling in the depths of his ice blue eyes, but it isn't directed at me.

"You are not a freak, what you can do is...out of this world. Why do you hide from it?" I get a little choked up at his question, no one has *ever* asked me something like that, they all just assume I love getting visions and think I'm above everyone else, but that isn't true.

"Because everything must have balance, I never asked for these visions or wanted them, I hate being able to see people's darkest hour or their most intimate moments. These visions..." I clamp my mouth closed, I can't believe I was about to tell him the truth, what the hell was I thinking? I cover my face with my hands and berate myself for letting my guard down for even a second, some may think I'm nuts for opening up to my captor, but the freaking truth is my captor is the only one who doesn't treat me like I'm a basket case and handle me with kid gloves.

"Why do you hate them so much?" That is another question no one has ever asked me; I feel like I'm an onion and he is peeling back my layers one at a time until I'm bare and exposed.

"Because they hurt." I drop my hands and swivel around until I'm facing him, he doesn't react, just sits patiently and waits for me to continue. "You know how I told you about my vision with Sky?" He nods. "Well, I felt everyone's pain from that vision, every vision I feel the anger, pain, hatred, I feel everything, and I hate it."

"Have you ever tried to change the course of someone's life because of what you have seen?" Cairo and I spend hours sitting out here talking, it's so weird for me to have someone actually care or curious enough to ask about my wants and needs. I've never had a friend before and being out here with him makes me feel like I may actually have a shot at making my first ever friend, in him. Cairo pauses mid-sentence and jumps to his feet; I follow his lead not sure what has caused his carefree look to be replaced by his normal unemotional mask. I stifle a gasp when he moves in front of me blocking me from whoever is coming into view. "She's fine, now fuck off." I peer around him to see my three brothers who all wear looks of rage, I smile sheepishly at them then quickly dart back behind Cairo. I know this is ridiculous, but I don't want to deal with my overbearing brothers and have them ruin this day for me.

"I don't think so, Belle is coming with us." I can see Cairo's shoulders tense and without thinking I reach out and lay my hand against his back, I gasp, and he stiffens. I can't tear my gaze from my hand that lays against him, I'm tense and frightened waiting for a vision to assault me.

"Belle?" I can't answer Blake, I'm stunned silent at the fact I willingly touched someone, and no vision has crippled me. Cairo begins to slowly turn around; my hand remains in the air and winds up against his chest as he faces me. My eyes are still rooted to my hand, how is this possible? I hear movement around us, but I ignore it as I slowly lift my gaze to his and see a war raging inside him, anger, intrigue, curiosity all shine in his eyes but I just know he is about to pull the rug out from under me. I can see it in the way his eyes crinkle in the corners and how the side of his lip lifts in a half smirk, half snarl, I've stunned him, and he doesn't like it. I quickly yank my hand back and drop it to my side, I stand tall and wait for his verbal lashing.

"*You* touched *me*." Huh? That was not what I was expecting to come out of his mouth!

"How are you still standing Belle?" I shake my head and turn to Hunter confused.

"What?" I ask.

"You can never stand through your visions, how are you still on your feet after touching him?"

"I-I...uh, I don't know." I sound like an idiot, but this is all new to me, this is the first time *I* have touched someone of my own free will and not had a vision. The only people I can touch and sometimes not be affected is my family, why is Cairo different to everyone else?

"What do you mean, *you don't know*?" Cairo growls out a warning, he doesn't like Cass's tone.

"Don't fucking talk to her like that!" All three of my brothers growl and begin to close in on us, for the second time today I don't think, I just act and spin around, so my back is to Cairo's chest and glare at my siblings.

"Stop! He didn't do anything; I'm confused because *I* touched him, and I didn't have a vision." Cass exhales loudly, Blake and Hunter both look taken back, I turn to my oldest brother and plead with my eyes that he hear me. "Cassius, I touched him!"

"Yeah, you said that." I can hear the annoyance in his voice but choose to ignore it.

"Cass, he is the first person outside of you three and dad that I have ever touched and not had a vision."

"Oh Jesus Christ." Hunter throws his hands in the air in exasperation. "Don't be so naïve Gabrielle, this is some Stockholm syndrome or some shit."

"Huh?"

"You think because you touched him that he is your Prince Charming? Newsflash sister, he isn't!" The way Hunter is looking at me and shouting hurtful things has me flinching, and taking a step back, I stifle a gasp when I feel Cairo pressed against my back––again, no vision assaults me. His breath fans the back of my neck and a shiver travels down my spine, I sag back into him slightly.

"Hunt, that's enough!"

"Stay out of it Blake, she has to hear this––." Hunter snaps his mouth closed when Cairo's hands land on my hips, my eyes widen in shock and I instinctively brace for impact, nothing happens. I'm so confused. "Fuck me sideways, are you crushing on the asshole that tore us from our fucking home and nearly killed our father?" I shrink back and drop my gaze to the ground, I feel the growl vibrate in Cairo's chest, he sounds vicious and angry.

"Unless you want me to teach you a lesson in manners, you should shut the fuck up." Hunter laughs but there is no humor to it.

"Oh yeah? You and what army? We're out here in the woods, three of u against one of you." Cairo chuckles but the sound sends dread pooling in my belly, Hunter has to stop antagonizing him.

"You never learn, do you?" I hear a twig snap and lift my gaze, walking out from the trees behind my brothers is none other than Sky and Zeke. Each of them have a murderous look on their faces, Sky looks ready to burn shit, Zeke cracks his knuckles and bends his neck side to side while eyeing my brothers. "You have two options, leave, or get your asses handed to you." Hunter scoffs and growls at Zeke.

"You think you can take us?" Z throws his head back and laughs before stepping backward behind Sky.

"Nah my man, I'm gonna leave the ass kicking to this badass." He lays his hands on Sky's shoulders and smirks triumphantly, the way the men around here look to her for advice and how they trust her is awe inspiring, Skylar Cage is a rarity. Her beauty is only amplified by the fact she has no idea how stunning she truly is, I can see why he feels the way he does. I don't want this to escalate any more than it already has, so I try to pull from Cairo's hold but his grip tightens and he grunts in disapproval. I swoon a little inside at his display of dominance, but these are my brothers that he is toying with, and I will not allow anyone to do that, I relax my body into him and feel his body lose some of its tension, then I yank forward breaking out of his hold, Cass reaches for me, and I go willingly.

I spin around and meet Cairo's glare. "We can talk later." I mutter.

Chapter Fourteen

Cairo

"**D**id she just...walk away from you?" I glower at her retreating form; I don't miss the way her brothers shield her as they move. I'm pissed at myself for being annoyed that she left with them, today...I opened up to someone which I never do and I even...laughed. She isn't jaded or bitter like most people in this fucked up world, she sees everything through rose colored glasses and I don't know if that is a good thing or not.

She sees the real you.

The hell does that mean, Bex?

If you have to ask, then you're not ready for the answer. I clench my fists in anger when Bex closes the link between us, he is a cryptic motherfucker and knows I hate it when he speaks in riddles.

"Let's head back–." Sky cuts me off.

"Ro, why were you out here with her?" The accusation is clear in her tone, no point lying when she already knows, she just wants to hear me say it.

"You know why." Her eyes widen slightly. "I did what I had to do; I just hope your right about her because if you're not..." I trail off and leave her to stand there and stew on my words, I never would have said anything to Belle if Sky hadn't pushed me to. I don't trust anyone with knowing the truth about Sky let alone some girl I just met, she may be *special* and able to see things but seeing them and knowing about them are two totally different things. Zeke chases after me but I don't slow my pace, I'm getting more and more irritated by the second, I'm angry I let her get under my skin and drop my guard for even a moment. To make it worse, she didn't even try, I just...let her!

"We need to talk, Ro."

"About what Z?"

"Bodie and the pack went on a run––." I growl in annoyance.

"I'm aware, I'll debrief with him shortly." Zeke growls and jumps in front of me, I grind to a stop, so I don't plow into him. I grit my teeth and glare at the bastard, he has some balls to pull a move like that. I still don't trust him fully after what he did.

"Bodie picked up a scent." The fucker quirks his brow prompting me to ask him, he'll pay for this later.

"Whose?"

"Vamps, but he also picked up a shifters with it." I scrunch my face in confusion.

"That bitch sent someone ahead—." I cut myself off when Z begins to shake his head, I feel Sky press up beside me. "It's not Davina's people, is it?" Z shakes his head.

"Bodie said one of the others recognized the scent, belonged to Jacob daughters, Kayla." *Shit!*

"Does my sister know?"

"Nah, I told Bodie to keep it quiet till I had a chance to speak with you." It clicks then.

"That's why you and Sky were out here?" He shrugs his shoulders.

"Perfect timing on your part then, now let's get back and figure out what the fuck is going on."

Dread begins to pool inside me as we make our way back, if it isn't one of Davina's vamps then that can only mean—Alexander is here and come for Belle.

After the three of us finish talking with Bodie we make our way back to my sister's house, now is the perfect time to speak with Belle's brothers while everyone else is out and it's only the Wilders home. My chat with Bodie was as helpful as a clit on a dick, he only confirmed what I already knew. I can feel the tension radiating between the three of us, none of us know anything about this Alexander and I don't cope well with the unknown. I hate situations where I have to go in blind hence why I made sure to research Belle and scope out her pack for days before I even made my move. I will never put my pack in a situation where I know we cannot get out of, it's my job as their...alpha. I never wanted to be alpha or to lead but I had no choice after what Sky and I did, Bex wouldn't allow me to stay hidden after that.

As soon as we enter the house I spot the four Wilder siblings in the lounge room, their conversation stops upon our arrival and we're met with angry glares from the three boys, Belle won't meet my stare and it pisses me off. I can tell her brothers have said something to cause her to retreat inside herself again.

I thought you didn't care about her?

Fuck off, Bexley!

I slam the link closed between us and grit my teeth, it's great being a shifter except for times like this when your wolf is being a bitch!

"My sister will not be your puppet any longer." I meet Cass's stare and laugh, there is no humor to it, and it comes out rough and course thanks to Bex rising up and breaking through my barrier. I feel my vision shift to his and zero in on Cass, he rises to his feet slowly and holds my gaze.

Big mistake, asshole.

"I accept your challenge, Cassius." Chaos breaks out, Hunter and Blake are on their feet and shouting, Sky and Zeke push forward as the three Wilder brothers' step around the couches toward us. Excitement thrums through me at the prospect of a challenge, Cassius knew what he was doing when he decided to hold eye contact with me, and I relish in his stupidity. It's been a hot minute since I have been challenged, Bex is preening inside me ready to roll at a moment's notice. When they are two feet from us, I meet Cass's gaze and smirk, he growls and clenches his fists at his side I see the flicker in his eyes and know his wolf is right there below the surface. Hunter places a hand on Cass's chest stopping his movements.

"Cass, this is not a good idea brother." Cass ignores his brother's plea and smacks his hand away as he meets my gaze.

"I'm ready now, *when* I win, we leave here immediately, and you never come near my family again *or* my sister." I smirk and allow Bex to speak through me.

"Deal." My voice is thick with warning, there is no way he will win, I'm not being cocky, I'm just keeping it real. No one, not even Credence-fucking-Reeves has ever beaten Bex. Bexley isn't like most wolves; he has no urge to submit or control, he just wants to excerpt his dominance over other wolves and that is all thanks to Sky.

I yank my shirt over my head and pop the button on my jeans, I can feel Creed's glare in the back of my head but ignore him as I quickly undress.

"She is going to flip her shit Ro――."

"Fuck off Creed, he challenged me, and I accepted, end of story." He's just got his panties in a bunch because my sister is pissy, the alpha challenge will take place on Jacob's old pack land, as mine and my sisters wolves can't be near each other. Sheba is a dominant mother fucker and Bex won't let her get one up on him so it's easier to keep them apart, Creed is only here because she made him come. I grip the waistband of my boxers but freeze when I feel Sky beside me, I turn to her, but her gaze is focused on my opponent.

"He favors his left, must have done his ACL, so his hind leg is the best bet to take him down quick." She tears her eyes from Cass and looks up to me, unease shines in her eyes.

"What's that look for?"

"He's not as weak as you think he is Cairo; I saw him and his brothers run the other night, and I observed his wolf, they follow him naturally and their wolves bow to him with no hesitation, even Bodie and Z felt the alpha within him."

"I can't be led Sky."

"No, but you can be beaten, so do not underestimate him Ro, or it will be your downfall. Attack his left flank and put him down quick, if he gains momentum, he will plow through you." Bex growls but Sky ignores him as she makes her way back to her mate, I pull my gaze from them as Callie leans in for a kiss. Seeing that has anger coursing through me, I have to let that shit go and move the fuck on. I roll my shoulders and crack my neck side to side as I push my boxers down, I spot her between her brothers and fight the smile that wants to break free when I notice she has averted her gaze, so she doesn't see my cock. The shift happens instantly, I love the feeling of my muscles stretching and tearing as they reform, I don't even bat an eye at my bones snapping. Shifting now takes less than two seconds, I shiver as all my senses switch onto full alert, sights, smells and sound are all fully heightened. I move toward the center of the circle which my pack has formed and freeze, I snap my gaze up and stare.

Bex...

I know.

This can't be!

How can it be?

I don't fucking know! This shouldn't be happening Bexley, something isn't right.

Once our gazes lock, I feel it deep inside of me and irrational anger burns through my veins, I release a loud long growl in warning. *Get us the fuck out of here now Bex!*

That would mean––.

I don't give a fuck what it means, I said now!

You will regret this Cairo.
I will regret nothing, now go!

Bex meets the eyes of Cassius's wolf and growls before turning and running, he snaps his jaws at the bystanders, and they stumble out of the way. I ignore the shouts for us to come back, I don't stop knowing that they will shift and follow me, if I do, it will all catch up with me and I...I just can't deal with that right now.

I don't know how I ended up here, I retreated inside myself until Bex forced us to shift, I stand here in the clearing naked and spin in a slow circle. Out of all the places to run and escape to, he chose here, why?

Bex?

This is the last place you felt any real emotion. I scoff.

Bullshit, I have felt plenty.

No, you haven't, you let yourself and others think you have, but this was the last time you truly felt bone deep emotion.

Huh?

All those years ago when Jess was at the mercy of Creed and the council, you were scared. You didn't know how you would take them down if it came to it, you knew she would have to do it in order for you to save your sister.

I think back to that day and sigh, he's right. I would have asked Sky to do it even knowing what the outcome would have been, does that make me a shitty person? I spot a fallen tree and decide to park my ass on it while I figure out what the fuck I am going to do from here. Everything has turned to shit, all of my planning and scouting just fucking went up in smoke hours ago, did she know?

I don't know.

How is this even possible Bex?

I don't know, she can't shift and isn't one of us.

I know!

Then you need to figure out why this has happened.

How?

Ask them, and maybe it's time to tell her the truth before it's––.

Bex is cut off when the sound of a twig snaps, I'm on my feet within seconds and shifting. I scent the air and turn ridged when the stench of rotting flesh assaults my nose.

Vampire.

The scent is coming from the left Bex.

Bexley turns so our back is to the tree in case of an ambush, I strain my hearing to try and pick up on any other sounds but find none. The sound of footfalls and the stench of death is getting closer, my hackles raise as I crouch low and wait for the source of the stench to reveal itself. A second later a figure emerges, a man wearing a black trench coat, black dress pants and white button up shirt. He's tall and has the build of a NFL player, no stubble coats his jaw, he has a square chin, straight nose that fits his face perfectly, dark brown eyes that almost seem black, and shaggy black hair that is slicked back on top of his head. I growl out a waring and the fucker smirks before moving toward the middle of the clearing, I turn with him making sure to keep my back to the tree. As if he doesn't sense the danger he is in, he turns in a slow circle taking in his surroundings, then runs his gaze over Bex.

"My oh my, out here all alone with no one to defend you. Here I thought getting to you would be a lot harder than this, you made it too easy Mr. Cruz." I tense, if he knows who I am then that means only one thing.

He's Alexander, the only living original vampire on Earth.

"You can shift back Mr. Cruz; you have my word that I did not come here to harm you. I only wish to speak with you, and then I will be on my way." I growl at the fucker; he meets my unflinching gaze and holds it as he says. "You have my word...alpha." Call me stupid but I can hear the truth ringing out in his words.

It's too risky Cairo.

What choice do we have Bex?

We don't shift, we are weak on two legs.

I need to know what he wants Bex.

Bex relents control and I shift back; I stand before him bare. He keeps his gaze on mine as he shrugs out of his coat and throws it at me, I breathe through my mouth or risk gagging at the stench of rotting flesh. Not wanting my cock out for this talk I slip the coat on and fasten it before meeting his gaze once more.

"I assume you're Alexander?"

"I am."

"Why are you here?" His eyes crinkle on the sides, his face takes on a hard edge.

"I came for my daughter; I hear she is in your care?"
Well fuck me, that wasn't what I expected.

Chapter Fifteen

Belle

I watch as his wolf runs from the makeshift circle with my mouth agape, what the hell is going on? Everyone shouts for him to come back, some chase on two legs while others strip down and shift to chase after their alpha. Once he hits the woods and I can no longer see his black and white wolf with the piercing onyx eyes I turn toward Sky, I shudder when I find her gaze already on me. Her mate and her twin move toward Creed, but her gaze still remains on me, the look she gives me has dread pooling in my belly. The sound of bones breaking shakes me out of my stare off with Sky, Hunter hands Cass his basketball shorts as I look anywhere except at my brother's nakedness.

"The fuck just happened?"

"No idea Blake, Cairo Cruz isn't known to run from a fight ever." The worry in Cass's tone has me on edge, my brothers may be rash and think with their fists more often than their heads, but they are noble. Cass winning an alpha challenge like this is a blow he won't accept, he spins on his heel and heads toward Sky, Cairo's beta. Blake, Hunter and I follow after our oldest brother. "The fuck was that?" I move to stand beside Cass, Sky doesn't look threatened or intimidated by the three giant men breathing down at her. I spy Callie, Cole and Creed out the corner of my eye moving toward us, they form a barrier around Sky in show of their silent support.

"You forget whom you are speaking to."

"I forget nothing, he just ran, so that makes me *your* alpha——." Faster than I can blink Sky has pulled a dagger from God-knows-where and has it against Cass's throat, my brothers try to move in but when she snaps her gaze to them, they freeze. I can see Cass's Adam's apple bobbing against the tip of the blade and I panic when I see a drop of blood trickle down his neck.

"Say it again...I dare you." The threat is clear as day in her tone, Blake and Hunter are tense and darting their gazes around trying to figure out a way to get our brother out of this mess, but they won't find one. We are amongst Cairo and Creed's pack, who of course, would be loyal to Cairo being that he is family.

"Babe, put the knife down and use your words like we discussed." Callie speaks as if she is talking to a scared animal, these two are polar opposites and I would never have guessed they were mates if I hadn't seen it in a vision. Sky is all badass and rocks leather kind of chick, while Callie is a girly girl who loves skirts and make up, but somehow, they...work.

"You didn't win shit, something happened, and I will get to the bottom of it, but mark my words. You. Are. Not. Alpha." Sky drops her arm back to her side and storms off toward the vehicles, Callie gives us an apologetic smile before turning and chasing after her mate.

"You wanna tell me what the hell that was all about?" I jerk back in surprise to find Creed is accusing me.

"I-I had nothing to do with...whatever the hell just happened." I snap, flailing my arms around, to my surprise Cass moves to stand directly in front of Creed meeting his gaze.

"I don't know what happened or why, but I give you my word that my family and I will help you locate Cairo and get to the bottom of this."

What the hell?

"Why would you help us?" Cass straightens to his full height.

"Things change when missing puzzle pieces fall into place." Cryptic much?

I continue pacing the length of the porch and fight the urge to chew on my nails–– it's my nervous tick, sue me! It's been hours and still no one has called or even come back, my brothers went with Creed, Jess and their pack, Cairo's pack is being led by Sky and Zeke.

What the hell is wrong with me?

My brothers and I should have run the second Cairo left, we may never get another opportunity like this again and we have just wasted it! I groan out loud and stab my hands through my hair, and here I was helping them map out routes that he could have gone, even encouraged my brothers to help. I must have Stockholm-syndrome or something. It's times like this that I hate the fact I can't shift! More than anything in the world I have always wished that I would find my wolf someday, but that day hasn't come, I turn twenty in less than six months. I know my dad says I'm a late bloomer but even he can't get his own lie to sound believable. I'm a dud, the alpha's only daughter and I can't even shift–– I'm a joke!

I drop into one of the chairs and clasp my face between my hands, why do I feel like there is this huge part of me that I am missing? Is it because I don't have a wolf but are born from two, or is it because I'm the pack freak, thanks to my visions? I feel like an idiot because ever since Sky did...whatever she did, I am able to go outside, and it's the first time I have actually felt... alive in years. Just to have the sun on my face or smell the fresh crisp morning air is something I thought I would never be able to do. Worry and frustration is warring inside me but another part of me is giddy.

I'm losing my damn mind!

"Nah, everyone is bit cray cray sometimes." I squeak in surprise and snap my gaze up to see Cairo leaning against the porch railing in a... trench coat? Whatever he must see on my face prompts him to add. "You were talking out loud?" A whoosh of air escapes me and the tension I was feeling seconds ago drains from my body, I run my gaze over his chest and begin to heat. His tattoo's peek out from the opening in the top of the coat, I curl my hands into fists to resist the urge to reach out and trace them. Cairo is hot, no ifs, ands, buts or maybes about it.

"What's with the coat?" *Really?* I mentally facepalm myself.

"I...uh." He reaches up and rubs the back of his neck, as if my eyes have a mind of their own, they zero in on the small sliver of skin on the top of his thigh that is visible through the part in the buttons.

He's naked!

"My eyes are up here beauty." I snap my eyes back to his and immediately feel the blush coating my cheeks, he smirks and my breath hitches. "Why are you out here pacing?" He doesn't give me a chance to answer as he pulls away from the railing and looks around. "Where is everyone?"

"What?" He turns to meet my gaze again, the carefree look he sported just a second ago is gone and replaced by his usual emotionless mask.

"Where the bloody hell is everyone?" I recoil at his harsh tone; I'm still thrown at how he can go from zero to a hundred in a matter of seconds.

"They're out looking for you. You've been gone for hours Cairo, everyone is worried." He runs his hand through his hair and his shoulders slump slightly.

"Right, I'm going for a shower––." I stand pinning him with a harsh glare that has him clamping his mouth closed.

"My brothers are out there searching for you and all you can say is you need a goddam *shower?*" I'm vibrating with anger, his blatant brush off of how his disappearing act means nothing pisses me off, everyone has been running around searching for him worried that he was injured or worse. His eyes burn bright with anger, he stalks toward me and doesn't stop until we are chest to chest, I have to crane my neck back to meet his eyes. He reaches out and grips the back of my neck, his fingers dig in but I refuse to cry out in pain, I grit my teeth and let my rage shine through my gaze.

"I could shatter your world right now beauty." He reaches up with his free hand and tucks a stray strand of hair behind my ear, the act is so intimate for the words he just spoke.

"Why would you want to?"

"Because I need to see you burn in order for this to break."

"That makes no sense."

"It makes perfect sense, you would have fit me perfectly beauty, but I have to save her, and in order for that to happen, I have to give you up." He whispers the last part, and it takes me a moment for his words to finally register before I yank free of his hold and gape up at him. I can see the regret in his eyes and my stomach drops as dread begins to fill my veins.

"What did you do?"

"Made a deal with the devil." I mull his words over in my mind and then it finally clicks.

"You traded me to someone because they said they could stop my vision from happening." I shoulder past him to head inside; he snakes his arm out to stop me, but I yank free. I grind my teeth in anger when I see him looking at me with sadness and pity. "Don't you dare fucking look at me like that! You had no right to do what the fuck you just did——."

"You forget who captured who, Gabrielle!"

"I forget nothing asshole, you didn't capture shit. I chose to leave with you so I could help ease some of the hurt inside you."

"That wasn't your fucking job, you are here to help Sky that is it."

"She will never love you! I've seen her life Cairo, California is it for her, she is Sky's first and last love, she will never love you the way you want her to." He scoffs.

"Let me guess, you would love me like I should be loved?" I balk at me.

"Full of yourself much? I don't even know you to love you, so no——."

"You don't need to love me to fuck me."

"Oh please, you think because you're good looking I would fuck you?"

"Say *fuck* one more time."

"You're not my father——."

"You don't even know who your fucking father is!" I stumble back a step; his eyes widen in surprise that those words flew from his mouth.

"W-what does that mean?"

"Cairo!" We don't take our eyes off each other as we hear the others approach, I can see it in his eyes that there is more that he's not telling me. Our staring is broken when Jess slams into her brother, he shakes his head and wraps his arms around his sister. I look around the porch and see Cairo's pack and loved ones are here, I spot my brothers on the lawn and quietly sneak around everyone to head toward them. Blake spots me first and gives me a reassuring smile, I nod my head for them to follow me, I don't stop until we are far enough away from Cairo and the others that they can't hear.

"What's up Belle?" I try to muster the courage that I will need to answer Hunter's question, but a lump begins to form in my throat when I run my gaze over each of my brothers. Cairo has to be lying, I know I don't look like my brothers but that's because I follow my mom's side of the family.

But you can't shift.

I try to silence the voice inside me, but it won't shut up, tears begin to build behind my eyes and I try to stop them from falling but I fail. As soon as Hunter spots my tears, he wraps his arms around me and hauls me against his chest resting his chin atop my head.

"What's wrong Belle, did something happen?" I hear the worry in Cass's voice, but I still can't get the words out. What happens if they are true? My whole life will change, and I don't think I would be able to handle that, I already feel like a freak without being an orphan to add to the list. "Belle?" Hunter pulls back and I wipe my nose with the back of my hand as I meet Cass's gaze.

"I'm sorry, Cairo just said something that upset me and––." I clamp my mouth closed when Cass's eyes narrow, Blake goes ridged and Hunter growls. I turn around to find... Cairo prowling toward us, except he's in wolf form with Sky beside him, an irrational sense of jealousy courses through me when she runs her hand through his coat.

"For God's sake! We weren't running, didn't we earn some form of trust from you people by helping you look for him!" Blake snaps while pointing at Cairo, when the wolf's eyes meet mine, I move back a step, Hunter wraps his arm around my shoulders and pulls me into his side. The wolf growls and beings to snap its jaws, I've seen this wolf so many times in my visions but seeing him now while I'm conscious is different, he seems different, in my visions he is always fighting and searching for something.

"Bexley wishes to speak to Belle." My eyes widen in fear, I turn to meet each of my brothers' gazes and give a subtle shake of my head. I know shifters share the same body but have separate souls, rationally I know this but right now after what Cairo just said I don't want to be alone with any part of him.

"That's not going to happen." Blakes voice holds authority, and it makes me proud.

"It is and it will, allow Bex to meet with her and trust me when I tell you things will change." She meets my gaze and I feel like she is imploring me to try and read between the lines somehow.

"How am I supposed to talk to him if... you know." I gesture to the black and white wolf wildly.

"You'll be surprised Belle, trust Bex––." I scoff and roll my eyes.

"Trust is earnt not given, you may trust the bloody wolf and its human counterpart, but I don't." Sky scoffs and gives me a look that has me glaring back.

"You allow everyone to believe you are meek and came here because you were forced, but that isn't the case is it Gabrielle?" I stiffen and try to mask it, but she notices and smirks. "My hunches are never wrong."

"What hunch?"

"I see your sister doesn't tell you everything Cassius." Cass attempts to step forward, but I grip his arm and he allows me to pull him back.

"Your hunch may be right, but you don't know everything Skylar, I'll stay here with the wolf but not alone."

"Your brothers––." I raise my hand stopping her.

"You can stay but I refuse to be alone with him." My brothers moan and groan, but I refuse to let them tell me what to do.

Sky and I walk side by side with Bexley trailing behind us, my brothers are pissed at me, but I have to do this.

"Why didn't you tell them you called Cairo to you?" A whoosh of air escapes me.

"Why didn't you tell everyone you're not a Shifter?" Sky stops walking, I do the same and meet her gaze. It takes everything inside me not to cower under the pressure of her stare, this woman is a warrior and a badass, I have to stop antagonizing her.

"Don't do that."

"Do what?"

"Back down, speak your truth and stand your ground, never back down Gabrielle."

"Um...okay."

"Answer my question first and then I'll decide if I'll answer yours."

"Honestly, I didn't even know I was doing it until it was too late. I have never pulled someone to me before from a vision, I knew he was getting closer and closer every vision I had but I didn't realize I was showing him the way to me until it was too late." Sky smiles knowingly which throws me. "Why are you smiling like that?"

"It wasn't your visions pulling him to you Belle."

"What do you mean?" She turns and looks at Bexley, I do the same and furrow my brow in confusion.

"He has to be the one to explain it to you." I groan as I tear my gaze from the wolf and focus back on her.

"He made his point earlier, why am I out here Sky, and please don't lie to me."

"You're out here because Cairo did something that pushed Bex too far and he took control."

"What's your point?" Her gaze spears me and I fight my urge to back away.

"Bex has never stolen control from Cairo like that before, whatever happened between the two of you caused a rift between man and beast." I throw my hands up in frustration.

"I'm over this bullshit, I came here to save your life Sky, not for Cairo or his freaking wolf. A part of me felt drawn to him from the moment I saw him in my visions——." I contemplate lying but decide to go with the truth, enough lies have already been told. "I've been having visions of Cairo for months, even before he realized I was calling for him."

"We know, that's how we found you." I shake my head.

"I saw the battle that was fought here, I know you all fled to an island——." I'm cut off when the wolf shifts back to man and Cairo stands there naked and puffing, with his fists clenched at his sides. Sky moves subtly till she is standing slightly in front of me, any normal human would have missed that move but not the greatly feared Cairo Cruz, he sees everything.

"Why did you send that letter?" There isn't anger or malice in his tone, I make sure to keep my eyes on his as I answer, so they don't stray down...south.

"Because I knew that man Jacob and your council were coming after an innocent child——."

"Bullshit!" I flinch, he moves toward us, and Sky shifts to fully block me, he stands before us glaring.

"Cairo––." He snaps his eyes to Sky and growls.

"You wanted me to talk and try this shit out, here I am Skylar, the fuck more do you want?"

"For you to stop self-sabotaging, my fate isn't on you! I'm fucking tired of having this conversation with you, grow some fucking balls and man up for Christ's sake, I am going to die Cairo, you need to face that fact!" I feel like I'm intruding on a private moment.

"The fuck you are! I told you I figured out a way to stop that from happening." Cairo screams at her; Sky throws her hands up in the air in frustration.

Chapter Sixteen

Cairo

My chest is heaving and I'm vibrating with unbridled rage, I clench and unclench my fists at my sides. I don't fucking do feelings and thanks to Sky being the pushy bitch that she is and making me face them I feel unhinged, Bexley forced a shift on me and stole control just to hunt down the nuisance that Sky now shields from me. I keep my glare on Sky while I ask her one last time for the truth, if she lies to me, she will learn really quick how far my temper will go.

"Why. Did. You. Send. That. Letter?" To my utter surprise she steps out from behind Sky and moves to stand in front of me, I search her gaze trying to gauge her next move. Gabrielle Wilder can't hide her emotions for shit, every thought and feeling is displayed across her face and if you miss it, you sure as shit can find it in her eyes.

"I learnt a long time ago not to interfere with my visions, no matter how many deaths I tried to stop, fate would always find a way to claim their pound of flesh. I made Cass drive out to meet that man and give him the letter because——." Sadness clouds her eyes as she turns to peer over her shoulder at Sky and then back to me. "I saw Sky lose control of her...energy?" Sky snickers as a blush coats Belle's cheeks, she has no idea what Sky really is.

"So, you tried to save me?" Belle doesn't take her eyes off me as answers.

"Yes and No. By sending you that note, I not only stopped you from losing control, I also stopped you from——." Unease creeps up my spine as a strange look contorts her features. "Killing Cairo." I stumble back a step, my eyes darting to Sky, her gaze is firmly fixated on the back of Belle's head. "I'm so sorry, I didn't know how to tell you earlier, I know it sounds cliché but there wasn't exactly a right moment for me, to you know, tell you." I turn my gaze to Sky.

"Can you give us a moment," I can tell she wants to fight me on this, I narrow my eyes in warning. "It wasn't a question Skylar." She darts her gaze to Belle who gives her a small smile and nod, Sky shoulder checks me on her way past, I grit my teeth to stop myself from lashing out at her.

"She cares for you deeply, that's why--."

"Don't pry into my shit, I don't care what you see or what you think you know, you may see things others don't, but that doesn't mean you know everything!" She flinches at my cold harsh tone, but I don't give a fuck, shit happened today that should never have! Bex is furious at me for cutting a deal with Alexander and putting her at risk, but what choice did I have? Before I can get lost in my own thoughts, a scream tears from Belle's throat and she sways on her feet as her eyes roll backward and starts to fall, I dart forward and catch her before she falls to the ground. I wrap my arm under her thigh and lift her, so she is laying bride style in my arms, she shakes and moans, a light sheen of sweat begins to coat her forehead--she's having a vision! "I'm sorry for what is to come." Staring at her like this in pain and agony because of something she can't control breaks something inside me. "I think I fucked up beauty, I fucked up really bad today." I lean down and press my lips against hers, when a hiss escapes her, I pull back and rush toward the house, it destroys me when she mumbles those three words.

"Help me Cairo." I kick the front door open; growls erupt as they ready themselves to face a threat but relax when they see it's me, Hunter rushes over and tries to grab her but I tighten my hold and growl right in his face.

"Back the fuck off pup." His eyes change to the color of his wolf, we stand here glaring at the other until a small moan escapes Belle, he reluctantly steps back and motions toward the couch. I gently lay her down and ignore everyone else, my gaze focused only on her until something hits me in the side of the head. I turn and glare at my sister who shrugs and says.

"I do not need to see your baby maker, thank you very much." I smirk and grab the black basketball shorts she throws at me and quickly stand pulling them on, I gently lift Belle's head and then rest it back on my thigh.

"What happened today brother?" I pull my gaze from Belle and look around to see, Cole, Callie, Sky, Jess, Creed, Zeke, Hunter, Cass and Blake all staring at me waiting for an answer. I run my hand through my hair and sigh before answering Creed.

"I fucked up."

"How so?" I meet Z's gaze and whatever he sees in mine has him nodding and dropping down into the couch opposite me. "Fix it brother, there is no other option here, because you know what happens if you lose *her.*" Everyone around the room is staring at Z and I, I am the only one who understands his cryptic meaning, I feel for him, I would never betray his trust by sharing his story with...anyone.

"What does that mean?" I smile sadly up at my sister who is tucked under Creed's arm, time to tell the truth and hope Sky is right.

"Gabrielle Wilder is my...mate." Gasps and shouts begin to break out, Cass tries to lunge for me, but Blake and Hunter hold their older brother back, I glare at the fucker.

"You stay the fuck away from my sister――."

"But she isn't your sister is she, Cassius?" Hunter and Blake still, their gazes darting between Cass and I in confusion.

"The fuck does he mean bro?" Cass ignores Blake as he continues to glare and growl at me, I smirk, knowing I have the fucker by the balls.

"Tell them, they deserve to know that Belle is a... I guess we can call her an original."

"What the fuck is he saying Cassius?" Hunter shoves Cass and steps into him, they're chest to chest both heaving in anger. Cass doesn't budge, and after a moment he finally steps back and curses under his breath before meeting my stare.

"How did you find out?" Cole beats me to answer.

"We all know, have done for a while now."

"Someone want to fill us the fuck in here?" Hunter snaps while looking to each of us before finally settling his sights on his older brother. A whoosh of air escapes Cass as he looks to each of his brothers and runs a hand through his hair.

"Belle...isn't our sister――."

"Fuck you, you're lying!"

"Bullshit, asshole." Blake and Hunter both start shouting at the same time. I actually feel bad for both of them, I had no idea they didn't know about Belle.

"She will always be our sister whether we share DNA or not but it's true." Hunter shoves Cass back a step and growls right in his face, I admit Cass has way more restraint and control over his wolf than I would have thought, Bex would have laid Hunter out by now.

"How long?" Cass quirks a brow in confusion.

"What?"

"How fucking long have you known about Belle, and don't you dare fucking lie to me!" Cass tears his gaze from Hunter to stare at Blake, I can see how tense he is and how much he hates this situation. Fuck him, that fucker deserves to sweat.

"Since the day we left to come here." Blake laughs but there's no humor to it.

"That's why dad spoke to you privately before we left?" Cass nods. "Here Hunt and I were thinking that you and dad were hatching an escape plan, instead you two were having a good old chat about our sister and never once thought to include us!" Blake is shouting, rage rolling off him in thick waves, it's so potent that I can taste his anger on my tongue.

"I didn't fucking have a chance to tell either of you––." Cass is cut off when Hunter lands a right hook to his jaw, he stumbles back a step and Hunter tries to launch at him again, but Z and Cole are there to pull him back.

"You fucking bastard! You stay the fuck away from our sister, as far as I'm concerned, you and dad can both go to fucking hell!" Cass drops his gaze to the floor and grinds his teeth.

"Hunter stop!" I snap my gaze down to the beauty in my lap, her eyes are open, but I can see the strain on her forehead, she's in pain. I help her sit up but when she tries to scoot away from me, I wrap my arm around her shoulders and haul into my side, she stiffens and turns to glare at me. I furrow my brow in confusion when the corner of her lip lifts in a snarl.

"Easy there tiger, I have bigger teeth than you." Clearly, she isn't in a joking mood, her eyes narrow to slits and tension begins to coil inside me. My mouth drops the fuck open when she smacks my hand away and throws her leg over my lap and straddles me. I hear gasps around the room, but my eyes are stuck on Belle, I'm smart enough to know that she isn't sitting on me because she wants me, she's up to something. She runs her hands along my abs and then up my chest, her tiny fingers splay over my pecs before trailing over my face and through my hair, she grips the strands and then tugs until my neck is tilted and I'm staring straight into her eyes.

"I tried to play nice, I tried to help, I even went as far as fleeing the only home I have ever known to help you." Her eyes darken, for the first time since meeting her I can't get a read on her emotions. "You pushed me away and hurt me with your words but yet I still stayed. Want to know why?" I suck in a sharp intake of air when she bends down and licks from my neck to my lobe, I fight the moan that wants to break out when she grinds down on cock and nibbles on my ear.

"Why, beauty?" Even I can hear how fucking horny I sound.

"Because I have known for months that you are mine Cairo." Her whispered words have me stiffening beneath her, I reach up and grip her shoulders pushing her back until I meet her gaze, she has a sly smirk on her face.

"You knew?" She shrugs her shoulders.

"I also knew what would happen today, Cass would never have harmed you because my brothers know who you are to me. You see, I let you think the ball was in your court this whole time until you overstepped today and made a deal behind my back."

"Belle——."

"I'll be with you in a sec Blake, just have to finish my convo with my *mate*." She spits the word mate like it means nothing as if it's a dirty word. "I have seen so many things Cairo, but I have never seen my own future, until I started seeing you, then things changed." Her eyes dart between mine trying to get a read on me and my thoughts, she bends down and whispers in my ear, low enough for only me to hear. "I will never go to my *real* father; I should have been the one to tell my brothers, not you!" She pulls back and I just stare at her stunned, who the fuck is this person sitting in my lap, because she sure as fuck isn't the innocent little girl I stole days ago. She climbs off me and turns to face her brothers, I move to stand beside her and that's when I notice her nose is bleeding, all three of her brothers rush forward, she halts them with a hand and then wipes her nose with the back of her hand. The look of fear on all three Wilder brothers has unease creeping up my spine.

"Belle, you need to rest." She shakes her head.

"Nah Hunt, I'm good, we have some matters to discuss." Cass recoils, Belle smiles reassuringly at him. "I knew he told you, I just hoped you would have come to me sooner." Regret and hurt flash in Cass's eyes, I can see that he and the other two truly love Belle.

"I'm sorry sis, I didn't know how and when I had the chance, I chickened out because I-I... I didn't want it to be true. You are, and always will be my sister Gabrielle, nothing and no one will ever change that, my loyalty will always be to you above all else, I swear it." Belle sniffles and then launches at her brother, the four of them stand there in an awkward four-way hug.

"Um, so, I get that I'm slow sometimes but...what the fuck just happened dude." I turn to meet Cole's stare; the bastard has a smile so huge that it'll rival the Cherisher cat. "I can smell how much she wants you from here." I roll my eyes and ignore him and Z chuckling, I turn to Sky to see her and Callie already staring at me, I quirk a brow at Sky, and she shrugs.

"Sue me, I had a feeling, and you know I always listen to my gut. Turns out it was right again." I glower at her, Sky has always said that the real Belle is hiding under all the fakeness, I didn't believe her and turns out she may be right.

I told you our mate is formidable.

Yeah, well bite me Bex.

Bex and I have been at odds because I thought my mate needed to be strong and forward and Belle just didn't seem like the type, I guess I was disappointed when the mate link clicked in.

"I don't mean to be the downer here but how is she your mate when she isn't a shifter?" Jess is right, I open my mouth to answer my sister, but Belle beats me to it.

"I don't know, truthfully I have no idea what I am."

"But you knew about him?" She smiles at Blake before focusing back on me.

"I only see things about myself through your eyes, I never see my own fate, if you get what I mean?" I nod, fully grasping what she means.

"For arguments sake, let's say some of us in the back don't get it, would you explain?" Everyone laughs at Cole's expense. Everyone takes a seat and just as Belle is about to drop down between her brothers on the opposite couch I reach out and grip her arm yanking her back to me, she falls into my lap and glares, I have no idea what the fuck came over me to do that but I'm not gonna tell her that.

Our mate needs to stay close to us.

How is she even our mate, Bex?

She just is.

I'm so over your cryptic shit!

If it's possible for a wolf to laugh, that is exactly what Bex is doing right now. Belle shifts and tries to squeeze next to me, but Z sensing what I want, he widens his legs so there is no room for her between us, Belle glares at him then shuffles until she finds a comfy spot on my lap, after a few seconds I grip her hips and hold her still, my cock cannot take anymore of her wriggling. She freezes when she feels my bulge beneath her ass, *that's right beauty I'm hard for you.* Someone clears their throat snapping her out of her stupor.

"Uh, yeah so, I never have been able to see my own future, I have never seen myself in a vision except for...Cairo's." I turn and share a look with Z, he nods and then asks.

"How much have you seen about Cairo?" She doesn't falter.

"Everything." *Fuck!*

I wrap my arms around her waist and stand with her flush against my front, shocked looks are cast our way, but I ignore them as I carry her toward my room. I slam the door closed once we are inside and then spin her so she is now pinned against the wall, angry eyes meet mine and I smirk. I might have been quick to judge her, she has fire and spunk and it's just taken me being a fuck up for it to come out.

"How much do you know?"

"Why did you offer me up to Alexander?" I growl, she bares her teeth at me.

"You answer first." She scoffs.

"That never works out in my favor, answer for an answer?" I close the space between us until our lips are nearly touching, mine skim over hers as I speak. "Don't push me beauty, you won't like the beast that you unleash." She smirks! She fucking smirks at me and before I can snap at her she throws her arms around my neck and smashes her lips against mine, something primal inside me fits into place, almost like a missing puzzle piece has finally fallen into place. This kiss isn't like anything I have ever felt before, I used to kiss girls to forget about Sky but this kiss, it grounds me, makes me feel like I'm...home. I run my hands down her sides and she shivers, I grip the back of her thighs and lift, she wraps her legs around my waist, and I turn heading toward the bed. My tongue pushes past her lips, and I moan at the taste of her, she scrapes her nails down the back of my neck I relish in the sting it causes. When I hear shouts it's like a bucket of ice water has been dropped on me, I pull back and unwrap her arms from around my neck and push her until she unhooks her legs, her pupils are dilated with lust, and I know if I scent the air, I will smell her arousal, so I breathe through my mouth. A look of hurt begins to cross her features but I ignore it.

"D-did I do something wrong?"

"What happened to that self-confident chick from minutes ago that jumped into my lap?" She smiles but it doesn't reach her eyes, I reach out and cup her cheeks in my hands. "You didn't do anything wrong." I grip her hand and place it against my hard cock, she gasps and blushes. "The only thing wrong is me having blue balls, but we have shit to sort out before I bury my dick deep in your pussy beauty." Her mouth drops open, I release her hand and wink.

"What do you want to know?"

"Okay, for a start why didn't you tell me straight away?"

"I told you before, that no matter what, destiny always finds a way, so I don't interfere with my visions anymore. I let them play out at their own pace."

"Why do I feel like there is a *but* coming?" She sighs and drops down on the edge of the bed.

"Because I've never done this before, seeing my future scares me, this is all new to me too. I'm trying to figure it out as I go."

"Your brothers help you?" She smiles and looks up to me, nothing but love shines in her eyes when she speaks of them.

"They may not be my blood, but they are everything to me, family runs deeper than blood, I don't have to share DNA with them to know I would trade my life for theirs in a heartbeat." Why does the thought of her dying cause something to ache inside me?

Because she is tethered to our soul and without a soul we cannot exist.

Well fuck, Bex. That was deep as shit. He growls his annoyance, but I ignore him and focus back on Belle.

"Okay, wanna make a deal?" She nods skeptically. "Why don't I send Z into town to get some Chinese take outs for us and we spend the night getting to know each other, no more lies or secrets." Her shocked gaze is almost comical.

"Why the sudden change of heart?" A whoosh of air escapes me, I remind myself that I just said no more lies and that shit starts now.

"Everything changed the moment Bexley uttered the word *mate.*"

CHAPTER SEVENTEEN

Belle

We have been talking for hours, the only break we had is when I showered, I never thought Cairo would be one for humor and laughter, but I was wrong. He isn't how I pictured him to be, he is kind, loyal to a fault, but he doesn't trust easily or love many. Those who are closet to him have earnt his respect and love and that is equal parts sad and beautiful. Now that I have five minutes to myself without Cairo sucking the oxygen out of the room, I start to think, I lied today. I didn't know for sure that I was his mate, it was hinted in a vision, and again when I saw him and Sky, something inside me knew she was talking about me, but one thing I can't get past is the fact she said *chosen mate*, not mate. Cairo is pulling me out from the walls I have hidden behind, and part of me loves that, but another part is scared. He asked me why I seemed so shocked today when he mentioned they weren't my brothers, I told hm the truth. My reaction was real, because I had never heard anyone utter those words out loud. It stings to know I have been lied to, but being blood related to them or not doesn't change my love for them or my father.

I know he wants to push me for information about Alexander, but the truth is, I don't know anything about him. All I have seen is that he is my bio father, nothing more and nothing less. A knock sounds at the door and I call out to come in, Hunter and Blake walk in with a shameful Cass trailing after them, Hunter darts his eyes around the room, and I smile.

"Cairo is in the shower." Hunter smiles but it doesn't reach his eyes, he moves over toward the bed where I am and sits down on the edge. I can see so many emotions swirling in his eyes and it hurts me that I can't take his pain away. I reach out and place my hand on top of his, hoping that a vision doesn't assault me, and I send a silent prayer up to whoever is listening and thank them for not letting it happen. "Nothing has to change, Hunt. I'm still me, and your still you, I love you and nothing will change that."

"I'm so sorry Belle, I didn't know...how I was——." I cut Cass off and slowly climb to my feet.

"You have nothing to be sorry about, you didn't do anything wrong Cass." I wrap my arms around my brother and rest my head against his chest, he wraps his arms around me and holds me tight as he rests his chin on my head. Cass is the quietest out of my brothers, he is strong willed, fiercely loyal, overprotective but he has the biggest heart. Hunter and Blake have no idea the sacrifices Cass has made so we could all have our freedom and live semi normal lives, Cass never had a chance to be young and dumb, he had to grow up real fast. He became a mother to the three of us and whenever dad was away, he would always fill our fathers' shoes. I owe Cass so much, which is the reason why I will never tell him that he won't be the next alpha for the Wilder pack. Destiny has something else in store for Cass, and I just hope he is ready for it when it happens, because he will do amazing things.

"I love you Belle; I'll always be here for you." His words seep into me, and I relish in the love I feel radiating off him, I feel my other two brothers at my back, and I turn to hug each of them. Cass sits in the chair by the window, Hunt and Blake hop up on the bed with me, I can see from the strain on Blake's face he has something to say, so I prompt him. "Just say it." He turns to me, but his gaze is focused over my shoulder.

"Your visions are slowing but getting worse, when you have one, I'm concerned Gabrielle." I open my mouth then clamp it shut when he glares at me. "Don't brush me off, I don't care if *he* needs your help. You are my sister and you come before everything and everyone."

"Blake, the visions are still coming I just haven't told you all about them except for the ones you have seen here. If this is the way I go, then so be it--." Hunter jumps to his feet cutting me off and shoving a hand through his hair as he paces the foot of the bed. He spears me with an angry glare, his lip pulled back in a snarl.

"Nah fuck that sis. You aren't going out like that. We'll fix this shit, the four of us--."

"This stays between the four of us, none of them can know." Each of my brothers exchange worried glances but I know they will agree with me. Cairo and I had a deal about no more lies, but right now this is my burden to carry not his, just because he finally admitted to me being his mate doesn't mean I feel the connection that he does. I blow out a huff of air and my shoulders droop.

"What's up?" I twist my hands in my lap and ask the one question I dread the answer to.

"If we aren't related--by blood, does that mean I'm not... a shifter?" I whisper the last part, like I said I only see myself through Cairo's eyes not my own. I hear sharp intakes of air from my brothers.

"I swear to you, we will help you figure this out sis." I fake a smile and nod. "Thanks Hunt."

Everyone is piling their plates with food while I hang back, just because I can be around people doesn't mean their touch--accidently won't trigger a vision. I smile to myself as I watch them, Cole, Callie and Creed banter back and forth like me and my brothers, Sky, Z and my brothers are lost in conversation and Jess is smiling at her son. I snap out of my staring when a round of congratulations burst from everyone, Jess thanks them and smiles shyly, not wanting to be the odd one out I jump in and say.

"Congratulations on your miracle, she is going to be beautiful--." I stop speaking when Jess pales and reaches up to cover her mouth with her hand, tears shining in her eyes. I gulp when Creed steps into her and hauls her back against his chest, his gaze bores into me and I begin to feel uneasy, what the hell did I do? I back up a step but I collide with something, I peer over my shoulder and release a whoosh of air at the sight of Cairo. His hands grip my waist, and he pulls me against him--protectively, whilst glaring at Creed, but Credence Reeves isn't looking at Cairo, his gaze is on me.

"What. Did. You. Just. Say?" I gulp and glance at Jess who has tears streaming down her cheeks, I start to shake my head not wanting to fight, because I have a huge mouth and don't know when to shut it apparently.

"Please Belle. Tell me what you know...please." I meet Jess's gaze and deflate, Cairo moves one of his hands and lays it flat against my stomach, I gasp but remain still, he's trying to reassure me that he is here, and I don't know how to feel about that. I have never had physical contact much in my life and having him this close is doing things to me that I can't even explain. Rather than focus on my own feelings I dart my gaze between Jess and Creed and blurt it all out.

"Your fertility treatment didn't work." A sob tears out of Jess, but I push on. "I know you have been trying and gave up five months ago--." Creed spins Jess around, and she buries her head in his chest as she sobs, I feel Cairo stiffen behind me, so I quickly push on. "You both stopped putting pressure on yourselves and your...at home remedy worked. Your about 6 weeks along, and she will be everything you hoped she would be." Creed's mouth drops open,

Jess spins out of his hold and stares at me as she swipes the tears from her cheeks.

"Are you saying?" The hope in her voice brings a smile to my face.

"That your about to be a girl mom in about 7 or 8 months? Yes." More sobs burst from her, she throws herself at Creed and locks her arms around his neck, his gaze still on me. He gently untangles her arms from his neck and moves toward me, he stops a couple steps away when Cairo growls in warning, still Creed keeps his eyes on me.

"I...Thank you Belle." His sincerity brings tears to the corners of my eyes, I nod not trusting my voice. "You have just given us...everything. In return, I offer you our help for whatever you need." I smile and nod again, I'm not used to people being okay with my visions, my pack hated me for it. I watch as everyone embraces Jess and Creed and touches her belly, even though she isn't showing, a pang of longing hits me, I will never get that joy of giving life to another. A shudder rolls through me when I feel his lips on the shell of my ear.

"You know, they were congratulating my sister and Creed because the dumbass finally took her advice and expanded his company interstate." I cringe, me and my big ass mouth. "Thank you, Belle." I try to move but he won't release his hold on me, I turn in his arms and stare up at him. For the first time he lets me see beyond his mask, his emotions on full display, and there is nothing but happiness and love in his gaze, but the longer he stares at me, I see...longing.

"For what?" I whisper just loud enough for him to hear.

"For giving my sister the greatest gift, she has been through so much and she deserves this more than anyone I know." I snort, his forehead furrows. I lean up on my tip toes with his hands still on my waist, he bends slightly to allow me to whisper in his ear.

"Pretty sure Creed was the one that planted that seed in her, not me." He pulls back and stares at me for a moment before throwing his head back and...laughing. Holy shit on a bible, Cairo brooding is sexy, but Cairo laughing and being carefree, is your panties destruction. Geez, even his freaking throat looks sexy when he laughs!

"Hey Belle?" I turn and peer over my shoulder to see Cole smirking at me, Cairo's laughter is cut off. "Your horny is showing babe." My mouth drops open and my eyes widen in horror, Cole, Z, Sky and Callie break out into fits of laughter at my embarrassment, I dart my gaze to my brothers to find the three of them are glaring at Cairo, if looks could burn you alive, Cairo would be ablaze right now. His fingers grip my chin and pull my face back to him, I fight the urge to close my eyes, so I don't have to look at him. He smiles at me but this one is different; I don't even know how to explain, I guess you could say it's a...genuine one?

"We're all shifters beauty, we can scent your...arousal."

Oh, for the love of Christ.

I feel the burn creeping up my neck, I can hear snickers, but I ignore them and drop my gaze to the floor mortified at myself! He grips my chin and lifts my gaze till I meet his, I cringe when I see laughter shining in his eyes. I tear out of his hold and head for the door, I squeal in surprise when he wraps an arm around my waist and yanks me against his chest. I hear growls erupt but I'm too focused on the way he is holding me.

"Come at me Wilder, and your sister won't be the only one I'm fucking up tonight." I gasp at his crudeness, but I would be a liar if I said his dirty words didn't have butterflies erupting inside my belly. The feeling inside me fizzes out when I realize that I will never be able to do that with him, he may be able to touch me now, but who is to say that having sex wouldn't change that?

"Say that again and I'll knock your fucking teeth down your throat and take your pack for real this time." Cairo drops his hold on me as if I burnt him and storms toward my brother, Cass stands tall and doesn't waiver. Creed blocks Cairo and within a split-second Sky is beside him with her hand on his chest shaking her head at him. Cairo thrashes against the two of them, Zeke and Cole quickly rush over while Jess grabs her son and leaves the room, Hunter and Blake are holding Cass back. Even Callie is trying to help my brothers with Cass, Sky snaps her gaze to me, and I freeze.

"Come and calm his beast or he will tear your brother apart!" I open my mouth, but she cuts me off. "Now!" Sky steps back as I approach them and place my hand flat against his chest, his growling stops and the tremors rolling through his body lessen at my touch, he drops his gaze to me and I hold it waiting to see if this bond is real between us, if it isn't, his wolf will see it as a challenge, but he doesn't. His eyes slowly flicker back to his own and he releases a rush of air, he grips my hand in his and then pulls me out the front door, I ignore the shouts coming from my brothers and quicken my pace to keep up with Cairo. His long legs eat up the ground so I'm near on jogging just to keep pace with him.

"I'm gonna fall––." I don't even get a chance to finish speaking when he turns grips me around my legs and hoists me up and I wrap my arms around his neck, and legs around his waist, he grips my ass to keep me from falling. He rushes us through a part of the forest I have never been and keeps walking until we come to a stop out the front of a small cabin nestled inside a small clearing. It's gorgeous and quaint, it reminds me of the house from Snow White and the seven Dwarfs. Cairo stalks up the small pathway and pushes the door open, he kicks it shut behind us and immediately I'm awestruck, this cabin has the feeling of memories and love inside it, I'm not an empath but you know when you just get those feelings? He moves past the small kitchen and lounge and heads down the hallway, he passes two doors and finally kicks open the third at the end of the hall and takes two steps inside then I scream as he chucks me, and I go sailing through the air. I expect to feel pain from hitting the floor but instead I land on a soft surface and bounce a couple of times––I'm on a bed.

I turn and glare at him, he has the audacity to stand there and smirk at me! "That was not funny."

"Actually, it was. You should have seen your face." To emphasize his point, he does this funny thing with his face and then begins to flail his arms around in imitation of me, I huff and sit up and cross my arms over my chest.

"Was it necessary though?" He comes closer and then stops in front of me, I refuse to lift my gaze to his because, A, I'm slightly embarrassed and B, I'm angry at him for laughing at me. He grips my chin and I try to shake out of his hold, but he grips it tighter, not enough for it to hurt but enough for me not to fight and lift till I meet his stare.

"Yes, it was. You were too far in your own head worrying about what was happening between me and your brother." His eyes begin to soften as he looks at me, like really looks at me. "I used to pray that I would find a mate one day just so I could have something to call my own. I had nothing growing up beauty, it was just me and Sky, until Z came along. I'm gonna fuck shit up between us, I'm a moody bastard and possessive as fuck, also..." His gaze bores into mine and I see him tense, I begin to gnaw on my bottom lip, he reaches up and pulls it out with his thumb. "Don't do that." I hear the slight growl in his voice.

"W-what?"

"Bite your lip while I'm speaking." The growl is still in his voice, but it isn't from anger.

"Why?" I'm genuinely confused. A mischievous twinkle enters his eyes.

"Because it puts images of you gnawing on my cock in my head." My eyes widen and I gasp as he chuckles. "Now like I was saying, I don't share beauty...Ever. You want to touch another man in front of me, fine, but just know you signed his fucking death warrant, because rest assured, no mother fucker will ever touch what is mine, and you beauty, are mine, make no mistake about that."

"I-I...uh." He smiles, and it damn near blinds me.

"Don't go all quiet on me now, I know you must have some shit brewing in that pretty little head of yours." All of a sudden everything becomes too much;

I push off the bed and begin to pace the room, raking my hand through my long brown locks. So many thoughts are swirling through my head, I don't even know if I'm a shifter, but I have a mate. I have a mate who wants to hurt my brother, he just admitted to me not long ago that he was in love with Sky, and now he drops the '*your mine beauty*' bomb, like WTF! I stop and look at him only to be more annoyed when I see him leaning against the wall with his arms crossed over his chest and a smug smile on his face. "Argh." I throw my hands in the air and continue pacing while I ignore his laughter. I'm trying to sort through all of the emotions inside me when he blocks my path, I stare up at him ready to yell or tell him to piss off, but his hands cup my cheeks, and he smashes his lips against mine. I freeze, then I feel his tongue probe the seam of my lips, I open for him, he swirls his tongue across mine and a small whimper escapes me, he shifts his hand to grip my waist and haul me closer, the other tangles in my hair so he can yank on it, a moan escapes me which elects a growl from him. He shifts hands and grips the back of my thighs lifting me like he did before, he carries me over to the bed but this time he doesn't throw me, he lays me down gently and then stands back gazing down at me, my breathing is erratic, and my heart is beating faster than it ever has in my life. The fire in his eyes has shivers wracking my body, he runs his hands up my legs and then pushes my shirt up so he can lay his hands flat against my stomach. A growl of approval slips from him when he pushes my shirt further and exposes my teal-colored lace bra. He slips his hands back down to the waist band of my jeans and smirks.

"I wonder if it's a matching set?" Embolden by the sheer desire that blazes in his gaze, I decide to taunt him.

"Pop the button and find out for yourself." His gaze snaps to mine and feel it more than see it when the tension in the room ramps up, it's not bad tension, it's sexual tension that is vibing off the pair of us.

"I pop this button, there won't be any going back beauty. I sink my cock inside you and there will never be any running from me, you ready for that?" I close off the rational side of my brain that knows this is a bad idea and go with the side that is pushing me to experience this type of intimacy that I thought was never possible.

"I have a condition first." He quirks a brow and licks his lips, I can see he is trying to fight the smirk that wants to break free when he says.

"Name it."

"Same applies for you, soon as your inside me, that means you're as much mine as I am yours." I sit up and run my hands under his shirt, his skin feels hot to the touch, and I smirk when he shivers. I glance up at him through my lashes and smile the sultriest smile I can. "Like you, I don't care much for sharing. I know you are an alpha, and a man who cannot be led, but heed my words Cairo, you fuck me over with another woman and I will turn your world upside down and make all your worst nightmares come to life. You know I have seen your fears and your struggles, I am petty, and would use all of those against you." A wide smile spreads across his face, he shoves me back so I'm lying flat on the bed, he nudges my legs open with his knees and crawls up my body resting his elbows either side of my face.

"You know you look sexy as fuck when you get angry." He leans down to kiss me, but I stop him with my words.

"I've never done this before." My cheeks flame at my admission but he doesn't laugh.

"Have you done other things?" I won't lie, this is a huge deal for me, so I have to be honest with him.

"No, you're the only person who can touch me without sparking a vision." His brow furrows.

"I thought your dad and brothers could."

"Sometimes, but when their emotions are running high, just their presence can spark a vision."

"We don't have to do this if you're not ready beauty––." I silence him by wrapping my arms around his neck and yanking him down to me so I can kiss him. This kiss isn't like the last one, this one is hungry and fueled with desire that knows no bounds. I pour everything into this kiss to show him I want this with *him*. I know without having a vision that Cairo is it for me, there will never be another that can replace him or even come close. He pulls back and grips the hem of his shirt then yanks it off tossing it to the side, he grips the bottom of mine and does the same, cupping both my breast in his hands, he squeezes them, and a small moan slips free. I reach up and run my hands down his naked tattooed chest, he pulls back and rests on his hunches as he pops the button on my jeans and slides the zipper down, he meets my gaze giving me one last chance to back out.

"Take them off." My voice doesn't sound like my own, it's breathy. I lift up as he peels my jeans from my body and throws them over his head, his eyes darken when they land on my G-string–That does in fact match my bra.

"Jesus Christ, I can scent how wet you are." I squirm beneath him needing him to relieve the ache and make me come. I'm not a complete prude, I have watched porn and made myself orgasm so I'm not a complete newbie. He leans down and captures my lips again, his arm snakes behind me and unclasps my bra, he pulls back and gently slides the straps from my arms and tosses it the side. He doesn't stop, he leans down and captures one of my nipples causing me to cry out in pleasure, he tweaks the other one his hand. He switches sides and I'm panting as I thrust my hips needing some sort of friction, he grips my waist and holds me down.

"Cairo…" He releases my nipple with a pop, and peeks up at me through his lashes.

"Something the matter beauty?" I narrow my eyes and growl; he leans back and chuckles while shaking his head.

"Baby, don't ever do that again, leave all the growling to me." He doesn't give me a chance to respond, he shuffles off the bed grips my ankles and yanks me down until my ass is balancing on the edge, he drops to his knees and then buries his face between my legs. He licks me through my panties, and I cry out, I've seen on the pornos how women rave about being eaten out, but fuck me, even with my panties on it feels amazing. He peppers kisses on my inner thigh and then does the same to other, I rest up on my elbows and peer down at him. I can't believe that I have Cairo Cruz on his knees right now, this man isn't the type to kneel for anyone, in yet here he is before me. "Are you fond of these?" He asks while tapping my panties, I shake my head unsure of what––.

"Holy shit!" I stare at him stunned, he holds my panties in his hand that he tore off me, yes literally tore them right of me! His eyes are focused on my pussy and I begin to feel self-conscious when he doesn't move or even blink, he just sits there staring at it. Before I can get lost too much in my own thoughts his tongue darts out to moisten his lips and a hunger blazes in his blue eyes. I spread my legs wider and bring my hands up to tweak my nipples, his gaze burns into me when he looks up and sees what I'm doing.

"Oh beauty, you will pay for teasing me." The snarky retort is on the tip of my tongue, but I'm silenced when he reaches up and parts my pussy with his fingers and blows across my enlarged clit, a moan of pleasure escapes me when he flicks his tongue across my nub and sucks it into his mouth. I cry out as he continues to fuck me with his mouth, I feel a fire burning inside me, the more he licks and sucks, it feels so fucking good! I feel his finger prodding at my entrance and try not to stiffen as he begins to push inside me, "got to stretch you out a bit baby." I nod and watch in a foggy haze of my sexual high as he eats my pussy and slips his finger inside me, it stings but it isn't bad, it feels… I don't even know how to explain, but God dammit I want more.

He inserts another finger, and my body reacts like it has a mind of its own and begins to ride his hand while chasing that euphoric high, Cairo picks up the pace and fuck the sight of him finger fucking me and lapping at my pussy like it's the best fucking meal he has ever had, pushes my orgasm closer to the surface, he flicks his gaze up to mine as I pinch my nipples.

"Come on my fucking hand and face beauty." He flicks his tongue across my clit one more time and then I'm crashing, I scream his name so loud I'm sure the whole pack can hear, he doesn't slow his pace as he continues to pump inside me while he sucks on my clit, I feel a strange pressure building inside me and I try to fight it, but he won't stop. "Let go baby, I got you." Within a second of him pulling his fingers out, liquid squirts out of me, my eyes widen in horror.

Oh, Jesus, did I just squirt?

Cairo growls his approval and then rams his tongue inside my pussy tasting me. "You taste so fucking good." I sit up and capture his face between my hands and then smash my lips against his, the taste of my release on his tongue has me groaning, he breaks our kiss when he stands. I'm now eye level with his bulging cock, still on a high from my orgasm and feeling like a bad bitch, I grip the waist of his pants and yank them and his boxers down. When his cock is finally freed of its confinement my bravado waivers when it slaps against his stomach, it's fucking huge! Granted I have only ever seen cocks on porn and not real life but fucking hell I didn't expect it to be this big! "Before you ask, yes it will fit inside you." I scoff and look up at him.

"That is not what I was thinking." He quirks a brow in question. "I was just thinking, how far I could suck you into my mouth before my gag reflex kicks in?" his head drops back as he stares up at the roof and groans.

"Fuck me beauty, don't tease me if you aren't ready to fucking suck my cock like——." I cut him off by reaching up and stroking him, he hisses, and I smile. I dart my tongue out to taste the drop of pre come on his head and we both moan, he tastes fucking exquisite! I wrap my lips around him and make sure to hollow my cheeks like I saw on the videos and suck him inside my mouth whilst simultaneously licking. His hand fists in my hair as he curses and moans, I breathe through my nose and try to relax my gag reflex but he's so big, there is no way I can take all of him. I'll admit I'm nervous that I'm doing this all wrong, but from the groans and the way he is gripping my hair and thrusting his hips, I must be doing something right. I gag around his cock when he slams his hips forward, saliva drips down my chin, but I can't pull back thanks to the grip he has on my hair, he shoves his cock so deep in my throat, my nails dig into his ass and my eyes water. He yanks his cock out and I drag in mouthfuls of air, he runs his thumb across my chin wiping it clean. "You look fucking beautiful like this."

I have no words as he leans down and kisses me, he gently pushes on me so I'm flat against the bed, our kiss never breaking. He settles himself between my legs and I feel his cock prod against my entrance, heat begins to fill my veins as he runs his hands all over my body and trails kisses down my neck to my collarbone, I moan when he sucks on the side of my neck. He pulls back and peers down at me.

"Last chance baby, pull out now or I'm about to be balls deep inside you and fuck you till you can't walk." His words cause a spark of desire to shoot through me and more liquid gathering between my thighs.

"I want this." Is all I manage to say before he's pushing me up the bed and then lining his cock up to enter my cunt, he holds my gaze as he gently starts to ease inside of me.

"I'll go slow, tell me if you want me to stop." I nod while I grip the bed sheets in a vice like grip, I bite down on my bottom lip as he pushes a bit deeper. A cold sweat breaks out over my skin, and I try not to tense, I thought his two fingers would be enough to not cause me pain, when it's his cocks turn, but I was wrong. He bends down and kisses me, distracting me from the pain, he reaches between us and circles my clit while continuing to push inside. Between him kissing me and circling my clit, it eases the pain slightly, but not much. I break the kiss and meet his gaze; I can see the strain on his face and know this is hard for him as well.

"Just do it, don't go slow, just––." I scream out when he slams the remainder of his cock inside me, I feel the exact moment he destroys my innocence. Sweat beads on my brow and I grind my teeth to fight against the pain, his eyes search mine, his jaw clenches, and his eyes keep flickering between his and his wolf's.

"Baby, I need to move." He grits out, I take a couple of shallow breaths before I nod, he sighs in relief then begins to move. Holy shit, it stings but the more he moves the pain begins to subside and turns into...pleasure. "Fuck beauty, your pussy was made for me." My back arches off the bed when he almost pulls all the way out and then slams back inside me again.

Chapter Eighteen

Cairo

"Cairo...fuck!" I love the way she screams my name; her pussy is clenching my dick like it wants me to live inside her. She is so much more
than I ever thought she would be, I stare down at her and watch as her pupils
dilate from the pleasure I am inflicting on her body, her perky tits bounce every
time I thrust inside her. I lean down and capture a nipple in my mouth without
slowing my pace, she arches up and grips the back of my head holding me there,
her other hand runs down my back scraping me with her nails. I hiss at the pain
but fucking love that I will wear *her* marks for all to see.

Mark her!

Fuck off Bex.

I close the link between me and Bex, I release her nipple and then pull back
gripping her legs and then resting them on my shoulders as I push forward and
bend her like a staple. I slam into her, and she cries out, her eyes begin to turn
glassy and start to roll back. I can feel from the way she is clenching my cock
that she is close; I want––no need us both to come together so I pull out of her
and leave her legs on my shoulders while I eat her out, she withers and moans
my name whilst riding my face like a fucking pro. When I feel her tense, I stop
and quickly line my cock up and push inside her, we both moan at the feeling
and fuck me if it isn't the best feeling I have ever felt.

"Cairo...shit...Jesus!"

"He ain't allowed in this room beauty." I grit out before plowing into her cunt
at a relentless pace. "Come all over my cock baby, I want to feel you wet the
fuck out of it." And with no hesitation she does screaming my name like it's a
fucking prayer, I pump inside her one more time before I throw my head back
and roar my release.

I slow my pace and bring us both down from our high, I drop her legs down
ravishing at the site of her, her eyes are closed but she has the biggest smile
on her face. I flick her nipple and she shudders snapping her eyes open. "I'm
gonna pull out beauty, it's gonna sting, okay?" She bites down on her lip and
nods, I slowly ease out of her and feel like an utter fucking dick when she

flinches in pain, as soon as the head of my cock is out, the front of my thighs are soaked from her come, I chuckle as she hides her face behind her hands in embarrassment.

"I want to crawl into a dark hole and die." I laugh as I reach forward and peel her hands away, I make sure she can see how serious I am as I hold her gaze and say.

"Baby, you being able to squirt is fucking hot, don't ever be ashamed of that, it means I've done my job right." I fight my smile; she looks so adorable with the pink stain coating her cheeks. I slip off the bed and wrap my arms around her legs, she locks them around my waist, and I lift her, she locks her arms around my neck as I carry her into the bathroom. I plant her ass on the bathroom counter and start the shower, I push her legs apart and slip between them as I cup her cheeks and kiss her, she melts in my hold and opens for me without a fuss. My cock is rock hard and ready to go again, but I know she won't be able to take another round. I pull back and help her off the counter and lead us both into the shower.

After I washed the both of us, yes, I'm that much of a controlling bastard. I'm sitting up against the headboard as she rests her head in my lap, I can't stop running my fingers through her hair. Seeing her in my shirt has my cock stirring in my pants, the sight of her bare thighs is making my mouth water wanting to take a bite.

Mark her, she is ours and others have to know.

No, I won't mark her Bex, not until... I know.

She is ours, not the other.

Enough!

I grit my teeth and slam the link between Bex and I closed, he is becoming a right fucking pain in the ass with his constant nagging and shit.

"So, how did Sky find you?" We have been doing this for the past hour, her asking questions and me touching her everywhere while I answer. We both keep dodging the elephant room, neither of us want to ruin the moment by bringing up what I just did. I acted rash and shouldn't have agreed to the terms, I was an idiot and acted out of——Nah, fuck that, I acted as my pack's alpha, not as her mate.

"She uh, it sounds corny as fuck, but she sensed me coming and followed her intuition is what she told me."

"How long have you two... been together?" I can hear the jealousy in her voice and a better man would ease her worry, but, I never claimed to be a better man, so I let her stew in it. If this *thing* is to work between us, she has to accept Sky as my beta and my go to, I don't make a move without Sky's input, and if I do it normally turns to shit, like today.

"Put it this way, I can't remember my life without her being in it, now, why don't you ask me the question you really want to ask about her." She sits up and turns to face me tucking her legs under herself, she gnaws on her bottom lip as she looks at me. I won't make this easy for her, she needs to embrace the fire inside herself, like when she jumped in my lap in front of everyone.

"Well, I'm avoiding asking about what happened today like you are, so, I'll ask you this one time. Have you and Sky ever slept together?"

"Yes." She tries to hide her shock but it's too late, I spot it before she quickly masks it.

Fix this before it is too late!

I won't handle her with kid gloves, she has to learn.

She is our mate!

No, she is your mate. I am just here trying to make this fucking work!

You feel something for her, you forget we share the one body, and I can feel what you feel.

Fuck off Bex, you know where I stand!

Things change and they have Cairo, stop fighting it.

Her shuffling off the bed yanks me from my argument with Bex, she walks around the side of the bed and finds her jeans. She refuses to meet my gaze and that just pisses me off, I jump up as she zips up her pants, and steps back, I growl each step she takes backward, I take one forward until she hits the wall. I cage her in with my arms either side of her head and still she won't look at me! I bend at the knees, and she turns her head to the side using her hair as a curtain, my restraint snaps and I clamp my hand around her throat and squeeze until she meets my stare. Her blue eyes spark with anger, but there is something else––hurt.

"You asked me a question and I answered it, now you stand here and sulk because it isn't the answer you wanted?" The hurt that shone in her eyes a second ago is overpowered by her rage––good, get angry beauty it makes my dick hard seeing you rage.

"What do you expect." She seethes, if she were a shifter, she'd be growling now.

"I expected you to behave like a grown ass woman, not a jealous—."

"Jealous what?" She rolls her eyes. "You can't even say it can you?" She shoves me, it doesn't do shit, but I appease her and release my hold taking a step back.

"What the fuck do you want me to say, that you're my girlfriend, or my mate? We fucked and it was great, but I won't teether myself to someone!" I shout, this woman brings out the fucking worst in me and my temper is forever flaring when she is around. She drives me fucking nuts. She locks her emotions down and keeps a blank look on her face, it irks me that I can't read her, but I don't let it show.

"Then let me go, I told you what you wanted to know—." I lash out and grip her throat as I slam her against the wall, I get right in her face and growl, but it cuts off when her eyes roll back and she starts to shake—Fuck, she's having a vision, I pick her up and carry her over to the bed and gently lay her down.

I'm such a fuck up, my emotions are running too high and I know because touching her I sparked the vision she is having.

It's been nearly two hours since her vision and she still hasn't woken, I gave up pacing and hopped on the bed resting her head in my lap. I can't tear my eyes off her, she still wears my shirt and it makes the beast inside me happy that my scent clings to her. If I had of let Bex mark her she wouldn't need my clothing, or me rubbing up on her every hour just to keep my scent on her. I rake my hand through my hair and tug on it when she releases another whimper, I can't take much more of this. I'm a piece of shit for putting her through this but I hate that I can't fight these visions for her. I shift her head slightly so I can slide my phone from my pocket and unlock it, my finger hovers over Sky's name and for the first time in my life I question if she is the right person to call in this situation. After a second of contemplation, I call the person I know who will help.

"This better be good."

"I need your help."

"Where are you?"

"The old cabin."

"I'm on my way."

I drop my phone and rest my head back against the headboard sighing, how did I let everything get so fucked up? Before I can spiral further, my phone rings, I don't bother looking at the caller as I answer it.

"The doors unlocked––."

"Not why I'm calling." I tense and sit up.

"What do you want Alexander."

"You gave me your word Cairo."

"I told you I would contact you once I have shit sorted, now back the fuck off."

"Tsk tsk, don't push me pup, I have lived a long life and know when someone is trying to play games. Hand over my daughter and your sisters pack won't be harmed." The sound of the front door opening distracts me for a second.

"I'll call you when shit is sorted." I hang up and quickly stuff my phone back in my pocket. The bedroom door swings open, and Creed's eyes shoot to me then to the unconscious beauty in my lap, he lets out a long whistle and shakes his head. I glower at him when I see Cole peeking over his shoulder. "The fuck did you bring him for?" Cole rolls his eyes.

"He isn't my alpha anymore, so I don't have to listen to him, plus, I was sitting next to him when you called."

"Just my luck." I mumble as the both of them amble into the room, the closer they get to the bed the more tense I become. Shifters are territorial of their mates, and it isn't Creed that bothers me because he is mated, but Cole, well he is a bachelor and Bex doesn't like him near Belle, so I can't stop the growl that tears out of me. Cole raises his hands and steps back.

"What happened to her?" Cole answers Creed before I can.

"If you can't smell the sex in the air then you my brother are losing your touch."

"Shut the fuck up Colton!" I snap, just because I don't want to claim her doesn't mean he can demean her.

"Dude, I wasn't being an ass, I was stating the obvious."

"Which is?" I grit out.

"That maybe by you two fucking, her emotions went into overload and put her to...sleep?" Creed releases a long sigh before shifting his gaze to me, quirking a brow.

"Yes, we did fuck but she was fine, and then shit got heated and––."

"What did you do?" I throw my hands up in the air, of course Creed would think this is all my fault. I should have just called Z.

"I touched her while I was ragging, and I think I sparked a vision."

"How long has she been out?" I drop my gaze from his to stare down at Belle, she doesn't look like she is in pain, I could fool myself into thinking she's sleeping.

"Couple of hours, but she keeps moaning like she's in pain and I––."

"Can't take seeing your mate in pain?" I sigh softly and nod as I stroke her cheek with my fingers, why does shit have to be so complicated? I always wanted to find my mate in the hopes that the feelings I have for Sky would vanish, and over time they have dwindled, but I'll always be loyal to her. I made her a promise many years ago, when she gave me my freedom, that I would always fight to protect her, and so far, I have done a shit job. "I can scent you on her, but Corbin can tell she is unmarked, why?" There's the question that I don't want to answer.

"Heads up, someone's coming." I don't question Cole as I slide off the bed and place Belle's head gently on a pillow and stand at the end of the bed when I hear a door open, Creed and Cole flank me either side to hide Belle. I scent the air and then relax; a second later Sky comes into view with a face like a smacked ass.

"What's wrong?" Sky and I are so in tuned with each other that we just know something is wrong from a single look. She meets my gaze as she answers me.

"You have about 3 minutes before Davina bursts through that door, you need to sort this shit with her Ro. If you don't put her in her place, I will be forced to do it for you."

"You will stay the fuck out of it, I told you no more after Jess––." She throws her hands in the air and growls, if she were a shifter, I'm sure it would sound menacing.

"Fuck you Cairo! I did it twice since your sister, just so you could have your mate at my own cost, do not lecture me." Consider me thoroughly chastised, she isn't wrong, she is the reason Belle is able to be around people and I haven't thanked her or thought of what the cost might be for her. "Sort this shit Cairo, I mean it. You have till morning to tell everyone because I'm telling California tonight."

"Wait, what the fuck is going on?"

"Nothing." I snap at Creed; the fucker turns on me and grips my throat, his eyes flick to his wolf's and I smile.

"If you have done anything to hurt my fucking sister, I will end you." I Tsk him.

"How will you explain that to *my* sister?" It isn't Creed that answers me though.

"Consider, said sister informed." Creed and I both turn to see Jess and Z standing behind Sky. "If you have done anything to put my best friend in harm's way Ro, I will cut your balls off."

"As entertaining as this is, we have incoming in about 45 seconds." I smack Creed's arm away and hold Zeke's gaze.

"Stall her for as long as you can, she can't get near Belle." I dismiss all of them as I move to the side of the bed and pull my phone out, I hit dial on Cass's number, it rings twice before he answers.

"Who the hell is this?""If you three want your sister safe, follow the path to the east of the house and trail mine and her scent here. You have 30 seconds to be here Cassius." I hang up and toss the phone on the bed, I turn to the others and nod my head at Sky. "Go with Z and hold Davina off, let Cass and the others in but that's it." I turn to Cole next. "Help the four of them out of here, meet me at the summit peak where Jess ran." He opens his mouth, but I cut him off. "Anything happens to her Colton; I'm coming for you." I make sure Bex is risen so Cole can see him in my eyes, he drops his gaze after a second and nods. I turn to my sister and Creed next. "I fucked up badly, I need your help to distract Davina until Belle and her brothers are gone."

"What the fuck are you hiding?" I scoff at the audacity of Creed.

"Your one to fucking talk *Mr. I never lied to my mate*. I'm doing this to protect her, you have no idea what the fuck she is and who Alexander is to her--."

"And you do?" Creed snaps back at me.

"Actually, yeah."

Chapter Nineteen

Belle

"*Skylar, please don't make me do this.*"

"*There isn't any other way out of this Cairo, you have to stop this, now!*" *I watch in horror as he shifts to his black and white wolf and then lunges.*

I startle awake screaming, hands land on me and I flinch away from the contact, I grip my hair and pull. This vision cannot come true. I have to stop it; it will kill him!

"Belle, you're okay we're here with you." I blink my eyes a few times to try and focus, the pounding headache makes it hard. I look around and realize I'm outside in the woods, my three brothers and Cole are crouched down in front of me with looks of concern on their faces. "You had a vision." If my head didn't feel like it was splitting in half, I would roll my eyes at Hunter.

"I got that part Hunt, what I don't get is why I'm outside?" I follow my brothers' gazes as they land on a sheepish looking Cole, I tilt my head slightly trying to get a read on him. He rubs the back of his neck and begins to whistle like there is nothing wrong with this situation I find myself in. "Where's Cairo, Cole?" He meets my gaze, and it throws me a little when I see pity shining in his gaze, what the hell happened while I was out?

"He'll be here as soon as he can, but for right now this is the safest place for you."

"Why Cole?" He sighs and runs a hand through his hair, his green eyes bore into me.

"Because my mother is here."

"Meg?" Cole shakes his head in answer to Blake but keeps his eyes on me.

"Our egg donor, Davina. She...uh wants you for something and we don't know what it is." I reel back in shock; my brothers climb to their feet, and I accept the hand Cass offers me. When I'm standing, he wraps his arm around my shoulders and tucks me into his side, it's like we're in a standoff. The four of us huddled together while Cole stands opposite us on his own, he shoves his hands in his pockets and scuffs his foot along the ground.

"What exactly does she want with Belle?" I can hear the unease in Cass's voice, we may have the advantage of my visions but that doesn't mean we know everything. Am I even a supernatural?

"That, I don't know. Cairo and Sky kept their cards close to their chest where you were concerned. We all may have helped locate you, but that's it." Something doesn't add up,

"I know why Cairo searched for me in the first place, I also know there is another reason, but he won't tell me. Can I assume it has something to do with this Davina?" Cole smiles sadly and nods.

"That would be my guess as well."

"Why does Cairo hate your bio mom Cole?" A whoosh of air rushes out of him.

"Take a seat, it's a long ass story, I don't know all the gory details, just what I learnt and saw from Jess and Creed."

"What does any of this have to do with your brother and Cairo's sister?" Cole meets Blake's gaze, the look in his eyes has me swallowing loudly.

"Everything." Cole heads over toward a tree and drops down so he can lean against it, Hunt and Blake follow him, but Cass pulls me back when I try to move away. He keeps his tone low so only I can hear.

"According to Cole you were out a couple hours back at that cabin and another couple here, that's four fucking hours Belle!" He grits out through clenched teeth, I cringe and try to mask it, but it's too late, Cass sees it.

"I'm not prepared––."

"Horse shit! This is too fucking much Gabrielle, you have told him what you know, correct?" I nod. "Then we leave at first light and get answers from dad because I will not let this shit kill you Belle." His tone escalates from angry to devastated, and that tears me up inside. Cass is the strong one, and self-assured so to hear him sound scared, puts the fear of God in me.

"I...I can't leave Cass."

"Yeah, you can, and you will. He isn't into you Belle, the fucker only used you to get what he wanted, and from the smell of things, he got his cake and ate it too." I flinch at the cold harsh tone and step back; his face drops when he sees the tears in my eyes. "Fuck. I'm sorry Belle, I didn't mean for it to come out like that––." I raise my hand to stop him and shake my head.

"To far Cassius." Is all I say before joining the others to hear the story of Jess and Creed.

By the time Cole is finished telling us everything that happened, the moon is high in the sky and there is a chill to the air, I rub my arms to try and warm myself. Cole's eyes shoot to me, and he jumps to his feet and heads toward the blacked-out Hummer that is parked near the road. He told us he didn't want us to go in any further in case of trouble and we needed a quick exit, makes sense since I will be the one slowing them down. He jogs back toward us with a jumper and chucks it to me, I smile my thanks and pull it over my head, I'm assaulted by the scent of Cole, he smells like pine trees and coffee which is weird but...soothing. The jumper is big enough for me to tuck my legs in it, I look like a cocoon, but I don't care, I'm warm and that's all that matters.

We have been sitting here for hours, Hunt and Blake have fallen asleep on the ground, and I can't stop staring at them. No matter what happens, or what we find out about my parents, I wouldn't give them up for the world. I turn to search for Cass and begin to panic when I don't see him, I go to stand but Cole's words stop me.

"He went to scan the area." *Oh,* that makes perfect sense. "What's on your mind, you've had a permanent frown in place for the past hour."

"I...uh, never mind——."

"Don't do that babe, I can see you are upset about something. Talk to me, I might even be able to help." He smiles kindly and I melt, why couldn't Cairo be more like Cole? I shake my head to rid myself of those types of thoughts, I knew what I was to him before I came here, and I even knew that things would be hard, but I didn't expect them to be like this.

"I'm confused and I have no idea what to do about it. I'm used to holding all the cards and being one step ahead, but since meeting you guys, I always find myself three steps behind, and I don't like it, at all." His eyes soften and he reaches out to touch me but stops himself, at least he has the courtesy to keep his hands to himself.

You weren't complaining when Cairo's tongue was inside you.

I block the stupid voice in my head and focus back on Cole. He is a ruggish sort of handsome, but he has that high school quarter back look as well, there is no denying that Cole is good looking, and seems to have a great personality to match.

"You will always be steps behind Cairo babe. He doesn't play by the rules, never has apparently. He knows and does shit without thinking of the consequences, he gets away with a lot of it because of Sky."

"What does she do exactly?" I want to confide in Cole about my visions involving Sky, but something inside me is urging me to remain silent, because Cairo will be mad.

"She balances him, Sky found Cairo when he was a lost pup. He was malnourished and scavenging for food. No one knows how they came to be so close, only that without Sky, Ro would have died, look there is more to them than––."

"Like Cairo being in love with her?" Cole's eyes widen and his shoulders droop.

"Yep, that'll do it. Who told you?"

"He did."

"Wow, that was...uh, big of him I guess." I roll my eyes.

"I knew there was something there between them, I just didn't know what, and he confirmed it for me. I know they slept together." Cole reels back in shock, he throws his head back and laughs. It takes him a minute to get himself under control, he swipes the tears from his eyes and points at me.

"You just gave me the best trump card; Callie is going to rip his dick off." I shrug my shoulders as I say.

"Break his face not his dick, that thing is like Harry Potters wand." He quirks a brow in question. "It's magic and makes you speak in tongues as well as making you see stars." Cole's laughter is cut off at the sound of his husky voice, I don't bother to turn or even acknowledge his presence. What he said before I passed out hurt more than I want to admit, how he could go from being so loving and attentive, to cold and detached in such a short time?

"Good to know my cock is more important than my face." Cole stands and walks over to him; I can hear them talking in hushed tones behind me. I choose to look back at my brothers and watch them sleep, my moment is shattered when legs appear in front of me. I sigh, I could keep looking at his Chucks or be a grown ass woman like he said and face the awkward conversation that is about to take place. I take a deep breath and stand, we're so close that I have to crane my neck back to meet his gaze, he's still shirtless which doesn't surprise me, the guy never wears shirts. As our eyes meet, I can tell he has his mask of indifference in place, I shake my head and push past him to wake my brothers. I'm hauled backward by the grip he has on my––Cole's jumper, he bends down and gets right in my face. Small growls rumble out of him, his eyes have changed to his wolf's. He grips the front of the jumper so our noses touch, I try to pull away, but he grips the back of my neck with his other hand and holds me still.

"What the hell is your problem?" I seethe.

"Why the hell do you smell like Colton-fucking-Reeves?"

"Seriously, that's what you have to say to me?"

"Answer my question." I can see the struggle on his face, he's fighting to stay in control when all his wolf wants to do is shift and attack Cole.

"Fuck. You. Cairo." I smile sweetly and bat my lashes at him, my bravado falters when he smiles and releases his hold, his grip on the back of my neck doesn't ease as he spins me around, one arm bands around my waist and with the other now gripping my throat. Cole stands there in shock, darting his gaze between me and Cairo, I try to keep my breathing under control, but I have a feeling I may have poked the beast a wee too much this time.

"Did you like hanging out with *my* mate, while I dealt with your mother Colton?" Cole stiffens at Cairo's mocking; he is acting like a real prick and I'm not having it. I try to pull away but his grip tightens on my throat, he leans down, and I feel his lips brush the shell of my air as he says. "Don't test me beauty, if I find out he has touched what is mine, I'll tear his fucking throat out in front of you." I snap, I'm done with this stupid game.

"You don't own me; I have a say in this fucking mate bullshit as well as you do. I will not be used by you so you can run back to that skank in the hopes she finally falls for you--." My words die in my throat, one minute my back is to him and then in the next second I'm flat on the ground with Cairo on top of me growling in my face. I'm so stunned that I lay here speechless as I stare up into the onyx eyes of Bexley, I can tell he is on the brink of losing control, and I know with my brothers and Cole all being here and unmated, it will be a shit show.

"Ro, you have to calm down--." Cairo turns his head to Cole and growls out a warning, I meet Cole's gaze and see he is pleading with me to calm Cairo. I reach up and cup his cheek, he whisks his gaze back to me, and I still at the anger swirling in the depths of his eyes. I bite my lip to try and temper my own rage, right now with his emotions being so erratic he can trigger a vision, and I can't handle another one tonight.

"I smell like Cole because I'm wearing his jumper, I was cold and--." He jerks back and sits on his hunches; I remain still waiting to see what he does next. He grips the front of the jumper and in one fluid move tears it in half. I gasp as I look from him to the ruined garment that is in tatters in his hands.

"That was my favorite Dickies jumper you asshole!" Cairo and I both ignore Cole, he leans down and rests his forehead against mine, I stiffen but he ignores it, physical contact is still new to me, and I don't know if I will ever get used to it.

"The only male scent I will allow to cling to you is my own--."

"Get the fuck off her now!" I flinch at the sound of Cass's voice, a sly smirk graces Cairo's handsome face.

"Tell your brothers to fuck off, you're coming with me." I shake my head but stop when he smashes his lips against mine, being the stupid wanton idiot that I am, I open for him and whimper when his tongue invades my mouth. When I hear a growl it's like a bucket of ice water has been dropped on me, I break the kiss and push against him until he moves back. I slide out from under him and climb to my feet, I nibble on the corner of my lip as I meet Cass's disapproving gaze.

"Just like that, huh?" I cringe at the disappointment in his tone. "He just needs to manhandle you a bit and then you're putty in his hands?" He's shouting now, the sound of his booming voice wakes Hunter and Blake, but I won't take my eyes off my oldest brother.

"What the fuck is going on?" I feel Hunt and Blake at my back, Cass looks to each of them before finally settling his sights on me.

"You're not going with him, you'll come with us so we can sort shit– –."

"I dare you." I stiffen at the sound of Cairo's voice.

"Dare me to do what?" Cass snaps.

"I dare you, to try and take her from me." A dark chuckle tumbles from Cairo, but there is no humor to it.

"She is my sister!" Cairo brushes past me and doesn't stop till he and Cass are chest to chest, Blake, Hunt and Cole rush over to intervene if needed.

"She may be your sister, but she belongs to me– –." Cass throws his hands in the air and growls; he begins to vibrate, and I know he is close to losing it. If either of these men were younger, they wouldn't have the control they do over their wolves, it's actually a beautiful sight to see.

"You don't even want her! She is a mere toy that you wish to play with, and when you are bored you will toss her away." Ouch, that stings.

"Are you getting this angry because I fucked her, or is it because you know she isn't *really* your sister and could fuck her too?" My jaw hits the bloody ground and my eyes widen to the size of dinner plates, how fucking dare he! Cass stands there open mouthed and in shock, he doesn't know what the hell to say that and I don't blame him. Cole pushes between the two of them and shoves Cairo back, Cole looks furious as he gets in Cairo's face.

"What the fuck is wrong with you Ro? You're a fucking prick, didn't you learn anything from your sister and what she went through with Creed? You wanna fuck this is up with Belle, fine, but do it by yourself, because I won't watch another innocent girl be hurt because of another dumbass guy who thinks fucking with them is okay." Cole turns toward me but stops and peers over his shoulder at Cairo. "In case I wasn't clear; Belle is coming with *me*, and you can find your own way back." Cole turns to me and smiles sadly as he flicks his head toward the Hummer, I nod and smile my thanks, I indicate to my brothers to follow.

CHAPTER TWENTY

Cairo

I drag my feet up the worn path to my sister's house, the lights are on inside and I know she will be waiting for me, but I can't deal with that shit now. I'm fucking pissed that Davina and her band of misfits are here, the bitch is hiding shit and her reasons for wanting Belle are bullshit. Something isn't right and I want to know what it is, Bex can sense the shift with her. I can't prove it, but something sinister is at paly with her, Vince even seems withdrawn. I veer left and head toward the creek out the back, I drop down on the bank and pull my phone from my pocket. I find his number and take a deep breath before I connect the call, if there is anyone who will know the truth about why Davina wants Belle, it's him.

"I didn't expect to hear from you so soon."

"That's not why I'm calling Alexander."

"Then what do I owe the honor of this call?"

"Davina Reeves just showed up and wants Belle." A beat of silence passes before he answers.

"I'll warn you once, you let my daughter anywhere near that vile cockroach, and I won't stop at killing you, I'll go for your pack, your sister, your nephew——." I growl.

"Threaten them again and I'll rip your fucking throat out with my bare hands."

"Keep her away from Belle."

"Why?"

"Because...Belle is special, and Davina will exploit that."

"Newsflash, everyone knows about Belle's visions." A tired sigh comes through the phone, and I grit my teeth in annoyance.

"I wasn't talking about the visions, bring her to me and I will tell you everything."

"Why the hell should I trust you near my——her?" I cringe at the fact saying *my mate* came so naturally to me.

"Because I am the one who hid Belle with Gabriel, I did it to keep my daughter safe."

"If you're this almighty original vampire, why the hell are you running scared?" He chuckles and it makes my hackles rise.

"Ah, you have so much to learn young Cairo. I don't run out of fear, I run to keep them distracted and off the trail of my daughter, plus, it amuses me. When you are immortal, you find things to amuse yourself so it makes the time fly by faster."

"Why not put a dagger through your own heart?"

"I would have, but nineteen years ago I was blessed with the one thing I thought I could never have." The longing in his voice tells me that he really does care for Belle, I wasn't expecting that.

"Can I ask you something?"

"What if I told you, I already know what you are going to ask?" I pause for a second.

"Do you have visions as well?" He laughs.

"I plead the fifth."

"Then how would you know?"

"Because I'm closer than you think, you want to know how you could possibly have found your mate in a vampire offspring?" Well fuck me.

"Yeah, that was...yeah, I was going to ask that."

"Because Gabrielle isn't full vampire, she is half shifter." Now that revelation has me stumped. "I must go now."

"Yeah, okay."

"Cairo?"

"Yeah?"

"You ever hurt my daughter again or throw her to the ground like you did tonight, I'll tear your fucking head off and send it to your sister." The line goes dead, I stare at my phone for what seems like an eternity, my vision becomes fuzzy. Alexander was in the woods tonight! He had to be, there is no other way he would have known that. Fuck I have to fix this shit with her, Cole is right, I'm being a dick because of things with Sky. It's not Sky's fault, its mine, I've known for a long time that the love I feel for her isn't how a man loves a woman, I love her like... I can't explain it. Belle makes my blood boil, and just seeing her gets my cock hard. With Sky, I will kill anyone who hurt her let alone go to war for her any day of the week, no questions asked.

"Why are you sitting out here?" I smirk.

"Should I add mind reader to your list of talents?" She scoffs as she drops down beside me.

"You forget we are tethered, and I can find you anywhere." I sigh. "What's going on Ro?"

"I fucked up Sky, I fucked up really bad."

"What happened?"

"She asked if we had ever slept together, and I told her the truth." Sky whistles and shakes her head, then laughs––She fucking laughs! "The fuck is so funny Skylar?" The little shit continues her charade of laughter, and it irritates the fuck out of me. I'm glaring at the side of her head and want nothing more than to wring her fucking neck.

"Did you tell her the *whole* truth?"

"No." I grit out clenching my teeth, she rolls her lips over her teeth to stop herself from laughing.

"Maybe you should have, if you did, you wouldn't be sitting here sulking."

"Geez, anyone ever tell you that you fucking suck at pep talks?" She smirks at me.

"Nah, Callie calls me her hype woman."

"Callie lied to you." She laughs and nudges me with her shoulder.

"What's really going on Ro? There has to be something else, because you wouldn't be this deep in your feels if it was just her finding out we slept together."

"It's...I don't even know Sky, she's, my mate." I laugh but there's no humor to it. "And I sold her to the devil to save...you." Sky releases a loud whoosh of air; I can feel the disappointment radiating off her.

"Nothing is set in stone Ro. Don't push her away because you feel obligated to save me, I can feel the power inside me growing unstable each day. I want to go out on my own terms, give me that...please." I want to be selfish and tell her no, but the truth is Sky has always lived each day like it's her last, and I've made sure she had a great life.

"How am I supposed to let you go?" I meet her gaze and allow her to see everything I am feeling. "How do I do that Sky? Part of you lives inside me, and because of you, Bexley was freed from needing a pack and going rogue." She smiles sadly and stands; she offers me her hand and I stare at it for a moment before she sighs and says.

"I think it's time I tell them my story, and you need to realize that I wasn't the one who gave you a gift." I furrow my brow in confusion. "Cairo, you gave me a family and a place to belong, you have protected and loved me when you didn't have to. I love you Ro, but it's time you stop this madness and focus on yourself and your mate. Whatever you have done or said, you can change it, don't do this to yourself." I climb to my feet and pull her to me wrapping my arms around her, she rests her head against my chest. I place a kiss to the top of her head and try to control my emotions, it's her story to tell, and I won't hold her back anymore.

"I love you too Sky." The sound of twigs snapping has me spinning around and pushing Sky behind me, Bexley pushes forward so I'm able to see in the dark, but I can't see anyone. The hairs on the back of my neck raise, and a shiver races down my spine, someone is out here. "Let's go, it's not safe." I grip her hand and drag her behind me, I can see the break in the trees that will lead us to the path at the back of Jess's house, but a growl sounds out and I freeze.

"Cairo, we're not alone and they're not from our pack." Sky and I move so we are back-to-back, I open the link I have with my pack.

Get to the woods behind my sister's house, rogues are here, alert Jess and Creed now!

I close the link and dart my gaze around and see shadows moving, I've counted at least a dozen so far.

"Sky, I have to shift, the pack is on their way, as well as Jess and Creed. You use your knives and that's it——."

"Cairo no——."

"That's a fucking order!" I drop my pants and allow Bexley to take control, the pain doesn't even register when I shift. Bex throws his head back and releases a howl alerting all the packs that there is an intruder, Bex catches the sound of leaves rustlings and turns toward the noise——Sky knows the drill, she turns so her back is to Bex's and makes sure she always has our six.

"Bexley, why are the others taking so long to reach us?" Knowing Bex is unable to speak, Sky reaches behind her and places her hand on our back——it's the only way we can communicate in this form.

I don't know and I can't hear anything beyond the woods, something is blocking me.

Bex, do you think they could have a...witch?

The thought hadn't even crossed my mind until she mentioned it, it'll make perfect sense given their scent is hidden from us until moments ago, and no one from my pack has answered my call.

If they do, you remain silent and you do not engage.

What...what if this is the moment Belle saw? Bex growls.

You won't be dying tonight, Skylar!

Before she can answer, figures emerge from the dense brush in front of me, Bex crouches low and drops his head slightly exposing his teeth and growling. Saliva drips from his teeth, hackles raised, Bex is ready to fight and show whoever is out there why he is feared world-wide. He has never been defeated in battle or an alpha challenge, we don't play to the same rules like the others,

Bex and I are not bound by law like other shifters, my sister included. Six figures dressed in black with rifles drawn step forward, the lasers from the guns are trained on me, I hear noise behind me but don't shift my gaze.

I have nine rifles trained on me, what's your count? I answer this time instead of Bex, he needs to concentrate, or we risk being caught off guard.

Six and their wearing night vision googles.

Ro?

Yeah.

I don't see another way out of this.

I'm about to shut her down when out the corner of my eye I see another eight guys come from the left and six more from the right––we're surrounded. Lasers from all the guns are trained on us, Bex looks for an opening, but I shut him down.

We may be able to get out, but Sky can't.

His only reply is to growl, he may be pissed, but he knows I'm right. Bex loves Sky and would never leave her behind.

Fuck!

She's right Ro, there is no other way out of this. Either we go down by bullets, or we let her end this.

The rational side of me knows Bex is right, and Sky using her magic to save us is the only option that guarantees we both make it out of this alive. However, the overprotective side of me would rather take a bullet than allow her to do this. Thing is, whenever Sky uses her gift, it gets harder for her to pull back in. Sky is dying because of the magic inside her, each time she depletes herself she has to siphon power from me––well Bexley. Her grip on our coat tightens pulling me from my internal debate.

Ro? Bex remains silent and allows me to give the okay, if I say *no,* Bex will fight, no questions asked. Before I can ponder it any longer, the masked bastards all move forward as one.

Do it Sky.

Ro?

Yeah?

Bring me back, okay?

Always! Sky is the baddest motherfucker that I know, so hearing the tremble in her voice puts me even more on edge. I won't let it get as far as it did last time. I force Bex to shift back and he does so willingly, knowing I need to be in human form for what comes next. I yank my pants up and notice that the fuckers are within twenty feet of us now, I peer over my shoulder when the wind begins to pick up, and the tree branches begin to creak. The *unit*––yeah that's what I'm calling them, pause and peer around them. Sky's head drops back as she looks up to the sky above, she raises her arms out wide and the wind around us begins to pick up rapidly. It's risky as fuck, but I have to do it in order to keep her grounded, I turn my back to the fuckers and place my hands on her hips. I hear the tree branches crack, as a white cloud begins to circle me and Sky, this mist will protect us from their bullets, the cloud like mist is halfway up our bodies when the sound of a gunshot rings out. I grit my teeth and grip Sky harder when the pain in my shoulder begins to register––The motherfuckers shot me!

"Sky, you need to do it now, before the rest of them get trigger happy." I dart my gaze around us and see them all exchanging looks and shifting their weight from side to side, half of them seem like they want to run, while the other half seem like they want to shoot now and ask questions later. The mist around us begins to pick up speed like a cyclone, it all happens so fast. One second the mist is circling us and in the next it shoots out around us and wipes every single one of them on their asses! I shake my head to clear it and quickly spin Sky toward me, her eyes are pure white, and I see the vile green and purple veins marring her face and body––fuck! I reach up and cup her cheeks, her expression doesn't change, the chaos that she has created is only intensifying, the wind is so loud I have to shout.

"Sky, baby you have to bring it back." I wait for a response, but I don't get one, I know shit is bad when a slow smile begins to grace her beautiful face. "Skylar, you fucking stop this now! Come back to me Sky, don't fucking go out like this." I'm pleading with her now, the mist begins to circle us again and I worry this time it will be aimed at me, I can hear the erratic beat of her heart and know she doesn't have long before the magic consumes her. Out of ideas I decide to go with the only one I have; I smash my lips against hers.

This isn't a kiss of passion or love, this is kiss of panic and distraction, I'm hoping by doing this, she siphons enough from me and use my strength to fight off this evil inside herself. She opens for me and when her tongue invades my mouth a small groan escapes me, a small voice in my head is telling me how wrong this is. I hate that I'm agreeing with the voice, kissing Sky before, I never felt bad or guilty, even when she got with Callie, but as I stand here and kiss her, all I can picture in my mind's eye is Belle. I don't break the kiss as I open my eyes and look around us, the wind is starting to ease and the tension in her body is lessening, I band my arms around her and hold her close. It feels like hours but is only mere minutes when the wind stops and the power she pushed out stops pulsing out of her. Her magic pushes the bullet from my shoulder, I tense from pain but know that my shifter healing will kick in. I break the kiss and peer down at her, her eyes are closed, I bite my lip hoping and praying that when she opens them, they are back to her normal muddy brown color.

"Skylar, come back to me." I whisper as I lean my forehead against hers, she blinks her eyes a couple of times and sways slightly on her feet before meeting my gaze. I sigh in relief when I see her eyes are back to normal, I smile sadly. I know this one took more out of her than either of us comprehended. A muffled sob has me pulling away and shoving Sky behind me, my mouth drops open in shock and my eyes widen. Belle stands there with her hand covering her mouth and a devastated look in her eyes, Sky moves hesitantly out from behind me and stands by my side. It takes me a second to realize why she looks so betrayed; she saw me kissing Sky!

"This isn't what it looks like." Belle scoffs dropping her hand to her side as she glares at Sky.

"Spare me your bullshit." Belle turns and runs back toward the house; I stand there stunned and confused as to what the hell I should do.

"Go to her Ro. Explain everything before she conjures up more shit in her head, she's your mate and you need her." I don't reply, I take off after Belle, my long legs eating up the space between us, she is only a few feet in front of me when I break through the trees. She bolts toward the cabin, and I know as soon as she is inside, I'm going to have to fight her brothers in order to get to her, I quicken my pace and tackle her to the ground, she lets out a scream of surprise, I flip her over and rest my legs either side of her waist, I'm not quick enough to stop her when she smacks me across the face. I grip each of her wrists and pin them above her head on the grass, I lean down so our noses touch and growl. Her shock quickly wears off and is replaced with sheer rage.

"The next time you slap me beauty, I'll chain your ass to my bed."

"Oh please, you don't have the balls." I smirk at her futile rebuke, I can hear how breathy her voice is, the idea turns her on.

"Baby, you and I both know I have the balls and the stamina to back my shit up."

"How about you *back your shit up* the hell off me!" I glare at her.

"You need to listen and let me explain."

"Explain what? You fuck me and then hook up with the chick you are in love with only hours after declaring I'm your mate? Oh, pray tell Mr. Cruz, did I get anything wrong?"

"Yeah, you did actually."

"Bullshit, I saw you kiss Sky!" She screams at me, but I snap my head up when I hear a gasp and curse under my breath. The cavalry has arrived and of course they heard what Belle just said, the looks they shoot me promise pain.

Chapter Twenty-One

Belle

I fight against his hold but his grip on my wrists tightens, I feel the others nearing us and with each step they take the more and more Cairo grows tense. I'm behaving irrationally right now but see it from my point of view for a second. I have dreamt about this man for months, for well knowing who I am to him, and I guess I came to have feelings for the...idea of him. Seeing Cairo for the first time took my breath away, I didn't expect him to look so...perfect. I know he has a lot of issues from his childhood, I hoped I might have been able to help him work through it, but things went south real fast between us. When I realized he could touch me, all thoughts of helping him flew out the window, everything I had planned went to shit. I thought if we came and helped him win this battle and saved Sky, he would take me as his mate, and I don't know...live happily ever after? I never expected or even saw that he was in love with Sky until it was too late!

"You better hope to God that she is lying Cairo, if I find out that you put your scummy ass lips on my mate, I will fucking tear you to shreds!" The anger that coats each of Callie words has Cairo flinching, but it's the hurt I also hear that has me feeling like shit. I shouldn't have blurted that out, I knew they would come running when they heard my scream, but I was so consumed with anger, I just didn't...think. Cairo turns his gaze back to me and I can see the threat in his eyes.

"*If* I let you up, you gonna keep your hands to yourself?"

"You gonna keep your lips to yourself?" I deadpan. He doesn't respond as he releases his grip on me and stands, I dislike the submissive position I'm in, but I refuse to show him that. He shocks me when he extends his hand, I stare at it for a beat before accept and allow him to help me to my feet. I dust myself off and fix my shirt before facing the others, Creed, Jess, Cole, Callie, Zeke, Cass, Blake and Hunter all stand their wearing varying looks of confusion, anger and hurt. I feel Cairo shift, till he is standing beside me, Cass glares at our close proximity but I shake my head subtly urging him to remain silent. Callie steps forward and darts her gaze between me and him, then behind us, it's then that a sinking feeling settles in the pit of my gut.

"What the hell did you——." I cut Callie off as I turn and run back toward the woods where I spotted Sky and Cairo.

"Belle!" I ignore Hunter and push on, seconds later I feel his presence at my back with Cass and Blake.

"Where are you going?" I'm panting and don't have the lung capacity to talk and run, so I ignore Cairo and keep going. I skid to a stop when I notice all the men that littered the ground are gone, but so is Sky. My brothers spread out around the area and stare in awe at the carnage that Sky caused, I never got the opportunity to see Sky at her peak, but my god, what I did see, took my breath away. No vision could have prepared me for that.

"Sky?" I cringe at the worry in Callie's voice. "Skylar, get out here now, this isn't funny." I drop my gaze to the ground; the others join my brothers and begin to scan the area for Sky, but they won't find her. "Sky?" The watery tone in her voice is like a knife to my heart, I turn around to tell her but come face to face with Cairo, he's a couple of steps away but his gaze spares me. He has an inkling that I know where she is but he's too scared to hear the truth, I take a step toward him, but he takes one back shaking his head.

"Just tell me beauty, what did you see?"

"I didn't see anything per se, this is new to me but it's a feeling of sorts."

"What does that mean?" I turn and see Jess standing near us with a look of concern. I meet Cairo's gaze as I answer his sister.

"It means that I've been getting these *feelings* in the pit of my gut and not a vision. Sky isn't here, whoever those men were had someone else with them." I close my eyes and try to focus, I have only managed to do this a few times with my dad and brothers. I take some deep breaths and open my mind, concentrating on blocking out all the noise around me, I don't tense when I feel my brothers surround me. If need be, they will pull me out of it, entering someone else's mind isn't easy, and it's risky for me. The pain that follows is very intense, one hundred times worse than a vision.

"You have five minutes and then I'm ending it Belle, you don't owe this fucker shit." I nod with my eyes closed, Blake is overprotective, and I love him for that.

"What is she doing?" My brothers growl.

"Trying to find your side piece, fuck knows why though." I mentally fist bump Hunter, Cairo deserved that.

"How risky is it?"

"Shut up Cairo, I can't do it if you keep yapping!" I grit out. Silence descends and I focus on trying to feel for Sky, I know this is going to hurt so I'm preparing myself hoping that it will help fight the pain long enough to locate her. "Show me what she saw." I whisper, being shifters means they can hear my whispered words. The daydream or vision slams into me, I'm unsure as to what I'm doing right now. The pain is instant, and the stabbing in the back of my head has me hissing, I feel hands on me and know it's my brothers.

"Tell me Belle, what happened?"

"She fought Blake, she fought but they had someone else."

"Who B?"

"I can't see them Hunt, they were in the bushes. Cairo was the distraction; he was never the target...Sky was."

"What?" Someone snaps.

"Shut up, or I pull her out now! carry on Belle, where are they?" I shake my head bending my neck side to side trying to alleviate the pain, but to no avail.

"Someone in a red robe came out, the men rose. They carried her, swirls circled her, and she fought. He came for her to take him down––ahhhhh." I scream out.

"Belle enough, stop it now!" I fight through the pain, if I pull out now, I won't see the man's face, and we will never find her.

"No!" I whimper.

"Your nose is bleeding and we're holding you up, stop." I ignore Cass, I push through the haze of pain and follow the vision of Sky fighting with all she has, she is magnificent and a force of nature. She has beams of light shooting from her hands, she moves swiftly, this woman is awe inspiring! "Stop her!"

"How do you expect me to do that?"

"If you don't Cairo, your mate will...die." I'm too far gone to scold Cass, reaching out for Ro's help, tells me it must be bad. Six sets of hands are replaced by two, and immediately the tension that was running through my body is gone, Cairo lowers my body to the ground, holding me.

"Beauty, can you do this?" I can't talk or I risk losing Sky, so I nod instead. "Tell me what you see baby?"

"She speaks in riddles you won't––." I cut Hunter off.

"Red robe, men on their feet, you're the distraction, she's their weapon to lure him out because of me."

"Who do you see baby? Anyone you recognize?" I feel my body begin to tremble and know I don't have long before I pass out.

"Seven people, suit and tie leader, ugly teeth, Sky hates him."

"Is it the council?" Before I can nod or do anything, the vision in front of me stills. Sky spins toward me as everything around us freezes, and I'm pulled into the vision, I'm no longer a by stander. The men with guns are frozen, bullets hang suspended in midair, the man in the suit has spittle flying out of his mouth, but its stuck, it's like someone has paused a movie.

"Belle, tell him it's the council and they have a witch."

"What?" I'm so confused this has never happened before.

"Belle!" I snap my gaze to Sky. "I'm a witch, Gabrielle. I summoned you here so you can go back and tell him that––." She pauses and her eyes cloud with tears causing me to gasp, Skylar Cage isn't the type of woman to cry. "Tell him to put me down, I don't want to be what destiny said I would be."

"Where are you Sky? We'll come––."

"No Belle, it's too late for me, the witch they have will make sure I don't have a choice." Tears begin to cloud my own vision.

"Sky please." She shakes her head.

"I don't have long Belle, tell California that I love her, and she was always the light in my darkest hour. Tell Cairo to tell her the truth about everything, make sure she knows she was my reason for fighting, and if I was given a choice...it would be her." Tears leak from the corners of my eyes; Sky is going to die.

"It will kill them, please fight." She smiles sadly.

"I've been fighting my whole life Belle; I can't fight anymore." A tear treks down her cheek. "Tell Cairo––Tell him I don't regret a thing, and I would do it all again." I nod my head and try to fight the sobs that tear from me, tears flow freely down my face.

"I'm sorry I couldn't save you Sky, I swear––." She shakes her head.

"It was never your destiny to save me, it is yours though to help him and love him even when he doesn't think he deserves it. His loyalty to me is holding him back from you, he will be everything and more for you Belle. Now go!"

Chapter Twenty-Two

Cairo

She trembles in my arms, shaking uncontrollably, I dart my gaze to her brothers, the three of them wear looks of horror. Whatever she is doing right now clearly is dangerous for her, the blood from her nose hasn't stopped running, Jess hands me Creed's shirt. I stare at it for a moment, it's irrational for me at a time like this to even consider not using his shirt because his scent will be on her. I snatch the shirt and thank her before wiping the blood from her face, my stomach is in knots, I've never felt so helpless like this, it's worse than when Jess was taken, which is fucked considering I have only known Belle for a short time. When she screams out in pain a part of me dies inside, her brothers rush over and drop down by her side. Her body is growing cold, and her lips are beginning to turn blue. I look to Cassius and see water in the edges of his eyes––Fuck.

"What's happening to her?" Cass doesn't take his eyes off her as he answers.

"She's dying." He whispers, I reel back, and my eyes widen.

"The fuck do you mean?" Hunter lifts his tear-filled gaze to mine and shakes his head.

"We learned a few years ago that each vision she has or when she does stupid shit like this, trying to save someone, takes a toll on her. It's her story to tell, but if we don't get her out of this, she...won't get a chance to tell you, her story." I brush my knuckles along her cheek.

"Come on beauty, come back to me." I wait for any form of response from her but get nothing, panic seeps in and I start to shake her. "Wake up!" I yell but she remains limp and cold in my arms.

"Mark her." I turn toward Cole.

"What?" He sighs and shrugs his shoulders.

"You marking her will be a shock to her system and hopefully pull her from her...trance?" I dart my gaze to the three brothers, to my complete shock they all seem open to the idea. Right now, I think they would let me do anything if it meant saving their sister. I brush her hair back and pull her shirt down slightly exposing her shoulder, Bex is pushing against me to allow him to mark her as his mate, but I keep him at bay. "Ro?" I turn to Cole and glare; I don't have time for his shit right now but the look on his face gives me pause.

"What?"

"You do this, there is no going back. She will be yours forever, and yours alone to care for, she deserves that, so can you give it to her?" I stare at him for a moment before cutting my gaze to Creed, he holds a sobbing Callie to his chest with Jess stroking her back. His eyes meet mine and I know he is just as stunned by Cole's declaration as I am, I turn back to Belle. Can I give her what she needs, can I be what she needs me to be? I have only just met her, but this amazing, beautiful, selfless girl has been tracking me for months and doing what she can to help me without even knowing me, all because she knew she is my mate. The decision should be an easy one, but fear grips me, I lost everything as a child, and to take her as my own, will I lose her to? The trauma of my childhood has haunted me every day since I was nine, I like to think it is honor and courage that lead me daily, but it isn't, fear is my biggest motivator. Right now, though, I can't let fear rule me.

Do it Bex.

Bexley pushes forward causing a partial shift, my eyes change to his and my teeth are exposed to those of my wolf's. I grip her chin with one hand and shift it to the side while I bend down and lap at the exposed skin of her shoulder, then Bex sinks his teeth in, ecstasy explodes inside me, my vision loses focus as mists of colors take over my sight. My body pulses with need, lust, completeness and belonging, this feeling is euphoric. Bex releases her and then laps at the blood that trickles out of her mark, her body stops convulsing causing me to pull back and forcing Bex back to allow me control again. I watch with bated breath as color slowly starts to return to her body, her lips slowly change from blue back their natural pinkish color. I release the breath I didn't know I was holding, when I brush her cheek and feel heat against my fingers.

"Did it work?" I keep my gaze on Belle as I answer Z.

"I don't know." I wrap my arms around her and stand, I sway on my feet slightly as exhaustion starts to take over my body. I tighten my hold on her when Cass reaches for her, I shake my head. "If you try to take her from me right now, Bexley will tear you apart and I'm to fucking wrung out for all of that." To my surprise he drops his arms and nods as he steps back to allow me to pass.

"Wait, what about Sky?" I turn and face a tear-stricken Callie, my heart hurts for her. I hate myself for what I'm about to say.

"We don't know where she went Callie, our best option is to wait for Belle to wake, and then find out what she saw――."

"No! I'm not fucking leaving her out there when she needs us, she fucking needs you Cairo and all you care about is *her*." I growl, a rage takes over me in a way that I have never experienced before, I know instantly it's because of the mate mark and Bex is extra protective of his mate.

"You know I won't rest until she is back here, we need to be smart California––."

"Fuck you, she needs us, she can't even shift––." I cut her off with a growl so loud and ferocious that it has her stepping back and dropping her gaze, a growl comes from Creed, but I ignore him.

"Sky can't shift because she isn't a fucking wolf. You think you know your mate, but you don't know shit, Skylar Cage is a witch Callie, you're mated to a witch because she wanted you and made sure it happened. I would die for her in a heartbeat, so don't you ever fucking question me when it comes to Sky, because I will burn this whole fucking world down for that girl." Zeke steps in front of me and shakes his head in annoyance.

"Take Belle back, I'll get Davina and the others to help me and Callie search for Sky. That should buy you some time to sort out what you need to with that whole situation." I nod stiffly, I forgot all about Davina being here for a brief moment.

I startle awake when I hear the creak in the floorboard near the door, I look up and see Cass standing there in a pair of sweats and nothing else. He and the other two have been coming in every half hour to check on her, it's after dawn and she still hasn't woken. None of us have managed to get more than ten-minute power naps, here and there throughout the night. Z has been keeping me updated on their progress, they lost Sky's scent ten miles out of town. Creed and Jess have prohibited Davina from coming anywhere near the old cabin currently occupied by the five of us. Cass moves toward her and sits on the edge of the bed, the rational part of me knows he loves her like a sister but the jealous wolf inside me hates that he is an unmated male and touching our mate, Cass just smirks when a growl slips out of me.

"I'm no threat to you alpha."

"Try telling Bexley that." Cass laughs lightly.

"Atticus doesn't think much of you or your wolf either." *Atticus*, nice strong name I like it. "But he and I both can admit that you are a good strong alpha."

"Ah, so I get your blessing?" I tease. He pins me with a tired look and shakes his head.

"Never. No one will ever be good enough for my sister, know this though Cairo, you ever hurt her, or fuck her over like your brother-in-law did to your sister, I will never let you within five feet of her again. Your wolf is strong, but so is mine, I will challenge you, and I don't back down like Creed, it will be to the death." I extend my hand toward him; he eyes it for a beat before placing his in mine.

"Believe it or not Cassius, I respect the hell out of you for saying that." He pulls his hand from mine and scoffs. "Nah, I'm serious. I wanted to rip Creed apart when he turned up on my pack lands, but I couldn't do that to my sister or my nephew. I'll fuck this up Cass, there is no two ways about it, but I'll try to make it work."

"What's this shit with you and Sky? You dropped a huge ass bomb back there and then just clammed up and refused to say shit, I ain't asking to be nosey. I'm asking as a brother who is concerned about his sister being caught in a love triangle." I hate to admit it, but Cass is growing on me, I respect any man who doesn't beat around the bush and gives it to me straight. I sigh and run a hand through my hair as I look down at Belle, she's still out cold but she looks peaceful.

"Sky is...she is me but with a pussy." We both chuckle at my attempt to explain what Sky means to me. "She is a bad bitch and saved my life, I was in love with Sky for more than half my life."

"What happened?" I laugh as I answer.

"We had sex and she realized she preferred *bun* to *sausage*." Cass laughs along with me; our laughter dies off and silence descends for a while before I break it. "I always wanted to be with Sky, but she never entertained the idea. She said one day I will find a mate, and I would forget all about her, I suspected that Bex's obsession with Belle was more than him, and I wanting to know what Davina was up to. I won't lie and say meeting Belle caused my feelings for Sky to disappear, my feelings for her started to lessen when her and Callie became an item. I saw the way Sky looked at Callie and knew I never stood a chance, did meeting Belle help? Fuck yeah, she pushed me out of my own head and made me see her. I didn't sleep with her to get at Sky, I did it because...it felt right."

"I don't want to hear––."

"Let me finish, I wasn't going to give you a play by play. I love Sky and I always will but it's a different kind of love now, part of Sky lives inside me, and I will always be loyal to her till the day I take my last breath."

"What does that mean?" I sigh, I have never told anyone this, but I have to start being honest or risk fucking things up with Belle before we even get a chance to start.

"Sky cast a spell on me when we were kids, the purpose for that, was for me never needing a pack, so I wouldn't have to go rogue and be put down. It also meant that I could never be led, Jacob could never come after me and use me to do his bidding, Sky gave me my freedom and my life. Without her I would have died in a ditch somewhere."

"I don't doubt that the two of you share a bond no other will understand, my worry is my sister will be caught in the crossfire. I know Belle isn't telling us everything because of some blind sense of loyalty to you, my sister and I know that something big is going to happen. Believe me when I tell you, that Blake, Hunter and I will follow her to the depths of hell."

I roll over and wrap my arms around something, I'm to fatigued to wonder what it is until, my foggy brain registers *who* the warmth is. I blink my eyes open and stare down at her, I cringe slightly when I see Cass asleep on the other side of her. I tighten my hold so she's flush against me, Bex sighs in contentment at having his mate pressed against him.

"Come on beauty, please wake up, we all need your help." I whisper.

"And here I thought you just missed me." I reel back and stare down at her in shock, her blue eyes shine with tiredness, even though she has slept for hours. I don't overthink it; I cup her face and press my lips against hers, before I can deepen the kiss she pulls back and smiles shyly. "Morning breath is not my jam." I can't stop the laugh that breaks free, Cass stirs behind us and sits up swinging his gaze to his sister. The shock on his face bleeds into relief as he rips her away from me and hugs her, he buries his face in the crook of her neck.

"Thank fuck Belle, no more day walking. That shit was fucking hard to watch, and I won't do it again, promise me Gabrielle?" He pulls back and stares at her with an intensity only a brother can, they may not be blood, but I can see love and devotion each of these Wilder brothers have for her.

"Don't make me lie to you Cassius. If it means life or death for someone, I'll do it––." Bex surges forward and growls cutting off her reply, both of their gazes swing to me. Belle's eyes widen when she sees my eyes, Bex is right here just below the surface ready to lay the law down for his mate.

"You will do as your brother says, if you disobey me, I'll take it out on each of them." Her mouth drops open in shock.

"I'd like to see you try." Cass mumbles but I ignore him as I keep my focus on the brown-haired beauty. I see the defiance in her eyes and wait for her sassy comeback, but then her face contorts, and worry begins to cloud her features. I can feel her panic through the mate bond, I reach up and rub my hand across my chest trying to alleviate this odd sensation inside me at feeling what she does. "Belle?" She ignores him, the uncertainty in her eyes puts Bex on alert wanting to destroy whoever planted that look in her eyes. This mate thing is going to take some time, I'm not used to Bexley fighting me for control, normally we are in sync with each other.

"Sky...she, uh, needs us but doesn't want you to go after her." I act on instinct; I reach out and grip her on either side of her arms and haul us both to our knees and get right in her face.

"Where is she?" She doesn't flinch at the harshness in my tone.

"She pulled me to her and I have no idea how she knew about my abilities to do whatever I did. She wanted me to tell you that the council has a witch, and it was them that took her, she said it's too late for her and the witch wouldn't leave her with a choice."

CHAPTER TWENTY-THREE

Belle

P ain is etched across his features, and I wish I could take that look off his face but I can't. His eyes flicker back to their normal ice blue, Cass inches closer to me in case I need him to intervene. I hear the bedroom door open, but I don't dare take my eyes off the beast in front of me.

"What else did she say?" The brokenness in his voice is like a punch to my gut, I see his and Sky's relationship in a different light now. I know he has lingering feelings for her, but it's like he is confused in his love for her. He thinks he loves her because of what she did for him, I may have been out for a while, but I could hear everything that was said between him and Cass last night. I reach out and pry his hands from my arms and grip them in my own.

"She said." I take a deep breath and squeeze his hands in comfort, because I know what I'm about to say is going to break him. "You have to put her down." He tears his hands from mine and jumps from the bed, I scramble after him and block his path to the door. Blake, Hunter, Z, Cole and Callie are all in here. Cole has his arm wrapped around his sister who is silently sobbing into his chest, my heart aches for Callie.

"I won't fucking do it!" Cairo shouts, I steel my spine and meet his gaze, it's risky but he has to see the truth in my eyes.

"She fought Cairo, she fought hard to draw them away from the rest of us. She doesn't want to be what destiny said she would be––." He growls right in my face, and I'll admit, fear grips me at the murderous look in his eyes.

"Ro, that's––."

"Shut the fuck up Colton. You don't know shit about Skylar, beauty, she is the strongest person I know, and she won't go down without a fight!" I nod my head.

"I told her to fight, she said she has fought her whole life and she can't anymore." He opens his mouth, but I raise my hand to stop him. "I felt the power inside her Ro, it was like an explosion. Sky has wild magic inside her, and it's never been tamed––."

"What the fuck do you know about my mate?" I flinch at the anger in Callie's tone, I feel Cass at my back offering me his silent support. I face Callie and fight the tears that want to break free for her and the loss she is about to suffer.

"She wanted me to tell you that she loves you, and you were always the light in her darkness...she fought as hard as she did because of you Callie." A strangled sob tears from her, Cole wraps his arms around her and holds her up, just in case she crumbles. Creed steps into the room and rushes over to his siblings wrapping his arms around both of them, I turn back to Cairo and fight the shiver that wants to trek through my body at the look he is giving me. "She wants you to tell her the whole truth Ro." I face Callie again, and the pleading in her eyes has the tears falling from mine. "Sky wants you to know that if she was given a choice between you and Cairo... it would always be you California." Callie screams and sobs wrack her body as her brothers hold her close.

"No, no, no. You fucking bring her back to me Cairo! You son of a bitch, you fucking go after her now, you bastard, this is all your fault!" Cairo stands there and bares all her cruel words. I drop my gaze to the floor and wring my hands together as I get the last of it out, I'm too much of a coward to meet his gaze. "She wants you to know that she doesn't regret a thing Cairo, she would do it all again for you." Cairo doesn't answer me, he couldn't even if he wanted to, because Callie is screaming insults at him and blaming him for everything. I slowly lift my gaze to his, Jess moves to block her brother from Callie's view, but he gently pushes her away and moves to stand in front of her. Callie lunges for him, smacking his face then punching his chest, Creed and Cole attempt to grab her but Cairo shakes his head and allows her to continue wailing on him.

"I fucking hate you! If she dies, I will never fucking forgive you, you're a disease Cairo! She is everything to me, and you took her away because you wanted that bitch!" She screams while blindly pointing in my direction, Cairo snaps. He grips her face and growls. Everyone remains quiet, the only sound in the room is Callie's sobs.

"I'll take your fucking hate. You want to blame me, go ahead, but know this California, I would trade places with Sky in a heartbeat, not only do I love her, but I will never be half the person she is." Hearing those words out of his mouth stings, Cass places his hand on my shoulder, I reach up and place mine on top of his. "She gave me my life Callie; I would have died without her. I knew from day one that she was a witch, and I spent my whole life making sure her secret stayed hidden. I vow to you Callie; I will find whoever outed her to the council and peel the bastard's skin from his body. I won't leave her−−."

"Why does she want you to kill her?" She hiccups, Cairo flinches but tries to mask it.

"Because I am the only one who can." I can hear the pain in his voice.

"Why?"

"Because a part of Sky lives inside of me, she can't kill herself, so she made sure that she had a backup plan. I didn't know she did it until years later." Cairo tells everyone how Sky broke his bond to the pack and why Bexley can't be led. "Callie?"

"Yeah?"

"You won't like what I'm about to tell you, but I can't deny Sky her...last wish." His tone is watery as he says the last part. "Sky is a witch and that means she...can't have a mate." Callie recoils.

"What do you mean?" Cairo drops his arms back to his sides and refuses to meet her gaze, the tension in the room has ramped up as we wait for him to explain.

"She loved you like no other Callie, she wanted you from the moment she saw you but knew you would never entertain the idea because you wanted to wait for your mate." A sad smile graces each of their faces. "She did a spell," her brows furrow in confusion. "She invented it so you would think she was your mate––." Cairo places his hands on the tops of her shoulders, Callie slowly lifts her gaze back to Ro. "Your *true* mate is still out there Callie." She yanks out of his hold and slaps him across the face, gasps break out around the room.

"You're a fucking liar!" She screams at him before running from the room, Cole and Creed are quick to chase after their sister, Jess moves toward her brother and wraps her arms around his waist and rests her head against his chest. Hunt and Blake move toward Cass, and I motion for us to follow them out of the room, I take one step and I'm yanked backward, I stumble but arms band around my waist to save me from faceplanting. I tense expecting a vision to slam into me, but when he growls, I know exactly who it is.

"She isn't going anywhere!" The gruff tone of his voice tells me it's Bexley in control right now, Cairo is in the backseat for the moment. Blake and Hunter try to take a step toward to me but Cass's arm snakes out and stops them, he and Cairo clearly share a look, but I can't decipher the meaning behind it. His grip on my waist tightens when I try to wriggle free.

"Uh, Z and I will give you all a moment, but meet us in the living room. We have to come up with a plan about what we do next––." Jess is cut off when Cairo's phone begins to ring, he reluctantly drops his hold on me and moves to retrieve his phone from beside the bed.

"Yeah?" Cairo snaps, he pauses to hear whatever is being said on the other end, his body coils tight with tension. "Yeah, I'm on my way." I turn toward my brothers to ask what is being said on the other end but the anger radiating off each of them gives me pause, the three of them glare at Cairo. "We need to renegotiate the terms of our deal." Cairo's eyes meet mine as he speaks. "Everything changed yesterday when I marked her as my mate." My eyes widen and it's then that a slight pinch of pain in my shoulder registers, I reach up and push the sleeve of my shirt down and run my fingers over the *mate* mark!

"Holy shit."

"It was the only way to snap you out of the trance Belle, we didn't know what else to do." Cairo's phone call is completely forgotten as I go in on my brothers.

"You fucking knew?" Blake opens his mouth to speak again but I cut him off. "You all agreed to this?" Jess and Z slip out of the room, Blake and Hunter at least have the decency to appear remorseful but not Cass.

"What choice did we have? As usual you do as you please, and the three of us are left wondering how the fuck to save you Belle. I will not watch you die, I'm not even sorry I told him to do it because here you are, alive and well." A tinge of guilt settles inside me at Cass's words, I'm not angry that Cairo marked me. I'm pissed because...I wanted him to do it of his own free will, not because he had to, in order to save my life.

"I didn't do it to save you." I hide my shock as I peer over my shoulder at him, his phone call has ended.

"You a mind reader now?" He stuffs his hands in his pockets and then diverts his gaze to my brothers.

"Can you give us a minute?" A beat passes before I hear my brothers leave the room and close the door with a soft click. The tension between me and Cairo is upping each second that passes. "I can't read your mind, but because of the mate bond, I can feel what you feel." That's a fact I sure as hell forgot about.

"We had sex, you told me you loved your beta and then I catch you kissing her, but you still mark me? Tell me, am I supposed to be grateful that you saved my life––I am by the way, but I also can't forget what I saw."

"I don't expect you to." He motions for me to have a seat on the chair in the corner, I do it because I'm starting to feel dizzy. "Like I said earlier, a part of Sky lives in me, so when she uses her magic, she weakens, the only way to help her is to siphon power from me which is done through a kiss. There wasn't anything more to that kiss yesterday than her simply recharging, I will not apologize for anything because I'm not sorry. I will do shit without thinking, that is just who I am Gabrielle." Not *Belle* or *Beauty*, I don't know if I like the sound of my full name out of his mouth.

"You and I clearly have shit to talk about and work through, but for now that has to wait. I assume that was Alexander on the phone?" He nods. "What does he want?"

"Davina was supposed to help search for the council and Sky while I brought you back here last night, but she didn't. She caught his scent and instead her and her vamps chased him."

"Why is she after him?" Cairo grinds his teeth.

"I don't fucking know, that is one of the reasons why I need to keep you from her."

"Why?"

"Because I don't trust that cheating whore within an inch of you, she may have the others fooled, but not me. Davina Reeves is a slimy bitch, and I don't buy her mothering act for a second, she's here for her own gain. I threw a spanner in her plans though." He smirks triumphantly.

"How?"

"Because Davina has no idea that her precious Belle is my mate, and believe me beauty, I'll tear hers and anyone else's throats out if they think they can take you from me."

11 days.

We have searched every place, every ridge, every tree we could. We have been following the scents of everyone from the woods the night Sky was taken, every day we are no closer to finding her. Cairo's frustration grows each day, with no hope of locating his beta; unfortunately, our personal chat has to be put on hold due to other commitments, as well as dealing with Alexander and the council, Cairo's main priority is Sky. Each night we use each other's bodies to find comfort and relieve the sexual tension that simmers between us daily. We argue nearly every day and drive everyone nuts with our constant bickering, but at night it's a fight to see who can make the other come first. I know this isn't healthy for a relationship but right now it's working for us, we do get along sometimes though.

One thing I have noticed but haven't told anyone yet, is that since Cairo marked me, my visions have changed. I don't always drop and black out anymore, I could be having a conversation with someone, and then my mind just explodes with a movie of their life. It isn't painful but it is worrying me because I don't black out, *black out*. I sleepwalk or day walk or whatever you want to call it, and have no recollection of how I got there, Cairo and my brothers think I keep running away just to piss them off. With all the stress that everyone is under trying to find Sky and the council, I haven't found the right time to tell anyone. I've been trying to reach Sky without anyone knowing. Cairo forbids me from doing it, but that control freak has to learn really fast that I don't follow orders blindly. I can't explain it, but I can still feel Sky, I guess you could say I feel her soul? So that means she isn't dead, but each passing day I feel the tether to her weakening.

"Go to sleep beauty, we have to be up in a couple hours." I roll over and rest my hands under my cheek and stare at him, the moonlight is the only source of lighting in the room. Cairo, my brothers and I, all moved into the cabin where he took my virginity days ago, it feels more like months. With how strung-out Cairo has been, he and his sister thought it was best for everyone, if they stayed apart until Sky was found due to their wolves being both dominant, Creed is somehow able to be near them without any issues which surprises me because he is an alpha himself. He kindly explained that he isn't a threat to Jess because she is his mate and Cairo has been his friend since they were pups. I know Cairo feels guilty about putting his sister's wolf on edge with her being pregnant, but it isn't his fault. "I can feel your eyes on me." I smile as his lashes begin to flutter open, he runs his arm under the covers and grips my hip. I stifle the moan that wants to slip free, his touch sets off a raw need inside me. I can't seem to get enough of him and just want his cock to live inside me, he made me come four times already tonight and I want more, I'm ravenous for him. "Stop making fuck me eyes." He growls but there is no mistaking the lust in his voice.

"I can't sleep, and I know something that will help me, can you guess what it is?" He groans and I chuckle.

"You know that we share this cabin with three other shifters, right?" I cringe at the reminder of my brothers being in the two rooms next to ours. "That's what I thought, they get about as much sleep as we do with all the screaming you do." I balk.

"It's not fault burying my face in a pillow doesn't help!" He gives me a dry stare and I shrug.

"Don't get me wrong, I love losing myself inside you, but I also know what you're up to." I stiffen and he narrows his eyes. "Huh."

"What does *huh* mean?"

"I wasn't a hundred percent certain that my hunch was right, but your reaction right now, proves I was."

"Shit."

"Hmmm, now spill it."

"I don't know what you mean." I tartly reply. He splays his fingers wide and they skate over the apex of my thighs, I fight the shiver holding back how much his touch affects me, the sexy smirk on his face tells me I fail at hiding my emotions. "I know what you're doing." Even I can hear how breathy I sound.

"Hmmm, and what is that beauty?" I'm ready to sass him but snap my mouth closed when he runs a finger through my folds biting my lip to stop the moan slipping free. "Jesus, you're soaked already!" I turn onto my back and spread my legs open for him trying to entice him to get lost *in* me instead of questioning me. He growls and throws the blankets back as he rolls on top, I snake my arms around his neck and pull him down to me. I can see he is warring with himself whether or not to continue this, or push me for answers, I think fast and grip his hair with one hand and with the other I slide it between us and wrap my tiny hand around his hard cock. He hisses and I smile, I love that I have this effect on him, and that little old me can get this big bad wolf to lose control. I pump him slowly as I kiss him intensely moaning at the taste of him, strawberries and mint such an odd taste but I love it.

"Swear to God, if you two fuck again, I'll cut his dick off Gabrielle!" We break apart and laugh loudly, even I can hear the growls coming from the other sides of the wall.

"We're not Hunt!" I shout back.

"Bullshit! We're fucking wolves Belle; we can hear every breath and smell the scent, every goddamn thing coming from that sex infested room!" I cringe, that is slightly disturbing to know that my brothers can scent my...need.

"Go to sleep baby Wilder." Cairo say's, humor thick in his tone. He places a soft kiss to my lips, I try to deepen it, but he pulls back and I grip his cock tighter. He scowls at me. "Don't you dare––." He snaps his mouth closed as I smile up at him, stroking him faster, I push against his chest with my other hand, the fact that his dick is literally in the palm of my hand has him at my mercy, so he does as I say. When he's flat on his back I release his cock and marvel at it for a moment before I push my way between his legs and wrap both my hands around his length. If he bites his lip any harder, he is going to draw blood, when I see a dollop of pre come on the tip, my mouth waters. I swipe my tongue across capturing the drip, he hisses, and I moan at the taste of it. Not in a million years did I ever imagine that I would enjoy sucking dick, since having sex with Cairo and becoming attuned to my bodies wants and needs, I'm loving it, knowing we both have to stay quiet or risk my brothers interrupting again, and let's be real, it's quite the buzz kill! I swing around so my legs are either side of his face and slowly lower my wet pussy to his mouth, being the amazing lover that he is, he pokes his tongue out steadily fucking me with it, adding to the motion I lift up and down, when it becomes too much to hold my moans in, I run my hands down his chest and across his abs to cup his balls as I slowly swallow his cock.

Sixty-nine is my favorite position, me being able to be on top and in control of his release is such a power trip for me. I rock backward and forwards across his mouth, I feel his cock pulse in my mouth from the vibrations of my moans. He lifts his hips ramming his length further into my mouth, I fight the gag but fail, he's too big for me take all the way in. I roll his balls in the palm of my hand and shudder when he sucks my clit into his mouth, spit runs down my chin as I continue to suck the life out of his cock and milk him for everything he is worth. I push my pussy down harder on his mouth and ride his face, fuck I want to scream at the pleasure thrumming through my body!

I use my hand to wrap around the base of his dick and stroke him at a fast pace and I bob up and down on his cock at the same speed as my hand. He reaches up and grips the globes of my ass holding me in place as he eats the fuck out of my pussy and believe me, I see fucking stars when he shoves his glorious tongue in and out my wet cunt, he swirls it inside me, and I can't stop the loud moan that slips free. He freezes, but I don't, I continue to pump, and suck his cock but stifle my squeal when he flips us so I'm on the bottom, keeping his cock in my mouth he somehow maneuvers us to the edge of the bed so he is standing and my neck is off the bed, he leans down and tweaks my nipples as he thrusts his hips, causing me to gag at the same time. Spit is dripping down my face as I choke on his cock, I would be a liar if I said I wasn't getting wetter every second that he makes me choke. He rips his dick out of mouth and I quickly roll over and climb to my knees, he stands in front of me panting rapidly. Bexley's eyes stare back at me, I love provoking him, so I swipe my finger across the edge of my mouth then suck into my mouth and moan as I hold his gaze. The beast snaps.

He strikes, his hand is around my throat, and he flips me on my back. I widen my legs to accommodate him better, I feel him pressing against my entrance, I reach down and grip his ass as I pull him to me. When his head breaches me we both begin to pant, I love how we get off on denying each other what we want, it just makes coming so much better. Orgasm denial is a thing and let me tell you, when you're denied one repeatedly and finally do come, it's ten times more intense, and fuck I love it. He slams the rest of the way inside me, and I cry out, fuck being quiet, my brothers should wear ear plugs.

"I'm gonna fuck you hard and you're not gonna come till I tell you to." True to his word he fucks me so hard I swear I'll leave a body imprint in the bed. Every time I get close to falling over the edge, he stops pumping into me, I clench his cock with my pussy trying to hold him inside me. The bastard smirks down at me knowing exactly what I'm doing. "Your greedy cunt has to be taught a lesson." I growl which only causes him to chuckle.

"You win okay! You stopped me from coming three times and now I'm over it, so either fuck me or get off so I can finish it myself!" He drops down and growls right in my face.

"Not you or anyone else will be touching this pussy! It's mine and I'll do whatever the fuck I want with it, your pleasure belongs to me beauty." Jesus Christ, his control freak ways shouldn't turn me on, but they do, my pussy is throbbing from his words, I nod my understanding and to my fucking relief he slams inside me and doesn't stop pumping until I scream his fucking name loud enough to wake the whole damn pack. "That's right beauty, tell them all who you fucking belong to." His pace doesn't slow as he tries to find his own release, I can see he is close and if he doesn't slow down, he'll come before I do, again.

"Cairo…" He leans back and wraps one hand around my throat as he circles my clit with the other, still fucking me like a savage beast. "Oh god."

"Only my name beauty!" He grits out through clenched teeth.

"Cairo!" I scream out as I shatter beneath him, he roars his release a second later, both of us are dripping in sweat and panting rapidly.

I think Cairo just fucked the soul out of my body.

Chapter Twenty-Four

Cairo

Each day is the same! Wake up, search for Sky, sleep and then do it all again. Tensions are high between me, Jess and Creed. Jess and I can't be near each other much because our wolves won't allow it, I need to leave soon or risk fighting with my sister, and I won't allow that. Creed and I are at odds because I know for a fact Davina is a snake and he refuses to see it because he wants his real mommy to wipe his ass. That bitch is up to something, and the fact that she has made no attempt to come near Belle, puts me on edge, her obsession with Alexander seems to trump whatever it is she wants with my mate. I hate the unknown, so I decide to take a break in my search for my beta and drop down on the grassy bank and pull my phone out, I hit his contact and wait for him to answer.

"You're making a habit of calling me." I grit my teeth to tamper my rage, if I want answers biting his head off isn't going to get them.

"Why is Davina hunting you and not coming for Belle?"

"Because she is a vile bitch and doesn't want the truth to come out."

"What the fuck is the truth, Alexander?"

"None of you are ready for the truth Cairo. Keep my daughter safe and when the time is right, I will tell you what you need to know."

"I don't have time for this shit––."

"Make the damn time! Mark my words, my daughter is more special than your female alpha of a sister. Belle is the answer to everything, Davina wants to destroy the one hope my people have, and I will not allow that."

"You know I won't give her up." His dark chuckle has my hackles raising.

"Why, because she is your mate?"

"You fucking come near any of my pack––."

"Travel to Montana, you'll find your beta there." My mouth drops open in shock. "Cairo?"

"Y-yeah?" The detached tone of his voice sends a shiver down my spine.

"She doesn't have long. The witch in their company is very strong, I have someone inside their group."

"Why are you helping me?"

"It's not you I'm helping; I want that council of mutts gone. This is me helping my own cause, take my daughter with you, I'll see you in Montana." He disconnects the call and I'm left staring at the black screen of my phone, the fuck just happened? I snap myself out of my thoughts and scroll through my contacts again before finding her name, my finger hovers over it.

It's a trap.

What if it isn't Bex? He is the only lead we have had for Sky; it's been six weeks and I can't take not knowing if she is...okay.

Sky is strong, but our mate––.

I get it!

I close the link and ignore my phone for a moment, Bex is right. If this is a trap, then I can't risk Belle being caught in the midst of...whatever the fuck this is. The problem is the little spitfire won't hear of me hopping on a plane without her coming. She is everything to Bex and I admit I was against this *mate* bond at the start, but now, she has grown on me, and every decision I have made lately is always with her in mind. I rake my hand through my hair and tug on the strands, I owe my life to Skylar Cage. I'm torn between my love and loyalty to Sky, in the midst of everything trying to protect my mate from––well, every fucking thing really.

"Eat a dick Cairo! I am not staying behind while you go off and do whatever it is you plan to do." I throw my head back and groan, I knew this would turn to shit as soon as I decided she had to stay back.

"It's too dangerous to take you with us––." Her eyes narrow, she places her hands on her hips and cocks her head to the side slightly.

"Whose *us*?" Ahhhh, fuck! I rub the back of my neck and try to smile sweetly.

"Just a few of the others, Cass and Hunter." Her face begins to flush red with anger, I quickly dart forward and grip her waist pulling her to me, but she begins to beat on my chest with her tiny fists.

"You asshole, you take my brothers but not me!"

"Beauty, be reasonable––."

"I'll give you reasonable." The dirty little minx has me crying out within two seconds, when she grips both my nipples and twists them giving me a double fucking nipple cripple!

"Stop it now!"

"Take it back, say I can come." I grit my teeth and shake my head; I will not relent. I grit my way through the pain and reach up to wrap my hand around her throat and slam her against the wall. The shock has her dropping her vice like grip on my nipples and I sigh in relief, that fucking hurt, and the fact that the she devil is batting her lashes and smiling up at me sweetly right now, has my anger soaring.

"I could break your fucking neck for that!" I hiss, the dirty little devil has me tensing when she reaches up and cups my face, she chuckles at my reaction which earns her a growl.

"You wouldn't dare, who would you sink into every night if I wasn't here?" *Checkmate*, I smirk cockily down at her, and she cringes. "Answer that, and the next thing I'll be twisting is your balls." I swear my balls shrivel up slightly at her threat. These past six weeks have been hard and discouraging with Sky missing, but the time has allowed me to get to know Belle, and actually not letting Bex influence me, because I'm not ruled by pack law or under the control of my wolf, unlike the others, the mate bond works differently for me. When a wolf mates with someone, they are in agreeance, and the deal is done, but for me, Bex chose her, not me, so it gave me time to get to know Belle. Don't get me wrong, I have felt a pull toward her and definitely attraction, from the first moment we met, but that doesn't mean I wanted to spend forever with her. Now though, I actually enjoy being around her and hanging out, her brothers are growing on me as well. The sex is fucking amazing and sometimes I wonder if this girl is more interested in my cock rather than my personality, ever since I took her V-card, all she wants is me inside her, she says she loves fighting because I fuck her harder when we make up. I really think fate got it right with her, I wouldn't be able to handle having a meek mouse as my mate, someone who follows and doesn't say shit. Belle makes sure you know what she wants and isn't afraid to voice her opinions, she really is incredible and I'm starting to fall headfirst down the rabbit hole, that is Gabrielle Wilder.

"Beauty, the only person I'm sinking my cock into each night is you, now wipe that hurt puppy look from your face." I can tell she needs reassurance, so I take a deep breath and give her that. "You're my mate Belle, I will never cheat on you, and I sure as fuck will never share you." She yanks me down to her and captures my lips in a searing kiss, within two seconds she climbs me like a pole and wraps her legs around my waist which has me chuckling. I know she wants to fuck, but we don't have time, I pull back and smirk when she pouts. "I have to go sort––."

"You have to fuck me hard and fast, I'm wet and needy and I want to come on your cock, not my own fingers." Jesus Christ, I groan. What red blooded shifter could deny a request like that?

"You're a huge distraction that I can do without." I growl, she smirks and winks.

"I know, now come play on the wild side with for me a bit, then I promise I'll help pack and book *our* plane tickets." I choose to ignore the fact she said *our* when she kisses me, my cock hardens, and I know if I don't get balls deep inside her wet heat in the next five seconds I'll combust. I move toward the bed and toss her onto to it, she giggles but it quickly dies off when I peel my shirt from my body. Not wanting to be left behind, she races to tear her clothes from her body, I stand there and marvel at her beauty. She isn't self-conscious or tries to hide from me, her self-confidence is awe inspiring and a fucking turn on! "Pants off, now!" I smirk at the bossy little minx and do as she says, I push my jeans and boxer shorts down, then smirk when her hungry lustful eyes land on my cock, she moistens her lips as I take my heavy cock in my hand and begin to palm myself. Her greedy eyes watch every stroke and when a small hiss falls from my lips, her eyes snap to mine, not one to be teased, she lifts her fingers to her mouth and sucks them. I growl.

"Get over here and suck me beauty." She yanks her fingers out and spins around so her neck is over the edge of the bed, she doesn't muck around, she opens her mouth and sucks me in as deep as she can. She opens her legs wider and my mouth waters at the sight of her pink pussy, I lean forward and push her legs open wider as I run a finger through her folds. "Fucking hell baby, you're soaking wet." She hums around my cock and the vibration causes my balls to tighten, I have to taste her. I ram my cock down her throat and love the sound of her choking on it, besides, who am I to deny her what she wants. I bend forward and rest my arms on either side of her inner thighs, spreading them so far apart, I dive in and feast on her pussy, she moans around my dick, and I hum my approval. She sucks dick like a fucking pro. I lap at her clit and don't stop until I feel her begin to tense, she releases my cock with a wet pop groaning loudly.

"Fuck yes, suck my clit and make me come!" I do exactly as she says and suck on it––hard. "Cairo!" She screams my name as she comes, I don't stop sucking until she squirts all over the bedsheets. I release her clit and lick down toward her opening, when the taste of her come hits my tongue I growl my approval. It's so fucking hot that she can squirt! "Get on your back, I wanna ride you so fucking hard." I smirk, I've created a sex demon and I'm not even mad about it. I move off the top of her and lay down on the bed, she repositions me, so my legs hang over the sides. I lean up on my elbows and observe as she spreads my legs slipping in between them, but she doesn't climb on like I expect. She turns around and positions herself to ride me...fuck yes, reverse cowgirl! I shuffle down the bed further until my ass balances on the edge to make it easier to guide her onto my cock, I push inside her and we both moan in unison, she sinks down on me slowly, its fucking torture but I love feeling her cunt adjust to me and shrink around my cock, her pussy was made for me. Once I'm fully sheathed inside her she groans in pleasure, I grit my teeth trying not to blow my load like a pubescent teen.

"Baby, I need you to move." She peers at me over her shoulder, her eyes are blown wide and filled with lust, she nibbles on her bottom lip.

"Can you make a replica of your cock?" I reel back confused as fuck at her request.

"The fuck you want a replica for?" She shrugs her shoulders and bats her lashes as she swivels around on my dick, short circuiting any thoughts I just had.

"Because I want to keep you inside me." She begins to bounce up and down, I hate that I can't see her tits, so I sit up as much as I can without disturbing her movements and cup them. She peers over her shoulder the reaches her arm back to wrap around my neck, so she's slightly turned on the side and captures my lips in a heated kiss. "I want you inside me 24/7, your cock is my addiction." I don't bother with words, I smash my lips against hers and match her pace, she pushes down and I slam up into her cunt.

"Keep riding me like that baby, I'm gonna cum in your greedy cunt."

"Fuck yes!" I release her waist and reach down so I can circle her clit, I'm not coming without her.

"I want you to squirt all over my cock beauty." She throws her head back and moans, I lean my head down and capture her nipple between my teeth, she cries out in pleasure. I suck it into my mouth as I pinch her clit.

"Oh, just like that. I'm coming baby, don't stop." I slam into her harder and when she screams my name, I feel her come at the tip of my cock, I pull out slightly to let it drip all over me. I release her nipple and grip her waist as I slam her back down, she bounces on it and takes every fucking hard thrust I give her.

"Fuck yes beauty, like that baby." I hold her in place as I slam into her two more times before I roar out my release. We stay here panting and out of breath for a few minutes before she speaks.

"I love you." I freeze, three little words that blow my euphoric bliss to smithereens and shatters everything.

"I know."

Chapter Twenty-Five

Belle

I *Know!*
That's what he has to fucking say to me, I'm so angry that I'm surprised I haven't brought on a vision myself! To be real though, I think I'm angrier with myself for assuming he would actually repeat it back to me. We haven't said a word to each other, we cleaned up and then we left to for Jess's house. Creed's mom just left with her beautiful little boy, admitedly I just sat here on the couch and marveled at him. I never thought becoming a mother myself would ever be a possibility, but now with Cairo and I being able to touch and have sex, it's on the cards for me. The trouble with that is I don't even know if kids are something he wants, I mean it's not like I am on birth control, and we haven't exactly been safe when we're having sex.

"So where are we going?" I shake my head to clear my thoughts and focus on the conversation going on around me.

"I got a lead and apparently Sky is in Montana." Cairo says in answer to Cole's question, I may be pissed off at him but even I can admit that he looks fucking hot. Black tee, ripped jeans, combat boots and a snapback with NY on the front. He has the cap pulled so low on his head that it partially shields his eyes, he seems so on edge and unreachable right now and it makes my heart sink. He's been so caught up in trying to find his...Fucked if I know what Sky is to him but I know she is important. Callie plonks down beside me and I peer at the teddy she is holding, it's a Naruto plushie. I had no idea she was into anime, she smiles and hands it to me, as soon as my fingertips graze it, I'm sucked into a vision, this one hits me hard. I cry out as the world turns black.

I look around the dark damp room, the only light source is the moon coming from the window on my left. I move toward the light and hope from this vantage

point I will get a better view; a door opens across from me and the lights flicker on. I blink my eyes a couple of times to adjust and when I do I have to muffle my scream. Sky is bound to a wooden chair, her wrists and ankles are cuffed to the arms and legs of it, her blonde hair is filthy and covered in mud, the man with the ill fitted suit grips her hair and yanks her head up, Sky's eyes snap open but they don't go to the man——she stares straight at me and winks.

Her lip is busted, and her nose is at an odd angle, her eyes have faded bruises around them, my lip begins to tremble, and tears start to gather behind my eyes. I run my gaze down her body and see her shirt is torn open, her bra is still in place, but she has cuts all over her chest and stomach. Her pants are missing, she only has her panties on, oh god please no, please tell me they didn't do what I think they did to her!

"You ready to play on the dark side Miss Cage?" Sky pulls her gaze from me and looks over the seven other people whose faces I can't see with a look of disgust, she turns back to Phillip I think his name is and spits at his feet. He yanks her back by her hair and slaps her across the face. I scream out for him to stop but it's no use, they can't hear me. He releases his hold on Sky, she turns to the side and spits out a mouthful of blood then laughs——she sounds so unhinged.

"When I get out of here, your wannabe witch isn't going to be able to save you, I'm going to rip you motherfuckers apart. You want the animal inside me to come out and play?" The eight of them begin to exchange looks but the only face I can see is Phillip, he tries to mask it, but I can see the fear in his eyes.

"You will be under our control——."

"You think because you have me in iron chains that it will keep me here? In three days' time it will be the harvest moon, and when it is at peak, you will all fall!" Sky laughs again and the sound sends shivers down my spine, The eight of them turn and exit the room, they all seem more tense than when they first walked in. When the door is closed behind them, I move toward Sky, I don't know if she can actually see me. "I know you're here Belle."

I sigh in relief. "Can you hear me?" She nods then a small hiss escapes her, I cringe unsure what I should do.

"Over there by the window is where they keep the water, bring me some." I do as she says and quickly grab a couple of bottles before returning to her and uncapping it, I place it against her lips. She finishes the first one in seconds and gets halfway through the second before she starts coughing and heaving. I drop the bottles and try to find a way to unlock the chains that bind her, but its futile! "They are sealed by a spell, only the witch that cast it can remove them."

"Then what was that bullshit about three days' time?" She smiles but it doesn't reach her eyes. "Why am I here, how am I here?"

"In three days', time the darkness that I fought to keep at bay will take over, you're here because I need you to keep Cairo from coming. I pulled you here."

"How? If these chains stop your magic, then how can you bring me to you?"

"I have someone helping me, he is the one who told Cairo where I am."

"Who is he?" She ignores my question.

"Gabrielle, you need to listen to me and listen carefully." I nod my head. "Davina is after you because you are the one who can end the vampire race." I open my mouth to protest, but she carries on. "Just listen, we don't have much time; Alexander is trying to protect you from her. He isn't the bad guy like Ro thinks--."

"I've heard of him; you said his name in a vision when I first met you all."

"That's because our destinies are intertwined."

"I don't need to hear anymore, let me go back Sky so I can warn the others, we can stop this--."

"No!" I flinch at the anger in her tone and look toward the door worried that someone might have heard her shout. "This is my ending Belle, it's a long story okay, and I will explain everything. Tell Callie everything she needs to know is inside her favorite plushie." I furrow my brow in confusion.

"That's confusing as shit Sky--." I snap my mouth closed when a wave of dizziness hits me, and I begin to sway on my feet.

"His scent clings to you, in another life maybe, he and I could have been, but not in this one Belle. You are his perfect match; I saw it in the way he gazed at you. You and Cairo are one in the same, be there for him when he tries to throw you away, and believe me, he will. He will need you for what is about to come."

The sound of a really large engine is the first thing I hear when I come to, I slowly blink my eyes open and begin to panic, when I don't see Jess's living room.

"You're okay beauty." I sit up and look around, we're on a plane! No, not just any plane a private jet, the others are scattered around sleeping on couches and chairs, I look to my left and see my three brothers asleep in the seats next to the window. I shake my head and turn back toward Cairo; I furrow my brow at the napkin he holds out for me. "Your nose is bleeding." I snatch it from him and quickly dab the blood away, I really hope it's not a bad bleed because I don't want to shove this napkin up my nostril, that would so not look hot. Thankfully I don't have to shove it up my nose, I look around again to give me something to do other than sit here in awkward silence with *Mr. I know.* Creed, Cole, Callie, Zeke, Hunter, Blake and Cass are the only other people on the plane aside from us. I look down at myself and notice I'm wearing Cairo's black Nike jumper, someone even put on my Canary yellow low-cut Chucks for me. "You looked cold."

I snicker before tartly replying. "*I know.*"

A low growl sounds out, but I ignore him, I know I should tell him about my vision, but I still feel dizzy and I'm tired. I stand ready to move near my brothers and hopefully get some rest before we land, but his arms band around my waist and yank me back against his chest. I still in his hold, he pulls his jumper down exposing my mate mark. He darts his tongue out and licks it, shivers wrack my body and I have to bite down on my lip to stop myself from moaning. Whenever he kisses, licks or bites the mark a euphoric feeling spreads throughout my body and it's ten times more intense when I'm about to come, and he clamps his teeth on it.

"Those three words are so overrated and hold no meaning." The blissful feeling evaporates within seconds, his words are like a bucket of ice water.

"Bullshit." I whisper shout not wanting to wake the others. "You're just too much of a coward to say them." He spins me around and then clasps my face between his hands, his eyes search mine, but I make sure to keep my emotions from my face.

"Do you know how overused those three stupid words are?" I narrow my eyes at him.

"In yet you can say them to Jess, your nephew and even Sky." He bends so we are nose to nose, a soft growl tumbles from his lips but I don't pull away. I'm a sucker for punishment and have to hear what he says next.

"Because those words are fitting for them－－."

"But not me?" He smiles like a cocky prick.

"No beauty, not you." I deflate, that stings. As I said before "Those three words are so overused and don't even come close to how...I feel for you." Tears leak from the corners of my eyes, he brushes them away with his thumbs, hearing the vulnerability in his voice has them flowing continuously. "I was a dick earlier, but I was also in shock, Bex knew instantly the moment he shifted in front of you that you were our mate, it just took me a bit longer to catch on than either of you would have liked. These past six weeks have been hell for me baby, Sky isn't just my beta, she is my best friend and so much more. I know this may hurt you and I don't mean for it to, but you are Bex's mate through and through. But my human half, Sky is my soulmate." I recoil and try to pull away from him, but he doesn't let me. "Please let me explain before you runaway." I reluctantly nod, like I said, sucker for punishment over here. "I *thought* I loved her; I really did. Everything I did, every move I made, I did so with her in mind, but meeting you and getting to know you, showed me differently. I couldn't have gotten through these past six weeks without you Belle, if you need to hear those three little words then I'll say them, but they will never hold as much meaning to me as they do you. My feelings for you," he blows out a frustrated sigh. "Cloud my judgment, everything I do now or any move I make, I do it with *us* in mind, because there is no more you or me anymore, we're an *us*, you're my co-captain, my teammate, and someone who will be by my side always." The tears run even faster down my cheeks, without saying the words I love you; he really did just say them without knowing it. He's right though, those words don't mean half as much as you think they do when what I feel for him is so much more. People will think I'm crazy for falling in love with a beast, when I have only known him for less than 3 months, but when ya know, you just know. "Can you say something?" A watery laugh escapes me, I bat his hands away and wrap my arms around his neck and kiss him. He moans into my mouth, that sound has me filling with need.

"Jesus Christ!" We break apart and I turn toward my brothers as he wraps his arms around my waist and pulls me back against him. Hunter, Blake and Cass all glare at us. "We are on a fucking plane and there is no doors or bedrooms in it, so for the love of Christ stop, please! No one needs to see that fucking PDA. Especially *when said* PDA is with my baby sister!" Laughter burst from me, and Cairo follows suit, Hunter sounds like my dad. My laughter cuts off, I haven't spoken to my father in weeks, and I really miss him, but I'm still hurt.

"What's wrong beauty?" I ignore Cairo and focus on my brothers, what I'm about to say is going to shatter the beautiful moment Cairo and I just shared.

"After we get Sky back and deal with those council scum we have to go home." Cairo tenses behind me and growls, this growl is deep and filled with dominance, so I know Bexley is right there below the surface. Cass ignores Cairo as he stands and moves closer to us, Hunt and Blake follow suit.

"Why?" My shoulders droop slightly.

"Because I need to hear the truth from dad." I whisper as I drop my gaze to the floor, fingers grip my chin and lift my head until my gaze collides with

Cass's. Anger simmers in the depths of his eyes and from how stiff his jaw is, I know Atticus is riding him right now.

"No matter what he has to say, you are our sister, nothing and no one will ever change that Gabrielle. You are a Wilder and you belong to us––."

"Correction, belongs to me." I elbow Cairo in the side and all that earns me is a dark chuckle.

"You'll pay for that beauty." Hunter and Blake groan while Cass glares over my head at my mate.

"As I was saying before I was rudely interrupted. We love you Belle. Now, why don't you tell us what you saw?" For a moment I forgot all about the vision, I sigh.

"Thank you, I love you all as well and we'll deal with this later. You should all sit down, what I saw wasn't good."

CHAPTER TWENTY-SIX

Cairo

I woke the others so Belle wouldn't have to repeat herself, she just finished telling us what Sky said and what she saw. Callie is a sobbing mess, again. She should have stayed home with my sister. Jess was pissed she couldn't come, but with her being pregnant Creed refused to even entertain the idea, and he has my full support with that. Once he reminded her of the baby she is carrying, she agreed under the condition he give her updates every hour. We didn't have time to waste so I carried Belle while she was passed out, we weren't sure how long she would be out and I couldn't leave her behind. Her vision and knowing that Alexander is going to be in Montana when we land has me on edge. Bex is pissed that I'm keeping this from Belle, but I don't know how to tell her. Hearing her say she needed to speak to her father and find out the truth made me feel like shit. I know the truth and still I refuse to tell her because I need her *real* fathers help to save my best friend.

"Wait, you said there were eight people?" Belle nods at Creed. "Without Shelley and Dela there should only be five council members remaining." *Fuck*, he's right.

"So, who are the other three?" I ask the group.

"Don't bite my head off." Z says to Creed. "Could two of those people be Davina and Vince?" That thought hadn't crossed my mind until now.

"What? No, Davina is out hunting Alexander!" Creed's defense is futile and judging by the look on his face he knows it as well.

"Why would she help the council?" Cole asks.

"If what Sky said about Belle is true, then it's the perfect plan." All eyes swing to Blake.

"How so?" Creed volleys back.

"Because she knows Cairo has been hiding my sister, which means drawing him out, would also bring my sister out of hiding."

"What does Sky have to do with this?" I grit out in frustration.

"I think she was just a pawn to coax you out so you would bring me." I meet Belle's gaze and the pitying look in her eyes annoys me.

"They could have taken Z." Zeke scoffs and rolls his eyes when I glare at him. "What?"

"Dude, there is no way you would have hunted for me as hard as you have done for Sky. The Reeves's pack is only helping because Sky is mated to one of the alpha's sister, she was the perfect target." I feel like someone punched me in the gut, Zeke is right as much as I hate to admit it.

"Why would your mother want me though?" Belle asks the three Reeves siblings.

"I honestly don't know; our best bet would be to find this Alexander and ask him." Belle's gaze swings to me and I stiffen at the knowing look in her eyes.

"Oh baby, you do know I have visions right?" I nod my head like an idiot. "I know you have spoken to him more than once, so why don't you start filling the rest of us in on what you *really* know about Alexander Maximoff."

"The fuck is she talking about Ro?" I swing my gaze to Creed and open my mouth, but no words come out. Does she know everything?

Bex?

No, if she did, she would have said something.

Are you sure?

No.

Thanks for nothing.

I'm a wolf not a fucking physic.

I deduce that if she really knew who Alexander is to her, she wouldn't be this calm and cocky, so I decide to play the game.

"Alexander and I met in the woods after the challenge with Cassius, he talked, I listened and agreed to...some of his terms." I can feel Belle's glare in the side of my head, I turn and smile at her which just earns me a blank look. "Fine, I agreed to trade Belle, but shit changed when I marked her. I ignore the growls and continue. "He called me and told me Sky is in Montana, he also knows Davina is after him." Everyone is shouting questions at me, but I focus on Callie who still hasn't spoken a word to me since she lost her shit. Callie's eyes are sunken in, she looks pale and has lost weight. She knows now Sky isn't her true mate, but I guess her love for Sky runs a lot deeper than I originally thought. "Callie?" Silence over comes the others, I wait for her to meet my gaze, but she doesn't. It hurts that she blames me, but I also don't hold it against her, I know this is all my fault and Sky has just been caught in––.

"What if she isn't just a pawn?" I swing my gaze to Blake.

"What do you mean?" He gives me a dry stare but answers me none the less.

"Think about it, they could have taken Jess––." Creed growls as Blake continues. "But they didn't, they took Sky because they want something from her."

"Like what?" Cole asks.

"I don't know, she is the first witch I have ever met, so I would imagine it has something to do with the magic inside her." I wrack my brain trying to think of what purpose they would have to take her for that purpose. Sky told Belle she can *cure* vampires, whatever the hell that means, but what use is she to the council? This is such a cluster fuck of lies, I hate that I can't figure out what any of this means.

"What if they just need her for her power?" All eyes are on Creed. "If they have Sky by their side, then that means they're able to work their voodoo and all wolves will have to submit to them again. Phillip is a power-hungry son of a bitch; we know he has another witch working for him, but what if she isn't as strong as Sky?"

"Sky would never betray us like that." I'm resolute in my answer.

"What if she didn't have a choice? Belle just said that Sky knows whatever is about to happen, is her destiny, I know you don't want to hear this, but what if Sky isn't in control anymore." I grind my teeth so hard my gums begin to ache.

"Sky once told me that there is this...other being that lives inside of her, and every day it tries to claw its way out. At the beginning I would brush it off and tell her it's just her wolf trying to break free after all these years, but then she told me the truth." Callie talks like a robot, there is no emotion in her tone. "She said that she was day, and the thing inside her is night, she wanted to take her own life, to stop it from ever breaking free, but that thing wouldn't let her. She knew that one day she wouldn't be able to fight and this being would want more power, so if what Creed is saying is true, then the council retrieving this thing to take over *my* Sky will mean the end for all of us."

After Callie dropped that bombshell, no one said a word, thankfully the plane landed half an hour later, so we didn't have to sit in tension filled silence for any longer. As we disembark from the aircraft on a private tarmac, thanks to Creed and all his new *associates* we were able to get a private jet. Waiting for us are two black escalades, as we approach the vehicles I pause; Creed stops next me and it's in this moment that it finally dawns on me.

"I have no idea where to go from here." He claps his hand on my shoulder and I peer over at him, he smiles smugly and shrugs his shoulders.

"Jess thought as much, she booked us an air BNB just out of the main town. We can head there, get some sleep and then hash out a plan in the morning." I nod and follow after him, Callie, Cole, Creed and Zeke occupy the first Escalade, and the rest of us get into the second. Cass rides shotgun next to me while Belle and the other two Wilders hop in the back. The drive passes by in a blur, conversation carries on around me, but I can't focus on anything they are saying. Now that we are here, and I know we are close, nerves wrack my body and doubt begins to creep in. We finally turn down a long drive that leads us to a two-story house that reminds me of Clark Kent's homestead, I don't bother to take in any details, we won't be here long enough for me to care. I pull the car to a stop behind Creed, everyone piles out and grabs our bags as Creed retrieves the key from a lockbox around the side of the house.

By the time I shower and crawl into bed beside Belle, it's nearly dawn, we'll only get a few hours of sleep before it's time to work out a plan and find Sky. This place is to big for us all to shift and try to catch her scent, it'll be like trying to find a needle in a haystack. Belle mumbles something incoherent so I wrap my arms around her an drag her back against me, I'll admit spooning her as I drift off is becoming an addiction. How she can fall asleep so fast after passing out for hours baffles me, I lay here and listen to her quiet breaths and once again, guilt eats at me.

"I swear once this is all over, I'll tell you everything and help you chase the answers you seek beauty." I whisper as I place a soft kiss to the back of her head, I freeze when she speaks.

"I know you will, I also know you're hiding things from me, but I know you must have a good reason for it." I have no idea what I'm supposed to say to that, I keep underestimating her and it's going to bite me in the ass hard, one day soon. Belle turns over so we are facing each other, she cups my cheek, and I see no anger in her eyes which causes the tension to flee my body. "We find Sky and take down these vile disgusting council members."

"Agreed." I growl.

"Then I want answers."

"I know."

"I want answers from you first Ro. I know there is something big you are keeping from me."

"I promise, I'll tell you everything once we find Sky and go back to my pack lands." She flinches and worry claws its way inside me. "What's wrong?"

"It's just...I don't know what I'm supposed to say to that, what about my brothers and––."

"Your dad?" A whoosh of air escapes her before she answers.

"Yeah, he won't leave my pack and Cass––."

"Is next in line to become alpha, I know. Cass also knows he and I can never cohabitate the same area, our wolves won't allow it. I would never stop you from seeing them, or visiting whenever you wanted, but beauty, you belong with me." She smiles and that throws me off my game a bit.

"Thank you."

"For?"

"Not asking me to leave my family and actually giving me a choice in your weird Cairo way." I chuckle.

"Baby, I never play fair and you need to learn that fast."

"Oh, I know you don't! Now let's get some sleep and we can work all this out after we get your BFF back."

"Thank you."

"Don't thank me, when it's the right thing to do *beasty*." I scoff.

"That is a shit pet name beauty."

"Is not, I'm beauty and you're the beast." We both laugh.

"Go to sleep." I say as I close my eyes ready to get some much-needed rest.

"Okay, I love you." I smirk.

"I know." She smacks me against my chest which just causes me to laugh, I cup her face and kiss her before pulling back and saying. "You are everything to me." Her eyes soften and melts against me.

"That was the best *I love you too*."

Chapter Twenty-Seven

Belle

I wake up to an empty bed, I'm used to it at this point, with him gone before I even wake. He searches for her from sun up, to sun down every day, I used to feel jealous about it but now I find it so endearing. I will never understand Cairo and Sky's relationship, but I can respect it. Cairo has confessed his thoughts to me about him and Sky, thinking he was in love with her, but now he knows it wasn't that kind of *love*. I stretch out before climbing out of bed and making my way to the bathroom. I relieve myself and then head for my toiletry bag on the counter so I can brush my teeth, when I lift the lid, I pause at the sight of my box of *Tampax*.

Did I miss calculate?

I've been under a lot of stress.

My visions have changed, so maybe that's the cause?

My thoughts spiral out of control as I stumble back and drop down onto the edge of the tub and clutch my head between my hands. My breaths are coming in short pants, I need to calm down or I'll risk setting a vision off. I scrub my hands down face and decide to panic later, without doing a test there is no reason to spiral, I mean there is a number of things why my period could be late. I stand and look at myself in the mirror as I turn side on and try to see if I can see a bump through my singlet.

You can't see anything idiot!

I scold myself yet again, *if,* and it is a huge fat *if,* I am pregnant, I will only be early. Like maybe 5 weeks. I shove all thoughts from my mind and go about my morning routine and head toward the kitchen after changing. I can hear bickering as soon as I round the corner to the massive country style kitchen, around the bench is sheets of papers and maps sprawled out in front of everyone. The only person missing from the group is Cairo, I look around to see if I can spot him.

"He left early this morning." I face the group again and smile my thanks to Creed.

"Did he say where he was going?" Before he can answer black dots begin to swim in my vision and I start to sway on my feet, shit.

"You want her back, then you do as I say!"

"I'll never give her up, she's mine!" I sit up and look around and furrow my brow when I notice I'm in a barn, hay litters the floor and bales of the stuff is stacked along the wall behind me. I climb shakily to my feet and move toward the railing at the edge, I look down and that's when I see stables below, with horses inside, and right there in the middle is Cairo and a man, I can't see the man's face because his back is to me, but I can tell through the thin cotton shirt he wears that he is tense. Cairo is grinding his teeth with his fists clenched at his sides in anger, his hair is a tousled mess, and his navy-blue shirt is crinkled, almost like someone has had it clutched in their hands, have these two been fighting? The man moves so he and Cairo are chest to chest, Cairo growls, his upper lip pulls back in a snarl.

"You will return my daughter to me––."

"Why now? You hid her and left her behind, so what the fuck was the point of that?"

"Because it is what kept her alive, I had your council chasing me, Davina and her goon squad hunted me. If they knew what she can do, then they would have killed her."

"What the fuck can she do that is so important?"

"Her blood is the cure for vampirism." I'm beyond confused, Cairo stumbles back a step and opens his mouth but no words come out. His eyes take on that glassy look which I have come to learn, it means he and Bex are conversing. Seconds tick by before he finally meets the man's gaze again.

"Is that why Davina wants her?" The man shakes his head.

"No, she wants to kill her."

"The fuck!" Cairo growls, he begins to shake, and I watch as fur begins to dot his arms. Bex is so close to the surface, and I see the strain on his face as he tries to wrestle control back from his wolf. "She said she wanted to protect her!"

"She is a born manipulator and lies with such ease you would never know. She makes out that she is the one to keep my daughter safe all these years, when

in reality, it was all me. Davina wanted her dead from the moment she knew my daughter is the savior of my people. I must have her returned to me."

"Fuck you——."

"I wasn't asking pup; I have given you everything you need to rescue your friend. You will keep up your end of the deal, if you cross me, I will start with your family, and then I will move onto her so-called siblings until she willingly comes to me. The choice is yours——."

I gasp.

I feel hands on me and snap my eyes open but groan when the ache in the back of my head intensifies. This is the worst part of having visions, the after effects suck hairy ass balls.

"Here sis." I feel someone grip my hand and slip something inside them. "It's Advil sis." I place the pills in my mouth and blindly reach for the glass Blake hands me. Water drips down the front of me, but I don't care, I keep my eyes closed as Blake places me back down. Silence ensues and I'm grateful for that, any loud noise right now will feel like a sledgehammer to my brain. After a few minutes when the pain begins to abate slightly, I blink my eyes open slowly, I dart my eyes around and notice I'm lying on the floor but my head rests on something firm, I tilt my head back and cringe slightly. I've been using Cole's thigh as a pillow this whole time! He smirks down at me, and I try to muster up the sweetest smile but fail terribly I feel so awkward in this situation.

My brothers, Creed, Zeke and Callie lean against the opposite wall and my heart explodes in my chest. I'm used to my brothers and dad being so caring and kind when it concerns my visions, but I have never had anyone else do this kind of thing for me. I gingerly sit up and unintentionally shy away from Cole's touch when he tries to help me.

"I'm sorry, physical contact scares me." He smiles kindly.

"I know, I wasn't thinking."

"Yeah clearly!" I dart my gaze toward the door, Cairo stands there fuming, at the same time clenching his fists, glaring daggers at poor Cole. My reply is right on my tongue, but I pause, he's wearing the same clothes from the vision I just had!

"Calm down——."

"Don't fucking tell me to calm down, you were ten times worse with my sister!"

"Huh!" I snap my gaze to Hunter in shock that he would join in on Creed and Cairo's verbal sparring match.

"Got something to say asswipe?" I stand and move beside my brother, Cairo meets my gaze and I allow him to see the anger swirling inside me, he doesn't get to take his anger out on my brother.

"Yeah, actually I do! You snap at Creed for being a douche toward your sister, and you think you can do the same to ours?" Cairo bares his teeth and takes a step forward; I dive out in front of Hunter causing Cairo to stall his movements. Cass reaches out to grab me, but I quickly move out of his reach.

"Low blow right there beauty." I scoff then place my hands on my hips. I feel the others gather around behind me and all of a sudden, the hallway feels cramped.

"Get over it, you come for one of my brothers and honestly think I would stand by and watch?" I don't give him a chance to answer. "I will *never* let you hurt them, you protect your sister with your life, and I will do the same for my brothers."

"Well, if this what coming home every day is going to look like, aren't I lucky?" I scowl at his lame ass attempt at a joke.

"You took your anger out on Cole for no reason——." He cuts me off.

"So, you'd be good with my head in Callie's lap?"

"Yes!" He throws his hands up in the air in frustration, Z, Creed and Callie brush past me to head toward the kitchen, I don't blame them for escaping. "Where were you this morning?" He tries to mask it and if I wasn't paying such close attention to him, I would have missed the look of panic in his eyes before he masked it.

"Trying to find Sky." The lie rolls easily off his tongue, and it grates on my nerves that he stands there, stares me in the eyes and lie. I can feel everyone's gazes on us, but I ignore them as I push him for more.

"Where abouts?" His eyes narrow to slits.

"Why?"

"Why dodge my question?" That earns me a growl, I refuse to back down especially when I run my gaze over him and see bits of straw from the hay bales around the cuff of his jeans.

"Don't try make out like I was up to no good."

"I wasn't!"

"Then what the fuck are you getting at?" He shouts. Cass and Blake move to stand either side of me, both of them release growls, I feel Hunter at my back.

Z moves toward his alpha and stands beside Cairo, eyeing my brothers up and down, Cole squeezes past us and moves into the middle of the showdown. He looks from the two of them and then to the four of us before releasing a sigh.

"Clearly Belle saw something in her vision why she is accusing you of something." He pulls his gaze from Cairo to look at me. "Right?" I nod my head confirming his suspicion.

"Well, did you want to share what you saw with the rest of us beauty or continue to rip me a new asshole?"

"As soon as you tame your big dick energy, then I will explain." I tartly reply as I head toward the kitchen with his gaze burning holes into the back of my head. I rummage through the fridge and let out a girly squeal when I spot the jar of pickles, I grab it and then move toward the butler's pantry and snag a jar of peanut butter.

Pickles dipped in peanut goodness!

I pop the jars of pickles and peanut butter on the counter next to Creed, unscrewing the caps I grab a pickle and dip one in the jar of peanut butter making sure to have a decent amount on it before closing my eyes and taking a bite, I moan as my taste buds go out of control at this amazing concoction. My eyes flutter open and the first thing I see is the horrified look on Creed's face, I look around and that's when I notice everyone's horrified at me eating my tasty treat.

"What?" I snap as I take another bite of pure heaven.

"Yeah, nah I'm not touching that one. Ro, Z, Callie, come with me for a minute." They follow after Cole when he leaves through the front door, my brothers follow after them not wanting to be left out of whatever is going on. I slowly turn toward Creed and smile as I offer him a fresh pickle with a large amount of peanut goodness, he chuckles and shakes his head.

"That's...a weird craving." I take a bite not chewing it properly as I swallow, the look Creed gives me is putting me on edge. He offers me his unopened bottle of water when I begin to cough, I take a few big gulps and try to regulate my breathing again. "I would pat you on the back, but I would hate to set off a vision in your *condition*." I freeze.

It's all in your head, he can't know.

I screw the caps back on the jars and return them in order to give me something to do other than facing Creed.

"Does he know?" His question breaks the tension filled silence; tears prick the corners of my eyes when we both stare at each other. I nibble on my bottom lip and begin to wring my hands in front of me, he releases a loud exhale as I shake my head. "You have to tell him."

"I don't even know––for sure, yet." I defend, his eyes widen and then he looks around the room. I have no idea what he is looking for, he turns and snags his keys off the counter then turns back to me.

"Come on, let's go."

"Huh? Where?" He rolls his eyes and reaches for me, but I flinch back, and his arm drops to his side again.

"Sorry, I spaced there for a second."

"It's okay––."

"No Belle, it isn't, if you are, then you have to be more careful because of your visions." I scowl at him.

"Don't tell me what to do!" He growls menacingly and I step back.

"Take it from someone who has lost a child, and never thought having another would be a possibility. What you carry inside you is a gift, a blessing, if you will so fucking cherish it." Guilt gnaws at me.

"I'm sorry."

"Don't be, now let's go before they all come back."

"Go where?"

"To the store to get you a test." I gulp.

Shit's about to get real!

The ride to the store was filled with so much tension, my nerves are frayed, Creed took pity on me and got the tests––yes, *tests!* As in plural, he said to be safe he brought one of each, so I sit here in the passenger seat with thirteen different tests on my lap. I can't stop my leg from bouncing, his phone rings and he connects it through the Bluetooth system in the car and answers.

"Hello."

"Don't fucking *hello* me asshole! Where the fuck are you, and Belle better be with you!" I cringe at the anger in Cairo's voice, Creed on the other hand doesn't even seem fazed by it.

"Doesn't it suck ass when your mate disappears?" Cairo growls and I cover my ears as the sound of it vibrates through the car, Creed laughs. I stare at him like he is a maniac.

"I'll fucking end you if you run with her––."

"Calm the fuck down dick." Creed darts his eyes to me quickly before continuing. "Belle needed––." I stop breathing, his gaze softens before he focuses back on the road. "Some tampons, I was around, so I offered to drive her to the store." A rush of air escapes me.

"Hurry the fuck up."

"Cairo?"

"Yeah?" A sly smirk crosses his face as he says.

"Eat a dick you little bitch." Then ends the call, I gape at him like he has lost his damn mind.

"He is going to be pissed at you." Creed shrugs his shoulders.

"Cairo is always pissed; you'll get used to it. From what I have seen, you seem to have a knack for pissing off the grumpy bastard." I scoff.

"He says *you're* the grumpy bastard." Creed chuckles.

"Nah, I used to be but then...Jess changed everything. She gave me a reason to smile, and then when I found out about Harlem, my whole world shifted. I have nothing to be angry about anymore, I have the most amazing kid and his mother is the light of my life. I have every reason to be grateful now." My heart longs for what he has, a family, someone that looks at me the way he looks at Jess.

"I envy you." I whisper as I stare out the window, I feel his gaze on me, but I don't want him to see the tears in my eyes.

"Cairo loves you Belle, anyone with eyes can see that."

"I know he does."

"Then why are you so upset?" I sigh, out of everyone in this group I have found myself a part of I never thought I would be having this conversation with Creed. I refuse to face him, I'm to chicken.

"Because what if these tests are positive? I overheard Cairo and Zeke talking a few weeks ago, he said he never wanted kids, plus, he has only just figured out that he isn't in love with Sky, never really was apparently."

"Okay, that is a lot." He chuckles but there's no humor to it. "Sky and Cairo are the dynamic duo; they share a love no one will ever understand, and honestly Cairo just loved the idea of loving someone. Sky is great don't get me wrong, but Ro never stalked her, chased her or even looked at her the way he does with you."

"How do you know that?"

"My wife is a well of knowledge." We both chuckle. "I think you will be surprised at his reaction *if* you are pregnant. If he clowns out, then Jess and I will be here for you and the baby, I'm sure your brothers and father will do the same thing. You and your family are always welcome at our pack Belle." A stray tear rolls down my cheek, I swipe it away and turn to face Creed.

"Thank you, I didn't know I needed to hear that."

"Don't get used to it kid, I'm not the deep and meaningful type." I cringe at him calling me kid. We pull into the driveway, and I can already see Cairo standing at the end.

"How am I going to get this past him?" I whisper afraid that his shifter hearing will hear this far.

"You're not, go to him and I'll meet you in your room shortly."

"Thank you."

"Your family, it's what we do for each other." Creed pulls the car to stop, and I slip out leaving the bag behind, Cairo's gaze trails all over me as if he is checking for any sign of injury. I stop in front of him and hold his stare, I open my mouth but am rendered speechless when his hand snakes out and wraps around my throat applying enough pressure to slightly restrict my airway. My eyes bulge as I begin to panic, I hear the car door slam behind me and heavy footfalls racing toward us. I spy Creed out the corner of my eye and try to implore him without words to help me, Cairo still hasn't shifted his gaze from me.

"Let her go."

"Where were the two of you?" The fact that Ro can sound so calm scares the shit out of me.

"At the store! I fucking told you that."

"She needed tampons, right?"

"Yes!" Creed snaps. A look I can't decipher is plastered across his face, his eyes are cold and vacant like he isn't really seeing anything aside from his rage. I reach up and try to pry his hand from my throat, but it just causes him to tighten his hold. He pulls me closer and bends so our noses touch, Creed wants to help but he knows if he touches me, it will set off a vision, I fucking hate these visions!

"I don't scent any blood beauty. Want to try again and this time tell me the fucking truth!" He all but screams in my face, his grip loosens enough so I can breathe slightly easier, but his hand remains on my throat.

"I-uh, I needed something——." His vicious growl has me clamping my mouth closed.

"Cairo, you're scaring her, let her go."

"Stay the fuck out of this, if I find out you have touched her I——." A fist flies out and clocks Ro in the side of his face, he drops his hold on me, so I quickly scurry away from the fight that is about to go down. Creed pushes against him;

they are chest to chest with Creed continuously growling. He grips the front of Cairo's shirt and then shoves him back a step.

"You ever, and I mean *ever*, insinuate that I would cheat on my wife, I will fucking kill you! Your sister is everything to me, you stupid prick!" Creed is screaming while Cairo just stands there with a look of shame on his face. I hear footfalls behind me, so I peer over my shoulder to see the others running toward us from the side of the house. My brothers are the first to reach me and shove me behind them, I want to argue but I know right now isn't the time. Callie, Cole and Z reach us, Zeke darts his gaze from me and back to the two alphas before asking.

"What the hell is going on?"

"Cairo is mad because Creed took me to the store." Zeke doesn't get a chance to answer.

"Why the fuck did you take her then?" Cairo roars.

"Because she needed help, unlike you, I would never disappear with your mate!" I cringe at the bitterness that coats Creed's voice.

"Stop lying!"

"I'm not lying Ro––."

"Yes, you fucking are! She doesn't have her period, so start telling the fucking truth!" How the hell does he know that? Creed turns to me, and his eyes plead with me to tell Cairo the truth, when I see Cairo's fist strike out and hit Creed across the face, chaos erupts. All the guys rush forward and pull them apart, both of them are panting and each of them got a couple of hits in before the boys intervene. "You son of a bitch––."

"He took me to get some tests!" I shout, Creed sages in relief, Cairo turns his angry stare to me, he pulls against Zeke and Cole's hold on him, but they won't let go.

"What fucking test?"

"Oh..." I turn to Callie and the look she gives me tells me she knows exactly what test we brought.

"I'm fucking waiting!" I cringe at the volume of his voice; I slowly pull my gaze from Callie to look back at Cairo. He looks rabid and slightly unhinged; I'm terrified to tell him the truth. I square my shoulders and hold his stare as I say.

"Creed took me to get some pregnancy tests." I say barely above a whisper, his brows furrow in confusion for a second before his eyes widen, I can feel my three brother's gaze's burning holes into the side of my head. I spin on my heel and march toward the car, I yank the door open, retrieve the bag and then head inside, footsteps follow after me, but I refuse to look and see who it is.

I head straight for my room; I dump the contents of the bag on the bed and still. I look at the scattered tests and a sob breaks free. The door closes behind me and before I know what is happening, I'm spun around and then crushed against a chest, I wrap my arms around Cass and sob into his shirt. He cups the back of my head and rests his chin atop my head.

"We'll get through this Belle, Hunt, Blake, Dad and I are always here for you."

"I'm scared Cassius." I sob into his chest, a sigh escapes him as he gently pushes me back and cups my face, he uses his thumbs to wipe away my tears as he smiles. I sniff and try to stop the tears from falling but they just keep coming.

"Belle, a baby is a gift and if that dumb-bastard doesn't realize that, then he can take a hike. The three of us followed you here because of the vision you had about being his mate, and Sky needing to be saved. Things have changed now." I shake my head as I grip his forearms.

"I can't...leave." His face morphs into an expression of annoyance.

"Take the test Belle. If it comes back positive then you have to think about your baby, and not yourself, it's not safe here right now for a kid––."

"You so much as *think* about taking my kid from me, and I'll end each and every one of you." Cass drops his hold on me and spins around to face Cairo whilst blocking me from his view. How he can move silently and open a door without a sound still baffles me.

"Your threats mean nothing!"

"It wasn't a threat; it was a fact."

"Touch my sister and see what I do to you." Cairo growls, I hear him take a step froward and I rush out from behind my brother and stand in front of him, Cass tries to move me out of the way, but I won't budge. I meet Cairo's gaze and his emotions are closed off, he's back to being the closed off cold as fuck alpha.

"Stop threatening my family." I say barely above a whisper, his expression doesn't change, he's ridged and tense.

"Stop lying to me!" He grounds out.

"I haven't––."

"When were you going to tell me that these visions you have are killing you?" I gasp but he doesn't stop. "Were you going to tell me after you found out you were pregnant and potentially put my kid at risk or before? Or what about you knowing that you were my mate this whole time and never told me straight up? Should I keep going beauty?"

"Cut your shit, she came here to help you, not fight you. All you have done is treat her like shit, either man the fuck up and step up, and be a true mate to her, or let her the fuck go and relinquish the bond!" My eyes widen in horror. Cairo's gaze shifts above my head to glower at my brother, he moves until his chest touches mine, I still refuse to move in case they take a swing at each other. He opens his mouth, but I cut him off.

"You lied to me." He still won't meet my gaze. "Who did you meet with this morning?" that manages to capture his attention, he takes a step back and meets my gaze.

"Alexander." I...didn't expect him to say that.

"The fuck——." I cut Cass off.

"Who is the daughter he was speaking about?" When a flicker of regret crosses his eyes, I instantly know, my hand comes up to cover my mouth and I start to shake my head. He rushes forward and grips my shoulders holding me in place.

"I was going to tell you." I yank out of his hold and move to the other side of the room; Cass darts his gaze between the two of us.

"What's going on?" Cairo won't answer him, so I do.

"Alexander Maximoff is my father, and Cairo hid it from me." Cass's eyes widen and his mouth drops open in shock, Cairo looks hurt, but I don't give a shit. "You stand there and scream at me for lying and yet you have hidden the biggest secret of all. So, when do you plan to trade me for Sky?" Cass turns to Cairo and grips the front of his shirt growling in his face, Cairo doesn't fight back he allows Cass to ram him against the wall.

"You fucking prick!"

"The deal was never going to happen." I scoff.

"Bullshit, I saw it all."

"You saw what you wanted to see; everything changed the day I marked you. Alexander thinks I'm going to trade you." He finally peers around Cass and looks at me. "I told you, you are everything to me Gabrielle and I will never let you go. I need his help and that is it, once this is over then I'll deal with him." I can hear the truth in his words and see it in his eyes.

"Cass, can you give us a minute——please?" Cass grunts before shoving Cairo into the wall before storming out of the room, slamming the door closed behind himself.

Chapter Twenty-Eight

Cairo

We stand here staring at each other, now all the cards are on the table, we have no idea what to do. I should have told her about Alexander earlier, but I didn't, I have no valid excuse, except I was...scared. Scared that if she found out she would hate me, I couldn't deal with that, I was a pussy and I have to own that shit. I also know I need to control my anger——.

Fuck! She could be pregnant, and I just choked her.

You didn't know.

That doesn't mean shit Bex.

I turn away from her and move toward the bed, scattered all over the place is at least a dozen pregnancy tests. I hate myself for accusing my brother-in-law of touching my mate, I know the only woman he desires is Jess, I have to fix that shit. I grab three tests and turn to Belle; she eyes me warily but says nothing as I approach and hold out the tests. She hesitantly takes them from me and cocks a brow.

"Take the tests and then we will talk while we wait for the results." She heads toward the bathroom, and I trail behind her, but she slams the door closed in my face, I grind my teeth together to stop the growl from tearing out of me. I pace the room waiting for her, she takes so freaking long I think I she may have fallen in the damn bowl. The door opens slowly, and she takes a hesitant step out. 'Did you take them?" She bites her bottom lip and nods. "How long does it take?"

"A few minutes." A whoosh of air escapes me.

"Good."

"Can I ask you something?" She still won't look at me and it's pissing me off.

"Yeah."

"Did you only change your mind about trading me because I might be pregnant?" Fuck it, I rush toward her and wrap my arms around her crushing her against my chest. Tremors wrack her body, and as soon as I feel her tears through my shirt, I hate myself a bit more. I hold her while she cries for a minute before speaking.

"I was never going to trade you; truth be told, I never planned to, even before I marked you."

"H-he's, my father." She hiccups.

"Yeah baby, he is." Another sob tears from her, and it's so loud, a moment later the door bursts open. I don't have to have eyes in the back of my head to know it's her brothers.

"What did you do?"

"Is it the baby?"

"Are you pregnant?" They all bark their questions in unison, I smile as I gently push her back and lift her face. I plant a soft kiss against her lips and wink.

"Want me to check the tests?" She nibbles that damn lip again, and it has my cock jumping to attention. She nods her head and I see the fear in her eyes, I cup her cheeks and bend, so we are eye to eye, I ignore her asshole brothers behind us as I speak. "Whatever happens, I'm here, and I'm not going anywhere Belle, I promise." She sniffs, then smiles meekly as she nods her head. I turn back to the three assholes and nod my head; they move inside the room and go to Belle as I make way inside the bathroom. Sitting there on the counter is the three tests, I stand there and stare at them for a moment, Bex tries to push me forward eager to find out if Belle will bare our pup, but I push him back down.

Shit will change Bex, no more running and no more fighting. We have to lay down roots and build a home if she is pregnant.

Agreed, we fight this last battle and then we go home.

I haven't been back to my pack lands since we ran from it, when the council showed up. I take a few deep breaths and move toward the counter; my nerves are going nuts and my palms grow sweaty the closer I get. The tests are face down on the counter, I take a couple of calming breaths and then do a mental count down before I flip them over.

3...2...1...flip.

Holy mother of mercy.

I stand there and just stare at the three of them, two pink lines stare back at me, and on the last one it says *pregnant.*

Belle is pregnant...with my baby.

The sound of their conversation shakes me from my moment of stupor, I'm going to be a dad! Holy shit, I grab the tests and shove them in my back pocket as I run a hand through my hair and try to compose myself. I make my way back into the room and find the three guys huddled around Belle, whispering––dumbasses.

"In case you all forgot, I'm a shifter and can hear every word you are saying." Belle drops her gaze to the floor at the sound of my voice.

"Did you hear the part about me calling you a drop-kick?" I scowl at Blake, the little shit is a pain in my ass, but truthfully, the loyalty the four of them have to each other is endearing. Cassius stands in the middle of the three of them, he turns to face me blocking Belle behind his back. He runs his gaze over me in clear disdain and I bristle at the accusation in his eyes, when he meets my stare. I brace myself for his threats and abuse, ready to strike at him if need be, Bex is dying to go a round with him.

"If those tests say what I think they do, then I need your word." I make sure to keep the surprise off my face as I nod curtly and ask.

"My word for what?" He blows out a loud exhale before squaring his shoulders.

"I know about your father and his...history." I tense at the mention of my father, he better make his point fast, that is a sore subject for me. "My sister will not be some side piece; I want your word that you will treat her right and do better than your father did for you and your sister." I can't hide the shock from my face this time.

"If you ever try to keep her from us or our father, I swear to God, we will wage war on you and your pack. Our sister means everything to us, and she is the apple to our father's eye." I turn my shocked gaze to Hunter and nod.

"She is not to be traded like chattel to Alexander, my brothers and I will help you with whatever you need to rid yourself of him. The baby that she carries may be half yours, and I don't give a fuck about logistics like DNA, that baby is still half of us. We will be here for her and the baby at any given time, we will visit whenever we want, and you will not stop us Cairo." I smile proudly at each of the Wilder brothers, their love and devotion to Belle and our baby, is something I'm in awe of. I will never keep them from Belle or our baby, even though they piss me off. I clear my throat and decide to be honest with them before breaking the news to my mate.

"I hid my sister for five years, helped her birth the twins, held her through the loss of my niece, and helped raise my nephew. I know how important family is, and I know I'm a bastard, but I would never keep her from you or your father, Belle's views on you three never changed, even when she learnt the truth." I suck in a harsh breath and say the words the three of them want to hear. "On my honor as alpha of the rogues, I, Cairo Cruz hereby swear to be faithful, loving and forever there for my mate. I cannot swear not to hide things from her——." They all growl and I hear Belle snicker, but I push on. "But only if it's something to do with her safety, I will always put her wellbeing first. Better to ask for forgiveness rather than permission I say. Now can you move, you big fucker, so I can talk to *my* mate." Cass moves toward me, and I ready myself for him to strike out, but instead he offers me his hand, I place mine in his and meet his gaze.

"As future alpha to the Wilder pack, I, Cassius Wilder, open my pack to you and welcome you onto our lands whenever you like." I stare at him for a moment before nodding, that was fucking huge of him to do, inviting another alpha to your lands is like opening it up to a lion. Blake and Hunter shake my hand before moving to stand behind me with Cass. Belle stands there nervously twisting her hands, staring at the floor with her chin on her chest, I make my way over to her and clasp each of her hands in mine, but she still won't look at me.

"Look at me beauty." She slowly lifts her watery gaze to mine and it pains me when I see the fear in her eyes. I will do anything to keep that look from ever gracing her beautiful face again. "Everything changes now, I'm not Creed, and I swear to you, I will never hide shit from you again. I know this is hard for you, because you don't have a wolf." She lowers her gaze in shame, I drop her hand and grip her chin lifting it, she needs to see the truth in my eyes. "I don't mean that in a bad way, all I'm saying is from the day of the challenge with Cass, shit shifted for me, you're my beginning, middle and end. There is no one else for me Belle, only you. I'm all in beauty, and I hope you are to?" I have just voiced my biggest insecurity, not only in front of her, but in front of her brothers as well, a small crease forms between her brows.

"You're not angry?"

"What would I be angry about?" She shrugs her shoulders and looks up at me with those innocent eyes. It hits me then, she is so much younger than me, and hasn't had a chance to live her life, I mean it's not like she was even going outside before me, but still.

"That you know, I could be pregnant?" I smile.

"Babe, I've lived and done all the young and dumb shit teenagers do, so the real question is. Are you angry?" She smiles wide and shakes her head. "Do you want to know if there is a little CC in there?" I move my eyes to her tummy; I hear the dicks behind me groan but ignore them.

"Yes!" I drop my hold on her and grab the tests from my back pocket then hand them to her.

"Congratulation's beauty, we just created a miracle." She bursts into tears and jumps into my arms, I return her embrace and hold her close, slightly panicked as to why she is crying so hard. I give her a few minutes to let it out before pushing her back and asking. "Are you crying happy tears?" She laughs a watery laugh and nods.

"A couple of months ago, I never thought I would ever get to kiss a boy, not to mention ever...ya know." A growl slips from me and the assholes behind me snicker, she smiles up at me and winks. "So, the thought of having a baby was never on the cards for me, it hurt, but I was slowly coming to terms with it, until I met you." I smirk smugly down at her. "You changed everything for me, I can go outside and be near people without my head feeling like it will break open. You have given me the greatest joy of my life Ro; you made the impossible, *possible* for me. I want this baby with you––." I don't let her finish, I've heard enough. I smash my lips against hers and pour all my joy and love into this kiss, so she will know that I... that I... I love her.

I pull back and search her eyes for a moment before saying the three words I thought I would never say again.

"I love you, Gabrielle." Her eyes widen to the size of saucers, more tears streak down her face.

"I love you too."

After apologizing to Creed and filling him, Cole, Callie and Z in on the news about Belle being pregnant, we have all gathered in the living room. Callie has been doting on Belle nonstop and making sure she is comfortable; Cole has even been less of a prick and hasn't made any smart-ass comments. Creed had asked if he could call Jess and inform her of the news, I agreed. My sister is over the moon and so excited that she and Belle are both going to have babies around the same time, I'll admit, I'm excited as fuck about the prospect of being a father. Creed told us that we can get Belle in with the pack doctor when we get back and have an ultrasound done to find out how far along she is and our expected due date.

I hate that the joy of our baby is clouded by this shit, with the council and the one person I wish I could share this joy with, isn't here. I need my right-hand woman back, Sky is a badass and I don't doubt that she would be fighting each day she is with them, but with our lack of knowledge about witches and how many there actually are, we are going in blind. I filled everyone in about my meeting with Alexander this morning, I tried to call him twice, but he isn't picking up. Something isn't sitting right with me; the man can't stand the sight of me, but he has never not answered my calls and it's making me feel uneasy.

"What do we do now?" I run a hand through my hair and meet Hunter's gaze.

"I...I don't know, and I hate waiting. Our options are limited though, Montana is too big of a place for us to shift and try to find her scent."

We'll find her.

When Bex? It's been fucking weeks and still we are no closer to getting her back.

We have one option. I growl at him in my mind.

Not going to happen.

She is stronger than you think!

Fuck!

I scrub a hand down my face and try to shake off the thought that Bex is right. I don't want to risk her or the baby by asking that of her though.

"What did Bex say?" I look to the side and smile at her, she is so in tuned with me already.

"It doesn't matter."

"It matters to me." The innocence in her voice shatters me, I'm going to hell for doing this to her. I twist my body so I can face her head on, the relaxed easy going look on her face changes to trepidation.

"If you were to try, are you be able to find Sky's location and––."

"Jesus Christ!" I snap my gaze to Blake who is staring at me with hatred in his eyes. "You want my *pregnant* sister, who is carrying *your* child to put herself and the baby at risk to find your side piece?" Before I can even defend myself, a lamp goes flying toward Blake's head, he dodges it just in time and it shatters on the wall behind him. I'm on my feet in a second and turn toward where it came from and find a seething Callie standing there, her eyes––They are turquoise, and fur begins to break out on her arms. Creed and Cole rush to her, but she snaps her teeth at them and growls. Everyone knows that both Reeves brothers are pussy's when it comes to their baby sister having a meltdown and clearly right now, is one of those moments.

"Call her a side piece again...I dare you." Blake's eyes are wide, Cass moves to block his brother from Callie's sight, and it earns him a growl from the she-wolf. He raises his hands as if surrendering.

"He meant no offense to your...*mate*."

"You don't get to speak to me." A look of hurt crosses the big fuckers' eyes before he masks it. The fuck is going on between these two. The tension between them is palpable and I have no idea why.

"Then don't throw shit at my brother, you have a problem, you take it up with me! I agreed to help you find her, but I didn't agree to let you take your anger out on my family." Okay, I know I have pissed Cass off––a lot. But he has never spoken to me with so much disdain in his voice like he just did with Callie.

"Someone's here!" I spin back toward Creed and see he has his gaze on Belle. "Go to the room and stay there, Callie, go with her and don't come out till we say." I can't help the growl that slips out, Bex doesn't like him ordering our mate around.

"Sorry." I say with a sheepish smile, Creed shakes his head and ushers the girls to hurry up and move. I place a quick kiss to Belle's lips and say.

"Hide, do not come out whatever you hear." She nods, I place my fingers against my lips and then lay them on her stomach. She gasps but I don't meet her gaze again as I hurry out the door after Creed, if he dies, my sister will fucking kill me! Z and I stand shoulder to shoulder as we scan the drive, Creed and Cole stand slightly in front of us with the three Wilder brothers blocking the entrance to the house.

"There!" Creed points toward the tree line, two figures come toward us and that's when I notice that one of them is injured with his arm around the other. Bex pushes forward to allow me to use his sight, but it isn't needed when I catch their scent. I rush over to them with Z at my side and the others behind me. I screech to a stop when they're mere feet between us, I dart my gaze between them and notice the blood that coats his mid drift is still coming out and not healing.

"The fuck are you doing here Vince and who the fuck is that?" Cole asks, the unease in his tone is clear. I meet the injured man's gaze and answer for him.

"Everyone, meet Belle's dad." Gasps ring out behind me; Alexander's gaze meets mine and the ominous look he gives me sends chills down my spine.

"Hide my daughter, they are coming for her."

CHAPTER TWENTY-NINE

Belle

Callie and I are peering out the window of my bedroom and watch as the guys approach the two men, Callie gasps at the sight of the uninjured man.

"Do you know him?"

"Y-yea, he is my bio-moms boyfriend, Vince." My gaze strays to the other man and when he lifts his head, something inside me pulls. He's a large man, his square jaw is taught with tension, his black hair is a mess, from here his eyes look black. A shudder runs through me, something about this man seems so familiar. "They're asking why they are here––Oh, shit!" I turn to Callie to find her eyes on me and whatever she has just heard, has her in shock.

"What is it?"

"I think we should–uh–come on." I follow her out of the room and out the front door, I have to jog to keep up with her, the guys all turn toward us and before we can get within ten steps of them, Cairo rushes forward and plucks me from the ground, I have to wrap my arms and legs around him or risk falling. I look over his shoulder and don't miss how my three brothers move to block the two men's view of me, I pull back and stare down at Cairo.

"What's going on." He moves his hands to grip me on my ass and squeezes.

"I told you to stay inside!" He grits out through clenched teeth. I keep struggling in his hold, he tries to grip me tighter but has no choice but to stop or risk dropping me. He places me on my feet and gets right in my face, his grip on my waist is bruising, I flinch, and he immediately releases me and steps back. "I'm sorry––I didn't mean to––."

"I'm fine!" I try to reassure him, but he isn't having it.

"Did I hurt the bean?" My mouth hangs open in shock.

"Did you just call our baby a *bean*?" I bite out. He rubs the back of his neck and nods, he looks so unsure and it's so cute. "I'm sure the baby is fine; you have to stop man handling me––." I don't even get to finish that sentence before he is crowding me and gripping the back of my neck, applying enough pressure to cause me to crane my head back and look up at him.

"Never beauty, being gentle with you isn't an option. I do however promise not to handle you roughly anywhere that can injure our *bean*." I roll my eyes heavenward; we are not calling our baby a bean for the next however many months!

"Fine, now can you tell me why Callie said I should be out here, or why you are making sure to keep me hidden?" His face remains neutral, no flicker of emotion at all.

"Can I lie to you once more?" He tries to smile but it looks pained, I place my hands on my hips and scowl at him. "Fine, one of the guys is Vince, he is Davina's right hand man or lover or whatever the fuck you want to call him. The other guy, well that one is complicated."

"Uncomplicate it then." I know that his apprehension has something to do with the other man and it's making me uneasy, especially when he releases me and takes a step back.

"The other guy is...Alexander, your father." I don't react, I honestly don't know how I'm supposed to react to that statement. I thought I would feel anger toward the man who gave me up, but I don't, am I curious about him? Yeah, I am, but that's as far as I can feel right now.

"Is he here to help find Sky?" My question must throw Cairo, he frowns down at me but has a skittish look in his eyes, like I'm about to explode or something.

"Uh, maybe, I don't know. Are you okay?" I nod.

"Can I meet him?"

"Soon, he's injured so we have to sort that first and figure out a few things."

"Like?"

"One, how he found us, two, why is Vince with him and three, how the fuck an original vampire ended up injured.""Okay, I'll wait inside." His face is scrunched up and clearly, I have shocked the shit out of him, but I don't have the energy to fight right now. All I want to do is find out from Alexander where Sky is, save her and then go home...but, where is my home now? I'm about to have a baby and I know Cairo said we would go back to his lands, but what about my family, I'm going to need them when this baby comes. I sigh as I drop down on the couch and rest my feet up on the coffee table, I thought having visions gave me an edge, but clearly I was wrong.

As I sit here and wait for the others to join me, my nerves start to go haywire, what if meeting him sparks a vision? A ton of bricks settle inside me, how could I have been so fucking stupid! How did I not put this together sooner, Alexander Maximoff is a vampire––an original vampire to be exact. He's my father which means...I'm a fucking vampire! Holy shit, my heart is beating erratically, how the fuck am I vampire? I don't drink blood and I don't burn in the daylight. I know Cairo said that they can go in the sun, they just get sunburnt fast, but I don't burn, I tan! I stand and start pacing the living room, is this why Cairo didn't tell me who he was to me? Do my brothers know or am I the last to figure this shit out? I stop pacing and stare down at my flat stomach, is my baby a vampire?

Oh, sweet baby Jesus!

Is my baby going to be a mutant half breed?

"What's wrong sis?" I snap my gaze up to see my brothers entering the house, followed by the Reeves siblings, Cairo, and the two men. They both turn toward me, and I swallow loudly, all the noise around me is muted as I scan over the man with the dark eyes that almost seem black, his gaze runs over me.

"Am I a vampire?" I blurt, my question is met with silence, I spy Cairo out the corner of my eye walking toward me. When he reaches out I back away, he frowns at me, and I shake my head. "You never told me once, you never helped me connect the dots when you dropped the daddy bomb." I turn to look at my brothers. "Did you know?" Cass drops his head, Hunter looks at the roof, but Blake meets my stare and I see remorse––They knew.

"We thought you got it Belle, we had no idea you didn't put two and two together yet." On top of feeling betrayed I now feel stupid, how did I let this go over my head? I mentally facepalm myself, I got so distracted by Cairo, that I didn't even think on the matter much.

"You're half." I face Alexander, he smiles tenderly and some of my anger abates. I run my eyes over him and that's when I see the blood-soaked shirt and how he has his hand clutched to his stomach, trying to stop the flow of blood.

"You're bleeding." I state even though it's bloody obvious. The other man Vince and Zeke help him over to the couch and lay him down, Creed and Cole chat with them but all I hear is white noise as my brothers and Cairo surround me.

"If this is too much we can leave." I shake my head and Cairo releases a relieved sigh. "I'm sorry Belle, we should have said something but shit just...spiraled and I guess we just didn't care. We see you as our sister and that's it." Hunter's words have tears gathering in my eyes and I quickly blink them away.

"I'm sorry beauty, I never thought to tell you." I look to Cairo.

"Am I even a wolf?" He smiles sadly.

"Yeah babe, your half shifter and half vampire, but I swear that is all I know about your heritage." I believe him, I thank each of them and push through so I can go to Alexander, I have need to hear the truth from him and find out what the hell I am and why he gave me up. Sky told me a small amount about him and so has Ro, but the man is still an enigma to me. Cole and Creed have his shirt open, and the slice down his abdomen looks severe, my knowledge of vampires is very minimal, I assumed that they didn't bleed because ya know––they're already dead! I take a few calming breaths, Cole rushes away to grab some towels, Vince and Z block my view of Alexander's face. I catch Callie's eyes on me, but I just stand here, numb. Cairo approaches me and grips my hand, I turn my head to look at him, he smiles comfortingly, and I appreciate his support.

"Vince, why the hell are you here?" Creed asks as he grabs one of the towels from Cole and applies pressure to the wound.

"Because your mother has turned."

"What the hell does that mean?" Cole snaps. Vince doesn't answer as Callie cuts him off.

"Dear old mom decided to work with the council and wants Belle for some reason, and they agreed to help, right?" To say I'm taken back by her words is an understatement, Vince meets her gaze and the sorrowful look he gives her is answer enough.

"No, she was changing and doing good." Vince places a blood-soaked hand on Creed's shoulder trying to comfort him, but Creed shakes him off with a growl.

"She isn't who you think she is."

"How the fuck would you know Vince? You think because you were fucking her that you know better than me?" Vince glowers at Creed.

"He knows she is a traitor because I planted him with her." My eyes bulge at Alexanders whispered words, Zeke whistles and it is the only sound for a beat before Cole snaps.

"I fucking knew she was a good for nothing bitch!" Creed lashes out and shoves Cole, he stumbles backward toward me, but Cairo is fast to react. He hauls me behind him and steadies Cole before growling at Creed.

"I get your pissed, but if you hurt my mate or my kid in anyway––."

"You're pregnant?" Silence, I'm ever so thankful for the fact Cairo's hulking form is blocking me from Alexander's view. I meet Vince's gaze over Cairo's shoulder, and I'm weirded out at the fact that he is smiling wide. I wrap my arms around my stomach protectively, I don't know why I feel so insecure about him knowing I'm with child. I haven't even told my *dad*. I don't care what anyone says, Gabriel Wilder is my dad, and that is the end of it.

"That's none of your business." Blake snarls.

"If she is pregnant, then yeah it actually is my business." Alexander's voice waivers, clearly the pain is getting to be too much.

"Let's deal with this later, right now we have to figure out how to stop the bleeding and then we deal with getting your beta back." At the mention of Sky, Z and Cairo offer their help and assist Creed and Cole.

You learn something new every day, apparently vampire blood can heal you except with Alexander being an *original* vampire it doesn't work on him. Unfortunately for us there is no pack doctor here, they have managed to stop the bleeding. Zeke and Cole went to the store earlier to get some supplies to stich Alexander's wound, I couldn't stomach the sight and even being a supernatural, he wasn't immune to the pain of it and screamed for a bit until he passed out. It took, Cairo, Cole, Zeke, Cass and Vince to hold him down, while Creed stitched and bandaged his wound. He's still currently passed out and it's nearly evening, Cairo has been pacing nonstop, anxiously waiting for him to wake up so he can grill him for answers. Cole, Callie, Blake and Zeke decided they couldn't just do nothing, so they left an hour ago to scout out the area in hopes of catching a scent. Creed ordered them to remain in wolf form in case the council has spies out and spotted them, clever thinking on his part.

Cass, Hunter and I are all sitting on one of the couches, Creed occupies one of the single seats and Vince is just leaning against the wall with his arms crossed over his chest. He is a handsome looking man, Caramel eyes, light brown hair and his teeth are perfectly white and straight. I also noticed he has an accent which is pretty cool, Alexander has one too, but I can't place his. The silence is suffocating, so I decide to break it.

"How do you know Alexander?" Vince's kind eyes soften as they land on me.

"Ah, that one is a tricky question to answer." I roll my eyes.

"Make it not tricky then." He smirks.

"I see you got his no-bullshit attitude." I squirm at his assumption.

"I'm nothing like him, his DNA may flow through me, but that is where our similarities end." Vince nods, then darts his gaze to Alexander before returning it to me, I can see he is torn between telling me something or not, so I push.

"Just say whatever it is." I can feel the others staring at us, but I keep my focus on Vince, this guy knows something.

"You sure you don't want to hear this from him?" I quirk a brow at him, and he chuckles. "Guess not." He sighs and runs a hand through his hair before looking to Creed and then Cairo who has now stopped pacing and is paying attention to the conversation. "I lied to you all back on the island."

"About?" Creed's tone is stern.

"I don't have a sister." Cairo scoffs and mumbles.

"Figures."

"What's your point Vince? Don't give me the long story, just give the cliff notes, because I am out of patience, I'm anxious to get the fuck home to my mate and son."

"Okay, Alexander is my half-brother, and I am also an original vampire." Yeah, wow okay. He has stunned everyone silent; Creed's gaze burns into Vince.

"Start from the fucking beginning!" Cairo grinds out.

"He was raised in Romania, and I was raised in Australia by my human mother until she died, then I sought out my father. You see being a born vampire, means you don't thirst for blood like a turned vamp, or even have any of the abilities of one."

"What does that mean?" Cass cuts in.

"It means that in order for your vampire side to...awaken I guess you could call it, is to kill." I gasp. "I unintentionally activated mine, once I landed in Romania, I saw a woman being assaulted by a group of guys, I found a steel pole and beat them off her, but I got one in the head, and he later died in hospital. Needless to say, I became a vamp and caused enough damage to garner the attention of my brother who found me, Alexander isn't a bad guy."

"Then why the fuck has he been a cagey bastard, and not giving the whole truth?" Cairo demands.

"Because knowledge is power, and you knowing too much would cause others to come for you." All Eyes swing to Alexander who is now awake, Vince rushes to his side and helps him sit up. Alexander asks Vince to help him remove his blood-soaked shirt and when his chest becomes visible, my eyes widen, and I cover my mouth at the sight of the tattoo on his pec.

Miracolul meu, Gabrielle

My name is tattooed across his chest! I have no idea what the inscription before my name means, but my freaking name is right there! My mouth is agape, and my eyes are stuck staring at his chest, silence begins to descend and I'm pretty sure it's because everyone else has noticed my name as well.

"W-why do you have my name?" His dark gaze swings to me, I still at the intensity in his eyes.

"So, I could keep you with me always." It's such a raw and honest answer that I didn't expect it.

"What does it mean?" I whisper slightly embarrassed by everyone being here and listening in to this private conversation.

"My miracle, Gabrielle." I don't have a response; I don't know what I'm supposed to say to that. If I was such a miracle to him, then why the hell did he throw me away like a piece of trash? "I can see you are hurt and angry, and you have every right to be mad. I did what I did in order to assure you had a chance at life."

"What does that even mean, and how the hell is this possible? We saw our mother pregnant, and she went into labor with Belle." The disbelief in Hunter's voice is understandable.

"Yes, you saw all of those things, but it wasn't as it seemed."

"Explain this to us, now!" The command in Cass's voice is alpha worthy, Alexander smiles at him and it sends a shiver down my spine.

"You will be worthy of your title when the time comes, but you will not be the only one that vies for her affection." I frown confused as hell as to what he means. "The child your mother birthed, died, I offered your father a replacement, and in his grief-stricken state, he agreed."

"Wait, so, dad just...took Belle?"

"Yes Hunter. Your father couldn't bare the loss of a child, so he agreed, I took the deceased infant and allowed Davina to find it, so she would think that my child didn't survive." I'm sick to my stomach, an innocent baby was used to make everyone think I had died. What the hell is wrong with him, no, what the hell was my father thinking? "Gabriel is a good man, I trusted him to do right by my daughter——."

I scoff. "I am not your daughter; you and I may share blood, but that is it. I have a family and a father; you gave up your right the moment you discarded me." I'm pissed that I can hear the hurt in my own voice, still no flicker of emotion crosses his face.

"It was either place you with the Wilder's, or have you hunted your whole life; I chose the lesser of the two evils. I knew what was coming and I couldn't change it, no matter how hard I tried——I couldn't." My eyes widen.

"Holy crap!"

"What is it sis?" I shake my head in answer to Hunter and keep my gaze on Alexander who is now smiling like he won the lottery. "You have visions as well?" Gasps ring out around us.

"You get your gift from me; I had hoped that you wouldn't but——." I cut him off with a tirade of questions.

"How are you able to be touched? How can you be around people? Did a witch spell you as well?" He raises his hand to stop my onslaught of questions,

I clamp my mouth closed and wait. I feel Ro come up behind me and place a comforting hand on my shoulder, both my brothers are sitting up straight waiting for his answer.

"At first, I was much like you, but over time I learned to control it with the help of Vince and my father––your grandfather. Each original is born with a...gift." I look to to Vince and ask.

"What is yours?" Alexander chuckles, which earns him a glare from his brother.

"I have the power to evoke feelings." I furrow my brow in confusion.

"What does that mean?" Creed asks.

"It means I can control the way someone feels, I cannot create love, but I can manipulate it. I feel what someone is feeling and use it against them, like Davina."

"Holy shit." I turn to peer over at Creed. "You made Davina fall for you so you could get closer to her, didn't you?" Vince nods.

"She already had feelings for me, I just enhanced them for my gain." In a sick twisted sort of way, that is pretty cool, not if you're the one having it done to you though.

"Your visions can be led––." I cut Alexander off again.

"I'm not just having visions." I feel my brothers and Cairo's eyes burning holes into my head but ignore them. I may be pissed at Alexander but if this is my only chance to get details and help with my visions, I'll take it.

"Elaborate, please?"

"I get feelings now, like in the pit of my stomach and sometimes I am able to... I guess rewind time and see what someone saw. The penalty for that causes me pain, and with the ticking time bomb hanging over my head with these visions I don't like to do it."

"What do you mean *time bomb*?" I release a long exhale before answering Alexander, Vince drops down beside him and focuses on me.

"My visions are killing me." The three guys around me tense, I can almost taste Creed's shock at my admission. Vince and Alexander share a loaded look before turning back to me.

"Explain what happens––please?" Comes from Vince, I tell them about the headaches and the blood noses and how sometimes I cry tears of blood when I'm in the trance like state.

"Hmmm."

"What does, *hmmm* mean?" I snap at Alexander; a sad smile graces his face as he answers.

"You my dear, are very powerful, but you are in a human body." I take offense to that and glare at him, Cairo and my brother's growl. "I mean no offense." I cross my arms over my chest and slouch back into the couch.

"What are you trying to say?" Alexander moves his gaze over my head to look at Cairo.

"What I mean Cairo, is that she is neither wolf nor vampire, so she is in a fragile body with supernatural gifts. Being a shifter means you age slower but do eventually die, being a vampire means you are immortal, Belle is neither of those. She will age, she will die––." Four growls sound out, and it warms my heart.

"She isn't going anywhere!" Cass grits out.

"Damn fucking right."

"You can say that again." Hunter and Cairo say in unison. Alexander's gaze moves back to me and this time a grave look enters his eyes which has me tensing in my seat.

"You have a choice Gabrielle, evoke your shifter side, lose your gifts and have no visions, or, activate your vampire side, live forever and keep your gifts." I don't even have to think about it.

"How do I become a wolf?" A flicker or regret passes his gaze and I snicker, did he really think I would want to be a vampire because of him?

"Nature always has a balance my dear, a price––."

"I don't care, I hate these visions and want them gone no matter the cost––."

"Even if the cost is your child's life?" Cairo growls, Hunter and Cass still beside me, I stare wide eyed at him. "Becoming a shifter requires you to shift, the first shift is the worst as I'm sure these four can confirm for you. The toll it would take on your body would cause a miscarriage." Tears prick my eyes.

"I'll do it after the baby is born." I relay stubbornly, he smiles sadly and shakes his head.

"You weren't supposed to have fallen pregnant this early, I thought I had more time."

"The fuck does that mean?" Cairo shouts causing me to flinch at the anger in his tone.

"It means you should have kept your dick in your pants and stayed the fuck away from my daughter like I told you to." I recoil, Alexander is on his feet and vibrating with rage, Cairo moves from behind us to face off against him. Vince and Creed are on their feet pushing their way between the two men to stop the confrontation. "I warned you there would be a price, I never wanted this for her!"

"You didn't even fucking want her!" I wince, Cairo's words sting more than I want to admit. Alexander hisses, his eyes turning almost black.

"I gave up the most precious thing in the world to me to keep her safe, I just didn't count on her falling in love with the likes of you." He spits out at Cairo, I can't take this anymore, I stand with Cass and Hunter mirroring me.

"Why can't I wait till after the baby is born?"

"The pregnancy will kill you; your child is still half vampire, even without the curse being activated. It will feast on your blood and drain the life force from you, if you did manage to survive that, then the labor will kill you." I nod my head numbly, the conversation around me becomes white noise as I begin to spiral, I place my hands protectively over my stomach.

CHAPTER THIRTY

Cairo

I stand in the doorway and stare at her sleeping form, after Alexander's admission today she has been quiet. Her brothers have tried to talk to her, so has Callie, fuck even Creed tried, but she won't utter a word. I'm about to lose my shit soon, I have to find Sky and finish this shit with the council, only then can I focus solely on Belle and the baby and do what needs to be done. I always thought having a baby would be an exciting experience, and it wasn't until Alexander dropped the news that the mother to my child would die. It's only been a short time with Belle, but I love her, she has calmed the raging storm inside me and made me see things from a different perspective. Bex is fiercely devoted to her and everything there is to love about her, she is the end to our story, and I couldn't handle losing her. My phone vibrating in my pocket pulls me from my turmoil, I close the door quietly, then fish the phone from my pocket.

Unknown caller.

I hit the green button. "How did you get this number?"

"Ro it's me." I stumble back a step at the sound of Sky's voice, I brace myself against the wall in the hallway.

"Where are you? Are you okay?"

"I don't have long––."

"Tell me where you are, I'm coming now." I say as I head for the front door.

"You can't." I Freeze with my hand gripped around the handle of the front door.

"Why not?"

"Because it's...it has to be this way."

"No, it doesn't––."

"Cairo, listen to me!" I clamp my mouth closed. "This wild force inside me isn't staying buried any longer, I can use it to take them out."

"Skylar, please." The meek sound of my own voice has anger swirling inside me, I turn toward the kitchen to see the guys all huddled around watching me. I turn my gaze to Alexander who has a knowing look in his eyes.

"Cairo, it has to be this way. I don't have time to explain it." She cries out in pain and recoil at the sound of it.

"Sky!" I shout, her rapid breaths come through the phone, and I wait with bated breath to hear her voice.

"It's pushing through me Ro; I'm surprised I've lasted this long in control. Two nights from now under the harvest moon, they are going to try draw the power from inside me and harness it. They have two witches, my powers are stronger, they are meeting near Mount Wood, you need to be there to take out the witches and...me."

"Fuck off, I'm not doing it——."

"Hurry, we don't have much time." I still at the sound of the strange female's voice.

"Who the hell is that Sky?"

"A...friend, Cairo, You are the only one who can get to me."

"I'm begging you Sky, please don't make me do this."

"I'm so sorry, there is no other choice, they cannot have the power inside me Ro, If they get it, they will use it against all of you, and I won't let that happen."

"Use it now to get the fuck out of there!" I growl.

"I wish I could but the room I'm in is blocking my magic somehow, my...friend will send you the coordinates of the meet——."

"Sky, please——."

"I love you Ro——."

"Don't you dare say that like it's a goodbye!""I wish it wasn't, but it is, we can't outrun our destiny's, no matter how much we try. Tell Callie I love her——."

"Give me the phone." At the sound of her voice, I spin around to spot a tear-stricken California standing behind me with her hand outstretched. I grip the phone tighter not wanting to let go of the only part of Sky I have right now, but I know Callie needs this. I spot Belle leaning against the door jamb to our room with tears in her eyes, she implores me with a look to give Callie this moment with her...mate.

"I love you Skylar, and I'll find a way around this——I promise."

"Don't give me hope Ro." I hand the phone to Callie who shakily places it against her ear, Cole and Creed move closer but stay back giving her space. We all stand here with our gazes on Callie eavesdropping.

"California." Callie sobs at the sound of her voice. "Don't cry babe."

"You're not coming back, are you?" The brokenness in her voice tears me up.

"Not this time babe, I don't have long——."

"How the fuck do you expect me to let you go?" I hear Sky's sharp inhale and I know without a doubt what she is about to do, and I wish with all my might, that she wouldn't, but she knows this is the only way Callie will let her go.

"You're going to let me go because I'm not your mate, I tricked you––." Callie's tears run down her cheeks like a stream.

"Don't do this Sky, I love you."

"I used you––."

"Stop it!" Callie shrieks. Cole and Creed move closer, but I raise my hand to stop them, she has to hear this, no matter how much it hurts.

"California, your mate is out there and I'm not it. I tricked you."

"I don't care, please Sky, please don't do this to me, I need you to fight baby. Come back to me." The sharp exhale from Sky tells me that this is killing her, she never wanted to hurt Callie, but Sky is like me, we use our anger and don't do feelings.

"Let me go California." Callie sobs and begins to shake. "Move on with your life because I won't be part of it anymore, I loved you before you even knew I existed. I'm not sorry that I tricked you, I would do it all again in a heartbeat. Be strong baby and know that my heart was always yours, it's always been you California." I hear the line go dead. Callie screams in agony and drops, but I catch her in time, she wails on me punching, slapping, kicking out and clawing my face, but I still hold her. Creed and Cole try to pry her from me, but I won't let them, she needs this outlet.

"I fucking hate you! This is all your fault; you get your fucking mate and a kid, but I don't get mine! If you do what she says and kill her, I'll fucking hunt you down and tear you apart." I take her anger; I take her hits and her kicks because everything she just said is true. I still have Belle and my baby, but she is losing the woman she loves. It is of no significance that Sky tricked her and made her believe that she was her mate, Callie still fell head over heels for my best friend.

"Don't cry for her." Callie pulls against my hold, and I let her go, so she can turn and face Cassius.

"Don't fucking speak to me!" He moves forward and grips her shoulders, Creed and Cole stalk closer, ready to take him down if he harms their sister. "You don't get to say her name!" She screams.

"You dishonor her by your actions, your...mate is a warrior and there is no greater honor for her than dying in the midst of a battle. I never got the chance to know her, but from what I have seen and heard, she is fierce and courageous; she wouldn't want you to cry over her."

"You know nothing about her, I told you before to stay the fuck away from me Cassius." She shoves him, but he won't budge, so she growls in warning, crouching low, ready to strike, her growls intensify the longer he stands there. The tone of her growls shifts, and I know her wolf is just there below the surface we have to stop this now!

"Sky has always known that this was coming." Callie stops growling, Cass moves to face Belle, who is walking toward us wearing only one of my shirts. I growl and quickly move toward her trying to shield her nakedness from the others, she rolls her eyes and sidesteps me as she continues toward Callie. "The first day you all came to my pack and Sky chased me down, I had a vision then, and a few after. They all gave me an insight of what is about to happen, she never knew of the exact time, only that it was getting closer. She instilled her magic in Cairo, so nature had its way of balancing things." She takes a shaky breath and steels her spine. "Sky made sure that there was always a way to...end herself, if the need should ever occur, and I believe she knew it would happen. I'm so sorry that this is happening to you Callie, I wish more than anything in the world that I could somehow give you more time with her." Callie breaks out into gut-wrenching sobs, Creed and Cole are there within a second to hold her. I move toward Belle and see the look of anguish in her eyes, she wishes she could comfort her friend, but thanks to these visions she is unable to do so.

It's nearly dawn, and I still haven't slept a wink, I tried but every time I closed my eyes, all I could picture was Sky. Hearing her voice tonight broke something inside me, she pushed me to believe in myself, and that I have the makings of a leader. Becoming an alpha cost my father his life, his best friend turned on him and I guess a part of me always worried that Sky would do the same. Instead, she proved me wrong by fighting alongside me, constantly watching my back, no matter what. Even if I was wrong, she would always be there for me, and then when no one was around she would rip me a new asshole until I finally saw the error in my ways. The sound of footfalls tears me from my trance, I watch as Alexander makes his way over to one of the empty couches and drops down, I lift my glass of whiskey and down the rest. I grab the bottle from the floor and pour myself another, maybe if I drink enough, I'll be able to forget about everything and finally sleep.

"You can't save her." I place the bottle back on the table and take another drink before answering him.

"I know."

"If you know, why do you fight it?" I narrow my gaze at him.

"Because unlike you, I don't drop shit and run when it gets hard, I'll never abandon her like you did Belle." I can hear the venom in my own voice, he doesn't show an ounce of emotion.

"I did what I had to do in order to ensure my daughters safety, will you do the same for your own child?" I take another gulp of my drink and relish in the burn as it slides down my throat.

"I thought we were talking about Sky?" That gets a reaction, he scowls at me, and I smirk. "You see, I know that we have a mole in our midst, I also know that Vince wasn't your only plant. So, who is the *friend* you have with Sky and what do you gain out of her death?"

"Your very intuitive. Skylar's end is the beginning of a plague, that none of you are prepared for. She is someone special and very powerful, the fact that she gave you a *key* to end her existence is something I didn't foresee."

"Why do you speak like you worship her?"

"Because Skylar Cage is someone to be worshipped. She is a witch who grew up with no guidance, she is the human raised by wolves and lived to tell the tale. You sit here and pity her, but she doesn't need it, Sky was never meant to live, she was hunted by the covens."

"What?"

"Skylar Cage is the daughter of two of the most powerful coven leaders." She could never remember her parents, we tried to find them but came up empty.

"How do you know all of this?"

"I've been around a long time; you tend to meet people and learn things." His cryptic answer has me grinding my teeth.

He knows more than he is saying.

I Know Bex,

"Your wolf will be the one to do it." I close the link between us and stare at him. "Your human side can't stomach the thought of hurting her, when the time comes your wolf will take control. Don't be too harsh on him, he will make the choice to save one and set the other free,"

"The fuck does that mean?" He smiles but it doesn't reach his eyes, the notion puts me on edge.

"If I told you, it would change the course, my daughter has yet to learn that. She sees things and should keep them to herself, but she shares it, therefore changing every one's paths. She will learn that less is more over time." We sit here in silence for a long while lost in our thoughts, until a question burns on my tongue.

"You know where Sky is, don't you?"

"Yes." He answers without hesitation.

"Where is she?" I growl, he shakes his head. I grip my glass so tight that it shatters in my hand, amber liquid drizzles down the arm of the chair.

"You're bleeding." He grits out.

"So?" I snap.

"I'm a vampire you fool!" *fuck!* I Jump to my feet and head for the kitchen, I turn on the faucet and place my hand under the running water. I shut off the faucet then grab the dish towel and wrap it around my hand, my shifter healing will kick in and close the wound in a couple of minutes. Deciding not to tempt fate, I wait until the wound has healed before rejoining Alexander.

"I cannot tell you where she is." I growl, my eyes flicker to my wolf's but he isn't fazed by the sight.

"Why?"

"Because things are set in motion that can't be changed, hate me all you want, but just know that this is the only way to ensure my daughter's safety."

"She is mine to protect, not yours!" Anger clouds his features.

"Then start by protecting the life that grows within her!"

"I am!"

"You are not! You want her to act pretty and be seen, but not heard, she is going to die, and so will the child, if she doesn't transition to a vampire!"

"How the fuck do you know that?"

"I have seen it; She doesn't have a choice Cairo, she needs––."

"Bullshit, you just want her to be the same as you!"

"You stupid fool, becoming a vampire is something I never wanted for her. Being immortal isn't a gift. Living and knowing that your days are numbered makes you appreciate the life you are given, death is what makes life enjoyable, because you live for the moment. She will never get that when she transitions, her life will lose the joy she is used to." I can hear the truth in his words and that pisses me off. "You may hate the idea of her changing, but it is her only option." Instead of cursing him out and storming off, I decide maturity is my best bet.

"What happens to the baby if she changes?" His gaze locks onto mine.

"The child will live, but I don't know if the change will affect its...race." A whoosh of air escapes me.

"So basically, you just came out here to give me more questions than answers?"

"No, I came out here to tell you that in two nights time, you will do what you swore you would never, and that I need you to convince Belle to transition."

I got jack shit sleep last night, I'm moody and irritated, and have been snapping at everyone all morning. I can't just sit here and do nothing; Callie won't even look at me and the guilt I feel about this whole situation is killing me. I'm also pissed, because I woke up to an empty bed and found out that Belle had left to go for a walk with Alexander so they could *talk*. She should have spoken to me about this before leaving!

"Brother, you have a face like a smacked ass." I glare at Creed from my seat on the porch step. The beefy fucker drops down beside me and hands me a sandwich, I want to refuse but Bex growls, so I take it and scarf it down. "I heard you and Alex talking last night." I stiffen.

"And?"

"I don't know what to make of what he said. I heard the truth in his words about Belle, is that a risk you want to take?" I deflate at the reminder.

"I don't know, what happens to my kid? Will it be okay if she becomes a vampire? Will she still be her?" I have all these questions and I can't seem to regulate a fucking proper emotion because I'm so sidetracked constantly thinking about this shit with Sky. The guilt I feel is eating away at me daily, and I don't know how much more I can take before I break!

"I can't answer any of those, I wish I could, but I can't. I know you have a lot on your plate with everything that is going on, so don't beat yourself up too much. Let's deal with the Sky situation first, huh?" A relieved sigh escapes me.

"Okay."

"What's the plan?"

"I don't have one." I admit.

"Well, we have the day to come up with one, where do you want to start?"

Chapter Thirty-One

Belle

We continue to stroll along a worn path through the wooded area surrounding the house, birds chirp and wildlife tracks can be spotted. I was in shock when Alexander asked me if I would take a walk with him, I didn't want to disturb Cairo because I know he hasn't been sleeping, so I asked the others to tell him of my where abouts. I know he will be angry, but honestly, if this is going to work between us, he has to trust my judgment. Alexander has made sure to keep enough space between us, so his close proximity doesn't set off a vision. I have so many questions for him in regard to my visions, but I haven't the courage to ask him. I know that seems stupid, since I'm literally out in the woods with a stranger, but a part of me trusts him. The man could kill me a hundred times over, but hasn't, so that has to count for something, right?

"Do you mind if we sit?" I nod and follow him over to a patch of grass beneath a huge tree, he leans back and stretches his long legs out in front of him. I sit cross legged and pluck at the blades of grass to give me something to do other than sitting here awkwardly. "If you have questions, I'm happy to answer them?" His tone is light and inviting, it calms my nerves slightly, allowing me time to conjure up the courage for my questions.

"How can I control the visions?" I ask without meeting his gaze.

"That's a catch twenty-two situation, it can be done, but it takes practice, and a lot of it."

"So, I'm screwed?" He chuckles.

"No, not at all."

"If I become a shifter though, that means I won't have to worry about them, right?" I turn to him, and when a look of hesitation passes through his gaze, dread starts to pool in my belly.

"I don't want to lie to you Belle––."

"Then don't!"

"If you choose to shift, your baby will die, you won't last the term of your pregnancy, because the child will drain your life force." To say I'm in shock is an understatement, my mouth opens and closes like a fish out of water. "Your only option is to activate your vampire side ––."

"No!" I snap whilst shaking my head vigorously.

"You don't have a choice; I had hoped to arrive before you and him...*mingled*." I cringe at his innuendo.

"Well, you didn't, plus how the hell would I activate my shifter side? I'm over eighteen, and isn't that the cutoff date or something?" He smiles but it's a sad one.

"Witchcraft my dear." I scrunch my face in confusion. "I know a few witches and would have asked them to perform a spell that pulled your wolf out and muted your vampire side."

"Where's my mother?" I blurt out, I'm startled at the question that came out of me, I slap a hand over my mouth. Sadness lingers in his features for a long while, before he answers, the tone of his voice is coated in heartbreak.

"Your mother died giving birth to you." That stings, I have lived with the guilt of thinking I killed my mother since I was young, and now, I thought maybe if my real mom was alive, it would wash away the guilt, I was wrong. "She was amazing, a force to be feared and adored, all at the same time. She was the most beautiful woman I had ever laid eyes on."

"It sounds like you really cared about her." He laughs, but there is no humor to it.

"She is the reason for who I am today, she was all my reasons, if it wasn't for her, I would never have sought peace with the shifters."

"What do you mean?"

"I approached Austin Cruz because of her, the existence of vampires isn't widely known, only a few shifters know of our existence. I thought they were savages and beneath us, until I met Kiara, I sought to try and find peace among the races so we could all live...peacefully. It all changed when Austin was murdered, I thought taking Davina Reeves would change that, but she is the worst of them all."

"Wait, I thought she was trying to help the vampires and shifters?" He growls but it doesn't have any effect, he isn't a shifter, so it just sounds comical.

"She is a vile pathological liar, she made out that we tortured her. I never met Davina until about twenty years ago, Vince was the one who intercepted her when she ran. She wants to destroy the shifters and make vampires the superior race."

"I don't see how that doesn't benefit you though?" I know I sound like a bitch, but why would he fight for the shifters when he's a vampire? His eyes take on a sympathetic look, and it baffles me.

"How could I let the race that gave me the love of my life and the most precious miracle be dammed?" That shocks the shit out of me. "I fight against her because if all shifters are to be dammed, then that means my daughter would be to. She let the others believe that *she* hid you to keep you safe, the truth is, she had no idea where you were. I mean why would a vampire hide one of their own with the race they hate. Those vampires on that island are all created by my blood, and it sickens me."

"Wait, what?"

"You see when a wolf bites a vampire, their venom is lethal to our kind, the only blood that can heal a wolf bite is an original. I left vials of my blood with Vince, so if that occurred, he would have a cure to save them. A drop of my blood can turn anyone into a vampire, if they die with it in their system."

"So, like the Vampire Diaries?" He rolls his eyes and shakes his head.

"That show is lies."

"Why is Davina really hunting me?" All expression vanishes from his face, causing me to tense.

"You're special−−."

"So help me God, if you say it's because of my visions, I may stake you myself!" I grumble, which earns me a chuckle.

"If you want to kill a vampire, go for the head."

"Noted."

"She wants you dead because your blood is the cure for vampirism." My eyes bug out of my head as I stare at him.

"Say what now?"

"Nature always finds a balance. You are the balance to our kind; a drop of your blood will cure any vampire and transform them back to a human." My mind is reeling with this knowledge.

"But, how?"

"You are the first of your kind Belle, it is never heard of vampires reproducing, because technically we are dead, but somehow, here you are."

"How does Davina know about me?" He shakes his head.

"I truly do not know; from what I can deduce, she doesn't exactly know that you are my daughter, only that your blood is the cure. She wants to eliminate you, because you are a threat to her army. She even orchestrated the capture of Cairo's mother and the original alpha to the Reeves pack. Kane and Shelley wanted peace like I do, Davina couldn't have that, so she handed them and Dela over to the council without hesitation." Before I can process what he said, a vision slams into me.

I'm standing outside an abandoned old building, glass is scattered along the path outside. Screams can be heard from inside; the sound sends shivers down my spine. The door to the building opens and a group of people run out, various cuts and grazes line their bodies.

"What the fuck is she?" One-man shouts.

"There is no way they can cage that bitch anymore." Another answers, the five of them take off running, and I decide to take a look inside. I make my way up the staircase and can hear shouts over the top of screams, shivers roll through me. I stop at the first landing and peer around only to find it empty; I take the stairs again to the next floor and cover my ears. The anguish in the scream is tangible, whoever this is must be in a lot of pain. Once at the top I move around the side to what used to be a conference room and pause. Sky is on her knees with her head thrown back, hands bound behind her back and four men stand around her with cattle prongs, they each take turns ramming the devices into her. Tears flow from my eyes; they are treating her like a wild animal!

"Release it now and this will all end!" I flick my gaze to the side of the room to see who spoke, lining the wall is the shifter council with the man Phillip at the front.

"You fool, it needs to be under the harvest moon." I snap my gaze to the other side and my jaw nearly hits the floor; Davina Reeves stands there with an angry look on her face. "She cannot do the transfer until the moon is at its peak, isn't that right Kayla?" I can't make out the girls features; she is shrouded by the shadows in the corner of the room.

"Tomorrow night is when this has to be done."

"I'll kill you all before I ever let you have my power!" Sky screams, I gasp when I see her eyes, they are pure white. Black veins course through her pale white skin, I can sense the power wafting off her in waves. Who the hell is Skylar Cage and what is she really?

"You don't have a choice, once you are dead your power will go to the one it deems strongest, and that will be me." Davina's eyes narrow at Phillip, clearly, they don't like each other but are working together out of necessity, not want.

"Take her back to her cell." A woman standing near Phillip barks, I watch as the woman Kayla comes from the shadows and hauls Sky up by her bound arms.

She has short blonde hair just past her ears, her blue eyes are devoid of emotion, if we weren't in this horrible situation, I would peg her as a cheerleader who thinks their own shit doesn't stink. I follow her and Sky from the room and down the stairs, this woman doesn't rush Sky and even wraps her arm around her waist to try ease her struggle.

"You better have a plan." Kayla whispers.

"I do." Sky answers.

"Care to share it with me, because Phillip or Davina cannot be the one to get your power Sky." She speaks to her as if they are familiar with one another.

"They won't get it."

"Why the fuck don't you just bust out of here?"

"Because this is where my path ends, I cannot outrun my demon any longer. I wish I could, but I cannot. I know now why it had to be at this exact moment, I have to die in order for another to live. Just do your part and all will end as it should."

"Cairo and Creed are going to kill me!" Kayla grits out.

"Are you worried about them or another Reeves sibling?" Kayla growls and Sky chuckles, but then begins to cough. We are now on the basement level in the room that I saw Sky in before.

"Tomorrow night——."

I bolt upright gasping; hands clasp my face and I shriek in fright until my eyes meet his and I relax. Worry lines mar his handsome face, I'm trying to regulate my breathing while he runs his eyes over me checking for injuries. I notice we are back in the living room; I pat his hands indicating for him to release me and he does. I swing my legs over the side of the couch and hunch over.

"Beauty, what happened?" The tone of his voice has guilt swirling inside me, I hate that he is worried about me because of my visions. I slowly sit up and look around noticing everyone is here, and I cringe, I spot Alexander leaning against the far wall with a worried look in his eyes.

"It was just a vision." I whisper, my throat is dry and coarse, Blake moves toward me and hands me a bottle of water, patting me on the head which earns him a glare from me. I didn't realize how thirsty I was nearly draining the whole thing.

"Is...did you fall? Is the...bean okay?" Oh shit, I place my hand against my stomach and berate myself internally for forgetting about the baby.

"She was seated when it begun, no harm has befallen the child." I snap my gaze to Alexanders.

"It didn't hurt when it happened, my head isn't aching now, why?" He holds my stare as he answers me.

"Because I guided you, your visions are powerful, with the correct guidance and help, they won't harm you."

"So, she won't die?" Cass asks.

"With the correct training, no, left unchecked it can cause a brain bleed from the pressure of them."

"Then train her!" Hunter growls.

"It isn't that simple pup; training takes time, and right now we don't have that."

"Alexander!" Vince reprimands him sternly. "Do not give false hope where there is nothing to be found." I tune Alex and Vince out as I turn to face Cairo, his eyes are on me already. I reach out and grip both his hands in mine, he pulls free and then wraps his arms around me hauling me onto his lap. I smile and run my fingers through his hair, he places his hand against my stomach, and I stop breathing for a moment.

"I'm sorry I worried you." A whoosh of air escapes him.

"I didn't expect to be so overcome by my emotions when I saw Alex walking toward us with you in his arms. Fuck beauty, I had to fight my wolf just to stay in control." Guilt gnaws at me once again.

"I'm okay, I swear."

"Just...let me hold you for a bit." I nod my head and lean into him. Conversation around us becomes white noise as I get lost in the feel of him, he has become somewhat of a safe haven for me, in such a short time.

"Belle?" I answer Creed without moving my head from Cairo's shoulder. "Hmmm."

"Can you tell us what you saw?" I tense, Cairo being the ever observant being that he is, notices and tightens his hold on me. I'm not sure how to explain what I saw, it was horrific and disgusting, no one––I mean no one, should ever have to go through what Sky is going through right now. Cairo draws soothing circles on my back with one hand and has his other splayed across my abdomen protectively, I swoon a little. I take a few deep breaths trying to build the courage, I need to tell them what I saw.

By the time I finish telling them wat I saw Cairo is tense and vibrating with anger, growls continue to tumble out of him, Creed and Cole have their sisters sobbing form wrapped in a tight embrace with looks of murderous rage plastered across their faces. Zeke looks like he is ready to smash something, my brothers even look angry. Alexander and Vince look...impassive. It almost seems like this is something they were expecting, which confuses me.

"I knew she was a spineless cunt from the moment we met her on that fucking island!" The venom in Cole's tone has an icy shiver sliding down my spine.

"I-I left her alone with my son, I trusted her." The devastation in Creed's voice has my heart aching for him, out of the three Reeves siblings, he is the one who let her in. I know her betrayal will be hitting him the hardest, and my heart goes out to him for that.

"I'm going to tear them apart piece by piece until they die *slowly* from blood loss." Zeke sounds so resolute in his vow and the look in his eyes tells me he means every word.

"What the fuck is Kayla doing there?" My gaze swings to Callie, tears continue to stream down her cheeks. "What else was said about tomorrow? Did they say a time?"

"I don't know who the woman is, she was helping Sky from what I could see. When the moon is at its peak, the power transfer will be done, my vision cut out before a time was confirmed—I'm sorry." Cairo growls again.

"You have nothing to be sorry for beauty, we know more than we did a few hours ago." He moves his head, so he is staring straight at Alexander. "Why do I get the feeling that Kayla is another one of your plants?" Cole gasps and his eyes widen as he stares at Alexander.

"Holy fuck! Ro is right, she was with you that night when Jacob died, so was Phillip." Cole starts growling, Creed and Zeke move to restrain him while Alexander sits there with a blank look on his face.

"You need to explain yourself now." I snap at Alex.

"I was there that night because I had recon to do."

"You stood by and did nothing!" Cole shouts.

"I needed the council leader to believe I was on his side; Kayla was Jacob's captive, and no one expected him to transfer his alpha power to her." Creed's face morphs from anger to shock.

"Wait, so Kayla is an alpha? That means Jess isn't the only female anymore."

"No Mr. Reeves, your wife is the first and Kayla Michaelson is the second. I made a deal with her, if she agreed to work for me and infiltrate the council, I would make sure that her father never made it out of that fight with your wife alive."

"Why Kayla?" Cole growls, he's vibrating with anger, and I don't understand why he is so upset over this woman being a mole.

"Because once Phillip realized that he could have a female alpha of his own, it wasn't hard to get her in. Phillip believes that Kayla wants to be part of the *new* council, in reality she hates them about as much as she hated her father. She blames them for her father having free reign to do whatever he wanted with her, she is an asset, and without her, none of us would've known where Skylar is being held."

"So, you know when they will move her?" He shakes his head in answer to my question.

"No, she is still not part of their inner circle yet, so all details concerning Sky are kept close to the council's chest. What we do know, is they have two other witches with them, from the information we know, they have no desire to be there and wish to return to their coven."

"Kayla told you that?" Z asks.

"Yes, she made a deal with the witches and guaranteed their safety home, if they agreed not to participate in the event tomorrow night."

"Why the fuck would they agree to that?" Creed snaps at him.

"Because they were taken from their covens against their own will, how Phillip managed to accomplish that is beyond me. He's under the impression that if Sky's power transfers over to him, he'll be able to eradicate all other races and rule over the entirety of the shifters."

"Why are all men ruled by the need for power." I grumble.

"Phillip is a pest; he is only on the council because his father and grandfather were fierce and respected warriors, so their kin are automatically granted a place on the council. Phillip has never fought a battle or seen a war, his father did him the disservice of keeping him sheltered, but in reality, all it did was create an entitled pest."

"From what I saw, Sky is battling to remain in control of her own power. Even with these witches agreeing not to take part in whatever it is, how do we stop Phillip from taking it?" I ask, I'm shocked when it's Cass that answers and not Alex.

"She's already chosen her successor." All eyes are on my brother.

"You're correct, Skylar may not be able to harness the power inside her, but make no mistake, whoever she chooses will have to be trained by a coven or they will meet the same fate as Sky. I believe Phillip has known about Skylar from the start, I would even go as far as to hedge that he is the culprit who ordered the deaths of her parents." Growls and curses sprout out around the room.

"Fuck me. Jess was never the target, was she?" Creed's gaze swings to Cairo in confusion. "He didn't know I was alive until Jess came back, I served Sky up to him on a silver platter when I came for Jess." Alexander's eyes soften as he looks at Ro.

"Yes, he was never able to locate her until you came out of hiding to save your sister. Your sister was a target, he wanted to have the first female alpha, but she no longer matters to him as he *thinks* he has Kayla." Ro shudders beneath me and I know he is warring with his wolf internally over the guilt he is feeling. He didn't realize saving his sister would cost him the life of his best friend.

"Ro, you didn't know––." Cairo cuts Creed off.

"I should have fucking known! It was my job to protect her, I promised her I would find a way to stop this shit from happening and I failed!" The anguish and pain in his voice guts me. Z steps forward and stands in the center of the room with his gaze fixed on Ro.

"Skylar wouldn't have changed a thing about her life, she always said she would never die laying down. Don't you dare sit there and act like this isn't the way she wants to go out, she is no fucking pussy!"

"Shut up!" Everyone stares at Callie. "All of you shut the fuck up, she isn't dead, and we can find a way to stop this––we have to!" Vince moves toward Callie with his hands raised, he places them on her shoulders and bends, so they are eye level.

"As a young pup, you shifted because that is what nature intended for you. Sky is much the same, she doesn't have a choice she has to expel this power inside her, if she doesn't, she will become an unstoppable force that none of u will be able to contain. Sky knows this and is willing to sacrifice herself in order for us to live. How she knew this time was coming I don't know, not even my brother knows the answer to that. Your mate is a selfless hero, and this is solely her decision, so what she is about to do, is honorable."

CHAPTER THIRTY-TWO

Cairo

I sit on the front porch and look up at the night Sky, I couldn't bring myself to dine with the others. The vibe inside that house is dull and broken, it's hard to sit in there without snapping, at them when they look at me with pity. I can take the hatred in Callie's eyes when she looks at me, I can handle anger and rage, but pity and guilt for my situation is something I can't stomach. I jump up and head inside when I hear Belle shout for me, I kick the door open and scan the area heaving, looking for the threat. I frown when I see her on the couch with Alexander and Callie sitting opposite them with a hopeful look, I look to the left to see the rest of the guys standing there smiling.

"What's going on?" Belle turns to Alex and nods her head encouraging him to speak.

If he doesn't speak soon, I'll tear his throat out.

Our mate won't like that Bex.

We can make it up to her.

I fight the smile that wants to break free, Bex can't stand Alexander and I'm glad we are both on the same page because I don't trust the old fucker.

"I have a way, with the help of Belle to send you and California to Sky."

"How?" I ask, I hate that hope blossoms inside me.

"It would only be in a dream like state, almost like Astro projecting, Sky will be able to see and hear and vice versa. You won't have long though, and this will be the only time it can happen." I narrow my eyes.

"Why?" I snap, he sighs and turns his gaze to Callie.

"Because Sky has agreed to use her power to funnel you to her, but only this once. She doesn't have much control over her power at the moment, this is risky and if it goes wrong——." Callie cuts him off. A growl comes from the kitchen, and I turn to see its Cass, why the fuck is he growling?

"Do it!"

"I'm in." I answer as I take a seat next to Callie, Belle's eyes move to me, and I smile reassuringly.

"I've never done this before——." I cut her off.

"I trust you beauty, you're stronger than you think babe, you got this." She beams at me, and I shoot her a wink. Callie tenses when I drop down next to her, I can take her looks and snide remarks but even for me being this close to her is––uncomfortable.

"Okay, I'm going to channel Belle as my anchor, the two of you need to join hands." Before I move and inch, I glare at him and ask.

"Why are you doing this? You don't like me, and you don't give a shit about Callie, so why?" He smirks.

"Because Gabrielle asked me if I could help in some way to give you both a chance at a proper goodbye, instead of that last phone call." Belle has a shade of red that coats her cheeks as she drops her gaze, I stand quickly and make my way to her clasping her face in my hands. I smile down at her and place a chaste kiss against her lips, ignoring the groans coming from the kitchen.

"Thank you." I whisper low enough for only her to hear, she smiles and shoos me back to my seat. Callie and I link hands––awkward is an understatement, but we grit our way through it. We close our eyes as Alexander instructs and wait for something to happen.

"Don't you have to chant or something?" I groan internally at Cole's dumbass question.

"No, you fool, this isn't a soap opera––." The rest of Vince's reply is cut off as I begin to feel like I'm falling.

I snap my eyes open and turn my head to the side to gag, it felt like I was in a dryer spinning around for hours. Nothing comes up but I continue to gag, I hear Callie beside me doing the same. When I finally get myself under control, I turn ready to lose my shit at Alexander but snap my mouth closed when I see a smiling Sky sitting on a couch. I jump to my feet and rush to her; she leaps into my arms, and I crush her against me. Tears cloud my vision as I inhale her scent, I feel her tears against my neck, I grip her hair and hold her closer.

"Sky––."

"Move asshole!" I chuckle, we release each other, and I step to the side allowing Callie the chance to move forward. They stand there staring at each other for a long moment, a sob tears from Callie as they rush into each other's arms. A whole lot of tears are being shed right now, so I decide to tune out their

hushed whispers and scan our surroundings, I furrow my brow in confusion. It is literally black; everywhere is black except for this little spot we stand in that has light--where it comes from, I have no idea. Two couches sit in the middle and that's it, I spin around in a circle thinking I've missed something, but I haven't. This place reminds me of something from the Matrix.

"Where are we?" I ask, I hear sniffling and then Sky leads Callie over to the couch she vacated, and I sit on the other facing them. Callie is wrapped around Sky like a blanket, I smile at her. I haven't seen her smile like this since she was taken; guilt is eating me alive as I meet my beta's gaze.

"Don't Ro." I can't help it though; I feel tears prick the backs of my eyes as I stare at her. Without her saying it out loud I know where we are. She didn't want us to see her beaten and bloody, so she brought us to another place where we would see the Sky we know and love. "It's nearly over." A gut-wrenching sob comes from Callie. I feel for her--I do, but all she bloody does now is cry! I mean can't a person run out of fucking tears.

"Don't say that, please don't say that. I can't--."

"Shhhh." Sky cups her face and brushes the loose strands of hair back as she places a soft kiss to her lips. "You can do anything Callie, your strong and sassy as fuck babe, you are a queen baby. Don't ever let anyone tell you otherwise." I smile at them, it's in this moment right here, right now, that I know I never loved Sky. I mean yes, I do love her, but not like how I love Belle, I latched onto her because she was all I had. I conjured up a love in my own head for her that never existed, She is my best friend, my sister, my...fuck, I can't even put what she means to me into words.

"Can we stop this from coming to pass?" Callie glares at me for cutting off their conversation, but I have to know the facts.

"No, I'm not myself anymore. You're in my mind right now because this is the only small space I occupy of my body, the Sky you will see isn't me Ro." I clench my hands into fists trying to fight off my rage. Sky pushes Callie and tells her to give her a minute before standing, I do the same and meet her in the middle. I peer down at her and my gut twists.

"How can you smile at me like that? I couldn't fucking stop this Sky, I-I couldn't save you." I can't stop them; tears leak from the corners of my eyes. She wraps her arms around my waist, and I do the same to her holding her close. I inhale her scent and cement it to my memory. Neither of us will say it because we don't want to upset Callie, but this is the last time either of us will see Skylar Cage as we know her. She pulls back and looks at me with tears streaming down her cheeks, I cup her face and brush the tears away with my thumbs.

"I've erected a bubble around us so Callie can't hear."

"Why?"

"Because she can't handle the truth Ro, I need you to watch over her and make sure she is okay."

"You have my word; I'll be there for her after your...gone." I choke the last part out and clear my throat, I need to be strong for her.

"It has to be you Ro." I shake my head denying her claim. She grips my face in her hands and holds my gaze. "It. Has. To. Be. You." I open my mouth to protest but she pushes on. "I know it's not fair and I'm so sorry, but you are the only one who has part of me inside, which is why you can get close enough to do it." I grip her face tighter as tears cascade down my face, I grit my teeth to try and stop the sob that wants to tear out of me.

"I can't Sky, I can't––."

"You must, if you don't Ro, I will kill everyone."

"Is there a cure?" She smiles sadly.

"No, the only way to have stopped this was to be trained as a child to control the wild magic inside me. Over time with it not being channeled, it turned dark, we knew this day would come. We can't bury our heads in the sand anymore, I love you and I'm so sorry it has to be you. Just know, giving my life means another will live. Trust me one last time Cairo, and I swear you will thank me for this heartache one day." I sob, I rest my forehead against hers and both of us stand here with our gazes locked, crying for the other. I can't even decipher what she just said, because my heart is breaking inside my chest. My best friend is no longer going to exist.

"I don't know how to live without you, since I was a child, all I have ever had is you." She smiles sadly and her grip on my shirt tightens.

"You have a mate now; she will guide you and be there for you Ro. Don't push her away, promise me."

"I won't, she's pregnant and I'm about to have a kid Sky, and you..." I can't talk past the lump in my throat.

"I will always be with you Ro, always. My power is draining, and I need time alone with Callie." I suck in a shuddering breath; I want to be selfish, but I know Callie needs this and so does Sky. I make sure she can see the love and devotion I have for her in my eyes as I say.

"I owe you my life, my pack, my alpha status. I owe you everything Skylar Cage, you will never be forgotten, do you hear me?" She nods as a sob rips out of her.

"I love you brother, more than anything." I pull her against me and wrap my arms around her, I meet Callie's gaze and the devastated look in her eyes kills me.

"I'll always love you Sky, always."

I come to, back on the couch, an ache so foreign to me forms in my chest and I feel like I can't breathe. I can't do this, I jump to my feet and run from the house ignoring everyone's shouts for me to come back. I don't even undress, I allow Bex control, and he shreds my clothes as he shifts, we take off toward the woods and don't stop running, my heart is breaking in half, I can't deal with it. This pain is like nothing I have ever experienced before, I feel like my chest is cracking open. Bex throws his head back and releases an agonizing howl, letting everyone know our agony.

Shut me down Bex. I beg of him; I need him to lock me away in the back of his mind and take away this excruciating hurt.

Only for a short time, you can't run from your hurt.

Just do it!

I scream at him, and he does, I welcome the sweet bliss of nothingness.

By the time Bex allows me out of my cage in his mind, I see the sun peeking over the horizon, we must have spent the night outdoors, and I know I should feel guilty for worrying the others, but I don't. I needed to be alone and just forget for a while. I wish with it being a new day that the feeling of what happened last night would lessen, but it doesn't, because today is *the* day. I don't know how I will be able to do as she asks, I could no sooner harm myself than Sky. If I could trade my life for hers, I would in a heartbeat.

We must return.

Not yet.

We are miles away and need to return so we can prepare for tonight.

Bex––.

I will not allow you to bear the burden, I will do what needs to be done and block you from the memory of it all.

Gratitude swells inside me.

I want to remember it all Bex, I just can't be the one to deliver the final blow.

Are you certain?

I take a moment to think on it, because I'm a sucker for punishment and love to self-sabotage, I tell Bex I don't want to be locked away when he does it. If Sky can sacrifice herself, the least I can do is be man enough to watch it happen. Bex takes us back, neither of us speak on the long trek back. By the time we break through the tree line, the sun is in the sky, I spot Creed and Belle on the porch steps with tired looks on their faces, Cole and Z are leaning against the house, the three Wilder brothers are at the other end of the porch and guilt gnaws at me that they waited out here all night. At the sound of me approaching they all turn tired eyes to me, once I'm at the base of the stairs Bex relinquishes control and I shift back. I take a few deep breaths whilst I'm on hands and knees naked, I try to ready myself for the onslaught of questions that they are going to ask me.

"We'll give you guys some time alone." I'm forever grateful to Creed in this moment, I hear their receding footsteps at the sound of the front door clicking shut, I finally stand. Belle has her hand outstretched with a pair of my sweats dangling from her hand. I thank her and quickly pull them on before I take a seat next to her. The silence between us isn't uncomfortable, each of us are lost in our own thoughts. Rather than use words I use actions, I wrap my arm around her shoulder and pull her into my side placing a kiss to the top of her head.

"Whatever happened last night is between you and Sky, you don't have to tell me." My gratitude and love for her swells inside me, fate sure didn't fuck up when they chose her as my mate. "I need to tell you something though." I tense at the seriousness in her voice. "Last night, after you left Alexander made me a proposition."

"What is it?" My voice is gruff.

"He offered to help me with my visions, as well as my...transition" I recoil away from her, she turns and faces me, the sadness in her eyes pisses me off.

"Don't you think we should have discussed this? I mean it is my fucking baby too!" She flinches at the anger in my tone, but I'm to pissed off right now to care.

"I won't survive the pregnancy if I don't do this Cairo, I can't shift because it will kill the baby, so that leaves me with one option." I scoff.

"Leaves *you* with one option, right. I mean it was only my cum that made the baby, so why should I get a say right?" I stand and glare down at her. "Do what you gotta do Gabrielle, I mean you're going to anyway right?" When she doesn't answer I shout at her. "Right?" The front door slams open, and I'm not surprised to see it's her brothers that come running to her defense.

"She didn't make the decision lightly." I snap my gaze to Cass and growl low in my throat in warning.

"And I'm sure the three of you were all to willing to help her make that choice, right? I mean after all; she will have to go with him, for well knowing that I can't abandon my pack, so it's a win *win* for everyone." I turn back to Belle and my anger rises further when I see tears trailing down her cheeks. "You do this, and I will never forgive you." She gasps but I'm done with this shit. I shoulder check Cassius on my way inside and head straight for my room so I can shower to try and get my head in the game in preparation for tonight.

I stare out the bedroom window watching the sun, in a few hours' time, I'm about to do the unthinkable, and the one person I wish was here to comfort me, has betrayed me. How the fuck could she make such a huge decision without me? None of us even know if it will be safe for the baby if she transitions, I growl and launch my fist through the wall of the room. I curse at the hole in the wall and then begin to pace to try get my anger to simmer down.

"You'll be paying for that." I growl and glower at Creed, he closes the door and leans against it with his arms crossed over his chest.

"If you're here to tell me she made the right choice, you can fuck off!" He scoffs and rolls his eyes.

"You stupid bastard, me of all people would be the last to agree with what she is doing." That causes me to pause my pacing. "I missed seeing my twins grow inside my wife, and I missed the birth of them, not to mention I missed ever getting the chance to meet my daughter." Once again guilt eats away at me, I'm such a fuck up! "I don't agree with her leaving with him and going to Romania, I know you can't follow her because of your obligations to your pack. I wouldn't wish what I went through on anyone, don't get me wrong, I know I fucked up, but I didn't deserve not to meet my daughter. That is something I will have to live with for the rest of my life." Sadness laces each of his words, I know it kills him that he never got to meet Katie. That is why Jess being pregnant again is such a blessing for them, after her complications with the twins.

"I'm sorry."

"Don't be, I made my bed, and now I have to lay in it. Learn from my fuck ups Cairo, don't miss this, because it will eat you alive from the inside out."

"How the fuck am I supposed to do that? I can't just up and leave my pack because my mate wants to run away with her daddy." I can hear the bitterness in my own voice. "I mean, why the fuck do they have to go to Romania? Why can't they just fucking stay here and who knows, I might even be able to help her."

"Have you thought about this from her point of view?" I narrow my eyes at him.

"Nah, not really. Plotting the murder of my best friend has kind of taken over my train of thought at the moment." He flinches.

"I know you are dealing––."

"You don't know shit!" I yell.

"Yeah, I fucking do! I was ready to kill my best friend if it meant getting to my mate, or did you forget that?"

"What happened between us isn't the same thing, we had a choice." My voice cracks. "She doesn't have a fucking choice and nor do I, I fucking hate that it has to be me." All the anger evaporates from his features and is replaced by understanding.

"My heart goes out to you brother, it really does, but it has to be you."

"You don't think I know that?"

"No, you're angry that it is you, but would you really trust anyone else to do what has to be done? Sky chose you for a reason Cairo, she knew you would be the only one strong enough to deliver her final wish. You are doing her a favor by ending her misery, if only I could change this outcome, but I can't. I wish I could do this for you Ro, I would give anything to take this burden from you brother." His words puncture a hole inside me, I drop down onto the edge of the bed and bury my face in my hands. A second later I feel the bed dip and Creed places his hand on my shoulder in support.

"I can't do this." I don't look up when I hear the bedroom open.

"Sky chose you, because she knew she could trust you to do it." I snap my head up and lock eyes with Callie. She stands in the middle of Zeke and Cole, who each wear looks of sadness. "I'm going to hate you for taking her from me." Her voice is watery, and I know she is close to tears. "She has to be set free Cairo; you are the one who can grant her that final wish. Lock your feelings down or do whatever it is that you need to do, but you set my girl free and end her suffering." My mouth drops open in shock. "Do you hear me? You end this for her!" Cole wraps his arm around her shoulders as the first tear falls from her eye, I stand leaving a foot of space between us as I hold her gaze.

"I'll take every ounce of your anger and hate, just know that when I do this, I won't just be killing her." She flinches at my words, but I push on. "I'll be killing a part of myself that I will never get back, let alone living with it for the rest of my life, this event will change everything California." She sniffs and wipes away her tears with the back of her hand.

"I know, which is why I am here telling you to do this, because I know you tried to stop it from coming to pass. You can't fight destiny Cairo, I fucking wish you could, but you can't."

Chapter Thirty-Three

Belle

My brothers, Vince, Alex and I all travel in one car while Cairo and the others travel together. We follow their taillights through the darkened roads heading toward the mountain ridge that Kayla told Alex about. Cairo hasn't said a word to me since I told him about my decision, it wasn't an easy one to make. I want to live and watch my baby grow, Alex made it clear that I was a once in a lifetime thing, he still doesn't know how he was able to procreate, part of him believes my mother had a witch cast a spell. He assured me that no harm would befall my child if I transitioned and call me stupid but I believe him. He told me that once the change has commenced, I will never be able to conceive again, this baby is the only child I will ever bare. I never thought children were a possibility for me a few months ago, so the thought of even having one is perfectly fine by me.

I know I should have consulted in Caro, but I'm the one who is at risk of dying, not him, so therefore I thought it only fitting I get to decide. I don't know why we have to travel to Romania, but it is part of the deal. I agreed to go, as long as I got to go and speak to my father before we left, he agreed. He also agreed that my brothers could accompany us if they wished and of course––they did. The only thing that's not in our favor is the transition has a time limit, Alex said I have to do it before my second trimester, because of the babies growth and its hunger, so I have to be strong enough for when it happens. Call me stupid but I thought you just kill someone and then––boom––you're a vampire, obviously I was wrong. I told him I couldn't kill anyone, that's not something I am able to do. He said we will go to a hospital and find someone in unbearable pain and offer them a humane way to end their life. It sickens me to think of doing something like that, but its kill or be killed, as he put it.

"Are we sure this is the right way?" Vince questions Alex.

"She said it was this mountain."

"What if they deceived her? Alex look, the moon isn't brightest on this side." I peer out the window from the backseat and Vince is right, the moon is brightest behind us. I close my eyes and wrack my brain for something from one of my visions about Sky and this night, I remember seeing a lot of peaks, and there were lakes as well as glaciers––I'm sure of it! I tell the guys what I saw and Alex and Vince both curse.

"We're going the wrong way!" Alexander snaps.

"How do you know?" Hunter asks.

"Because she just described Bare tooth mountain, not Rocky Mountain. Someone call the other car, we're turning around now." Vince pulls his phone out at his brother's orders and then passes it to me; I stare at him for a moment before meeting his gaze.

"He is acting like an ass, but he has to hear this from you." I nod my head and shakily grip the phone, he has Cairo's number punched in already, so I hit dial and wait, on the third ring he answers.

"What?"

"It's me." There's a pause, and I decide not to let the silence carry on as this is time sensitive. "We're turning around."

"Why?" I can hear the unease in his voice.

"Kayla was given the wrong information, what I saw in my visions doesn't match the surroundings she described." Another pause.

"Are you sure?" I sigh in relief that he isn't doubting me.

"Yes, the moon was so bright and practically above us in my vision, the way we are heading is away from the moon." He curses and then tells Creed to turn around and follow us, I grip the handle on my door as Alex spins the car around, the tires squeal in protest. He doesn't miss a beat as he slams his foot down on the gas and then we are heading back the way we came.

"Belle?" *Not beauty.*

"Yes?"

"Will we make it in time?" I take a shuddering breath and decide to be honest.

"I think we'll arrive at the end, there will be no more of *your* Sky by the time we reach her."

"Okay."

"Ro?" I hear him sigh.

"Yeah?" He sounds so defeated and it's crushing me that I can't help him.

"I'm sorry." I whisper, I wish we could have had this conversation in private but unfortunately with them being supernatural's, we can't escape their hearing.

"I know. I can't focus on that right now; I have to keep my focus on Sky."

"Okay." I say barely above a whisper.

"I have to go."

"Okay." I sound like I'm on repeat, but I honestly don't know what else to say. He ends the call and I hand Vince back his phone, my stomach is in knots, and I hate the feeling of uncertainty that is coursing through me.

"He'll come around sis, he just needs to get through his." I lean my head against the glass and sigh.

"I know Hunt, I just wish there was more I could have done to help him."

"You have done every fucking thing possible for that asshole Belle. He needs to pull his fucking head out of his ass and realize that, fucking quickly or he and I will finish what we started at the alpha challenge." The conviction and love in Cass's voice should make me feel better, but it doesn't. I rest my hand against my stomach and close my eyes.

I'm doing this for you Bean, I just hope your daddy can accept my decision and be there for us.

Yes, I have taken to referring to our child as *bean*.

"We're fifteen minutes away." Alex announces, my palms begin to grow clammy, and I know without a shadow of a doubt, Cairo will be feeling anxious and unsure. I wish I could go to him and try comfort him but I'm not able to do that, I know right now he needs to be in his own head ready for whatever is about to happen. We head toward the steep incline to the peak of one of the mountains, I'm about to ask Alex if he's sure this is the right way, but when I spot the broken gates, I bite my tongue. Clearly no one is supposed to be up here at night and the council didn't care. The tension in the car is so thick you can taste it, the closer we get, the more dread festers inside me. An ear shattering *boom* sounds out and Alex swerves from the shock before aligning the car, to avoid slipping off the narrow road.

"What the fuck was that?" Blake shouts.

"I believe Sky has just succumbed to the magic inside her and unleashed it." I answer, from what I saw in my vision, Cairo doesn't arrive until after she has taken out the council, and I'm assuming that is what just happened. We spot other cars and Alex slams the car in park before we all burst out of the vehicle, it's so dark out here, the only light we have to focus on is from the moon. Creed parks haphazardly near us, and they all pile out of the car, Cairo doesn't stop like the others, he takes off through the woods and I follow after him ignoring my brothers shouts to come back. I was supposed to remain behind in the car because I'm pregnant, but in my vision, I have to be there, I know in my heart that I'm right.

I can just make out his figure in the distance and make sure to watch where my feet are landing so I don't trip. I have no idea how he knows which direction to go, but I don't question it, I hear the others behind me gaining on us, willing my legs to go faster. If my brothers catch me, they will march me straight back to the car and I cannot allow that to happen. I hear screams of agony and cries for help––we're getting close. I see Cairo's figure disappear through the brush of trees, quickly following after him, when I break through, I slam to a stop and gawk at the carnage around me.

Oh my god.

My hand flies up to cover my mouth, the rancid smell of burnt flesh and singed hair assaults my nostrils. Wolves lay on the ground whining in agony––dying. I spot some of the council members littering the ground, nearly gagging at the sight in front of me. Some of them are missing limbs and the remainder of them are burnt, the others break through the trees, and I hear their gasps. I scan the area and that's when I spot them, Sky is standing on a dais at the other side of this clearing with Phillip kneeling in front of her, Cairo stands about ten feet away with his gaze fixated on Sky.

"You really thought you could control me?" Sky laughs but it sounds horrible, it reminds of the coughing sound a fifty-year-old smoker would make.

"You cannot––." Phillip doesn't get to finish, with a flick of her wrist a white light slices through him and I muffle my scream behind my hand when his head topples from his body. Sky finally turns to face Ro, and I gasp again; her face is so pale––translucent like. Black veins litter her once beautiful face, her eyes are black and that right there is the sign I needed. When Sky has used her magic before her eyes were white as I saw in my visions, the Sky we know is no longer here, the darkness has taken control of her.

"You are foolish to have come." Ro shakes his head and takes a tentative step forward but stops when she narrows her eyes.

"I will always come for you Sky." The devastation in his voice tells me he knows his Sky isn't with us.

"You are too late."

"Never! Let me fix this, I can help you––."

"I don't want your help!" She screams at him, her hair whips side to side as she shakes her head. "I have been repressed for far too long and I will not be caged any longer."

"Sky, I can help you." She glares at him.

"I will kill you."

"Let me help you." Her black eyes crinkle at the corners.

"You promised me you would never let this happen––."

"Please let me help you." She's toying with him, using his own guilt of not being able to save his best friend against him. The way he deflates, with his head drooping forward, shows me that she is getting to him, it's all and act and he needs to realize that.

"Your council is dead; your *chosen* mate is next––." A growl tears from his chest and he begins to vibrate with unbridled rage.

"You take me! You leave her out of this and take me instead, I'm the one you want, not her." Cass grips my arm and yanks me back until I'm behind him, I peer around his frame and watch as a nasty smile spreads across her face.

"I might just take you all." She hisses and before we know what is happening, she throws her head back and in seconds the wind is whipping around us and the sounds of trees cracking fill the clearing. I scream when one topples over inches away from us and smashes against the ground with a deafening boom.

"Get her out of here!" Alexander shouts at my brothers, none of us can move, the wind is so strong, I'm fighting to stay on my feet. Hunter fights against the force of the wind and wraps himself around me, I hate that he is using his own body as a human shield for me. I peer to the side and see Cole and Creed frantically looking around, that's when I notice what they are looking for. Callie is missing, and I would bet my life on the fact I know exactly where she is, I turn my head the other way and squint my eyes. The dust and leaves blowing everywhere is making it difficult to see, I spot a figure along the tree line near Cairo and just know that it's Callie.

"There!" I hear Cole shout, none of us will be able to get to her in time, the sound of fabric tearing has me turning back the other way, standing there in wolf form is both Reeves brothers, they take off toward Callie, but the wind keeps knocking them back. I look to Ro and see him struggling against the wind to reach Sky, for every step he takes he gets pushed back two, it's like he is going the wrong way on an escalator.

This is so much worse than my vision.

CHAPTER THIRTY-FOUR

Cairo

I fight against the force of her wind and try with all my might to reach her; I hear another tree fall in the distance and cringe. If I don't get to her soon, she is going to bring this whole forest down and we will all be caught in the crossfire.

Shift.

What?

I can fight against this force better than you can.

I have to talk to her Bex, I can––.

She is gone Cairo.

No!

You need to accept it, she is gone.

She said before though that––.

She is playing on your weakness for her, she is gone Cairo and we have to end this before she kills our mate and pup.

I turn to peer over my shoulder using Bex's eyes, I spot her huddled between Blake and Hunter, Alexander and Vince are gripping onto a nearby tree, Z is doing the same. I look for Cassius and the Reeves siblings but can't spot them, I dart my gaze around to see Creed and Cole in wolf form trying to come around behind Sky, I spot another wolf gaining on them from behind––Cassius. What the fuck are they doing? I turn back to Sky and watch in horror as I see Callie approaching the Dais from behind, she has scrapes and cuts littered across her face and arms from the debris that's flying around, she drops to her hands and knees clawing at the ground so she can get to Sky. My stomach drops when Sky spots her, she spins away from me and from the horrified look in Callie's eye's, she knows she's in deep shit. Bex is right, our Sky is gone.

Take control, don't shut me out Bexley.

I try to relax and grant him control, but my fear of what is about to happen makes it unbearable and I unintentionally fight against him.

Stop fighting me.

I try to do as he says but I know deep inside myself that when I let him take over, he will end her, and I don't know if I can live with that. My moment of distraction cost me, Callie is sent sailing through the air and smacks into a tree near Cassius, his wolf leaps on top of her, trying to protect her but it's futile, Sky throws him next, and then sets her sights on Creed and Cole.

"You will all perish and bow before me." Her voice has changed, its deeper and gruff, hearing it makes the final decision for me.

Do it and lock me away Bexley.

Are you certain?

I take a shuddering breath, the sounds of Creed and Cole's wolves whining in pain is like a bucket of ice water.

Yes, lock me down and do it Bex.

CHAPTER THIRTY-FIVE

Bexley

I force the shift and push Cairo back; I lock him away and grant him the small mercy of not being present to what is about to take place. The feeling of my fur billowing in the wind is what pulls me from my thoughts, I open the link between Zeke and I, issuing an alpha order.

Get my mate out of here now.

Alpha, we can't move. If I try to take her from here, there might be a chance of injury.

I growl.

Guard her with your life.

Yes, alpha.

I close the mind link and use Cole and Creed as the distraction that I need. My paws sink into the dirt beneath my feet, I push with all my strength to get closer to her. I grind my teeth in frustration, the wind is picking up and if I don't end this soon, we will all be crushed. I hear trees in the distance falling, two more near us drop to the ground with a deafening crack. I peer out the corner of my eye and see a naked, she is about to shift so she can get closer to Sky. Callie braces herself against the tree she hit, her gaze is focused on Sky and for a brief second something transpires between both of them, the wind dies down enough for me to make my move. I take off running as fast as my paws will carry me, and when I'm a foot out from her she spins around, surprise clouds her gaze as I launch through the air. She has no time to strike out or use her power, I clamp my jaws on the side of her neck, her shocked intake of breath has her blood oozing into my mouth through the puncture wounds. Not wanting her to suffer, I yank backward and spit her flesh from my mouth.

I meet her gaze and watch, as the black begins to recede from her eyes, the wind around us dies out completely. The choking sound she makes will haunt me for the rest of my days, blood splatters from her mouth and I wish I could look away, but I can't. For a brief moment as her eyes return to their normal color, I see the real Sky before she is gone, and the scream that tears from Callie will haunt me. I release Cairo from his cage and shift back so he can deal with this as he sees fit, I'm prepared for his anger and hatred toward me when he sees the damage I have done.

Chapter Thirty-Six

Cairo

My heart is shredded, a million tiny little pieces of that artery are floating throughout my body as I stare down at my best friend. I rush forward and drop down on my naked ass as I pull her onto my lap. Her muddy brown eyes are vacant, her soul has left her body. I throw my head back and scream! I never wanted it to end this way, I was supposed to stop this from happening, I promised her——I fucking promised her I wouldn't let this come true! I run my hand over her lids and slide them closed, tears pour from my eyes as I brush her cheek, I can feel the warmth beginning to leave her body. I look around me and find a discarded cloak, I grab it with my free hand and pull it over her like a blanket.

"Don't worry, I'll keep you warm and then you'll be back to normal in no time. You're Skylar Cage, you were born to t-torment me forever, remember?" I fight back the sob that wants to break free, an idea hits me. "I'll bring you back Sky, I'll bring you back!" I lean down and smash my lips against hers, I wait for the feeling of tingles to spread throughout my body like it always did when she siphoned me, but it doesn't happen. I pull back and then kiss her again...and again...and again. Frustrated that my efforts are proving futile I grip her face and shake her. "Wake the fuck up!" I scream.

"Babe." I snap my gaze to the left and growl; this is all her fucking fault! If she had stayed the fuck away from me and never pulled me to her, Sky would still be alive. I turn away and focus back on Sky. "She's gone Ro." Her words are like a dagger to my already shattered heart.

"Shut the fuck up! She just needs time to recoup and then she will be fine. You take all the time you need Sky; I'm right here, promise I won't leave you." I whisper in her ear, I use the cloak to cover the gaping wound on her neck, I can't stomach to see what I fucking did——no, what my fucking bastard of a wolf did!

I did it to save our mate, I'm sorry Cairo——.

Fuck off Bexley. I hate you.

And I will take all your rage and hate if it means you still live.

Bexley closes the link and I feel him shrink back giving me the space from him that I need, I hear footsteps approach me from behind and I stiffen when I catch their scents. A small delicate hand lands on my shoulder and I tense when she crouches down beside me, she reaches out and runs her hand through Sky's blonde her, a gut-wrenching sob tears from her and I die a little more inside. Z moves to the opposite side of Callie and grabs Sky's hand from under the cloak, I can feel both their emotions radiating off them.

"It was my honor and privilege to fight alongside you Skylar, you are the strongest fiercest warrior I have even known. Your fight is over now my friend, give them hell up there and hold nothing back." Zeke's words cause the lump in my throat to expand. He and Sky had their differences, but at the end of the day they both knew that when push came to shove, and shit hit the fan, their backs would always be covered by the other.

"I would trade places with you in heaven in a heartbeat, your time wasn't now." Callie leans down and places a kiss against Sky's lips...like a goodbye! I growl, her gaze snaps to mine and I glare at her.

"She's coming back! she just needs time to--to rejuvenate and then she will be back! Stop acting like she's--like she's--."

"Like she's dead?" I flinch, Callie squeezes my shoulder in support. She's barely spoken to me since Sky was taken and I hate that I feel like I didn't just...do what I did to Sky but also to Callie. She turns to Z and nods; he tries to pry Sky from me, and I growl.

"Touch her Zeke and I'll rip your goddamn head off!" Callie cups my face and applies pressure until I reluctantly face her, tears stream down her cheeks like a broken faucet. The look of hollowness in her eyes kills me.

"Let her go, Z is going to take her back to the car and then we can go be with her again." I open my mouth to argue but she pushes on. "I will not have my *mate* on this disgusting blood-soaked earth any longer, Zeke take Sky now!" Before I can argue or protest, I feel arms banding around my own and my neck, I'm yanked backward and roar when Z stands with Sky's limp body in his arms. I fight with all I have and turn side to side to see, Cole, Creed, Cass and Hunter holding me back.

"I'll fucking kill you all for this!" I scream, I fight harder than I ever have before when Zeke turns to walk away with Callie at his side and Sky in his arms. "Bring her back to me!" They ignore me as they continue to leave, the further they get the more reality begins to sink in, Sky is gone. I hear screams sound out around me, and it takes me a couple of minutes to realize the screams are my own, the four of them release their hold on me and I drop to my knees burying my face in my hands. I may have a mate, but I swear to the gods above that

Skylar was my soulmate, she was me, but without a dick, she gave me my life back. She was with me through everything, she loved me when no one else did, stuck with me through all the lows and never once abandoned me. I feel her in front of me, but I can't look at her, my eyes will say everything I'm feeling, and I'll lash out. She needs to get away from me before I destroy her.

"She knew this was going to−−."

"Belle, I don't think now is the right time."

"I'm sorry Creed, but Sky told me it had to be now, and no offense but I think she knows him better than anyone." I don't lift my gaze as I ask.

"What did she say?" My voice doesn't sound like my own, it's broken and raspy.

"That you will lash out and blame me, that you would push me away because you would blame yourself for this−−." A dark chuckle escapes me, I feel all their eyes on me and relish in the way they are all on edge and scared of what the beast will do next. I lift my gaze slowly to hers and smile darkly, she tries to hide her fear, but I can see it, taste it even.

"Oh beauty, I don't blame myself at all." Shock beings to cloud her features and when I see her begin to relax her shoulders, I deliver the final blow. "I. Blame. You!" Her eyes widen as she gasps, I push off the ground and slowly climb to my feet never taking my gaze off her, she trembles under the pressure of my stare. "Go home, go back to your daddy and take your brothers with you." Fresh tears roll down her cheeks.

"You don't mean that!" She argues but it's futile.

"You don't know shit, I just murdered my best friend, she was everything to me. Imagine the damage I will cause to you and that *thing* inside you−−."

"Cairo, stop."

"Shut the fuck up Cole, leave now and don't come back Gabrielle." I ignore her sobs as I brush past and take off after Zeke and Callie, I have a funeral to plan and my sisters bitch ass mother-in-law to kill. I couldn't scent the cunt when we entered the clearing, that slimy bitch is hiding away somewhere and when I fucking find her, I'll kill the bitch slowly and relish in her screams of pain. I won't grant her the mercy of death until I am ready, Davina Reeves thinks she is cunning and smart, but she has no idea who she just fucked with, I have nothing to lose and everything to gain. If I stay here all I'll do is blame and hurt Belle, I have roughly six months before I have to be back and ready for the arrival of my baby.

Run run as fast as you can Davina, because I'm coming for you, bitch!

CHAPTER THIRTY-SEVEN

ONE MONTH LATER

Belle

I sip my lavender tea as I gaze out over the landscape below us, it is such a cliché, but Alexander lives in a castle. He told me this place has been passed down through the generations and will one day be mine, the thing is I don't want it. Alex has been great at helping me try to control my visions, I don't sleepwalk or black out completely now. He says that once the transition is complete the pain will lessen, my human brain can't the force of my visions. The bonus about becoming a vampire is that my visions won't kill me. It's weird being here with him but I won't lie, I am beyond grateful for his help. I have never felt in control of my *gift* before, and within just a few weeks with him I can now navigate through them without passing out for hours. I'm still learning, but honestly for the first time in my life, I have hope.

There is only one thing I want right now, unfortunately that can't happen. Thoughts of him plague my mind daily––hourly––if I'm being honest. I miss him so much it hurts, the last time we saw each other was at Sky's burial. He and Callie agreed that she should be laid to rest where both their families are buried. He carried her casket but refused to speak, he stayed at the very back of the crowd and once it was over, he was already gone. We all learned that it was Davina that set up the attack on her Island, Creed is livid and out for blood because he now knows, his bio mom was the one who allowed Jess to be taken. Jess and Meg were distraught to learn that Davina is the reason that Kane and Shelley are dead, A shiver runs down my spine at the thought of this woman.

I haven't heard from him or seen him since the funeral. Jess, Cole, Creed and even Callie checks in with me regularly. Last I heard from Jess was that Zeke returned in the middle of the night taking half of Cairo's pack with him but wouldn't give them any details concerning his whereabouts. Jess told me Creed is taking Davina's betrayal hard, Cole and Callie have stayed back with them until Davina is found, their whole pack is on lockdown.

I visited my father before we left for Romania, I expected him to be angry that I was leaving and choosing this way of life, but he wasn't. He told me that he would love me no matter what, and that he will always support my decision. I didn't have the energy to get into any deep conversation about my upbringing and him not telling me about Alexander so we left it. We both know we will have to speak about it one day but until then we just deal with awkward elephant in the room.

"It's getting cold Belle." I peer over my shoulder and smile at Hunter.

"I want to feel everything before I can't anymore." In two days' time, Alex and I will visit the hospital and do what needs to be done. An elderly man wishes to die, due to being diagnosed with a brain tumor which is terminal, but the doctors forbid it, when Alex approached him about our situation the man eagerly agreed and even *thanked* us. My stomach is tied up in knots, but with Cairo MIA at the moment, I'm all our baby has, and I have to survive. Hunter drops down beside me and not a second later Blake and Cass are joining us. We sit here in silence as we watch the sunset.

"Thank you guys."

"For what?"

"For dropping everything and coming here with me, Blake. I know it's hard for you guys to be away from the pack and I just want you to know, I'm so grateful." I'm so emotional these days, thanks to my hormones; I brush away the stray tear and ignore my asshole brother's laughter.

"We would follow you anywhere sister––."

"Gabrielle!" The four of us are on our feet and spinning around at the panicked tone of Alexanders voice, he rushes toward us and hands me a phone. I look at it for a second before grabbing it and placing it against my ear while I hold Alex's gaze.

"Hello?"

"It's me." My legs nearly give out, Cass wraps his arm around my waist to hold me up.

"C-Cairo, where are you?"

"I'm coming beauty but right now you all need to run!" My eyes widen and Alex keeps darting his gaze around. If he is worried, then something is up, not much rattles this man's cage, I mean he's an original vampire and stronger than anyone I know.

"Why? Cairo, what's going on?"

"She took Sky's power."

"How? Sky...died with her power." I hold my breath thinking that my reminding him of her death will anger him.

"Sky's body went missing three days after the funeral, a...friend spotted Davina crossing the border from Serbia into Romania. I'll explain everything when I get to you, but right now you have to listen to Alex and run––." I don't get a chance to reply, a loud bang sounds out and the ground beneath us begins to shake. The phone tumbles from my hand, Cass plucks me off my feet so I'm bride style in his arms.

"She's here, you all have to run. I'll hold her off for as long as I can." Tears gather in my eyes as I look at Alex.

"Come with us, we can––." He cuts me off.

"Finish the transition Belle." He smiles sadly at me as he reaches out and brushes the tips of his fingers along my cheek. "You truly are a miracle, now go!" Cass takes off with the others following, I struggle in his hold and shout for Alex to come with us but none of them listen to me. Another boom sounds out and the ground under our feet shakes yet again, it sounds like bombs are being let off and I'm so freaking scared. I see the west wing of Alex's castle crumble; I gasp at the sight. Holy shit, they really are using bombs!

"They're gaining on us!" I peer over Cass's shoulder and fear grips me, more than a dozen vampires are chasing us. My brothers are fast, but they are no match for vampire speed, Cass curses and then stops, placing me on my feet. He cups my face and the serious look he gives me steals my breath.

"Run––."

"No."

"Belle, you run, and you keep that baby safe. We'll hold them off for as long as we can, get out of here now and find Cairo. We'll catch up to you!" Tears stream down my cheeks as I look to each of my brothers, I want to stay with them, but I know all I will do is distract them.

"I love you all, don't die, I need you three and so does *bean*." Those better not be the last words I say to my brothers, I think to myself as I turn and start running for mine and my baby's life. I break through the dense forest that surrounds Alex's castle never stopping, my breaths are coming in short rapid pants, and I curse myself for being so...human. I keep going until I spot a small stream, I stop trying to find the safest way across, without me slipping on the moss-covered stones and hurting myself or worse, the baby. I pat my thigh and freeze, I forgot about the dagger strapped to my leg that Alex gave me. He insisted since we got here that I always carry it with me. The noise of the battle behind me is nothing but a distant hum, I slowly trek across the stream and send up a silent prayer of thanks when I make it safely to the other side. I head up the incline and hope begins to blossom inside me, once I'm over this hill, the main town is only a fifteen-minute walk from here and I can get help. I push my tired legs to carry on, and just as I'm about to crest the hills peak, I smile.

I'm gonna make it!

The smile vanishes from my face, standing no more than ten feet away from me is Davina. She wears all black and has her long hair slicked back in a high ponytail. Creed and Cole look so much like her. I swallow loudly and try to control my breathing, but it's no use, fear has me gripped firmly in its clutches. It hits me then.

"They were all a distraction back there, weren't they?" Her smirk morphs into a full-blown smile.

"What gave it away?" All hope flees from my body.

"You knew they would make me run." I utter, my brothers and Alex are back there fighting for their lives and trying to buy me time, but the reality is that I'm already fucked and no doubt going to die. Cold sweat drips down my spine, I dart my gaze around trying to find a way out but to no avail. With her vampire speed she will be able to chase me down before I make it two steps, resignation settles inside me. If I'm to die here today, I won't go down without a fight.

"You have something that belongs to me."

"I have nothing of yours! I would rather die than give you anything." She tsks me like I am an errant child.

"Oh Gabby." I cringe, I hate being called Gabby. "I won't kill you until *after*, that baby is born." I stop breathing. "I'll even let you meet it before I kill you." I shake my head rapidly.

"No, no, no. I won't let you have my baby!" I scream, tears of frustration begin to cloud my vision. I don't know what my baby has to do with any of this, but I will never allow that vile woman to touch my child! I wish my mate bond worked like everyone else's, I can't communicate with Ro, and he can't track me because I'm not a shifter! All he can do is feel my emotions, if he was close enough now, he would feel how terrified I am, not for myself but for our Bean.

Before I can try to defend myself or run, she blurs so quickly that I gasp when she is an inch away and back hands me, I topple over but manage to land on my side instead of my front. I cup my cheek trying to ease the sting, she hisses at me and it's in this moment I see the monster lurking beneath the surface. The stories about her kindness and how she pretended to change run through my mind, Alex is right. Davina Reeves is a master manipulator and fooled everyone.

"I don't have time for your shit." She reaches down and grips a hand full of my hair and yanks me to my feet, I scream out in pain which just earns me another smack. I don't fall this time thanks to her grip on my hair, but my vision goes blurry. She stalks forward and drags me after her, I slip but she yanks on my hair to keep me upright. I try to fight her but it's useless, I'm not strong enough! Then it hits me, I'm not completely defenseless, I slide my hand under my sundress and grip the hilt of the dagger and yank it free, then without thinking I plunge it into her side. She screams out in pain, when she releases my hair, I take off back toward the castle and hope that the dagger did some permanent damage and gives me enough time to reach my brothers.

I make it to the stream and try to calm myself enough so I can pass it safely, I get one foot on the other side and then I'm tackled from behind. I land on my front and cry out when my head smacks against a rock. Dark spots appear in my vision when she rolls me to my back, I don't see it, but I feel it when she plunges the very dagger I used on her into my collarbone. A blood curdling scream tears from me, the burning sensation in my right side turns into and inferno. My fight or flight instinct kicks in and I begin to kick and throw my hands around trying aimlessly to hit her, I feel a couple of hits connect before my arms are captured and pinned above my head. The movement shifts the dagger and I scream out again, my vision starts to clear, and Davina is right there in my face with her fangs bared at me, fear takes hold and I freeze.

"You stupid bitch!"

"Fuck you!" I scream at her and then spit in her face, my triumph is short lived when she grips my hands in one of hers and punches me right in the nose with her other, I feel the bones break beneath her hit and cry out once again. She punches me again but this time in my eye, and the force of the hit turns my vision hazy, I feel dizzy, and I know I'm about to pass out. I try to fight it because then she will be able to run with me and I'll be at her mercy.

"I'm going to enjoy breaking you and then sending your father pieces of you." Her words sound like they are echoing. "You're an abomination––." A force I can't see slams into her, and she cries out, my body urges me to lay still but I have to get out of here or risk her getting her hands on me again. Cairo will never survive the loss of our baby, I grit my teeth as I push myself up into a sitting position, blood from my nose trails a wet path down my chin and the burning pain in my side is crippling. The sound of a growl snags my attention, when my eyes land on Davina and a wolf, everything freezes.

"No!" I scream when the pure black wolf launches itself at Davina, he isn't strong enough to take her down. She dodges his attack and swings around kicking her leg out and connecting against his ribs, the wolf whines and I know I need to do something to save him. I struggle to my feet and bite into my lip to stop the scream from tearing free. I sway on my feet but nothing else matters right now, I push the pain down and focus on saving the wolf, I can't lose him! Water from the stream splashes as they trade bites and punches, I scream when she lands a hard blow to the wolf's head, his eyes swing to me, and that tiny distraction costs him. Davina moves like a snake, she jumps and then flips through the air landing on the wolf's back, she reaches around and grips its jaws in her hold trying to pry them apart. He flips onto his back but it's no use, her legs lock around him and her hold tightens. I make my way toward them, I dart my eyes around for a weapon but can't spot one, the wolf makes a horrible sound and I know I have to do this in order to save his life. I reach up and grip the hilt of the dagger not giving myself time to think, I yank it out.

Son of a bitch!

I bite my lip that hard blood coats my tongue, I rush toward them and lift my arm over my head ready to stab her again but then the tension in her arms disappears as she rips the wolf's jaws apart, I freeze directly behind her at the sight, his yellow eyes land on me and then something inside me snaps. I plunge the dagger into her head, her scream is muted from the blood rushing in my ears, I yank it out and keep stabbing her anywhere and everywhere. When she flops onto her back in the stream, I jump on top of her like a woman possessed and continue to stab her over and over again in her face and neck. She tries to fight back but is weakened from the stab wounds, I can't stop myself. Tears stream down my face, she took him from me!

"I fucking hate you!" I scream, when my arms are so weak and boneless, I finally stop, the red haze I was just in, slowly disappears as I look down at her, wounds are seen all over her disgusting face, her head is nearly severed from her body. Stab wounds litter her face, head and chest, blood runs from her eye and when I see it is almost out of its socket, bile rushes up my throat and I quickly scramble off her and empty the contents of my stomach into the stream. I wipe my mouth with the back of my hand, then spin around, sobs wrack my body when I look over to him, I rush over and grip his arm trying to pull him with all my strength to the bank, I manage to get his top half out of the stream but I'm too weak thanks to the blood leaking from my stab wound and the blows to the head. I drop down onto the bank and lift his head until it rests in my lap, his bottom jaw is missing, and his vacant green eyes stare up at the sky above, I brush my hand along his cheek and sob. "I'm sorry, I'm so sorry, I'm sorry!" I scream out, my chest is on fire not only from the wound but from the burning ache of losing him.

CHAPTER THIRTY-EIGHT

Cairo

The castle is in shambles as Z and I run through with the rest of our guys following behind, I spot Alex fighting a group of vamps and signal for some of my guys to help. I jump over the stone patio's wall and rush toward where I can see her brothers fighting off another group of vamps. Z and the rest of my pack fan out and box them in, I allow Bex forward and we shift mid step. Bex jumps on the back of an unsuspecting vamp and as he hits the ground he leans down and swiftly rips into his throat. We takedown a couple more before finally reaching Cassius, I shift back as does he. Each of us has blood coating our chests and heaving.

"Where is she?"

"We held them off to give her a chance to run." Good, I shift back, as long as the fight is here then that means Belle is safe. We all work as a unit to take down each of the vamps, the taste of their blood on my tongue is like a balm to my battered soul. I haven't stopped hunting this bitch since we buried Sky, I vowed that day I wouldn't rest until that cunt is six feet under. Two vamps are attacking Zeke, I sprint toward them and bowl one of them from the side and make quick work of separating the fuckers head from its body.

Twenty minutes later we all shift back and look out over the carnage, dead vampires litter the ground, my heart sinks when I see three of my wolves laying there, lifeless in their human skin. Some of the fuckers managed to get some hits in and my ribs are burning, but unlike the three wolves, I will heal.

Fuck.

"I have to find my sister!" I spin around to see a worried Hunter ripping at the strands of his hair.

"What happened?" I snap, my worry hitting me in the chest.

"Blake heard a scream and took off mid fight to go after her——." I don't stick around to listen to the rest, Bex comes forward and I don't fight him. He'll get to her faster than my human self. He rushes through the woods following her scent, the further we search the stronger her scent becomes, but then...Blood!

Bexley...

I'll find her.

He skids to a stop by a stream and that's when I see her, I hear the others behind me as I shift back. She has her head thrown back screaming up to the heavens as she grips her brothers head in her lap. Her yellow sundress is soaked in blood and fear grips me by the throat as I rush toward her and drop to my knees. I look down at Blake and curse under my breath, he's dead. I focus on Belle as I cup her cheeks and turn her to face me, blood coats her face and my anger soars inside me, her perfect little nose is broken and her eye is swelling shut, I run my gaze over her and spot a stab wound on her shoulder that is dripping with blood. Bex growls and vows to kill whoever did this to her.

"Beauty." She shakes her head and rips free of my hold when Cass and Hunter drop down beside their brothers' body. Sobs tear from her, Cass and Hunter both have tears trailing down their cheeks, Cass reaches out and hauls his brother's lifeless body up wrapping his arms around him and buries his face into the crook of his neck as he screams. My heart breaks for them, I can't imagine losing my sister.

"H-he s-saved me." Belle hiccups. Hunter reaches out and grips the back of Blake's head.

"I'll kill the fucker who did this!" He says through his tears.

"I already did Hunt." My shocked gaze snaps to her, Hunter lifts his eyes to her, clearly in shock as well. We both follow her gaze to the stream, and that's when I see it, Davina Reeves's mutilated body lays in the stream with a dagger sticking out of her forehead, hers and Blakes blood is turning the stream red. I turn back to Belle and cup her face in my hands, she does the same to my face.

"I need to take you back so I can get you seen by a doctor beauty." She shakes her head.

"I'm not leaving Blake." Fresh tears pour from her eyes.

"I'll bring him back." Cass's gruff emotionless tone has me tensing, the loss of his little brother is going to destroy him. I wrap my arms around her and lift, the cry that tears from her destroys me inside, I should have been here to protect her. I'm scared to even think about the baby and if it's okay, so I don't ask.

Thanks to Alex and all his contacts we were able to fly out of Romania and bring Blake's body back to the states in record time. Belle and the other two haven't really said much the past four days, Belle had to have her nose reset and obviously needed stitches for the stab wound. Her body is covered in bruises and cuts, the doctor Alexander hired did an ultrasound and when I heard the heartbeat of little bean, my legs gave out. I'm not religious or even believe in God, but you best believe that I thanked the heavens above for the life of my child. We found out Belle is now 11 weeks pregnant. The drive back to the Wilder pack has been silent, Alex and I ride up front with Belle and her brothers in the back. None of them have uttered a word the whole flight and even when we transferred Blake's casket from the plane to the hearse. I informed my sister of what's happening, so her and the others are meeting us back at Belle's pack. The sound of Alexander's phone ringing breaks me from my thoughts.

"Yeah?" Thanks to being a shifter, I can hear the whole conversation.

"I know who took the witches body." I tense at the mention of Sky. I peer in the rearview mirror and find all three in the back are focused on Alex and his phone call.

"Who?"

"Her coven came for her." I grip the steering wheel tight until my knuckles are turning white. Who the fuck do they think they are, to uplift her like that! I thought it was Davina, we all did. What the fuck was that crazy bitch playing at then?

"She doesn't have a coven." Alex snaps.

"Apparently she has a sibling and they wanted to consecrate her properly." I have no idea what the fuck gibberish this bitch is spewing.

"Is there anything else?"

"Yeah, I've been staking them out and trying to work my way inside. From what I can gather, her power has been passed down, whoever it instills itself into will wear a circle brand with all the elements inside it."

"Keep me updated." Is all he says before he ends the call, I grind my teeth to try and keep my anger in check. I have to be here for Belle today as we lay her brother to rest, I'll figure out what happened to Sky tomorrow.

"Tell them." I dart my gaze to the rearview mirror at the sound of Hunter's whispered words. Belle shakes her head and that pisses me off.

"Got something to share beauty?" I grit out. She looks to each of her brothers before meeting my gaze in the mirror.

"I know who has Sky's power." She says it barely above a whisper.

"Who?" Alex and I ask in unison. She takes a deep breath; I tear my eyes from hers to watch where the fuck I'm going. I follow the hearse as it turns left, we are nearly at the Wilder pack.

"Sky transferred her power to our baby." I choke on my own spit, Alex gasps and runs a hand through his hair in surprise.

"I didn't see that coming." He mutters.

"How do you know?" I ask.

"I had a vison a week after we buried her, she told me it was the only way to ensure nothing happened to the baby. She said her magic would protect the unborn child and that I would have a choice now, either shift or become a vampire. Guess I blew that choice when I killed your sister's mother-in-law." The bitterness that coats her tone is tangible, she completes her transition in three days' time, when she has to drink blood. Because Belle is from the original line, she doesn't need her father's blood to transition, she only had to make her first kill. Being an original means Belle will now be able to create vampires and I don't know how I feel about that.

"We get through today and lay our brother to rest, and then we research the shit out of what is going on with the baby. I swear to you Belle, I won't let anything happen to your baby." My respect for Cassius just skyrocketed.

"Why didn't you tell me?" I ask her, her eyes narrow and her upper lip pulls back in a snarl.

"How the fuck would I have done that, huh? You took off for a month and left me! Not the other way around asshole, don't pull your bullshit on me today Cairo when I'm about to bury my fucking brother!" I flinch, everything she just said is true and I have to make it up to her. I should never have pushed her away and let my anger take control. "By the way, don't act like you care about this *thing* inside me. You want to fuck off and chase down your demons, go for it. I don't need you to raise this baby, I have my brothers and father that are all too willing to help." I growl and smack the steering wheel, my vision shifts to Bex's, I need to control my emotions or risk killing us all by shifting in the car.

"You can talk about this later, we're here." I grind my teeth in annoyance at Hunter's words, cars are parked everywhere, and I spot Creed's car in the distance. I'm thankful that they came today, they aren't here just for me, they came to show their love and support for Belle.

Chapter Thirty-Nine

Belle

My brothers and I head for the hearse that carried Blake's body; I don't have it in me to look around at all the people that have gathered here today. The driver opens the door and there inside the mahogany casket lays the body of my brother who died so I could live, I swipe away the stray tear that falls without my permission. Cass and Hunter reach in to grab the handles on either side, Creed and Cole step up to help grab the next two handles and then to my surprise, Z and Cairo come forward to help. Once they have the casket out, we turn to head toward the cemetery where Blake will be laid to rest next to their––mom. We all pause at the sight of my father, he moves slowly toward us with red rimmed eyes, I stand tall and square, my shoulders ready for him to blame me for the loss of his son.

I stand shoulder to shoulder with Cass and the closer dad approaches the more tense I grow; Cass was the one who called and told our dad what had happened. I was too much of a coward to even speak to him, guilt eats at me daily over Blake's death. Dad doesn't speak to any of us, he places his hands flat against the casket and then rests his forehead against it, quiet sobs fall from his lips, all the guys holding the casket keep their gazes forward offering my father some semblance of privacy as he says his final goodbye to his son.

"I loved you from the moment you were born, and I loved you till your last breath, and I will love you till my final days. You will be remembered as the hero that you are my son, thank you for choosing me as your father." He breaks down and I have to suppress my own tears, a lump is forming in my throat.

Cairo stands beside me the whole time in silent support as we bury Blake, I have avoided my father like the plague, but felt his gaze on me every so often. I can't find the strength to meet his stare and see the hatred that shines in his eyes, I appreciate that Creed and the others came here to pay their respects. I stand here in a daze as they pile dirt on top of his casket, a numb feeling washes over me as I watch the coffin slowly disappear. People start to disperse but my eyes remain fixed on the pile of dirt in front of me, with a tombstone that I haven't been able to bring myself to look at.

"I'll give you some time alone, I'm here if you need me beauty." I nod like a robot at Cairo's words, when it's just me left, I kneel down and rest my hand against the mound of dirt and finally let my tears fall, I bite my lip to simmer the sobs that come from me.

"I'm so sorry Blake. I would trade places with you if I could——."

"He wouldn't want that." I gasp and stand as I turn around and finally face my father, his eyes hold none of the hatred I expected to see. He closes the space between us and cups my cheek, I nuzzle into his touch. "Why are you hiding from me?" He whispers.

"Because I don't want you to hate me." I choke out, he growls and then wraps his arms around me, I hiss in pain thanks to the wound on my shoulder. He releases me and frowns, I pull my shirt down slightly so he can see the gauze that covers my wound. His eyes darken before meeting my stare again.

"If you hadn't slaughtered that good for nothing leech, I would kill her with my bare hands."

"It's all my fault, Blake saved me——."

"Don't do that——."

"You don't understand, it's my fault you lost your son!" I shout in frustration. His eyes narrow at me, and I see the anger covering his face, good I deserve it.

"*My* son lost his life because he was protecting *my* daughter. I don't care if you share DNA with someone else Gabrielle, you are my child, and nothing will ever change that." I cover my mouth with my hand, his words are a balm to my tattered heart. "Read the headstone Belle." I nod my head and turn around; I lift my gaze slowly and read.

Blake Wilder
Beloved son of Gabriel & Kirsten
Brother to,
Cassius, Hunter, and Gabrielle.
"God gained an angel, we lost a piece of our hearts."

Dad steps beside me and rests his hand a top of my good shoulder and squeezes.

"You are my daughter Belle, those boys would lay down their lives for you in a heartbeat, Blake proved that, blood means nothing to them." I cry silently, I turn to my dad and hug him ignoring the pain in my shoulder.

"I'm so sorry for leaving and not sorting things with you." He rubs my back soothingly.

"Don't be sorry, I was too scared to tell you the truth because I was afraid you would leave us, and I couldn't face that." I hold him tighter.

"I would never leave you, I love you too much for that to happen." We pull apart and he smiles down at me as he wipes away my tears with his thumbs.

"You're on your own path now Belle." I gasp.

"Cass told you?"

"Yes, now tell me why haven't you completed the transition. I hear you have three days left to drink, and you haven't yet." I won't lie to him.

"Because I wanted to wait until after today, and I wasn't sure how you would feel about me, ya know?"

"It hurts my pride that you won't be a shifter." We both chuckle. "But being a vampire isn't bad either."

"How can you be so sure?"

"Because you becoming a vampire means I get to keep you longer, call me selfish but I'm okay with that."

I sit up in my room and marvel at it, I used to feel so at home in this space. It was my haven at one point but now it just reminds me of a cage. Since the transition has begun, I haven't had a vision, Alex assures me that it's normal, I hope that once its completed, they will become minimal. Alex believes that they will, but he promises to help me manage them, he even agreed that since his home in Romania will need to have parts rebuilt thanks to the bombs that day, that he would prolong his stay in the US. I don't know where I go from here though, Cairo and I have a lot to work out and I also know that he needs to help his sister and Creed sort the packs as they no longer have a council. The night Sky died; she eradicated all the council members; she did the shifters a favor if you ask me. A knock on the door pulls me from my thoughts.

"Come in." I turn away from the window to see a nervous looking Cairo standing there with his hands shoved in his pockets. We stand here silently staring at each other for a moment, he looks beautiful as always in a plain white tee, dark wash jeans and black Chucks. His hair is a tousled mess but it's just the way I like it.

"I'm sorry." I quirk a brow at him, I'm not letting him off that easy. What he said to me the night Sky died hurt me really bad. "I never should have said any of the things I did, and I sure as fuck didn't mean what I said about our baby. I want––no, need to be a part of my child's life Belle. I never got to know my parents, and I don't want my child to go through that, I'll do whatever I have to so you can trust me again, but please, I am begging you Gabrielle, don't cut me out of my kids' life."

"I need assurances."

"Like?" I want to throw my arms in the air, but I know it will hurt like shit.

"When shit gets hard, are you gonna run again? Will you continue to close me out and lash out at me when your upset? I won't raise our child like that, this baby deserves better." He closes the distance between us and I'm like a moth to a flame, I can't move when he looks at me like this. Nothing but love and devotion shines in his ice blue eyes, he reaches up and tentatively cups my cheeks, he makes sure not to touch my injured eye or apply enough pressure to hurt it. If I just drunk the blood like Alex said, then my wounds would heal, but I couldn't do it without speaking to my father first.

"I'll run to you, not from you. I'll work on not closing you out, I won't lash out at you, but I'll tell you about things. Our baby deserves the best of us both, and I promise to give *bean* everything Belle, you both are everything to me. If you could just give me another chance I can prove––." I cut him off by kissing him, I ignore the burn in my arm when I wrap my arms around his neck. His tongue swipes out and I open for him, we both moan in unison at the taste of each other. He grips the backs of my thighs and lifts me; I wrap my legs around him and bask in this moment. "I need to be inside you baby." He mumbles between kisses; I groan and grind down against his cock, he hisses, and I smile against his mouth.

"Jesus Christ." I pull back and when I see who's standing at the door, I quickly scramble to get out of Cairo's hold, he places me on my feet laughing while I try to straighten my drees before meeting my father's gaze with rosy cheeks. "Dinner is ready, sort yourselves out and then please join us."

"Yeap." I squeak out mentally facepalming myself.

"Cairo?"

"Yes?" I feel the tension in the room amp up the longer each of them holds the others gaze.

"Cassius is strong and loyal, so is Hunter, but compared to me, they are puppy dogs, remember that, the next time you even think about hurting my daughter." My eyes widen and I nearly choke on my own spit.

"Dually noted, sir." Dad turns to leave but stops and peers over his shoulder and sternly says.

"Three other shifters live in this house, and the last thing I want to hear unwillingly is what my daughter does at...night." My jaw hits the floor, Cairo laughs, and I want to crawl into a hole and die from embarrassment.

"Yes sir, none of...that will be happening in your home." Dad grunts and then finally leaves, Cairo breaks out into fits of laughter while I stand here and glare at him. I am beyond mortified that my father caught us in such a compromising position and then proceed to insinuate that we can't have sex here!

Kill me now!

"It's not funny!" I hiss at his hunched over form. He gets himself under control and then stands smiling at me.

"Babe, it's going to happen. I have fucking blue balls and need to fuck you as soon as possible, but the least I can do is grant your father the small mercy of not hearing his daughter scream my name all night long."

Fuck, my panties are soaked.

Chapter Forty

Two Months Later

Cairo

Belle is 19 weeks along now and has a tiny bump, my new favorite thing to do is lay between her legs and just watch my baby move. It pisses her off because she naturally assumes that I'm about to eat her pussy——I do, but only after I get to watch my baby for a bit, I mean happy mom, happy baby, right? Belle and I decided to spend some time at Jess and Creed's before returning to my pack lands where we plan to raise our child, it's been utter chaos trying to get all the alphas to agree to a meet, the shifters have been out of control since the news of the council's demise spread. Packs have been raiding others lands and killing each other. That is something we cannot let go unchecked, my patience is thin at the moment because I'm anxious to get home and set things up for our baby. Belle has no idea the surprise I have for her, I asked Creed if he could build me a house on my pack lands and he agreed. He told me last night that they are about six weeks out from being done. I appreciate the rush he put on making this happen, Jess and I need our space——soon as possible. My phone rings and pulls me from my thoughts, I pull it out and glare at the unknown number but answer none the less.

"Who the fuck is this?"

"Is that anyway to speak to your friends, Cairo?" I growl, I take a quick look around the cottage to make sure Belle is still with Jess and I'm alone before I answer.

"What do you want Kayla?" The friend that told me about Davina crossing the border was Kayla, I don't know what her end game is in this, but I won't question it when she is the only source of information I get about Sky. I need to be careful though, ever since Belle completed the transition and started training with Alex, she is now able to bring on visions, she caught me out when she thought I was closing her out again and had a vision of me asking her father for her hand in marriage. Needless to say, she felt like shit after that, and promised not to do it again, but if she thinks I'm in trouble, I know she won't hesitate to do it again, contrary to what she says.

"I saw Sky's body." I lean against the wall for support.

"What the fuck does that mean?" Pictures of her decomposing body run through my mind, and I begin to feel sick.

"Cairo, I don't know how to explain it but she––she looks the same." I frown.

"What does that mean?"

"I mean she doesn't look like she has decomposed at all, whatever they are doing, they have clearly preserved her body somehow. I mean she isn't even fucking pale; she looks exactly the same!" I can hear the intrigue in her voice and that sets me on edge.

"What else?"

"Sky has a brother."

"Say that again?" She growls in annoyance.

"Her brother is now the leader of their coven; it was him that took her body." I hear laughter and curse beneath my breath.

"Stay on them and keep me updated."

"I don't work for you." She snaps.

"Why the fuck are you doing this then?"

"Fuck you." The line goes dead, Kayla is a weird one. She has to be getting something out of this, what that is, I have no idea. Her only terms for information were that I don't let anyone know where she is or that I have spoken to her. I mean, I don't even know how to contact her, she forever changes her number and is constantly on the move. Fuck it, not my mate, not my worry. The front door opens, and I quickly shove my phone in my pocket and smile when I see my mate walk through the door with Z following after. The two of them have become close and I think it's good for the both of them.

"No way!"

"Yes, it's a boy!" I furrow my brow and ask.

"Do I even want to know what the two of you are arguing about now?" Belle glares at Z and lifts her lip exposing one of her fangs. I think it's so fucking sexy when she does that shit.

"Belle thinks the baby is a girl and is clearly delusional." I chuckle and then quickly close my mouth when she swings her glare my way, she is so moody and easily angered these days. I think it's so cute, but it pisses her off when I say that, so I choose to keep my balls attached to my body and glare at Z, he throws his hands in the air and then storms out of the house.

"Pussy." She mutters.

"I heard that you demon!" Z shouts from outside, I shake my head at their antics. I open my arms and she comes willingly, resting her head against my chest.

"Ro?"

"Hmmm?" I answer as I inhale her scent and hold her close.

"I'm craving again." I roll my eyes and pray for patience; her cravings change daily.

"What does the bean desire beauty?" She pulls back and then smiles up at me sweetly while batting her lashes.

"Your cock down my throat?" I choke on air; the dirty little devil laughs at me. I cut her off when I pluck her off her feet, her arms and legs wrap around me. Once her belly gets bigger, I won't be able to do this.

"I told you, no choking until after the baby." She pouts.

"You're not going to hurt the baby––."

"My cock, my rules!" Her eyes narrow and I gulp, fuck!

"Oh baby, you still don't learn. Give me what I want, or I promise you, I'll finger fuck myself and make you wait till after the baby is born before you can fuck *my* pussy." I growl up at her.

"The only thing you will be squirting on is my cock, my mouth or my hand." She smiles wickedly.

"Use your mouth to make me come and if it's good, I might even let you fuck me––." I cut her off when I smash my lips against hers. I move us toward the bedroom but my hunger for her won't allow me to wait that long, I place her on her feet in the hallway then kneel down in front of her pushing her dress up. My eyes widen when I see she isn't wearing panties. "You keep ripping them off me, so I thought I would make it easier for you."

"Fuck, I love you." I lean forward and inhale her musky scent, Bex growls approvingly. I lift her leg and place it over my shoulder, her pussy is open and dripping wet for me. I can't draw this out, I need to taste her. I dart my tongue out and lap at her juices, she moans, and I relish in it. I reach around and grip the globes of her ass and pull her against me, she rides my face like a fucking porn star. I keep eating her until I know she is close, her moans are loud, and her body is slick with sweat, I love winding her up until she breaks, but today it won't be by my mouth––I don't have time. I pull back and chuckle when she growls at me, I stand and make quick work of undoing my jeans and pushing them and my boxers down. I grip the backs of her legs and hoist her up, her hands grip my shoulders as I slowly lower her onto my aching cock. The tip of my cock prods her entrance, her eyes are glassy and filled with lust. I slam her down and we both cry out at the feeling of being joined once again.

"Fuck, you feel so good wrapped around my cock baby."

"Fuck me hard and fast Ro." I smirk, she has been insatiable since we got back, we fuck at *least* four times a day and twice a night until she passes out.

"Hold on tight baby." She hums her approval as I begin to slam inside her relentlessly, the wall behind us creaks and groans from holding our weight. He pussy clenches my cock and I know she is about to shatter and squirt all over my fucking cock.

"Fuck yes, don't you dare stop, I'm gonna come all over your dick." I slam into her hard and the only reason I'm giving her what she wants is because Meg told me that us fucking hard wouldn't hurt the bean. "Fuck yes!" She screams, when I feel her cunt suck the life out of my cock I pull out and she gushes all over me and the wooden floors. I growl my approval and then slam back inside her; I fuck her harder against the wall. She tilts her head to the side offering me her mate mark, Bex surges inside me and clamps his teeth into her. She cries out again and I follow suit spilling everything I have inside her and claiming her once again as mine.

Creed's knowing smirks greets me as soon as I walk into the town hall where the meeting is being held. Belle and I tried to clean up as best we could but without showering everyone is going to know why we are late. I pull her along behind me and claim my seat beside Creed, Belle drops into the chair next me. Jess and Cole sit opposite her, and Cass, Hunter and Gabriel sit on the other side of Belle. Her brothers both send me looks of malice and I smile and wink, Cass growls but I shrug it off. I mean what the fuck can they say? she is pregnant with my kid and mated to me, of course we're gonna fuck like rabbits. I pull my gaze from them and count out thirty-two alphas, holy shit! This is either going to go well or end up in a fight.

"Why is there a vamp present?" I snap my gaze to the other end of the table and growl in warning. Cedric is a fucking piece of shit; he may lead over a large pack in Alaska, but he is weak as shit. I open my mouth to tear the cunt apart with my words, but I'm shocked when I see Alexander step out of the shadows beside us with Vince at his side.

"Because she is an original vampire and my daughter, speak ill about her and I promise I'll wipe your entire fucking pack out, without blinking an eye." Cedric is smart enough to know that Alexander speaks the truth, being an original means, he is fucking strong. That day at his castle he had laid waste to nearly twenty vamps before we turned up to help them.

"Belle is mated to Cairo and has just as much right as any of your mates to be here, she is also my sister-in-law to be, so if you want to get sexist about shit, I'm down to fuck shit up!" I smirk at Cole; Belle isn't technically his sister-in-law, but he says we are brothers, so I guess it fits.

"Look, we didn't come here to fight. We have to form an alliance and make sure that our race stays hidden from the norms." Jess suits being in charge, I know Creed is pissed that she is here, considering she is due to give birth in a few weeks, but no one wanted to deal with my sister and her attitude, so he relented when Cole offered to come as extra protection for her.

"What is it that you propose, Mrs. Reeves?" Alaric has always been fond of Jess since she called him here to fight against Jacob, why, I have no idea.

"I propose that we elect an alpha that rules over us all––." She doesn't even get to finish before shouts and arguments break out around the room.

"You would choose yourself."

"She can't lead."

"Your pack is weak."

"Your pack is a mixed breed."

So many insults are hurled around the room, and I can't stand it, I smash my fist down on the table and growl loud enough to hurt the ears of every shifter in this room. I shoot my sister an apologetic look, but she smiles thankfully at me as I turn back to address the alphas.

"All of you, shut the fuck up."

"Why should we listen to you? You can't even bee lead!" I glare at Curtis.

"My sister and Creed are alphas to two of the strongest packs in existence, I am alpha to all rogues. My mate is also the daughter to the alpha of the Wilder pack and from the original vampire line, do you really want to go to war against my family?" Cass and Hunter both growl out their agreement, Curtis the pussy shrinks back into his seat.

"So, you want to elect yourself or Creedence to be alpha over us all then?" I meet Alaric's gaze and shake my head. "What guarantee do we have that you will adhere to whoever is chosen, you cannot be led Cairo, so we need assurances." Creed doesn't want to lead, he told me so himself. He said it would take too much time away from Jess and their kids, Cole can't because he isn't willing to become an alpha, but there is someone else though. I push back and stand as I look to each of these alphas.

"If I pledge my loyalty to the new alpha, will you agree?"

"We will vote." Marcus pipes up. I turn to Creed and ask.

"Do you trust me brother?" Without hesitation he answers.

"With my life." I nod, I move back so they are all able to see what I am about to do. I have no desire to lead, never have and with my baby coming soon, I want to be present. I also have too much on my plate with trying to figure out what happened to Sky and trying to find answers about what is going to happen to my kid, now that the bean has Sky's power. I place my fist over my heart and take a knee as I say.

"I, Cairo Cruz, alpha to all rogues, herby pledge my loyalty to Cassius Wilder." Cass's eyes widen, his mouth open and closes at a loss for words. I feel like a fool kneeling here on my own––.

"I, Creedence Reeves." I turn to the side to see Creed kneeling beside me, and this is the reason why he is my best friend. "Alpha to the Hasting-Reeves packs, pledge my loyalty to Cassius Wilder as well," I spot my sister stand and she makes her way over to us and places a hand on each of our shoulders.

"I would kneel but, even Creed isn't strong enough to lift me at the moment." Her joke lightens the tension in the room and some chuckles can be heard. "I, Jessica Hastings-Reeves, alpha to the Hasting-Reeves pack, hereby pledge my loyalty and the loyalty of my pack, to Cassius Wilder." To my utter shock, Alaric is next to agree, then slowly the others follow suit. Five alphas refuse, but majority rules, so they can eat shit. Cass is yet to say a word, Gabriel stands next and draws all of our attention.

"My son knows he has my loyalty and always will, but it is time I pass on the honor." Belle and her brother's gasp. "I will be stepping down as alpha and placing my son Hunter in charge of the Wilder pack, clearly my eldest has other duties to attend to now." Gabriel smiles down at Cass who still looks like a lost lamb.

"Dad––." He shakes his head cutting Hunter off.

"It is my time son. Plus, I want to be there for my first grandchild, and I can't do that if I'm leading a pack, so now that is your burden and honor to bare."

We all sit around the fire pit at the back of Jess and Creed's house sipping beers, Belle is wrapped up in a blanket in my lap chatting with Jess who has a sleeping Harlem in her arms while I listen to Z, Cole and Creed talk about the hunt they plan to go on next week. As much as I love being here with them, it's time for me to return home, Bex can't be free here and my sister and I have tension between us when we stay together to long because of our wolves. It sucks, but it is what it is, I guess.

"Can I speak to you all for a second." Everyone goes quiet as we give Cass our attention, he stands there with Gabriel beside him. Cass looks nervous, his hands are shoved in his pockets, and he won't hold eye contact with anyone. He takes a deep breath and finally lifts his gaze; I hold his stare but there is no challenge in his eyes only...respect. "What you did today, I never expected that, and I'm honestly lost for words. Since losing Blake, I have been fumbling and trying to find a sense of purpose again, and today, you gave that to me. Thank you, Cairo." I nod my head and tip my beer toward him. He takes another deep breath and then turns his gaze to the two Reeves brothers, the serious look in his eyes has me on edge. "I swear that I will help you all find answers about my sisters' baby." Why is he looking at them and not us, Belle even seems confused? "And find answers about Sky...but from a distance, for now." Creed leans forward and rests his arms on his thighs as he locks his gaze onto Cass and asks.

"Why?" Cass blows out a loud exhale before answering.

"California has run away––." Creed opens his mouth and Cole jumps to his feet, but Cass raises a hand stopping them. "She left because she found out that I have become head alpha."

"Why the fuck does my sister care about that?" The anger in Cole's voice is palpable.

"Because she hates me."

"Why?" Belle asks, a sad smile graces his face and that's when it hits me. *Holy fuck!*

"California Reeves is my true mate, and she and I have both known this since the moment I shifted at the alpha challenge. Don't worry, I have taken precautions and made sure that someone I trust is with her until I can bring her back."

"How do you even know where she is?" Since the betrayal of Davina, Creed has kept his siblings close. He hates that he trusted her and let her in, Cole and Callie didn't give a shit that she died but Creed did. He was the only one out of the three of them that had any memories of their birth mother. Callie not being within his reach where he can keep an eye on her is going to set him on edge and right now, he doesn't need that with Jess due in a few weeks.

"Because of the mate bond." *Well fuck me sideways, I was not expecting that!*

"You've marked my sister?" Cole snaps. Cass meets his gaze and I respect the fuck out of him for being man enough to stand here and tell us this.

"Yes, I marked her a couple of months ago. She *is* my mate and I give you both my word that I will bring her back, no matter the cost."

CALIFORNIA

I couldn't stomach the thought of living near him or under his rule, I fucked up and made the biggest mistake of my life. I haven't been able to look at myself in the mirror since that night with Cass, I had never even been with a man before! So, I packed my shit and ran while everyone was distracted. I don't know if what she said in the text message is true, but if there is even a slim chance it is, I'm taking it. They may have all moved on from Sky's death, but I haven't! They each get to go home to their mates and families, but I go home to no one! Every day the pain inside me intensifies, I can't even breathe without it hurting. I hate that she left me here alone!

My phone begins to ring, and I fish it out of my purse and answer when I see who is calling.

"You better be right, if you're lying––."

"California, I have done some fucked up shit in the past but even for me this is low. I swear I am telling you the truth, get on the plane and come to New York."

"H-have you seen her?" She sighs.

"I have, she's here." I feel like a fool chasing after my girlfriend's body, but I need to do this in order to try and heal. For me there is no moving on from Sky, you only get one epic love story in your life, and she was mine. I fight back the sob that wants to break free and clear my throat.

"I'm at the airport now, my flight leaves in an hour."

"I'll be there to pick you up."

"One more thing."

"Yeah?"

"If you try to fuck me over Kayla, I'll kill you."

"I know, get on the plane Callie. There is a lot you have to learn about what is happening out here." I end the call; I've already checked my bag in, so I make my way through security and head for my gate. I find my seat on the plane 38C, I smile, window seat yes!

I place my phone on flight mode and then shove it in my purse as I push it under the seat in front of me. I close my eyes and rest my head against the window hoping that they will hurry up. I feel someone drop down next to me but don't open my eyes, I take a deep breath trying to relax and then freeze. I slowly peel my eyes open and turn to the side.

"Surprise."

"What the fuck are you doing here?" I whisper shout, Hunter narrows his gaze at me and leans forward so we are nearly nose to nose.

"Cassius is tied up but will meet us there as soon as he can, until then you're stuck with me."

"I don't want you here!"

"Too bad, you're his mate Callie, he isn't just going to let you go." The harsh tone of his voice and the hard set of his eyes tells me he isn't going to budge.

"I am not––."

"Keep running babe, he's a predator and the beast in him loves the chase."

I am going to kill Cassius Wilder even if it is the last thing I do!

T o be continued...

Book 4 – Brutal Beauty – Cass and Callie's story will be coming later this year!

Thank you!

Holy shit, are you still with me?

What a ride, right?

Cairo and Belle had some epic twists and turns in their book, twists I didn't even see coming! Cairo was hard to write, he would toy with me and then be like, "nah, fuck that, scrap it all and start again." This book is the first to make me cry while I was writing it. The loss of Sky hit me deep, but she was such a heroic badass, she needed a hero's ending and I think she got it.

Thank you so much for coming on this wild ass ride with me, Savage Lies was meant to be a standalone, LOL. Clearly that didn't happen––cue, Brutal Truth. It was supposed to end there...again. Clearly these characters don't like to be left in the past.

Callie and Cass's book will be a wild as shit journey, there *may* be a trigger warning for their book as Callie is on a dark path after the loss of Sky.

I hope you stick around for their book – Brutal Beauty. Xxx

If you would like to stay up to date with all my releases, follow me on the links below. If you loved Savage Beast, please leave a review on, Amazon, Bookbub, or Goodreads, your feedback will be much appreciated.

@authorsamanthabarrett

Acknowledgments

I have to give credit where it is due. None of the Brutal Savages books would be here today without my mum. She has Alpha/Beta read them, edited each of these books as well as helped me plot them. Shout out to you mummy for being a badass woman and my best friend, I love you!

Thank you to my girl Cyndi for alpha reading this bad boy! You are so appreciated, and I love you dearly!

My Savage Beast−−Marcus, I love you! Thank you for pushing me to chase my dreams and loving me through my meltdowns with each of these books!

Amber, babe I will be lost without ya! Why you put up with me I will never know, you constantly deal with my nagging and ass backward schedule. I appreciate you and cherish you immensely babe.

Kim...The woman who swears she would never read! Sucker, welcome to the dark side biarch and I hope you have fun falling down the rabbit hole of this series!

To my amazing readers, thank you!

your support and recognition to these characters is the reason that drives me to follow my dreams. Without all of you I wouldn't be able to live out my dream, from the bottom of my heart, Thank you!

If you loved *Savage Beast*, please leave a review.

Sam Xx

ABOUT THE AUTHOR

S amantha is a book lover and writer. She is originally from the land of the long white cloud, New Zealand.

Sam loves anything Twilight and is a TWIHARD proudly.#TeamEdward

She loves fantasy-romance novels with strong Alpha males.

Samantha loves to write complicated love stories with a twist. A strong and badass heroine is a must!She lives in Brisbane, Australia with her husband, two children, and four dogs.If her books leave you wanting more or you feel as if you connected with the characters in some way, she takes that as a win!!Sam loves writing anything that is out of the box!

You can find her on –

Amazon - amzn.to/3vsmuxy

Bookbub – bit.ly/2NvIJl4

Goodreads - bit.ly/2NsCSx2

Also By Samantha Barrett

The Dream Trilogy (Complete)
A Beautiful Dream
A Twisted Fate
A Beautiful Nightmare

The Dream Trilogy Spin offs (Can be read as Standalones)
Redemption – Brothers best friend
Anarchy – Best friends' daughter

Brutal Savages Series
Savage Lies
Brutal Truth
Savage Beast
Brutal Beauty